KU-687-614

Margaret Dickinson

The Fisher Lass

PAN BOOKS

First published 1999 by Macmillan

This edition published 2001 by Pan Books
an imprint of Macmillan Publishers Ltd
25 Eccleston Place, London SW1W 9NF
Basingstoke and Oxford
Associated companies throughout the world
www.macmillan.com

ISBN 0 330 37685 3

Copyright © Margaret Dickinson 1999

The right of Margaret Dickinson to be identified as the
author of this work has been asserted by her in accordance
with the Copyright, Designs and Patents Act 1988.

All rights reserved. No part of this publication may be
reproduced, stored in or introduced into a retrieval system, or
transmitted, in any form, or by any means (electronic, mechanical,
photocopying, recording or otherwise) without the prior written
permission of the publisher. Any person who does any unauthorized
act in relation to this publication may be liable to criminal
prosecution and civil claims for damages.

3 5 7 9 8 6 4 2

A CIP catalogue record for this book is available from
the British Library.

Typeset by SetSystems Ltd, Saffron Walden, Essex
Printed and bound in Great Britain by
Mackays of Chatham plc, Chatham, Kent

This book is sold subject to the condition that it shall not,
by way of trade or otherwise, be lent, re-sold, hired out,
or otherwise circulated without the publisher's prior consent
in any form of binding or cover other than that in which
it is published and without a similar condition including this
condition being imposed on the subsequent purchaser.

MM ALICE £1.25
A

The Fisher Lass

Born in Gainsborough, Lincolnshire, Margaret Dickinson moved to the coast at the age of seven and so began her love for the sea and the Lincolnshire landscape.

Her ambition to be a writer began early and she had her first novel published at the age of twenty-five. This was followed by twelve further titles, including *Plough the Furrow*, *Sow the Seed* and *Reap the Harvest* which together make up her Lincolnshire Fleethaven trilogy, *The Miller's Daughter* and her most recent novel, *Chaff Upon the Wind*. Married with two grown-up daughters, Margaret Dickinson combines a busy working life with her writing career.

This book is a work of fiction and is entirely a product of the author's imagination. All the characters are fictitious and any similarity to real persons is purely coincidental.

With the deepest admiration this book is respectfully dedicated to the fishermen of Grimsby, their wives and families.

Acknowledgements

Grimsby is the inspiration for this novel although the story is entirely fictitious. I am very grateful to Mr Richard Doughty, Director of Museums, Archives & Archeology, and all his staff and volunteers at the National Fishing Heritage Centre in Grimsby for their interest and help, especially Mike Cullum and Doug Richards for sharing with me their experiences aboard minesweepers during World War II; Ray Smith for his wonderful tours of the *Ross Tiger*; Bob Roach, Craig Lazenby, Fisheries Historian, and Russell Hollowood, Fisheries Officer, for general background information and patiently answering innumerable questions.

My special thanks to Mike Coulson, of Skegness, who served as a radio operator aboard trawlers for two and a half years in the early 1960s and so kindly read the whole script for me.

My love and thanks as always to my family and friends, especially those who read and helped edit the script in the early stages; my sister and brother-in-law, Robena and Fred Hill; my brother and sister-in-law, David and Una Dickinson; my friends, Pauline Griggs and Linda and Terry Allaway. Thank you all so much for your hard work!

Part One

One

'Let me go. I'm not what you think.' The girl's terrified voice echoed along the dark, wet streets. 'Please – no – please don't.'

'Don't lie to me. You're one of Aggie Turnbull's sluts.' The man holding her laughed cruelly. 'I saw you come out of her house just now.'

'No – no. I'm not.' The girl struggled but was no match for his grip.

From an alleyway opposite, Jeannie watched the figures silhouetted against the light that spilled out from the windows of the Fisherman's Rest.

She had been hurrying along the deserted streets, anxious to find lodgings, when she had seen five or six young men lurch out of the pub on the corner. The sound of laughter from inside followed them into the night. Immediately, she had melted into the shadows until they moved on. But the group stood on the pavement, gathered around one of their number who seemed even worse for drink than the rest.

'We should get him home,' one of the young men said. 'If he doesn't get to the church for eleven in the morning, upstanding and sober, there'll be hell to pay.'

'Oh give it a rest, Edwin,' was the disdainful answer. 'It's his last night of bachelorhood. Let the poor chap have a good time, eh?'

'Sorry, I'm sure. But I'd have thought you of all people,

3

Francis, ought to be looking after Robert. That's what a best man is supposed to do, isn't it?'

The other laughed loudly. 'Maybe, but it's high time our brother cut loose the apron strings and had a little fun. And if tonight's his last night of freedom then . . .'

Jeannie heard the one addressed as Edwin mutter some reply, but, from across the street, she could no longer distinguish exactly what he said.

His brother's voice was clear. 'Then you run along home to dear Mama, Baby Boy, and leave us men to drink this town dry before the morning.' She saw him raise his hand and pat Edwin on his cheek with such a condescending gesture that Jeannie herself almost stepped out of the shadows and slapped him back.

They were beginning to move off down the street, half carrying, half dragging the befuddled bridegroom-to-be between them. Still Jeannie stayed hidden. Then she noticed the figure of a girl emerge from one of the houses a few yards down the street. Pulling her shawl about her head and hunching her shoulders, the girl tried to scuttle past the young men, but a hand shot out and grasped her arm.

'Oho, what have we here?' Jeannie heard Francis's languid voice raised again. 'A little bit of skirt for you, Robert, my boy. One of Aggie's girls.'

It was then that Jeannie heard the girl's frightened denial. Instinctively, she moved forward out of the shadows.

'Leave her be, Francis,' came Edwin's voice, but his protests were drowned by the general shout of approval.

'If she's one of Aggie's trollops, she's fair game.'

There was laughter now from all except Edwin and the bridegroom who seemed barely conscious. He was unable

4

to stand without support and his head lolled against one of those who held him upright.

The girl began to struggle, her screams echoing down the street.

'Leave her alone,' Edwin persisted. Still fast hold of the girl with one hand, Francis turned and shoved his brother in the chest. Edwin fell backwards into the road as the others dragged the girl and the semi-conscious bridegroom towards an alley between two houses.

Jeannie dropped the bundle of her belongings and ran forward.

Pausing only a second, she heard their crude comments.

'Prove yourself a man.'

'Your bride'll thank you tomorrow night, Robert.'

'My turn next.'

And then again came the petrified girl's screams that now went on and on.

Enraged and without thought for her own safety, Jeannie ran past Edwin, struggling to rise from the roadway, and plunged into the blackness of the alleyway.

She pushed and shoved her way amongst them, her fists flailing, not caring whom she hit, just forcing her way through. 'Let her go. You're animals . . .' She was standing now above the two on the ground. The young man lay motionless, sprawled on top of the girl. Squatting beside them, Francis was tearing at the girl's clothing, ripping away her blouse to expose a white mound of flesh and then pushing the face of his drunken brother into her bosom. 'How's that feel, eh, Robert? Good, is it?'

Jeannie reached out and grasped Francis's hair with her strong fingers, jerking him with such unexpected force that he gave a cry of pain and fell backwards, clattering against a bin and its surrounding mound of rubbish. Then she bent and pushed the inert young man away. There was not an ounce of resistance in him and he slid off the girl and rolled over on to his back, his eyes staring up at Jeannie with a glazed, stupid look. She bent over him, straining in the darkness to see his features. She intended to remember him and all his cronies. He blinked once or twice as if trying to focus on her face.

'I dinna know who you are, but I'll no' forget you,' she hissed at him. 'You should be ashamed of yoursel'.'

She straightened and now pulled the girl up. Turning, she made to return to the street, but Francis had regained his feet and was barring their way.

Through clenched teeth, Jeannie said, 'Get oot of ma way.'

There was a strange silence for a moment and then Francis threw back his head and laughed. 'Why, it's only a fisher lass. A Scottie. And we all know about them, don't we, chaps? Following the herring fleet down the coast, like camp followers . . .'

'How dare you—' Jeannie began and then she did what she had been wanting to do since she had seen this man's attitude towards the young man called Edwin. She smacked Francis's cheek so hard that it stung her own hand.

For an instant he gawped at her, unable to believe her audacity. 'You little—' he began, but whatever he had been about to say, or do, was cut short by Edwin stumbling into the alleyway and calling urgently, 'Come on, there's a policeman walking down the street. Let's get out of here.'

Suddenly, there was a lot of pushing and shoving and scrambling towards the opening into the road and Jeannie and the girl found themselves pushed backwards so that they fell over the prostrate young man and sprawled on the cobblestones beside him.

The superior voice of Francis rang through the night air. 'Just a little fun, constable. Out on a stag night and we encountered these two street girls . . .'

Red rage misted Jeannie's eyes as she struggled to her feet once more. 'I'm no such thing. I'll tell you what happened . . .' Emerging from the darkness, she pushed her way through to stand facing the black-uniformed officer.

'Now, now.' The man held up his hand, palm outwards, placatingly. 'We don't want any trouble. You and your friends be on your way, Mr Francis, and as for you, young woman, you'd best not let me catch you on any street corners for the rest of tonight.'

'How dare—' she began again, but felt a warning hand on her arm and heard Edwin whisper, 'Leave it. For heaven's sake leave it, else he'll run you in.'

Jeannie clamped her mouth shut but her eyes flashed in the darkness. Edwin was pulling her arm and saying quietly, 'Come on. Let's get them out of that alley and home.'

To her surprise, when she walked back into the alley-way, it was to find the girl trying to help the young man up.

Jeannie paused. Had she made a terrible mistake? Was this girl what the young men had implied? Maybe she was known to them. At Edwin's next action, this thought seemed to be confirmed.

'Here,' he said to the girl. 'I'm sorry about tonight. You're not hurt, are you? Please.' He pressed something into her hand. 'Please take this. We – your dress is spoilt. I – I am sorry, truly I am.'

Silent now, Jeannie stood back, just watching as Edwin

pulled his brother to his feet. The young man stood there swaying, shaking his head as if trying to clear it.

'Come on, Robert old chap. What Mother will have to say about this, I dread to think.'

Staggering a little as the one leant heavily upon the other, they moved towards the street. As they passed close to Jeannie, the bridegroom-to-be raised his head and looked straight into her eyes. She saw him open his mouth, lick his lips and then in a cracked whisper, he said, 'I'm so sorry.'

'So you should be,' Jeannie muttered, still outraged. 'But I dinna suppose you'll mind anything about it by the morning.'

'I'm hoping very much that he won't remember,' Edwin said with feeling.

As they emerged from the shadows, the constable said, 'Oh 'tis you, Mr Robert and Mr Edwin. Ah well, I see now . . .' The man laughed and nodded towards Francis. 'But you'd best be getting him home, Mr Francis, if you're to get him to his wedding tomorrow.'

And then they were gone, lurching down the street to hail a cab on the corner and disappear.

'Good riddance,' Jeannie muttered and then turned to the girl, who was still standing in the shadows, sniffling miserably and trying to cover herself with the torn fabric of her dress.

'Come on,' Jeannie said, kindly but with a hint of the exasperation one might use to a wayward child. 'Let's get you home. Where d'you live?'

'Baldock Street.'

'Where's that? Is it far?'

'No, no. It's the next street but one.'

'Right. I'll see you safe home and then . . . Now, where did I drop ma things?'

Two

On her arrival in Havelock earlier that evening, Jeannie had felt compelled to go down to the docks, to walk along the quays out to the end of one of the piers until she stood surrounded by the sea, willing her father's boat to appear on the horizon. But in the gathering dusk, there was not a single vessel coming in from the heaving sea, past the lightship and into the mouth of the Humber.

Behind her, alongside the jetties, a forest of masts and funnels swayed with the motion of the water beneath them and the wind that howled around them. The local trawlers had all made safe harbour on the evening tide and already their crews were gone, enjoying their brief time ashore before sailing for the fishing grounds once more. But now came the lumpers, the men who unloaded the fish on to the pontoon for the early-morning fish market on the dockside. Already several were beginning to gather in the hope of a night's work.

And with the morning tide would come the Scottish herring boats. Perhaps her father's little steam drifter would be amongst them.

Jeannie clasped the shawl that was in danger of being whipped away and drew it around her head and shoulders. Instead of giving warmth, the sodden garment made her shiver and, with sudden determination, she picked up her bundle, turned and marched along the pier, without glancing back, even just once more, towards the sea. She hurried along the quayside, taking care to keep her bright red hair hidden beneath her shawl. Maybe this far south, she told herself, the fisherfolk did not have the same superstition, but back home in Scotland, she knew of two fishermen who refused to put to sea if they saw a red-haired woman just before they were about to set sail. Jeannie had no wish to upset the folk here. She needed to find work and even if it meant tying a scarf around her head so tightly that she appeared bald, then she'd do it. There was no way she could hide the peppering of freckles across her nose, nor her green eyes, but in the dusk of the September evening she was just a tall, slim figure hurrying home, even though, as yet, she thought ruefully, she had not found a place to call 'home'.

Ignoring raucous shouts from the men, she turned in the direction of the streets of back-to-back houses close to the docks where the fisherfolk lived. It was beginning to rain and, in the narrow streets, darkness had already closed in. She regretted her foolishness in staying so long looking out to sea for a boat that she knew, in her heart of hearts, would never come home again. Yet the compulsion was still strong. She could not believe, even yet, that the big, laughing man who had been her father – who *was* her father, she told herself fiercely – could be gone for ever.

Now, with her arm about the sobbing girl, Jeannie hurried her along, patting her shoulder every so often and murmuring, 'There, there, hen. You're safe now.' But inwardly she was cursing her own stupidity for having lingered so long at the docks. It was getting late and, soaked to the skin and still trembling with anger, Jeannie doubted she would find a place to stay for the night.

She glanced down at the thin little figure cowering against her and clinging to her arm. The girl only looked fourteen or fifteen. She ought to have more sense than to be wandering the streets alone at this hour, Jeannie thought. What sort of family allowed such a young girl to be out alone?

'This is where I live,' the girl said. 'Down here, second house in the row. Number four.'

'I'll see you to your door, then I must be away.'

'Go the back way, down the alley,' the girl said. 'Me mam'll have a fit if we knock at the front door.'

Your mam'll have a fit anyway, Jeannie wanted to say, when she sees the state you're in. She said nothing but rapped sharply on the back door of the girl's home and, when it was flung open, she found herself facing the tallest, broadest man she had ever seen. She had thought her father big, in every sense of the word, but this man would have dwarfed even Angus Buchanan.

'Grace.' His voice was as cavernous as his frame. He reached out towards her with huge, calloused hands, taking her into his arms as she threw herself against him and burst into a storm of weeping.

'It wasn't my fault, Dad,' Grace was sobbing. 'They – they attacked me. They – they thought I was – that I was . . .'

His mouth tightened and swift anger darkened his eyes as, over her head, his stern gaze met Jeannie's. The man didn't need to speak for her to read from his expression just what he was thinking.

Lifting her chin defiantly, she said, 'I ken your daughter is no' what they thought and neither am I. But if that's a' the thanks I get for trying to help her, then I'll be on ma way.'

'Wait!' The word was like the crack of a sail in a force nine gale. 'I'm sorry if I misjudged you, girl. Please come in. I want to know what happened.'

His arm still about Grace's shoulders, he turned and led

11

the way through the scullery and into the kitchen of the terraced house, leaving Jeannie to step inside and close the door behind her.

A woman straightened up from bending over the range and looked towards them, her glance taking in, with a look of horror, the young girl's dishevelled appearance. Now Grace pulled herself from her father's arms and flung herself towards the older woman, sobbing wildly, 'Oh Mam, Mam.'

The woman did not at once take her into her embrace, but held her firmly by the shoulders at arm's length. 'Are you hurt, hen? Tell me at once, now?'

The girl shook her head. 'No, no. Not the way you mean. Not – not that . . .'

Jeannie was staring at the girl's mother. In the warm room after the cold of the wet night and added to the fact that she had not eaten all day, Jeannie's legs felt suddenly weak. She passed the back of her hand across her brow and the room swam before her.

'George,' she heard the woman's voice say again. 'George, yon lassie's about to pass out. Catch hold of her . . .'

She felt as if she were waking up from sleep, but as she stirred and consciousness returned, Jeannie became aware that she was lying on a hard, horsehair sofa and that faces, in shadow from the light behind them, were bending over her. She struggled to rise, but gentle hands pressed her back. 'Lie still, hen. And drink this. Why, you're soaked to the skin.' The woman's motherly hands touched her shoulder.

Gratefully, Jeannie pulled herself up to a sitting position

and took the proffered steaming cup of tea. Sipping it, the sudden warmth to her cold body made her shiver.

'You'll be catching a chill. Drink that and then we'll get you out of those wet things.'

The woman turned now and addressed someone standing behind her. Looking beyond her, Jeannie saw a young man, his shoulders broad beneath his fisherman's jersey, who was almost as tall as the man who had opened the door to them. He even had the same colouring. Fair, springy hair and blue eyes, but without the beard that the older man had. He was obviously the son and so, Jeannie realized, the girl's brother.

Standing a little way back from the couch, the young man seemed uncertain what he should do or think. Every so often he glanced worriedly at the grim expression on his father's face.

But it was the mother who took charge. Small, with a well-rounded, comforting sort of body and with grey hair pulled back into a neat bun at the nape of her neck, she was quick and decisive in her movements. She wore round, steel-rimmed spectacles which constantly slipped down the bridge of her nose, so that for most of the time she seemed to be peering over the top of them. With a gesture that was obviously a habit, she pushed them back up her nose with her ring finger.

'George, fetch some blankets from upstairs.'

'I'm not moving, Nell, until I've heard what happened.' The father's voice was deep and booming but for all that, the woman shooed him away with a flap of her hand. 'Away with you,' she ordered, adding sharply, 'and do as I say.'

To Jeannie's amusement, her husband turned away to do his wife's bidding. When the older woman once again

13

bent over her, her tone was gentle, all severity gone, and the concern in her voice made tears spring to Jeannie's eyes.

'There, there, hen,' she patted Jeannie's hand. 'You're safe now. Both of you. Tom will see you home when you're ready to go.'

'I'll not be seen walking the street with the likes of her, Ma, so . . .'

The woman straightened up again and said fiercely, 'Away and fetch more wood for the fire, Tom.'

For a moment the young man's face was mutinous, but then, with a glance towards his sister and a glower towards the stranger in their midst, he, too, turned to do as he was told.

As the back door slammed behind him, the woman winked at Jeannie. 'He thinks himsel' beyond being ordered about, but he's still ma bairn and I'm no' about to let him forget it.'

Jeannie, revived by the warmth of the room, the tea and even more than that, by the warmth of the woman's kindness, smiled.

'What made you pass out, hen, because you look a strong lassie to me, not the fainting kind at all?'

Jeannie looked up at her and her smile widened to a grin. Now she was over the initial shock of hearing the woman speak, she could laugh about it.

As she opened her mouth and said, 'It was hearing another voice from home . . .' it was the older woman's turn to draw in a sharp breath and stare down at her. Then she, too, laughed and said, 'You're one of the fisher lasses, are you?'

They were the same words that one of the young men in the street had used, but there was a world of difference in the way it was said now. 'Well, you're very welcome in my home, hen, and not only because you helped our lassie.'

She jerked her head towards where the young girl was huddled close to the range, still trying to pull her torn garments together to hide her shame and embarrassment. She was a pretty girl, Jeannie saw now she had time to look at her properly, with a small nose, a sweet mouth and large, blue eyes that, at this moment, filled with easy tears. Her long, fair hair was coming loose from its pins and her face, streaked with dirt, was unnaturally pale from the shock she had just suffered.

Answering the girl's mother, Jeannie said softly, 'Then you don't think I'm a – a . . .'

'A Scottish fisher-lass a whore? Never,' the woman bridled indignantly. 'Never in a million years. And Tom will get a piece of my mind for even thinking such a thing.'

At that moment both men returned.

For the next half-hour, the kitchen of the small terraced house was a bustle of activity. The men were dispatched once more whilst the girls took off their wet, soiled clothes and wrapped themselves in the blankets and Mrs Lawrence set a pan of thick broth on the range to heat.

A little later, Mr Lawrence demanded yet again to be told the truth of what had happened.

'Ya should have told us straight away,' he said to Grace, but his glance of reproach was towards his wife. 'Then I could have gone out and found them.' He said no more, but he pounded one fist into the palm of his other hand and no one in the room was in any doubt as to what he would like to do to his daughter's attackers.

'Now, hen,' Nell Lawrence was saying to her. 'Tell us what happened?'

The girl gulped and, for a moment, hung her head. 'I

15

was just on me way home, Mam. They came out of the Fisherman's Rest and – and – well – they were drunk and . . .'

'Are you sure they didna hurt you? They didna . . .'

Grace shook her head. 'No, no, but – but they might have done if – if it hadn't been for her.' She looked across towards Jeannie who was now sitting up on one end of the couch and gave a shudder. 'I daren't think what might have happened if you hadn't come along when you did.' She gave a ghost of a smile. 'And I don't even know your name.'

'Jeannie. Jeannie Buchanan.'

Now it was the turn of the two men to look surprised and then George Lawrence let out a guffaw of laughter that lightened the tension and, for a moment, had everyone in the room smiling. 'There you are, Nell, one of your own. I didn't notice it when I opened the door to you, lass. I was too teken up with Grace. Well, well, a Scottish lassie, eh? I'll be damned!'

'And well you might be, George Lawrence, but . . .' His wife wagged her finger in the direction of Tom. 'But your son there certainly will be if he doesna apologize to this lassie for thinking what he did.'

Tom shuffled his feet awkwardly. His swarthy face reddened and then there was a sudden sheepish grin. 'I'm sorry, miss. No offence. I were just that mad – worried – about our Grace.'

Jeannie smiled and nodded. 'It's all right.'

'What I want to know is,' Mrs Lawrence said turning back to her daughter, 'what were you doing anywhere near the Fisherman's?'

Again the girl hung her head and, at once, Jeannie knew that she should not have been there.

'I was walking down Harbour Road.'

'Why? What were you doing down there? That's out of your way?'

'I – I'd been to Aggie's.'

'Aggie Turnbull's?' Now the mother's voice was raised in anger. 'I've told you to keep away from there. I won't have you going anywhere near *that woman*.'

Then Jeannie saw that Mrs Lawrence was looking, not at her daughter, but directly at her husband.

'You still haven't told us who the men were,' Tom was saying, emulating the older man's outrage. 'Cos if I know any of 'em, I'll . . .'

'No, no.' The girl's voice was shrill with terror. 'No, you mustn't do owt, Tom, please. Nor you, Dad.'

Her father was frowning at her. 'Why? Why ever not?'

'Because – because it was – they were out to celebrate – one of them, the one they were trying to – to make . . .' She gulped.

Jeannie, feeling a stab of sympathy for the young girl, said quietly, 'It was obviously a stag night. A group of young men were out on the town. One of them – Robert, I think I heard him called – is getting married tomorrow . . .' She glanced up at the clock on the mantelpiece above the range and, smiling wryly, added, 'Well, today now and . . .'

She became aware that the two men and the mother were exchanging glances, then George Lawrence leaned towards his daughter and demanded, 'Robert – and getting married tomorrow? You don't mean it was Mr Robert Hayes-Gorton and his pals?'

The girl nodded miserably and her voice was no more than a whisper as she said, 'Yes, Dad.'

In unison, the two men let out a long breath and George sat back in his chair. 'Oh well, that's it then, lad, there's nowt more to be said or done.'

Grimly, Tom said, 'No. Not now, there ain't.'

Jeannie was mystified. 'Nothing to be done? But surely, you're no' going to let them get away with it? I mean, what if . . .' She hesitated as three pairs of eyes glanced in her direction.

'What? What is it?' she asked.

Nell Lawrence said, 'There's nothing they can do, Jeannie. Not if they want to keep their livelihood. Mr Robert's father is a trawler owner and he owns the ship my husband skippers. He's his employer.' She sighed and added, her voice flat now with defeat, 'And Tom's too. He's a deckie on another Gorton boat.'

In a sudden, jerky movement, Tom got up, thrusting his chair away so that it fell backwards on to the floor with a clatter. 'It's ya own fault, Grace,' he said harshly, all sympathy gone now. 'You shouldn't have been anywhere near the pub at that time of night. Or going to Aggie Turnbull's. You brought it on yasen.'

He turned away and dragged open the back door, slamming it behind him as he left so that the pots on the shelf rattled.

Scarcely able to believe what she had just heard, Jeannie stared after him.

Three

Robert Hayes-Gorton woke with the feeling of a cold wetness around his neck. It was still dark and the room was illuminated only by a pale light that filtered in through the half open bedroom door from the landing. He raised his head but the room seemed to be spinning around him. Then he became aware of a vile smell and, putting his hand to his face, felt the sticky thickness of vomit caked around his chin.

He groaned aloud. In the dim light he could see the dark stain over the pillow and the sheets. Gingerly he put his feet to the floor and levered himself upright, but the feeling of nausea so overwhelmed him that he sat down again quickly and put his hands to his head. The vomit was all over his face, even in his hair, and the feel and the smell of it made him retch again. He grasped the bedpost and hauled himself upright and staggered towards the bathroom adjoining his bedroom. He bumped into the door jamb and then lurched towards the bath, banging his knees against it. Then he reached out and grasped the gold tap. Water poured into the bath but it was only lukewarm. Shivering he made himself climb into it and lay down, completely submerging his whole body. Then, sitting up, he soaped himself vigorously, furious now that he had allowed himself to get into such a state the previous evening.

'Bloody Francis,' he muttered. 'Some older brother he is.'

He couldn't remember drinking so much to get this drunk. But then, he couldn't remember much about last night at all. Suddenly he was still, his hands, covered in lather, suspended in the action of soaping his hair. Last night! Oh Lord – he could remember. At least, there was something . . . A wave of shame swept over him and yet he couldn't quite remember the actual reason for such a feeling. What was it that had happened last night that he couldn't recall and yet his subconscious mind was telling him that it was something awful? Was it just because he'd got so drunk? No, it couldn't be that. He'd been drunk before, though never as bad as this, he had to admit. No, there was something else. There was something shameful about the previous evening's escapades.

Slowly, he rubbed his hands over his hair, washing away the stench and massaging his aching head at the same time. Then carefully he stood up and stepped out of the bath, still a little unsteadily but feeling much better than when he had stepped into it. He dried himself vigorously until the roughness of the towel made his skin glow. Then dropping the towel to the floor he stepped back into the bedroom, wrinkling his nose in disgust at the smell coming from the bed. There was no way he was going to sleep there.

The eiderdown had slipped to the floor from the end of the bed and, thankfully, was unmarked. Picking it up, he wrapped it around himself and went towards the couch set beneath the window. First he opened the top of the sash window and then lay down on the couch, settling himself for what was left of the night. He closed his eyes and tried to will sleep to claim him. In only a few hours he'd be standing at the altar waiting for Louise and if he looked half as bad as he felt at this moment, there'd be hell to pay. His mother would have something to say about all this, never mind his bride and *her* mother.

His head still pounded, but the cooling draught from the window soothed his brow and he began to feel drowsy. But in the final moments before sleep overcame him, pictures flashed into his mind. Fleeting, disturbing images.

Darkness, shouting and laughing and then a girl. She was bending over him, saying something. Shouting at him. Yes, that was it. She was shouting at him.

'You should be ashamed of yourself.'

'Tom'll see you to your lodgings, hen,' Mrs Lawrence said, levering herself up. 'Your clothes'll soon be dry, except your shawl, that is. I'll put that in the tub for you and you can call for it another time. I'll lend you one of mine.'

'Thank you,' Jeannie said, but she made no move to divest herself of the blanket nor to rise from the sofa. She glanced up. 'There's just one snag. I've no place to go. I was on my way to find lodgings when . . .' she gave a slight gesture with her head towards Grace, 'it happened.'

'I see. Well, you can bide here for the night if you dinna mind sharing with Grace, that is. But we'd best be awa' to our beds. It's late and they're . . .' she gestured towards the two men, 'awa' on the morning tide.'

'That's kind of you, but . . .'

'No "buts",' the woman said quickly. 'We're grateful for what you did. It's the least we can do.'

The small terraced house bulged when the two men were home at the same time. With only two bedrooms upstairs, the son slept downstairs on the couch.

21

At five o'clock the following morning, Nell Lawrence tapped on the door of the bedroom where the two girls had shared the narrow bed. 'The herring boats are in, Jeannie. Get up. You too, Grace.'

Jeannie swung her legs to the floor and padded on bare feet to the window. Bending, she lifted the corner of the curtain and looked down into the street below. Already, the fisher-girls were emerging from the houses in ones and twos, tying the cotton rags around their fingers as they walked, laughing and calling to each other. Swiftly, Jeannie washed in the pink and white bowl and dressed. Carrying her heavy boots in one hand and her gutting knife and cotton bandages in the other, she went down the stairs to find a bowl of thick porridge awaiting her on the kitchen table.

'There you are, hen, made the Scottish way.'

'This is kind of you,' Jeannie said, picking up her spoon with relish. 'But I ought to be away down to the docks. The girls'll be getting together and if I'm no' there, I'll be left out.'

The herring girls worked in teams of three, two gutters and a packer. As one who had arrived a little later than the rest, Jeannie knew it was difficult to find work. She was an outsider, one who was not already part of a team.

For many years now, the Scottish herring girls had travelled together down the east coast, even as far as Great Yarmouth, keeping pace with the fleet as it followed the shoals of herring, beginning in the Shetlands in the spring and early summer and then drifting southwards through summer, ending up off the English south-east coast by November. The fisher lasses were a close-knit band and each girl jealously guarded her place within a team and each team fought to stay together. They knew one another's ways, each relying on the other's skill; the packer on the gutters to work swiftly and cleanly, the gutters dependent upon the packer to lay layer upon layer of salted silver fish neatly and tightly in the barrels so as to pass the foreman's strict standards. From the days of the luggers and their great flapping sails to the modern steam-driven drifters the fisher lasses had followed the herring fleet.

'What job do you do then, lassie?' Nell wanted to know, sitting down at the table opposite Jeannie and wrapping her hands around a mug of steaming tea.

Jeannie shrugged and said, between mouthfuls, 'I don't mind, just so long as I find work. Gutting or packing. I've done both, though I like the gutting best.'

Nell nodded. 'Aye, the packing's a back-breaking job. I was a gutter.' She smiled. 'Not tall enough to be a packer bending right down to reach into the bottom of the barrels.'

Jeannie pulled a face and laughed with her. 'Well, I canna make that excuse, Mrs Lawrence. But I dinna mind. I'll take what comes.' She did not add aloud, if anything does come. She would liked to have stayed chatting, to have asked Nell more about how she came to be living here in England, but reluctantly she rose and said, 'I must be away. I've lodgings to find and . . .'

'Ah, now about that, hen . . .' Mrs Lawrence interrupted. 'I had a word with George this morning and we're agreed. You can stay here, if you like. Just whilst you're with the fisher lasses. You'll be moving on soon anyway and our menfolk'll be awa' now for a while. And even if you're still here when they come back, well, you wouldna mind sharing the couple of nights they're home with Grace, would you?'

'It's kind of you, Mrs Lawrence,' Jeannie said again, but in her own mind she was doubtful about accepting the woman's offer. As a fisher lass, she needed to be with the other herring girls. When the boats came in, she had to be there, ready to work at once as part of a team, even in the middle of the night. Being separated from the others might mean that she would not be fetched and might be left out. Aloud, she said, 'I'll be away to the docks to see if there's work to be had.'

As if reading her thoughts and understanding her dilemma, Nell Lawrence nodded. 'Aye well, hen. See what happens. You're welcome to come back here if you want.' Then, almost as an afterthought, she added, 'I'll come with you, if you like? If Billy McBride is still one of the foremen, then . . .' she winked broadly at Jeannie, 'he'll find you a job.' Then, almost playfully, she wagged her forefinger, 'But dinna tell my George I said so.'

The herring boats had been sighted nearing the mouth of the Humber, the chugging of the coal-fired engines accompanied by the screeching of seagulls driven wild by the banquet of fish.

The fisher lasses were gathering on the dockside, standing in small groups, binding each other's fingers and chatting amiably together. Some had their hair drawn back into a bun on the back of their head; others, like Jeannie, covered their hair completely with a square of cloth. But they all wore oiled cotton skirts and aprons and short-sleeved, hand-knitted jerseys. A few had thick scarves wound around their necks against the cold wind that whistled in from the river and along the dock.

As they drew near, Nell stopped and looked about her. 'If I hadna seen it with ma own eyes, I wouldna have believed it,' she murmured shaking her head. 'There's hardly anyone here.' Puzzled, Jeannie too glanced around.

To her, there seemed to be a great many girls here – and all waiting for work.

'In my day,' Nell was saying. 'The place was just seething.' She waved her arm in a broad arc to encompass the area where the wooden troughs – the farlanes – stood awaiting the day's catch of fish and where the herring girls would stand at their work for the next twelve hours or so. Beyond them were row upon row of empty barrels where a few men – the coopers – stood waiting for the work to begin. They all seemed to be dressed in a similar fashion: open-necked shirts, the sleeves rolled up above their elbows; braces, holding up their trousers, covered by a waistcoat. Sturdy boots and a cloth cap completed their workaday attire.

As Nell seemed to be lost in her own memories, Jeannie squared her shoulders, lifted her chin and marched up to the nearest group. ''Mornin'.'

The girls glanced her up and down and then nodded in return to her greeting.

'D'you ken if there's work to be had?'

'Gutting or packing?' was the brief question.

'Either,' Jeannie said.

One of the girls jerked her thumb over her shoulder. 'See Billy McBride. He's the foreman. He'll know.'

Jeannie turned back to Nell Lawrence. 'He is here. Somewhere.'

The woman blinked and, pulled out of her reverie, gaped at Jeannie for a moment. 'Och aye, aye,' she said, suddenly remembering exactly what she was doing here. 'I thought he would be, but it'll be finding him that's the problem.' Nell chuckled. Then she glanced at Jeannie and pointed to her hair that curled waywardly on to her forehead, however tightly she tied it back beneath the triangle of cloth. 'Tuck your hair well oot of sight, hen. Billy's one of the old fishermen. He doesna trust red hair.'

Jeannie smiled and did as she was bade. She had every respect for the superstitions of the fisherfolk. Maybe, she thought sadly, I brought my own father bad luck when I went down to the harbour to wave him off that last time. The thought hurt, but she swallowed her private feelings, lifted her chin with a tiny gesture of determination and followed Nell.

They wandered amongst the throng asking, 'Billy McBride?'

A shake of the head, a shrug, and 'I havena seen him,' until one girl said, 'He was here a minute ago. Och, there he is.'

Jeannie looked where the girl pointed, but could see no one. Nell, however, threaded her way through and Jeannie followed in her wake until she came up behind Nell almost bumping into the woman as she stopped suddenly.

'Well, well, Nell MacDonald. Yer've no' altered a scrap, young Nellie.'

Jeannie watched the woman's shoulders shake and heard her laughter. 'You auld rascal, Billy McBride. You're still a right blether.'

Over Nell's shoulder Jeannie saw the man they were seeking. No wonder, she thought, he had been so difficult to find. Whereas on her first sight of Nell Lawrence's husband, Jeannie had thought him the biggest man she had ever encountered, now she found herself facing perhaps the smallest man she had ever seen. He was no more than four feet tall and whilst at the present moment he was greeting Nell like a long-lost friend, Jeannie could see that the man's sharp, beady eyes would miss nothing and that his mouth, at the moment stretched wide in a smile, was capable of contracting into a hard, thin line.

The girls who mingled around them were certainly in awe of this little man, for their jobs depended upon his say-so.

He would have hired the teams in Scotland, bringing them down the east coast, probably even arranging their travel and accommodation, keeping the girls tightly under his control. It was doubtful that there would be any work to be had, Jeannie realized with a sinking heart, yet he was her only hope, so she smiled at him and stood meekly behind Nell whilst the older woman chatted and almost flirted with her old friend.

Then his glance came beyond Nell to appraise Jeannie. 'And who's this, then, Nell? Your lass, is it?'

Nell shook her head. 'No, Billy. I have a daughter – and a son – but they're working. No, this is Jeannie Buchanan. She arrived last night and . . .' Nell's swift glance at Jeannie silently asked that she should not recount the circumstances of how she came to meet the Lawrence family. 'And,' Nell went on, 'I was wondering if you could find work for her.'

'Och, well now, Nell, that might be difficult.' The man stroked what looked like a three-day growth of grey stubble on his chin. 'The girls are already in teams, ye ken.'

'Aye, but if you could, Billy . . .?' Nell left the plea hanging.

Now the man addressed Jeannie. 'Gutting or packing, lass?'

'I dinna mind. I've done both.'

'Your first time in England, is it?'

Jeannie was obliged to nod, 'Aye, but,' she added swiftly, 'I went to the Shetlands last year.'

'Well, you're tall enough to do the packing, but, as it happens, it's a gutter we're short of. The lass cut herself

27

badly and it's gone septic. She didna bind her fingers properly. Now – let me see your hands.'

Smiling with a sense of pride, Jeannie obediently held out her strong hands for inspection, knowing that the tiny faint scars on her fingers were her passport to employment. Taking them into his own, he turned her hands over, his glance keen and knowledgeable. Jeannie knew that the foreman would be able to tell, just from looking at them, if she were speaking the truth. If she were a practised gutter, Billy McBride would know.

Then Billy looked up into her face, staring at her, shrewdly assessing her character. Her clear green eyes returned his scrutiny steadily and she allowed her mouth to curve in the hint of a smile, not so much as to be thought too forward, but just enough to give a small sign of self-confidence in her own ability. She was dressed like all the other girls mingling on the dockside and now as a final proof, if proof were still needed, from her pocket she pulled out the binders for wrapping around her fingers to protect them from the sharp gutting knife.

The man was nodding. 'You'll do, lass. Shall you be following us down to Yarmouth?'

There was the only slightest hesitation before Jeannie said, 'Aye,' but it was enough for the man to glance sharply at her once more. 'I need to be certain, Jeannie.'

'Yes, yes,' Jeannie said swiftly, but Billy McBride was still not wholly convinced.

'Some man here?' he probed bluntly.

If her heart had not been so heavy within her, Jeannie would have laughed out loud. She swallowed and, with a fleeting glance towards Nell, who was quietly watching and listening, said, 'Only my father.' As she said the words, she nodded seawards, towards the homecoming fleet.

'Och, I ken.' The man smiled now, satisfied.

It was not that she deliberately intended to mislead the foreman, who, though brusque in his manner, seemed fair enough, but Jeannie found it difficult to confide in anyone.

As he raised his voice and shouted to two girls standing together, binding each other's fingers, 'Flora, Mary, you've got a new gutter . . .' Jeannie lifted her head, smiled and moved forward to meet her new workmates.

'See you tonight, hen,' Nell called after her and Jeannie turned, waved and said, 'Thanks, Mrs Lawrence.'

Their glances held each other's for a moment as the older woman said softly, 'Thank *you*, Jeannie Buchanan.'

Four

The organ music seemed so loud. It reverberated through Robert's head, louder and louder, until he wanted to put his hands over his ears and run out of the church.

'You look awful. For God's sake don't pass out on me again,' Francis hissed at his shoulder.

'Thanks,' Robert muttered wryly. 'You do wonders for a chap's morale. Besides,' he added morosely, 'it's you I've to thank if I do look a mess.'

To the unobservant eye, Robert would have looked no different from what the guests might be expecting to see in a nervous bridegroom. Both he and the best man, indeed all the gentlemen of the wedding party including Edwin as usher, their father and the bride's father, were attired in black suits and waistcoats, with silk ties around stiff, winged collars. They each wore highly polished black shoes and white spats and carried a top hat and white gloves. A snowy handkerchief, neatly arranged in the top pocket, and a white carnation in the lapel completed the look and if the bridegroom's face was pale, his dark brown eyes shadowed, then they would say fondly that it was the occasion overwhelming the young man of only twenty.

But his brother was not so sympathetic. 'Serves you right,' Francis retorted. 'I can't abide a chap who can't hold his liquor.'

Robert glanced sideways at him, but the darting pain

behind his eyes made him turn his head back to face the altar.

'Nor,' Robert heard Francis snigger, 'a chap who can't rise to the occasion when he has a member of the fair sex – er – just handed to him.'

'Oh, for goodness sake, Francis. Don't be so crude. Not here, of all places.'

But his elder brother had no reverence in his being and Robert regretted having asked him to stand as his best man. In fact, now he came to think of it, he had not himself asked Francis nor even wanted him. It had all been taken for granted, all taken out of his hands by his parents and his future in-laws.

'Of course your elder brother must be your best man,' their mother had decreed and there had been an end of it.

He wondered if the fact that Francis, the first-born son and heir, had been the only one of the three Hayes-Gorton brothers to be sent away to boarding school, had set him apart. Robert, three years younger than Francis, and then Edwin, born a year after Robert, had both attended the local Grammar School as day pupils.

'I will not allow you to send all my sons away,' their mother had insisted.

But had Francis's time away from home given him his supercilious manner? And had he learnt there, too, from unsuitable peers, the dissolute life he now led? Francis had stated, with such determination that allowed no argument from their parents, that he had no intention of marrying. With a rare flash of insight into his own character, he had said, 'I suppose I could be quite fond of Louise, but I would not be cruel enough to marry her. My way of life would break her heart in a couple of weeks.'

And so Samuel's desire for a grandson had become a duty for the second son to fulfil.

Robert had been swept along on the tide of his family's machinations and in this bemused state he found himself standing before the altar in St Michael's Church at eleven o'clock on the morning of the fourth of September in the year of Our Lord Nineteen Hundred and Twenty-four waiting for the organ to strike the first triumphant chords in the music that would herald the arrival of his bride.

A girl, he realized with a shaft of horror, whom he hardly knew.

How on earth had it all happened? He wondered if she too had been inveigled into this marriage. Was she also feeling as he did at this moment? Utterly panic-stricken.

'I can't go through with it, Francis. I can't marry Louise. I—'

His brother's grip was vice-like on his arm. 'My dear boy, of course you must go through with it. Just cold feet, that's all.'

But this was more than cold feet, more than just wedding-day nerves. Robert made to pull away, to pull free, but Francis held him fast.

Now the older brother spoke through gritted teeth. 'It's all gone too far now. Think of the trouble you'd cause. If nothing else, think of the company.'

'The – the company? Is – is that all you can think about?'

Slowly Francis turned his head, his cold blue eyes a steely gaze upon his younger brother. 'The Gorton Trawler Company – and what this marriage will mean to it – is all that matters.'

Robert felt a cold sweat. It wasn't that he didn't like Louise. She was a sweet girl, with blonde hair cut short to frame her delicate features that were like those of a fine porcelain doll. Though he did not, he thought as another spasm of fear gripped his insides, love her.

'Francis, I really can't . . .' he began but when he turned his head again, the pain stabbed once more. Robert groaned aloud and then tried to stifle the sound that seemed to echo around the rafters of the church roof. 'I've never been this bad before.'

Francis gave a snort of laughter. 'Well, I lost count how much ale you had and then,' he paused significantly, 'you went on to the rum.'

Now Robert groaned again, making no effort this time to conceal the noise. 'Oh hell,' he said under his breath. 'You know rum makes me bad. Why didn't you stop me?' There was a pause, then bitterly, Robert added, 'It was you giving me it, wasn't it? Pouring it down my throat.'

'I thought you ought to have a good time on your last night of freedom.'

'You call that a good time?' the bridegroom said with feeling. 'When I can't even remember leaving the pub let alone anything after that.'

'What a shame. Then you have no recollection of the girl?'

'Girl? What girl?' Robert turned towards him again, ignoring the stab of pain this time. 'What – what happened? What did I do?'

At that moment, the organ broke into the bridal march and there was a stirring through the church as the congregation rose to its feet.

'Forget it,' Francis said. 'I think Edwin took care of it anyway. And if there's any further bother—'

'Bother? What sort of bother? Tell me,' Robert demanded as they got up.

'I said, forget it. It'll be all right. You're getting married and your beautiful bride is walking up the aisle behind you at this very moment. Just forget about what happened last night.'

'But I don't know what did happen . . .' he began but Francis was pushing him forward to stand before the steps at the end of the aisle.

As Robert fixed his gaze upon the huge stained-glass window above the altar, he was thinking, not of his bride walking slowly to stand beside him, but of a girl in the darkness of the alley bending over him and shouting at him.

Jeannie soon slipped into the work as a gutter alongside the other fisher lasses standing at the farlanes – the waist-high troughs overflowing with slippery herring. Mary and Flora were friendly, laughing and joking as they worked, but their hands moved like lightning. Flora was the other gutter in their team of three, slicing open the fish with a long, easy motion from head to tail, scooping out the insides and then tossing the fish to Mary, the packer. It was a bright, warm morning and soon the girls were taking off the thick scarves from around their necks. The fish dock rang with their laughter and their Scottish voices. Jeannie felt good to be amongst her own kin. The Lawrences had made her welcome in their home and not just because of the gratitude they felt but also because she was a Scottish lassie too and far from home. Nell would remember, even after all these years, what that felt like.

Jeannie half-listened to the gossip flying around her as she worked, but when Flora said, 'It's the Hayes-Gorton wedding today,' her interest sharpened.

Mary was laughing. 'Aye, and the bridegroom'll have a thick head this morning. They were pouring the drink down his throat last night in the Fisherman's . . .' And then, lest anyone should think she had been present, she added quickly, 'So I heard.'

'Och aye,' Flora teased, quick on the uptake. 'I bet you were there, Mary Fraser, with your man.'

Joining in the repartee, Jeannie winked at Flora and called back over her shoulder to their packer. 'You got a man then, Mary?'

'No, I havena,' came the quick reply, a little too quickly to be convincing and Jeannie and Flora laughed aloud.

'She'd've liked to be marrying Robert Hayes-Gorton hersel' this morning.'

'Who wouldna?' Mary's voice was dreamy but her busy hands never slackened their pace.

Careful to make her tone sound deliberately off-hand, Jeannie asked, 'What's he like then, this Robert What's-'is-name? Who is he anyway?'

Flora actually paused for a moment in her work and stared at Jeannie. 'You mean you dinna ken who the Hayes-Gorton family are?'

Jeannie shook her head. She had a shrewd idea from the conversation that had passed between the members of the Lawrence family the previous evening, but by feigning ignorance now, she realized she could learn more.

Behind her, Mary giggled. 'You'd better tell her, Flora.' She lifted her head and shouted to the other girls working close by. 'Listen, everyone. Story time.'

'Go on, then, Flora,' called a voice nearby. '"*Once upon a time . . .*"' There was a ripple of laughter, but then those within earshot fell silent, ready to listen.

The centre of attention, Flora preened herself. 'The Gorton Trawler Company is the second biggest trawler owner in Havelock . . .'

'And the biggest is the Hathersage Company,' put in another voice.

'Ssh, let Flora tell it.'

'Aye, she's a born storyteller. Go on, Flo.'

All the while a thousand bound fingers never stilled, sharp knives flashing. Hands plunged into the brine-filled farlanes to pick up the fish. Herring, their scales sparkling in the sunlight, were ever on the move being gutted, tossed and packed. The coopers moved amongst the girls, inspecting the packers' work, removing the full, heavy barrels and bringing empty ones. Thirty-five barrels a day, Billy McBride demanded from each team and with eight hundred to a thousand fish to each barrel, the fisher lasses stood there hour after hour with not a moment to waste. Banter and laughter, or a story, were welcome diversions.

Like an actress centre-stage, Flora began. 'The Gorton Company was founded in the 1880s by Thomas Gorton. He was just an ordinary fisherman then, but he married the daughter of the feller who owned the boat he skippered. The girl's father was against it.' She laughed. 'I s'pose he thought Thomas was just after his boat.'

'And was he?'

Flora shrugged. 'I like to think they really loved each other.'

'Did they elope?' a voice asked and the listeners laughed.

'To Gretna Green?' someone else joked.

'I dinna ken if they went to Gretna, but they did run away to be married.' Now Flora held their attention once more. 'They were awfu' happy together in their wee terraced house near the docks. But she was an only child so when her father died, she and her husband inherited the trawler.'

'I thought so,' muttered a voice, more cynical than the rest, but Flora ignored the interruption.

'Thomas Gorton skippered it himself for a while but then he bought another boat and another until he had a fleet of ten or so. They say he was a nice old man. A real fisherman through and through. Tough, but always fair. And he stayed all his life in the same house.' She nodded briefly in the direction of the rows of terraced houses where the fisherfolk lived and where the Scottish girls found lodgings. 'Old Thomas died about twenty years ago and his son, Samuel, took over the company.' Flora paused for effect, knowing she had her listeners spellbound, so she began, as all good storytellers, to embellish the truth a little.

'He was a different kettle of fish altogether.' She smiled at her own pun.

'And still is,' muttered a voice thick with resentment.

'He bought a posh house on the outskirts of the town and began to live the life of a laird. True, he carried on building up the company, but he cut the men's basic wages and their share of the catch to buy more ships.'

'Hathersage is worse, though,' came the voice again. 'He's a tyrant.'

Flora went on. 'The Hayes-Gortons now own fifteen boats and about a hundred-and-eighty families depend on them for a living.'

'Oh, good at arithmetic, isn't she?'

'Hathersage has got twenty boats.'

'And don't forget, if a catch is bad, or the price drops, the deckies barely earn a living wage.'

'I've heard of men coming back from two or three weeks at sea and they owe the company money because they've already borrowed against their wages.'

'Aye, and then the wages they expected don't come, so they're in debt,' another voice complained bitterly.

'How did it come to be *Hayes*-Gorton?'

The remarks flew back and forth, but Flora only

answered the last question. 'Samuel married a girl fu' of airs an' graces. She insisted on adding her maiden name to Gorton and making it a double-barrelled surname.'

There were groans of derision all round.

'That's not the young ones' fault,' Mary put in. 'The three brothers. Is it, though?'

Now the laughter was turned on Mary. 'Sweet on them, are you, Mary? Which one do you fancy then?'

Jeannie risked a brief glance back at their packer. The girl was blushing, but still she answered her tormenters. 'They're so good-looking. A' three o' them. I'd take me chance with any one o' them.'

'The younger two are fine, but the eldest . . .' Flora shook her head. 'His eyes . . .' She held up a fish. 'They're as cold as this herring's. And it's dead.'

Then slicing her knife through the flesh, she tore out the guts and held it up again. 'And he's as much "heart" as this has got now.'

She tossed the fish behind her as if flinging the man away from her too.

'You sound bitter about him, Flora?' Jeannie said quietly.

The girl glanced at her. Dropping her voice so that the conversation was now only between the three of them, herself, Mary and Jeannie, she said, 'He's nothing to me, if that's what you're thinking. Thank God. But two years ago, on my first trip down here, I worked alongside a girl called Rose. Bonnie wee thing she was, though not ever so quick at the gutting. Still, the men liked her and I reckon that's why she kept her place. Well, she got in with Francis Hayes-Gorton. You'll see him, in a day or so, strutting about the fish dock. He'll mind to keep his fancy clothes away from the fish, but he's eyeing up the girls. You'll see,' she said and nodded wisely. 'But if you pay heed to me, you'll keep away from him. Handsome he may be, but he's as rotten as a barrel of fish left out in the sun.'

'So it's no' him who's getting married today then?' Jeannie said, still feigning ignorance.

'I'm coming to that,' Flora said and raised her voice again to continue her tale. 'Samuel Gorton married into money, some say – and I would agree with them – deliberately. And,' she wagged her knife dramatically in the air to emphasize her point, 'today, he's making his second son, Robert, do just the same thing.'

Now there was a chorus of disbelief.

'Never.'

'Who's he marrying then?'

At Flora's side, Jeannie said, 'Well, he's the fool for allowing himself to be pushed into doing it.'

Flora laughed wryly. 'You dinna ken Samuel Hayes-Gorton, Jeannie. Nobody, but nobody, including his own sons...' She paused and then added with emphasis, '*Especially* his own sons, dare to defy him.'

Jeannie was silent, thinking of her own father. A big, gentle-hearted giant of a man, with a mane of fair hair with a tinge of red in it and a beard and moustache that covered most of his face. But not his eyes that twinkled and sparkled with mischief and merriment. Her mother's death seven years earlier had threatened to devastate the big man, but he had put aside his own grief to support his eleven-year-old daughter in the loss of her mother.

And now he, too, was gone. One day soon, Jeannie knew, she would have to come to terms with the awful truth. But not yet, not yet. Not until someone found a piece of the boat or . . .

The voices around her were invading her private thoughts.

'Who's he married then?'

'Why do you saý Robert's marrying for money?' Mary put in. 'He's too nice to do that.'

There was a chorus of laughter. 'Och, Mary, you missed out there. You should have netted him. It could have been you in the church today all dressed in white with all of us making an archway of gutting knives.' Gales of laughter echoed along the dockside.

'Because,' Flora said, enjoying creating the suspense, 'he's uniting the two biggest trawler companies on the east coast of England. Today, Robert Hayes-Gorton is marrying Louise Hathersage.'

Five

Herbert Hathersage rose to his feet in the long hall of his country mansion and glanced about him. The tables had been positioned so that the top table lay horizontally to the foot of the wide staircase, with three tables running the length of the hallway at right angles to the bridal party table.

At first-floor level the staircase divided and ran in a gallery around the hall, the ceiling high above them in a skylight at third-floor level. At the far end of the gallery, musicians played *pianissimo*, a genteel background to the muted chatter of the guests.

Catching the eye of the trio, Herbert nodded and the music stopped, but not until he had tapped the table with a spoon, did conversation cease and faces turn expectantly towards him.

'Dear friends, may I welcome you all to our home on this happy occasion which unites not only two young people, but two families and . . .' he paused for effect, 'the two major trawling companies in this part of the British Isles. I'm sure I speak for Hayes-Gorton's family,' he gave a small bow towards Samuel and his wife, 'when I express my delight at the union of our companies. In due time, it will be our mutual grandson at the helm of a great business empire . . .' His voice droned on and Robert bowed his head and suppressed a visible shudder. Oh, what had he done? He hardly knew the girl at his side. They had spent no more than a few hours alone together during the whole of their supposed courtship.

He didn't like to think of himself as weak so how had he allowed himself to be carried along on the tide of his father's enthusiasm for the match? He was not even twenty-one and Louise was only eighteen. There had been no reason to oppose the match, and yet . . .

He became aware of his surroundings again. '. . . And so dear friends, I ask you to be upstanding and to drink a toast to the bride and groom.'

There was a scraping of chairs on the marble floor and a murmuring like a breeze wafted around the hall. 'The bride and groom . . . bride and groom.'

And then it was Francis's turn, as Robert's best man. He made a few of the usual jokes, though Robert was relieved that he did not descend into crudity as he was wont to do in men-only company. Francis proposed the health of the four bridesmaids and then Robert found himself on his feet, and, to much laughter, heard himself say, 'My wife and I . . .' Dutifully he thanked everyone for coming, for their good wishes, paid tribute to his new in-laws and a lavish compliment to his bride, but inside his mind he was thinking, Yes, my wife and I. I am a married man. It's done and now I must make it work. As he sat down to the polite applause, he turned towards the girl at his side. She really did look very pretty, he told himself, beneath the chiffon veil and its headdress of wax orange blossom. Now he noticed that she was wearing his wedding-day gift to her; a pearl necklace and drop earrings.

Taking her hand in his, he raised it to his lips and she turned and smiled at him, her blue eyes sparkling, her nose wrinkling daintily.

Yes, he really would try to make this marriage work,

Robert promised silently, but first, there was just one thing he had to do.

'Edwin.' Robert gripped his younger brother's arm. 'I must talk to you. Come out on to the terrace. We shan't be overheard out there. Louise is upstairs changing and we won't be missed. I've got to talk to you.'

His brother grinned. 'What? Cold feet already? Or do you want a pep talk about the facts of life?'

But Robert did not even smile in return. 'Please, Edwin.'

'Let me get a drink first then. One for you?'

Robert shuddered. 'No, thanks. I reckon I've had enough to last me a lifetime,' he said with bitter irony.

Edwin laughed. 'Well, I'd not argue with that. Be with you in a minute.' He pushed his way through the throng to where the solemn-faced butler stood with a tray of drinks while Robert skirted the mingling guests, submitting *en route* to handshakes and kisses and good wishes until he came to the front door, which was standing open to the bright sunlit day. He blinked as he stepped outside and then drew in deep breaths of fresh air. Nodding to the footman who stood sentinel at the side of the door he moved along the paved terrace and leant on the parapet looking out over the lawn stretching down to a lake and beyond that a copse of trees. Behind him towered the square Georgian house; the Hathersage mansion, as every-one called it.

He was part of all this now, he told himself, but the thought gave him no joy. He groaned aloud and leant his elbows on the stonework.

'Still got a hangover, old chap?' came Edwin's voice at his elbow.

'A bit.' He straightened up and turned to face his brother. 'But it's not that. I must know what happened last night. Francis keeps making snide remarks and I really don't know what he's talking about.'

Edwin sighed. 'I wish you wouldn't worry about it, it's—'

'Edwin, I've got to know. I keep remembering flashes but not everything and it's driving me mad.'

His brother shrugged. 'If you insist then.' Briefly he recounted the events of the previous evening.

'. . . Then suddenly there was this girl, like an avenging angel, fists flying and shouting at the top of her voice. It must have taken some courage, you know, to wade in amongst the lot of us. For all she knew she could have ended up being – well, you know – too.'

'Raped, you mean?' Robert's voice was a hoarse whisper. 'You mean I was party to a rape?'

'Oh, you didn't actually do anything,' Edwin gave a wry laugh. 'You weren't capable.'

'That's not the point. This is terrible. What about that poor girl? And what if the police had come along?'

'Oh, one did,' Edwin said, as Robert groaned again. 'But luckily it was PC Parsons and he just sent us on our way. Advised me to get you home, which, incidentally, I was trying to do anyway.'

'And the girl?' Robert persisted.

'Which one?'

'The one – the one . . .' Robert gulped painfully. 'I attacked.'

'You didn't attack anyone. It was all Francis's doing. He's a vicious sod when he's had a drink.'

'But what happened to her?'

'Oh, the other girl – the one who came to her rescue – took her off. Home, I expect.'

44

'Who was she? The – the other girl?'

Edwin shrugged. 'By her accent, one of the fisher lasses. Nobody who matters.'

Nobody who matters. The phrase jangled around Robert's battered mind. Oh she mattered all right. For it was that girl whom he could not forget. Whose accusation still rang loudly inside his head.

'You should be ashamed of yourself.'

He was, oh he was, he answered her silently.

'The boats are leavin'. Shall we take our jilly piece and watch them go?'

It was the time when the girls took a brief respite. Jeannie smiled at Grace who stood on the far side of the farlane, holding jam sandwiches – their 'jilly pieces' – wrapped in a cloth. Grace Lawrence might not be Scottish born but with Nell for her mother there was some of the breeding there, the words and phrases of Jeannie's homeland.

Jeannie nodded, unable for a moment to speak. Standing all morning amongst her own kin had made her feel homesick and heart-sore for the loss of her own folks.

Linking arms, the two girls walked along the quay, eating as they went. Standing in the same spot where Jeannie had stood the previous night, they watched the ships easing their way out of the dock, heading for the open sea.

'There they go,' Grace murmured. 'Safe home,' she added like a prayer.

'Which one is your father and brother on?'

'Dad skippers the *Gorton Sea Spray*. But I can't see it. Maybe they've gone already.' She screwed up her eyes against the glare of the sunlight glittering on the water.

As they walked back, Jeannie glanced about her. 'Isn't that your father? Talking to that woman?' The figure of the stranger stood out in sharp contrast to the working fisher lasses. The woman wore a blue and white striped ankle-length dress made in a shiny fabric. Silk, Jeannie supposed, though she could not quite be sure from this distance. The woman's hair was covered with a close-fitting cloche hat trimmed with two white feather pompons that rippled in the breeze. She wore white silk stockings and pointed shoes.

'Where?' Grace asked and, following the line of Jeannie's finger as she pointed, added, 'So it is. And me mam'd go daft if she saw him talking to her.'

'Why?'

'That,' Grace said, nodding towards where the tall, broad figure of George Lawrence stood laughing down into the upturned face of the woman, 'is Aggie Turnbull.'

'Aggie . . .?' Jeannie began and then she remembered. 'Oh yes. The woman whose house you'd been to last night.'

Grace nodded.

'I ken your mother doesna like her?'

Grace gave a snort of laughter. 'You could say that.'

'Why?'

The girl smiled impishly. 'Me mam ses she's "Nae better than she should be".' Grace mimicked the Scottish accent perfectly, even though her own speech normally held no trace of it.

Jeannie laughed, throwing her head back so that the scarf tied around her head slipped down letting her red hair fly loose in the wind. George Lawrence turned away from Aggie Turnbull and walked along the quay towards them.

'My, my, that's a pretty picture for a man to take to sea with him,' came his cavernous chuckle.

Self-consciously, Jeannie touched her hair and then tried to pull the scarf up over her head again.

George put out his huge hand and touched her curls. 'Don't cover it up, lass. It's such pretty hair.'

'You – you dinna mind, then?'

George looked puzzled for a moment and then he laughed. 'Oh, old Billy McBride and his superstitions, eh? Nell been telling you, has she?'

Jeannie just smiled. She had known of the superstition from childhood.

'Well now,' George put his arms about both girls' shoulders and steered them down the jetty towards where his own boat was moored. 'I respect a man and his beliefs. We've got a few of our own, but red hair on a pretty girl isn't one of them, not in these parts anyway. Now, come and see me off. It's high time I was aboard.'

They couldn't stay until the boat nosed its way from the jetty towards the dock gates but they watched him climb the ladder and jump aboard the *Sea Spray*.

As they turned away they saw Tom hurrying towards them.

'I can't stop,' he said. 'I should be aboard, but . . .' He turned to Jeannie. 'You'll still be here when we get back?'

'I dinna ken,' Jeannie said quietly and her glance flickered beyond Tom's shoulder across the grey water to the Havelock boats moving out into the mouth of the Humber and towards the sea until they became distant specks on the horizon.

Tom, misreading her thoughts, said, 'If you're looking for the Scottish drifters, they were first out on the tide this morning. But they'll be back. They'll be using this port for a week or two yet, I reckon.'

'Uh?' She dragged her wandering thoughts back to the young man standing in front of her. 'Och no, it's no' that.

I mean, I wasna looking for the herring boats. At least,' her voice dropped to a mere whisper, 'not the ones that have just left.'

She said no more and avoided meeting Tom's eyes until his deep voice, the disappointment evident in its tone, asked gently, 'What are you watching for then? Or is it some*one* you're watching out for? Is that it, Jeannie?'

Now she had to meet his gaze and, though she tried to smile, she knew the haunted look was deep in her eyes.

Tom put out his huge hand and suddenly gripped hers. 'Tell me? What is it?'

There was a shout from a man standing midway up the gangway leading on to a ship. 'The gates'll be closing in half an hour, Tom.'

Jeannie heard his sigh. 'I'm sorry. I'll have to go . . .' Again he gave her hand a quick squeeze. 'I – I hope you're still here when we get back. And Jeannie, there's just one more thing. Look out for my little sister here, while I'm gone?' He smiled down at Grace and tweaked her nose playfully. 'I wish we weren't sailing today but I can't let me mates down. I'm just glad I've managed to get on a Hathersage boat this trip and not a Gorton.' Suddenly there was a dark anger in his eyes. 'That bastard is going to pay for what he did. Me dad – nor me – aren't going to forget.'

And then he was gone, striding along the quay and running up the gangway and on to the *Hathersage Enterprise.*

She was still standing watching when Grace touched her arm and said, 'We'd best get back to work, else you'll lose your place.' She gave a wry laugh. 'There's allus plenty of local lasses without steady work trying to get into a team while the herring girls are here.'

Jeannie gave one last glance towards the trawlers and then hurried after Grace. 'Doesna your mother come down to see them away?'

Grace shook her head. 'She's too busy. She's got to braid a net – part of a cod net, that is – in two days. She'll still be at it when we get home tonight. You'll see.'

And Jeannie did see, for when she unwound the ties from her fingers and walked wearily through the gathering dusk to Baldock Street, it was to find Nell Lawrence standing before the kitchen wall from which hung a fishing net, growing longer under her nimble fingers. Jeannie watched in fascination as the braiding needle flashed in and out of the mesh.

'I'm sorry, hen,' Nell said, her hands never slowing in their task. 'I havena had time to get you a meal ready.'

Grace winked at Jeannie. 'That's all right, Mam. You carry on. Me an' Jeannie'll get the supper, but you must stop and have a bite.' The girl, now fully recovered from her ordeal of the previous night, wagged her finger playfully at her mother. 'I bet you've never stopped all day to eat, have you?'

Nell chuckled and shook her head. 'This net willna braid itsel', hen.'

Jeannie moved closer, watching, and when Grace went from the kitchen into the back scullery, Nell asked in a low voice, 'Has she been all right today, Jeannie?'

'What? Och aye. She seems fine now. She seems to have got over it very quickly.'

Nell's lips compressed into a tight line. 'Only thanks to you coming along in time, hen. It might have been very different if . . .' She stopped and then shrugged her shoulders and said, 'Well, let's just be thankful you did. We'll think no more of it now and I just hope it'll all be forgotten by the time the men come home again.'

Jeannie turned away, anxious that Mrs Lawrence should not see the doubt in her eyes. She was sure that Tom would not forget Mr Robert Hayes-Gorton and his friends and what they had tried to do to his sister.

Six

News of the grand wedding was the talk of the fish dock for days. Gossip filtered back from the domestic staff who worked at the Hathersage mansion.

'It was a lovely wedding,' Mary told them dreamily. 'And they've gone away on honeymoon now. For a whole month.'

'How do you know?'

'The daughter where I'm lodging is a maid at the Hathersages' place and she was telling her mother all about it. Their servants have been run off their feet for weeks before, but she said it was worth it. Miss Louise looked a picture, Annie said. She wore a cream ankle-length gown with gold embroidery and beading round the neckline and hems. And she had a long train from the shoulders . . .' Mary swept her hand down the length of her own body to demonstrate. 'The edges were decorated to match the dress. And white silk stockings.' She sighed. 'Och, what I wouldna give to wear white silk stockings.'

'Dinna forget, Mary, that Aggie Turnbull and her like wear white silk stockings,' put in a voice at the next trough and Mary shot a venomous glance at the girl, who only laughed and nudged her companion. 'Our Mary gets carried away with herself and her dreams of living in high society.'

Mary sniffed contemptuously and turned her gaze away, determined not to let anyone spoil her romantic fantasies. Then she looked down wistfully at her rough clothes and at her hands bound with the ragged tapes. 'I dinna think anyone will ever say that about me. That I look "a picture".'

Flora sniffed. 'Shouldna think little Miss Louise has ever had to lift her dainty fingers to do a stroke of work in her life. 'Tis nothing to be proud of, leading such an idle life.'

'I could get used to it,' Mary grinned, her natural resilience and good humour rising to the surface once more. 'Married to Robert Hayes-Gorton, I could get used to anything,' she added, rolling her eyes comically so that all her workmates laughed.

Only Jeannie Buchanan did not join in their laughter, pressing her lips together to keep them from opening and spilling out exactly what she thought about the man who seemed to hold such a fascination for Mary Fraser.

On the second morning of their honeymoon, Robert Hayes-Gorton stood at the bedroom window overlooking Lake Windermere. The pale, early sun was just rising over the hills filtering gentle streaks of light across the water. The lake was peaceful, so opposite to the tumult going on inside the unhappy young man's mind. His gaze was upon the tranquil scene, yet he hardly took in the view.

He was reliving the night. The horror of it. Inside his head he could still hear Louise's hysterical screaming that had not subsided until he had given his solemn pledge never to try to touch his wife again.

It had begun with such promise. The previous night – their first as man and wife – had been idyllic. As they had driven away from the reception in Samuel Gorton's motor car, Louise had been laughing and flirtatious, waving happily to all their guests as the motor rounded the bend in the driveway of her home and turned into the road. Then she had tucked her arm through Robert's as his hands rested on the wheel and snuggled her head against his shoulder. 'My husband,' she had murmured. 'My handsome husband.'

That evening, they had dined in the small hotel where they were to stay for the first night. There were few other guests in the dining room, but Louise had sparkled and chattered throughout the meal.

'Weren't the bridesmaids pretty? Did you like my friend, Madeleine?' Robert opened his mouth to reply with a dutiful compliment, but Louise carried on, almost without pausing for breath. Her questions, it seemed to Robert, did not require an answer.

'She's my very best friend. She's asked us to go up to London and stay with her any time we like. Won't that be fun, darling? And Francis made a wonderful best man. He's very handsome, isn't he, with that fair hair and pointed moustache? Has he got a girlfriend? I'm surprised he wasn't the first to get married.'

'He's not the marrying kind,' Robert put in, 'so he says.'

Louise's laugh tinkled merrily. 'Oh, they all say that, but he'll change his mind, once he meets the right girl.' Coyly, she put her head on one side. 'Just like you.'

Robert smiled and reached across the table to touch her hand.

Later, as he slipped into bed beside her, she nestled against him. Knowing how tired they both were, he held her, kissed her gently but tried nothing more. Time enough, he told himself, even though the feel of the girl aroused him.

But last night, here in the hotel overlooking the lake where they were to spend the first two weeks of their honeymoon, he had taken her in his arms, his kisses becoming more passionate. His trembling fingers tugged at the front of her nightdress and at once she shrank from him.

'What are you doing, Robert?'

'You're my wife, Louise. You know what happens, don't you?'

'What do you mean "what happens"?'

'When a man and woman are married. You know about – well – that?' There was a silence until he added, with a growing sense of disappointment, 'Don't you?'

'I don't know what you're talking about.'

He released her then and rolled on to his back, letting out a great sigh. 'Oh,' was all he said, his voice flat.

There was silence as they lay side by side in the huge bed. Then she stirred beside him, raising herself on one elbow and leaning towards him, she said softly, 'You can show me, if you like.'

Hope surged within him and he reached out for her again, pulling her to him. 'I'll not hurt you,' he murmured, kissing her gently. 'I promise . . .'

His kiss became more urgent as his ardour heightened. He unfastened the front of her nightdress and buried his face in the soft fullness of her breasts and he moaned with pleasure, kissing and caressing. Then he was tugging at her nightdress again, pulling it up, his hand seeking her private place, his fingers searching.

'No, no, you mustn't do that. It's . . .'

But his urgency was too far gone now for him to pull back. He was astride her, lying on top of her, spreading her legs apart with his knees.

'No, no, Robert. You're hurting me. No, no!' She was pushing against him and her voice was loud and frightened.

And then suddenly it was as if he were back in the alleyway and beneath him someone was screaming. He almost felt the hand on his shoulder once more pulling him away.

His passion died and he was still, lying heavily on top of Louise, who was crying hysterically, 'You're hurting me.'

He rolled off her to his own side of the bed and lay staring up into the darkness, listening to his child-bride sobbing beside him.

And out of the blackness of the night, yet again, came the voice. 'You should be ashamed of yourself.'

Seven

'What were you doing at Aggie Turnbull's place that night anyway?' After a few days when Grace seemed to have recovered from the incident, Jeannie felt able to ask the question.

The girl glanced at her quickly and then her gaze fell away. 'I'd – er – just been round to see Aggie. Y'know.'

'Are you friendly with her then?'

'It's – it's . . .' Grace hesitated and Jeannie had the feeling that she was trying to scrabble around her mind for some plausible excuse. A defensive note crept into Grace's tone. 'Aggie's all right. Really she is. She's kind and friendly and – well – fun.'

'But your mother doesna approve.'

Grace looked at her and then suddenly she moved closer, glancing about her to be sure they could not be overheard. 'If I tell you summat, will you promise not – not to tell me mam?'

Jeannie studied the girl's young face, but she could not be less than honest. 'I canna promise you that until I know what it is.'

Grace blinked and faltered, 'Oh. Oh, then it's best you don't know.' She half-turned away, but Jeannie caught hold of her arm. 'Be careful what you're getting into, Grace. Aggie's house may seem like good fun, but . . .' Suddenly, Jeannie felt older than her eighteen years and much older than the naive sixteen-year-old standing beside her. Surely, she thought, living in this area, knowing Aggie Turnbull all her life, Grace could not be so ignorant? If she were, then Nell had kept her unenlightened deliberately. But there were consequences to be paid for for being overprotective. That ignorance could lead Grace into danger.

The young girl shook her head and at her next words, Jeannie knew a sense of partial relief. 'Oh, I know what Aggie Turnbull is.' A small smile twitched at the corner of her mouth. 'Everybody round here knows that. It's a wonder there isn't a pathway worn in the road by the number of fellers who make a beeline to her door when the boats come in. Aye, an' not only the single fellers either. There's married ones an' all whose wives don't . . .' Mischief danced in Grace's eyes. 'Make 'em welcome home, if you get my meaning.'

So, Jeannie thought with amusement, Grace was far from being as naive as she had imagined.

'But,' the girl went on, giving a mock shudder of disapproval, 'don't think I'm getting into anything like that. It's just that – well – I can meet me friends at Aggie's.'

Jeannie frowned, her mind racing and, quick to understand the underlying meaning to Grace's words, she said, her mouth tight, 'You mean, friends your mother wouldna approve of?'

Again the quick glance and then away again. 'She doesn't approve of me having boyfriends. Ses I'm too young.' Now Grace flapped her hand at Jeannie, 'Oh, now look what you've made me do.' Angry tears shone in her eyes. 'You've wheedled it out of me and you'll go and tell me mam and . . .'

'Only if I think you're – well – in danger of getting yoursel' into trouble.'

'No, no, it's not like that. It's – it's only a boy. He's not

57

from round here. I – I only see him now and again. When . . .' Again she seemed to be searching for a credible story. 'When his boat's in.' Now Grace seemed to be warming to her theme. 'Mam'd like him, if only she'd let me bring him home.'

'Mm.' Jeannie was thoughtful. It was an old problem and one that was hardly likely to change. When girls and boys got to a certain age and thought of themselves as grown up yet their parents still treated them as children, it could lead to this kind of deceit.

'You won't tell me mam?' Grace begged.

Jeannie sighed heavily. She had the uncomfortable feeling that whilst Grace may not be actually lying to her, she was sure the girl was not telling her the whole truth. 'I'm not making any promises, Grace,' she said. 'But just you mind what you're doing.'

Impulsively the girl hugged her new friend. 'I will, Jeannie. Honest I will.'

'They're back. Have you heard?'

The fisher lasses were once again standing at the troughs. Today they were all well wrapped up, for the wind lashed through the docks, rippling the surface of the water and whistling along the quays. Then it began to rain, soaking the girls, stinging their faces but still they stood there, working with no easing of their speed, stoically trying to ignore the cold.

'Back?' Flora said, never lifting her eyes from her flashing blade. 'Who's back?'

'The bride and groom.'

'Already? I thought you said the other day that they'd gone on honeymoon for a whole month?'

'So they had, but they're back. And that's not all.

They've gone to bide at the Hathersages' place and . . .'
Mary paused to achieve the most dramatic effect. 'And
they've got separate bedrooms,' she finished triumphantly.

There was a moment's silence until Jeannie said, 'Well,
don't a lot of the upper classes sleep in separate bedrooms?'

The other girl seemed nonplussed for a moment but
then said stoutly, 'Well, you wouldna think newly-weds
would want that, would you? Not even in the upper
classes. And what about coming home early from honeymoon then? Besides, I got it from Annie. She works as an
upstairs maid there and she ses . . .'

The girl prattled on whilst Jeannie was busy with her
own thoughts. She felt sorry for the child-bride. No doubt
Robert Hayes-Gorton had forced himself upon her on their
wedding night in the same way that he'd attacked Grace.

Oh yes, she felt very sorry for the poor girl and she
hadn't a moment's sympathy for him. Not one moment.

'Come in and close the door.' It was a command rather
than an invitation.

Robert did as he was bade and stood before his father-
in-law's huge desk in his study.

'Now, young feller, you'd better tell me what's going
on between you and my daughter.'

Robert felt himself blushing uncomfortably, making
him feel even more gauche and foolish than he already
felt.

'Well?' came Hathersage's bark. 'I'm waiting.'

'It's personal and – and delicate.'

'Oh, so Francis was right, was he?'

Robert's head jerked up to see his father-in-law nodding
knowingly. 'Francis? What has he been saying?'

'When you arrived back from your so-called honeymoon far earlier than expected, your brother guessed that you haven't – er – consummated the marriage yet, eh? Only Francis didn't put it as politely as that.'

I bet he didn't, Robert thought morosely. He was rapidly beginning to see his elder brother in a very different light recently. If it hadn't been for Francis, he wouldn't have been involved in that disgraceful incident the night before his wedding and now, it seemed, his own brother was not above tittle-tattling to Robert's new in-laws about what was a private matter between the newly-weds.

Robert lifted his head, squared his shoulders and faced the man across the desk. 'Your daughter, Mr Hathersage, is only eighteen and doesn't seem to have been told what to expect of married life.'

'What?' Now the red-veined face opposite him was growing purple. 'What are you insinuating?'

Calm now, Robert said, 'I'm not insinuating anything. She didn't know anything about the – well – you know what I mean.'

Hathersage let out a grunt of anger. 'I left all that sort of thing to her mother.' For a moment he was silent and thoughtful, as if he were thinking back and remembering. Slowly, he said, 'Mm, well, it's not as unusual as you might think, m'boy. You'll just have to be very patient with her.' Standing up he added, 'But I wish you hadn't come back so soon. It's set the servants gossiping. And the separate bedrooms hasn't helped either, but I'll have a word with her mother.' He moved round the desk and patted Robert on the shoulder with what was intended to be a fatherly gesture but to the young man it had the feel of condescension about it. 'Yes, yes, that's the best. I'll speak to her mother. It'll be all right.'

Eight

Robert weaved his way amongst the fish troughs ignoring the raucous shouts from the girls until he found himself standing opposite a tall, slim girl with her bright red hair tied back. Her hands never slowed in their movements, yet he was aware of her glances. He could not fail to see the anger and resentment in the flash of those green eyes that told him she knew exactly who he was and what he had done.

Surely this couldn't be the girl he had supposedly attacked? She looked too feisty, too spirited to have . . . And then suddenly he knew. She was the one who had flown to the other's rescue. This was the girl who had shouted at him and hauled him away.

Ever since the day of his wedding he had promised himself to come down to the docks to seek her out. But now, standing before her, Robert's mouth was suddenly parched. He ran his tongue around his lips and when he tried to speak his voice was little more than a hoarse whisper. 'Excuse me. Might I – er – have a word with you in private?'

'I canna leave me work,' was her curt reply.

Robert was immediately aware that close by all the chatter and noise had ceased and though the work never slowed, he knew that all who could overhear were listening hard.

He swallowed and tried again. 'I would like to speak

to you. Could I meet you somewhere when you finish work?'

'Meet me? Meet me?' Suddenly the sharp blade of the knife she was wielding with such effect on the fish, was being held threateningly only inches from his face. 'Like to meet me in a dark alley, would you?'

He stepped back to find himself up against one of the girl packers at the next trough.

'Mind where yer treadin', mister.'

There was laughter all round. 'Aye, he wants to mind where he's treadin' all right.'

His face reddening, Robert turned and blundered away, the sound of their suggestive taunts following him.

'I'll meet you round the back, mister, if she won't.'

'Fancied a bit of rough, did you?'

Jeannie bent her head over her work, thrusting the blade into the fish with a vicious delight. How she would like to have slashed at his face; marred those godlike good looks, that smooth, boyish skin.

Then suddenly a wave of shame swept through her. She had always known she had a quick temper, but until this moment she had never experienced such a passionate hatred for anyone. The violence of her feelings shocked her.

She paused a moment and glanced up to watch him hurrying away, his shoulders hunched.

She felt Flora's elbow dig her in the ribs. 'That the one who attacked Grace Lawrence, then?'

Jeannie turned wide eyes on her team-mate. 'How on earth . . .?'

The girl laughed. 'Och, news travels fast on the fish dock, Jeannie. You canna keep a secret round here for long.'

Jeannie said nothing until Flora prompted again, 'Well, was it him?'

In a quiet, flat tone, Jeannie answered. 'Aye.'

Flora nodded towards the corner of the building around which Robert had disappeared from their sight. 'You should have given him a chance to explain, maybe to apologize even. He's only a wee laddie, Jeannie. You should have given him a chance.'

'Him and his friends weren't giving poor Grace "a chance",' Jeannie retorted bitterly. Yet she was honest enough to admit that now she had seen him close to and in daylight, he was much younger than she had expected.

'Aye well,' Flora was saying, her tone philosophical. 'From what I heard, if Grace Lawrence goes visiting Aggie Turnbull's, then she can expect all she gets.'

'You two goin' to gossip all day,' came the truculent voice of their packer from behind them. 'I'm waiting.'

Jeannie guessed that Mary had seen what had happened and overheard every word, had learned the truth about the young man she had so admired from a distance. And Mary didn't like it.

'Sorry,' Jeannie said at once and again her knife blade flashed, but this time only upon the fish.

He was waiting in the shadows on the corner of Baldock Street when Jeannie and Grace made their way home.

'Excuse me . . .' When he stepped out in front of them, both girls jumped and Grace gave a little scream.

He glanced briefly at Jeannie but now it was upon Grace that his gaze rested.

'Please . . .' He put out his hand to catch hold of her arm and Grace screamed again, the sound echoing along the street.

'Don't you dare to even touch her,' Jeannie hissed and stepped between them.

'Please, you've got it all wrong. I've come to apologize – to explain—'

'What is there to explain, mister? You attacked an innocent young lass. A gang of you. What chance had she got, eh?'

Even in the fading light, she could see that he turned white. 'I was drunk. I can't even remember clearly what happened. I would never – ever – have done such a thing in my – my right mind.' He swallowed painfully and again he looked directly at Grace. 'Did – did I hurt you?'

Mutely, Grace shook her head but fiercely Jeannie said, 'Only frightened her out of her wits. And who's to know what might have happened . . .' She didn't add 'if I hadn't come along' for even to her own ears, it would have sounded boastful.

He was putting his hand into the inside pocket of his jacket. 'Please, let me . . .?' He opened a leather wallet and extracted a five-pound note and thrust it towards Grace, but before the girl could even reach out, Jeannie wrenched the piece of paper money from his fingers and tore it into shreds, casting it into the gutter. 'How dare you? How *dare* you insult her like that?'

'I'm sorry. I only wanted—'

'We ken what you wanted.' She grabbed Grace's arm now and hauled her along the street, calling back over her shoulder, 'You and your like! Think the fisher lasses are good for only one thing.'

Robert stood staring after them whilst, as Jeannie dragged her away, Grace twisted her head round to watch the little pieces of white paper float along the gutter and disappear down a drain.

Jeannie was still seething about the incident when they arrived home but Nell, her fingers still busy braiding a net, seemed to accept the news calmly. In fact, to Jeannie's annoyance, Grace's mother seemed almost to be taking the young man's part.

'I canna understand you.' Jeannie spread her hands, palms upwards, in a gesture of exasperated disbelief. 'Any of you. Just because he's the son of the owner of the ships, you're going to allow him to get away with what he did to Grace.'

'He didna do anything to Grace, did he? Not really?' And as Jeannie opened her mouth to retaliate, Nell held up her hand. 'Och I ken, lassie, what he – and all the others – might well have done if you hadna come along when you did.' For a moment, Nell actually dropped the length of sisal she was holding and moved towards Jeannie. Taking her hands between her own, Nell said gently, 'I ken how you feel, hen, and what you'd like to do to those – those . . .' The word to fit the description of what she felt for them defeated her and her sentence ended in a sigh. 'And I feel just the same . . .' She balled her hand into a fist and smacked her own plump chest. 'In here. Really I do. But there's nothing – *nothing* we can do. It's best left.'

'But to come down to the dockside today. To seek her out in front of everyone and offer her money. The final insult. How could he do that?' Jeannie burst out.

Grace, who had stood nearby quietly listening to every word, spoke up now. 'He was going to give me five pounds, Mam. A whole five-pound note, but – but Jeannie tore it up under his nose and threw it into the gutter.'

For a fleeting moment even Nell blinked and glanced from one to the other, a moment's unguarded hesitation on her features. Five pounds to a fisherman's family, even a skipper's family, was a lot of money. She gave a little sigh and a tiny shrug of her shoulders as if to dismiss it from her mind and then, looking once more directly into Jeannie's eyes, she said softly, 'Have you stopped to think, hen, what courage it must have taken for that young man to come amongst all the lassies on the docks today? They're the salt of the earth, all of them, I'll never say different, but they wouldna have been beyond turning on him if they'd all known the full story. He could easily have found himself rolling in the mud, his clothes torn from his back. They might even have thrown him into the water. Son of an owner or not, if they'd all done it, there'd have been precious little anyone, including the police, could have done about it.'

Jeannie, still unforgiving, her mouth a straight hard line, leant a little closer to Nell and said, with quiet deliberation, 'Aye, an' if I'd known that this afternoon, Mrs Lawrence, I'd have led them on mysel'.'

Nell gazed at her for a long moment and then nodded slowly. Her eyes softened as she smiled. 'Aye, I do believe you would have done, hen. For you're a brave, feisty girl, and I'll thank God every day of my life that you came along at that moment. But you know something, Jeannie lass . . .?' The older woman patted the hand she still held. 'You're always going to be the one that others lean on. Because you are so strong, you're always going to be the one they all come to. All your life, lass, you're going to have to carry the burdens for those nearest to you.' For another moment she held Jeannie's gaze and then she turned away, bustling back to her work. 'What am I doing standing here blethering on as if next week'll do. I've this net to finish by the morning and I'll be up half the night as it is.'

'I'll help you, if you like,' Jeannie volunteered and Nell glanced at her again, this time with surprise in her eyes.

'You know how to braid?'

Jeannie nodded and a lump came into her throat as she

said hoarsely, 'I had a very good teacher. The best. My father taught me.'

Aware that the girl was perhaps reliving painful memories, deliberately Nell pulled a comical face. 'Is there anything you *canna* do, lass?'

Now Jeannie laughed as she moved towards the net to watch Nell's quick fingers for a moment. 'Plenty,' she said and added wryly, 'I'm no great shakes in the kitchen. The man who takes me on'll have to have a strong stomach.'

The two women laughed together and behind them even Grace smiled as she turned away, the one, by the sound of it, to cook the meal again that evening.

Nine

'Tell me about your home, hen,' Nell said softly. 'Your mother and father and where you come from.'

They were sitting by the fire late one evening, just the two of them, waiting for Grace to come home.

'We lived in a small fishing village on the Fife coast,' Jeannie began and suddenly she could almost feel again the wind on her face as she had stood on the wall watching her father's boat becoming a mere speck on the horizon as he sailed away. A wave of homesickness for the white-washed, gabled cottages that clustered around the harbour, the ever-open doors of friendly neighbours in the tiny community where everybody knew everyone else, washed over her.

Faltering a little at first, Jeannie went on to tell Nell's sympathetic ear about her childhood, the loss of her mother, but when she spoke of her father there was a catch in her voice. 'My father's sister took care of me when he was at sea but I used to live for his time ashore. He'd take me into Kirkcaldy and buy me clothes and presents or even to Edinburgh. Och, he used to spoil me rotten. Once he took me on a real holiday to the Trossachs. D'you know, if I close my eyes . . .' she did so to demonstrate, 'I can still see the wet rocks and hear the rushing water of the Falls.'

She sighed and opened her eyes bringing herself back to the tiny, cramped kitchen that was miles from her homeland. She forced a smile and said, 'Mr Lawrence reminds me of him in so many ways. He even looks a bit like him.' She laughed. 'He has a beard like him.'

'Aye, he's a good man is my George,' Nell said dreamily as if she too were thinking back. 'The first time I laid eyes on him, Jeannie, I knew he was the man for me. I just never went home.'

'Have you ever been back to Scotland? For a visit?'

Nell pressed her lips together and shook her head. 'We couldna afford it, specially when the bairns came along. And now all ma family in Scotland are gone. There's no point in going home. I've been homesick many a time. But you see, hen, I loved George Lawrence. And he,' she ended simply, 'was here.'

'But you still call Scotland "home"?'

The two women exchanged a glance. 'Aye well,' Nell said. 'You never forget your roots, do you, hen?' She paused a moment and then asked gently, as if already half-guessing the answer, 'And your father?'

Mutely, Jeannie shook her head and then the words came haltingly. 'He – he didna come back from his last trip. He was with the fleet – the herring fleet. He has . . .' She hesitated and then deliberately said, 'Had – his own little steam drifter.' She bit her lip and fell silent.

'How long since his boat went missing?' Nell's soft, lilting voice was a balm to Jeannie's tormented heart. The sound of home and yet far enough away to lend a remoteness that in itself was a comfort.

'It's – it's been four months now. I know it must sound foolish, but that's why I came further south. I thought he might have put into another port for a wee while for repairs and then maybe moved on, following the herring fleet, y'ken . . .? Her voice trailed away. Then Jeannie pulled in a deep breath and with a determined effort, she said, more strongly, 'But I know I ought to face the fact that he – he's gone. If he'd been all right, I'd have heard by now. He wouldna have let me go this long without a word from him.'

'Aw lassie, I'm sorry.' Nell had reached out and gripped the girl's hand, but she probed no further.

The room was silent for a moment save for the ticking of the clock and the spitting of a log on the fire.

'How long was it before you married Mr Lawrence? After you'd met him, I mean?'

'Och well, I went on with the fisher lasses right down the coast to Yarmouth, but instead of going back home at the end of the season, I came back here and we were married on his next shore leave.' She smiled impishly at the memory. 'There were a few too many local girls with their eye on George Lawrence for my liking.' A slight shadow crossed her eyes as she murmured, 'One in particular . . .' Then she cleared her throat and was smiling again, 'And I couldna let him escape *my* net, now could I?'

As they laughed together, Nell glanced up at the clock and her expression sobered. 'It's time Grace was home. Surely she can't be working as late as this again?'

'Would you like me to go and look for her?'

'No, no, Jeannie. I'll wait up. You be away to your bed. Tomorrow's a big day . . .' Her face was wreathed in a happy smile again. 'The men will be home again.'

As Jeannie rose Nell reached up and patted her cheek affectionately. 'Sleep well, hen.'

When George Lawrence stepped into the house, Nell came alive. The big man brought light and laughter into the little terraced house and even the ever-present net lay limply, half-braided, against the wall whilst Nell bustled about after her husband. It wasn't that she was miserable when he was at sea, but the moment he came home there was a sparkle in her eyes, a smile on her lips and an extra spring to her step.

'Get yar bonnets on, girls. I've been for me settlings . . .' He spilled a bundle of notes and coins on to the table. 'It was a good trip, so I'm taking you into the town. You too, Jeannie.' He reached out and gathered most of the notes together. 'Here's your housekeeping, Nell. And this . . .' he picked up the remaining money, 'is to spend.'

He took them to Main Street, Nell, Grace and Jeannie.

'It's lucky there were no herring boats in today, else you'd have missed this,' Grace said, linking her arm through Jeannie's, but her new-found friend's reply was a heavy sigh.

'The shoals of fish are moving south. The girls will be going too soon.'

'Shall you go?'

Jeannie shrugged. 'I dinna ken.' Then she smiled. 'Let's no' think about it today. Let's enjoy ourselves.'

'Yes, let's,' Grace agreed.

And enjoy themselves they did. They had dinner in a fancy restaurant and George took them round the shops and insisted on buying each one of them a new winter coat.

'Och no,' Jeannie resisted. 'I couldn't possibly.'

'Go on, hen.' Nell nudged her and winked. 'Our Tom'll be home soon and I know he wants to take you out. You'd look lovely in that dark green coat with your pretty hair.'

Jeannie felt a lump come into her throat.

Spending lavishly after a good trip, George Lawrence reminded Jeannie even more of her father. Thinking of him, she felt the familiar ache in her chest. The only difference was when he spoke, for George's Lincolnshire dialect was nothing like the brogue of Angus Buchanan. But for today, she could imagine she had her father back with her, so she lifted her chin, smiled and thanked the big, generous man.

'I told you, didn't I?' Flora said. 'There he is.'

'Who?' Jeannie looked up, her gutting knife still for a few seconds.

'Francis Hayes-Gorton.' Mary nudged her from behind. 'Look, over there. Oh, but he's handsome. Just look at his fine clothes.'

Jeannie's eyes narrowed as she studied the man. He was, as Flora had predicted, strolling about on the edge of the area where the girls worked, idly swinging his cane, his thumb hooked into the pocket of his waistcoat.

'I wouldna trust that one,' Flora put in. 'Now, if you'd told me that he was the one who had attacked Grace Lawrence, I'd have believed it.' She shook her head. 'But, you know, I still canna believe it was the other one. Robert.'

'He was there.' Jeannie nodded her head towards Francis.

'Was he trying to stop what was going on then?' Flora probed.

'Well . . .' Jeannie hesitated. 'I think it was him who was the ringleader but, to be truthful, I dinna ken. I just waded in. I didna wait to see who was doing what exactly.' She grinned ruefully. 'Me and my temper.'

'There,' Flora said triumphantly. 'I didna think it would be Mr Robert. I've always thought he was rather nice. Though I'm not,' she added sharply and, with her knife, indicated the girl behind them, 'as smitten as Mary.'

Jeannie was thoughtful for a moment before she said,

slowly, 'There was one of them who tried to be, well, helpful.' She gave a sniff of derision. 'But only afterwards, when I'd broken it up.'

'Who was that?'

'I'm not sure.' She paused again, dredging back through the fleeting images and voices of that night. Then she asked, 'Is there another brother?'

'Yes, we told you. Edwin. He's the youngest.'

Jeannie nodded. 'I think it was him, then.'

'I still dinna think it was their fault. Not any of 'em.' Mary was still determined to defend all the brothers. 'She led 'em on, if you ask me.'

Jeannie half-turned and opened her mouth to make a sharp retort in Grace's defence when her attention was caught once more by Francis Hayes-Gorton. He was standing by the corner of a building, talking to a girl. His head was tilted to one side and he was looking down at her, a sideways, slightly sardonic smile on his thin mouth. Then he reached out and touched the girl's cheek with his fingers.

Jeannie drew breath sharply and then clamped her mouth together to stop the words she had been about to utter.

'There,' came Mary's triumphant voice from behind her. 'What did I tell you? See that?'

The girl, looking up into Francis's face and blushing prettily, was Grace Lawrence.

When the work was finished for the day, Jeannie went in search of Grace. As she moved amongst the throng of girls making their weary way home, she felt a touch on her arm and turned to look down upon Billy McBride.

'A word with you, lassie.' His face was serious and for

one moment Jeannie's heart leapt in her breast. He had news. News of her father.

'Jeannie, I'm sorry, but there's not enough work to warrant taking you with us on to Yarmouth. The catches are dwindling already. They've not been what they used to be for a few years now.' He sighed heavily. 'I reckon soon there won't be any Scottish lasses coming this far south. And besides, the lass who's usually with Flora and Mary will be well enough to work when we get to Yarmouth and back to take her place in the team.'

Jeannie nodded and smiled. 'It's all right, Mr McBride, I . . .'

'I could have a word with a few of the local employers, if you like, lassie. I know several of them. And you're a good worker . . .' He nodded and smiled, showing broken, uneven teeth. 'I've been watching you.'

It was a rare compliment, Jeannie thought, and her smile broadened of its own accord. Billy McBride was a hard taskmaster. That much she had seen. His recommendation would certainly be worth having. She thought quickly. She had been about to say, before his interruption, that she would go home, back to Scotland. But now, with the promise of a job here, she held her tongue. At least, for the present, it might be worthwhile staying in Havelock. She was overcome by a sudden longing for home and her resolve almost weakened. But news, her head told her, if any came at all, was far more likely to come here, to Havelock, for her father's vessel had been following the boats southwards.

Quickly, she made her decision, she would stay here. She would write home to one of their neighbours to make sure there had been no news there, but she would stay in Havelock at least for a while longer.

Her attention came back to the wiry little man and what he was saying. '. . . There's the kippers. There's work there for a while longer. Or the filleting, alongside Nell's lass. Maybe she could help you find employment.'

Ah yes, Jeannie thought, Nell's lass indeed. Grace Lawrence. Now there was another problem. It wasn't really any of her business, of course, but she meant to say something to the girl. She could not begin to understand how Grace could even speak to Francis Hayes-Gorton after what had happened. It seemed to Jeannie that she was far more angry and resentful about the incident than Grace. Wisdom told her that she should catch the first train back north of the border. And yet, she liked the Lawrence family. She felt drawn to Nell, who was one of her own, and to George. And to Tom Lawrence too. One day he would grow into a fine man like his father.

Jeannie felt herself being lured into the mesh of this family, like a fish entangled in one of their nets. Instinct told her to go; she ought to leave, right now, and yet something held her here.

It was more than just the vain hope that her father would one day come sailing into this safe haven. Now, it was more to do with the Lawrence family and, in particular, in saving Grace from her own foolishness.

So when the other Scottish girls moved southwards following the herring fleet, Jeannie stayed in Havelock.

'You'll easily find work in the fish docks, hen,' Nell had assured her. 'And you're welcome to stay here as long as you want.'

'But you havena the room when the menfolk are home.'

Nell gave a snort of laughter. 'And how long are they

at home? You tell me, as if I didn't know. Thirty to forty days out of a whole year, so you'll hardly be in the way, now would you?'

Jeannie laughed. 'No, I suppose not, if you put it that way.' Her eyes took on a faraway look, as she murmured. 'I should like to stay here a while longer.'

So, when Tom Lawrence came home, Jeannie was still there and his expression, when he saw her, left Jeannie in no doubt as to his pleasure at seeing her again.

'My word, what have you got, Jeannie, that the rest of the girls round here haven't?' Grace teased her archly as they undressed and got into their shared bed that night. 'He's never stayed away from the pub and his mates on his first night ashore. And taking you out for a walk, just the two of you.'

In the flickering light from the candle, Jeannie smiled grimly to herself but said nothing. She could hardly tell Grace that they had spent most of the time talking about her and that the conversation had almost turned into a quarrel.

'Have you been looking out for our Grace, then?' had been Tom's first words. 'Has she been behaving herself and keeping away from Aggie?'

The familiarity with which Tom spoke of Aggie Turnbull was not lost on Jeannie, but she made no comment. 'She's been out once or twice – to see friends – but she didna stay out late.'

Tom gave a grunt. 'Where did she go?'

'I've no idea, Tom. I promised you I'd look out for her, but I'm not her keeper.' Her anxiety about the girl made her tone sharper than she had intended. She had tried to keep a watch on Grace, but the girl was as slippery as one of the fish Jeannie gutted each day. Always, it seemed,

Grace had a plausible excuse. 'I was on an errand for me mam,' or 'I had to work late . . .'

When Jeannie had probed about seeing her talking to Francis, even then Grace had had a ready retort. 'I can hardly snub him if he chooses to speak to me, now can I? His company employs my father.'

'I'm sorry, Jeannie, but I worry about her,' Tom was saying now. 'She's only sixteen and a naive sixteen at that. And me mother, well, I think she sees no wrong in her.'

'Och, I think your mother knows more than you think,' Jeannie said, remembering the immediate reaction of Nell Lawrence on the night of the attack when hearing Aggie's name mentioned. 'I think she knows exactly what Aggie Turnbull is. And so does Grace.'

Tom stopped and turned to face her, catching hold of her arm and turning her to face him. 'What do you mean by that? "What Aggie Turnbull is"?'

She looked up into his face, seeing his fair eyebrows drawn together in a frown. The square of his jawline suddenly hard and his mouth down turned at the corners. For a moment Jeannie stared up at him and then with deliberate pointedness looked down at the huge hand still grasping her arm. Quickly, he released her and gave a quick, rueful, smile. 'I'm sorry, Jeannie . . .' He ran his hand through his thick, springy fair hair. 'But I get so wound up when I think about our Grace getting 'ersen into trouble.'

Jeannie felt her head reeling. For a moment, his quick spurt of temper and the sudden disarming apology had reminded her yet again of her own father; the loving, generous man with a heart of gold had nevertheless had a swift temper but it had always died just as quickly as it had flared.

Now she was just as quick to forgive Tom. 'It's all right. I do understand. It must be very difficult for you – and for your father – being away so much, to look after your womenfolk.'

'It's a strange life,' Tom murmured. 'Me dad always ses that when you're at sea you long to be home and when you're ashore you can't wait to get back to sea.'

Jeannie smiled, but the smile was tinged with sadness for his words still reminded her of her father. 'Yes,' she whispered, a little catch in her voice. 'That's what ma father always said too.'

And suddenly she found herself confiding in Tom, telling him everything that she had told Nell.

'I used to count the days off on the calendar to him coming home,' she said softly and her throat constricted at the memories. 'And then all too soon, he'd be gone and the counting of the days would start all over again.'

'And now?' Tom prompted gently.

Jeannie shook her head and said flatly, 'He – he hasna come back. Since May, on his first trip out with the herring fleet this year, the – the counting has never stopped.'

'Aw Jeannie . . .' Now the touch on her arm was surprisingly gentle. 'I'm sorry. Sorry about your dad. I – I thought it was – I mean – I thought you were waiting, watching for someone special . . .' He faltered. 'Y'know – a boyfriend.'

My father was special, she wanted to say, very special, but she said nothing. They walked on together for a while before Tom asked, 'What are you going to do?'

Jeannie lifted her shoulders in a shrug and there was reluctance in her tone. 'Go home, I suppose. Eventually.'

'Is that what you really want to do? I mean, is there someone back home. A feller?' Again, disappointment clouded his eyes.

Now Jeannie laughed. 'No, no feller. But there are a lot of friends. People who took care of me when my father was away. Although,' she hesitated again, 'my aunt died last year. Very suddenly, from a stroke.'

'Do you want to go back?'

There was a pause before Jeannie said slowly, 'I dinna ken. It's my home and yet – without my father . . .' She left the sentence unfinished for she was muddled in her own mind as to exactly what her feelings really were. Part of her was homesick for Scotland and yet another part of her dreaded having to go back to the house knowing he would never come home again.

'Then stay here, Jeannie, with us. Me mam'd love to have you and you'd be a friend for our Grace and . . .'

She looked up at him, a sharp retort on her lips that she had no intention of staying just to be nursemaid for his sister, but then she caught the look in his eyes and there was no mistaking the sentiment in his next words. '. . . And I'd like you to stay too.'

Ten

The screams echoed through the house bringing Mr Hathersage and his wife, dressed only in their nightwear, running to the bedroom which Robert and Louise now shared at her parents' insistence. Yet it was only to stop the servants gossiping, Robert thought resentfully. No one seemed to be making any real effort to help Louise act like a real wife towards him.

His blustering father-in-law flung the door open without even knocking. 'What on earth is going on?'

It was like a scene from a farce, yet no one was laughing. Louise lay on one side of the huge four-poster bed, drumming her heels and wailing whilst Robert slipped from beneath the sheet and reached for his dressing gown. As he pulled it on to cover his nakedness, Mrs Hathersage rushed forward to gather her child to her ample bosom. Rocking her, she crooned, 'There, there, my precious. I'll not let him hurt you again.'

As the girl's crying lessened to a hiccupping sob, the mother glared at the two men until they moved away and left the room.

'Huh, such a carry-on. Come down to the study, boy. I could do with a drink . . .' Henry Hathersage led the way downstairs, his bare feet and ankles poking out comically from beneath his white nightshirt.

In the book-lined study that reeked of its owner's stale tobacco smoke, Robert sat in one of the leather armchairs.

His father-in-law poked the fire into life. 'Doesn't look as if you're going to give me a grandson at this rate, m'boy. What are we going to do about it, eh?'

When Robert made no reply, the older man turned towards the array of bottles on the sideboard. 'Mind if I make a suggestion, young feller?'

'No,' was Robert's toneless reply.

Mr Hathersage came and stood in front of him holding out a glass with a inch of amber liquid in the bottom.

'Go and see Aggie.'

'For heaven's sake!' Robert burst out without pausing to think. 'You're as bad as my brother.'

'Eh?' The older man sat in the chair opposite. 'What's that supposed to mean?'

Robert sat forward, placed his drink on the small side table and leant his elbows on his knees. With a groan he dropped his head into his hands. 'Oh hell, what a mess!'

'Come now, my boy. It's not as bad as all that. Why, I remember . . .' Mr Hathersage made a coughing noise and changed the direction of his sentence. 'I've told you before, this is a common thing with the ladies, especially a young, sheltered girl like our Louise.'

Slowly Robert raised his head and looked at his father-in-law with a haunted, haggard expression in his eyes. 'Does she know nothing? About – about that side of married life?'

Mr Hathersage cleared his throat again noisily. 'Evidently not. My wife – er – finds such matters indelicate and could not bring herself to talk to the girl. Pity. It's hardly fair on you.' He shot Robert a keen glance. 'You – I take it – have little experience with women?'

Robert gave an involuntary shudder, remembering.

'What did you mean? About your brother?' Mr Hathersage persisted. When Robert did not reply, the older man's tone became coaxing. 'Come on, my boy, this is man to man stuff. It'll go no further than these four walls. I promise you.'

Still Robert hesitated. It seemed ironic to confide such a thing to the father of his bride. And yet, the young man thought, it would be a relief to speak of it. He let out a huge sigh and began to relate the shameful details of the night before his wedding.

'Ha!' Mr Hathersage slapped his knee with the flat of his hand. 'Francis took you to Aggie's, did he? Didn't I say that's what you ought to do. She knows a thing or two about how to please a man, does Aggie.'

Slowly Robert raised his head and was appalled to see his father-in-law give him a broad wink.

'And as for the girl, well, if she wasn't one of Aggie's girls then she should have known better than to be in that street, specially at night.' Mr Hathersage dismissed the whole incident as being of no consequence.'Your brother had the right idea, m'boy. You go back to Aggie's.' He tapped his forefinger against the side of his nose. 'But not a word to our ladies, eh?'

Sickened, Robert got to his feet, sorry now that he had foolishly confided in his father-in-law. 'Thank you for the drink, sir.'

'All right, m'boy. All right. And think about what I said, eh?'

Robert nodded, turned and left the room, closing the door quietly behind him. He had no intention of going anywhere near Aggie Turnbull's. Instead, he decided, he would try to talk to his wife. Perhaps, if he was very gentle with her, they could learn together. It was worth a try.

And she was not the only girl he wanted to talk to. He had still not had a chance to explain everything to that red-haired beauty, Grace Lawrence's avenging angel, Jeannie Buchanan.

'The boats are in. The boats are in.' The cry, and the excitement that the words always brought, rippled around the docks and the neighbouring streets. No one ever quite knew how it happened, but the news spread like a tidal wave, bringing wives, sweethearts, children, sometimes whole families, to the dockside to watch the armada of boats coming home with the tide.

It was not the herring fleet now that had appeared on the horizon this time, for they had moved southwards, but the home fleet of Havelock trawlers. Since Tom had last been ashore, Jeannie had found work alongside Grace, as a filleter, and now the two girls, in their break, stood watching the ships draw near.

'Me mam's still busy with a net, so I've come to see me dad's boat come in. And Tom's too.'

Jeannie was looking forward to seeing them both, the big man with his loud laugh and bluff affection, but especially Tom with his lopsided grin.

'Are they on different boats again?' Jeannie asked.

'Yes. Tom's still on the *Hathersage Enterprise*. He ses he won't go back on a Gorton ship.' Her face expressionless and without a trace of emotion in her voice, Grace nodded towards a building behind them. 'But they're all here today. I wonder why?'

Jeannie turned to see five men standing on the steps. They were all in formal suits with high-standing collars and black ties and the two older men had moustaches, twisted into points at either side.

Involuntarily, Jeannie felt her jaw harden. 'Two I

83

know,' she said, her voice tight as she recognized Francis and Robert Hayes-Gorton. 'The third young man must be their brother, Edwin.'

'That's right.'

'Who are the two older men?'

'The one standing next to Mr Robert is his father, Mr Samuel Hayes-Gorton. The other is Mr Hathersage.'

Jeannie turned her gaze away from the men for a moment and looked at Grace. Bluntly, she said, 'I saw you talking to Mr Francis a while back?' Sarcasm crept into her tone. 'Was he apologizing?'

Grace's face was suddenly bright red as colour flooded it. 'Oh Jeannie, please don't make any more trouble. It was nothing. Honest. He's always around the docks, specially when the fisher lasses are here. He's just a flirt. We all know what he is. And don't say anything to me dad. Please? Or to Tom.'

'We-ell,' Jeannie said slowly, trying to stop the teasing smile twitching her mouth. 'Just so long as you do as your mother says and keep away from Aggie's.' Then she allowed her generous mouth to curve in a mischievous smile. 'But d'you know, I keep hearing about this Aggie Turnbull. Her name seems to keep cropping up. I've seen her, but only at a distance. One of these days I'll have to meet her. I'm quite looking forward to it.'

'Oh you!' Grace said good-naturedly. She linked her arm through Jeannie's. 'Come on, let's go and meet Tom. That's his boat just coming in now.'

Tom was first off the boat, clambering down the ladder almost before the ship had settled its prow gently against the side of the jetty.

'He seems in a hurry,' Jeannie murmured, puzzled by the young man's haste. There seemed an air of agitation about him and his face was set in a grim frown.

'I don't think he's seen us,' Grace said in surprise. Obviously she had thought that her brother's haste was because he had seen them waiting for him, but as his feet hit the solid mass of the quay, he began to run, a little unsteadily at first, towards the dock office.

'Tom. Tom!' Grace shouted and began to push her ways towards him, with Jeannie in her wake.

The young man halted and turned to face them. At once, Jeannie could see the anxiety in his eyes.

'Jeannie, oh Jeannie. You're still here.' Tom came to her and put his arms about her, burying his face in her neck, not caring who saw.

'Tom, what is it?' Jeannie tried to ease herself from his embrace, but the young man held on to her fiercely.

Now Grace was tugging at the sleeve of his jersey. 'What's the matter?'

Against her, Jeannie felt Tom drag in a shuddering breath and then he lifted his head, loosened his hold on her and stepped back a pace. But he did not let go of her hands, still clinging on tightly as if he would never let her go.

'I'm that glad to see you still here.' And he gave her hands an extra squeeze. 'Has there been any news?'

'News, Tom?' Grace said. 'We don't know what you're talking about?'

Still his gaze was on Jeannie. 'You mean, you haven't heard anything?'

'Heard what . . .?' Then, as understanding dawned, Jeannie heard Grace draw in a sharp breath. 'Oh no, you don't mean Dad's ship?'

Wildly, Tom shook his head. 'That's the trouble. I just don't know. There was a terrific storm three nights ago and we heard that a boat had gone down. But I can't seem to find out which one. I don't know what to do.'

85

Gently, Jeannie pulled herself free of his grip. 'Won't the dock office know?'

Tom ran his hand through his hair. 'Yes, yes. They might. I suppose I'd better go there.'

Jeannie took hold of Grace's arm and said, 'We'll come with you, Tom.'

But Grace held back. 'You go. I – I'll wait here.'

Jeannie turned to look at her in surprise. 'But don't you want . . .?' she began and then noticed that Grace's gaze had gone beyond her, beyond her brother, to the building that housed the Gorton offices.

'I bet that's why they're here.' Grace nodded her head in the direction of the five men and as Tom turned his gaze and noticed them for the first time, Jeannie saw his body stiffen. 'I couldn't understand it. I've never seen all of 'em come down to the dock 'afore. That'll be why.'

'Right,' he said grimly. 'We'll see what Hayes-Gorton himself has to say.'

'Oh no, Tom,' Grace cried, catching hold of his arm. 'Don't make trouble. You know Dad wouldn't want that.'

Her brother turned to face her, whilst Jeannie looked on silently. 'I'm not going to make trouble, Grace. I just want to know what's happened to me dad's ship.'

'But you said yourself, you don't know that it is his. Not yet. Why don't you . . .?'

'Have you seen it come in?' Tom flung his arm out wide to encompass the steady stream of trawlers nosing their way through the narrow dock gates and towards their assigned positions.

'No, but – but – they're not all home yet. Not even all the ones that are due today. Likely his boat's just late. Maybe tomorrow . . .' Her voice, and her argument, fell away.

Tom's voice softened. 'There's no harm in me asking.

They can't do anything to me for just asking, can they?'
But now it was as if he were seeking reassurance too.

Jeannie stepped in. 'Then I'll go. There's nothing they
can do to me . . .' and added bitterly, 'at least, not in broad
daylight.'

Robert saw the girl pushing her way through the people
milling about on the dockside, coming directly towards
them, and his mouth was suddenly dry. Surely, she
wouldn't make a scene? he thought and then answered
himself at once. Oh yes, she would. He felt his breath
coming faster and then she was standing before them, on
a lower step, looking up at them, her bold, green gaze
resting on each of their faces in turn. And when she came
at last to him, Robert saw the contempt in her eyes. But
her glance flickered away from him and turned instead to
his father.

Becoming aware of her scrutiny, Samuel Hayes-Gorton
looked down and said, 'Well, young woman? What do
you want?'

'Sir, there's a rumour going around the dock that one
of the boats has gone down.'

Her tone was polite, but firm, deferential but certainly
not fawning. At his side, Robert felt his father stiffen.

'Nonsense,' Mr Hayes-Gorton growled. 'There are several not back yet. Whatever makes you think that?'

Jeannie opened her mouth to say that the son of one of
the men aboard the *Gorton Sea Spray* had heard it even
whilst still at sea, but she closed it again. The reason she
was standing here was because Tom himself did not want
to be the one to enquire.

'Then you're saying,' she said, 'that you have not had
word that a boat's gone down?'

'I've already given you my answer, young woman,' Samuel Hayes-Gorton said, but neatly avoiding answering her question, whilst, beside him, Robert cringed. He saw the girl glance again into the face of each of them as if she were trying to read the truth written there. As she turned away, his father muttered, 'Get down there, boy, and scotch this rumour. Edwin, you get back to the office. We must make sure word doesn't get out.'

'But I can't tell them nothing's happened when we know it has,' Robert said, aghast to think that his father cared so little for the families of the men aboard the *Sea Spray* that he would lie to them, just to ensure that, in two days time, his fleet would sail again, unhindered by the knowledge that a tragedy had befallen one of their boats.

'You can't . . .' he began, but his father cut short his protest.

'Don't you tell me what I can or can't do, boy. Get down there . . .' And without waiting to hear any more Mr Hayes-Gorton turned and stamped up the steps into the building.

'You'd better do as Daddy says, old chap,' came Francis's smooth voice whilst Mr Hathersage gave a grunt and turned to follow his fellow trawler owner up the steps.

For a moment Robert made no move but, from his vantage point, he watched Jeannie make her way back to where a young man and a girl stood together, obviously waiting for her. He ran lightly down the steps and followed her. As he neared the three, they turned to face him. Robert nodded briefly to Jeannie and then to Grace, feeling once more as he did so, the flush of shame creep up his neck. He cleared his throat with a nervous sound and turned to face the young man. Strangely, both Tom and his sister refused to meet Robert's eyes. Only the red-haired girl's green eyes met his challengingly. Despite his father's orders, he could not lie to these people, so instead he said quietly, 'If I promise to let you know, myself, immediately we have news, would you – I mean – could you, please, say nothing to anyone else for the present?'

Jeannie, quick on the uptake, said, 'Aye, I thought your father was avoiding answering my question.'

Keeping his voice level, Robert found himself replying to her, for the other two had not opened their mouths. 'Well, in a way, yes, he was, but I think . . .' He hesitated, for he was in danger of lying too now and he hated being forced into doing so. 'The truth is,' he began afresh, 'that we ourselves know very little at present and we don't want rumours to spread before we know the truth.'

Now Tom spoke, his tone deferential. 'But you think something has happened then, sir? To the *Sea Spray*?'

Robert swallowed again, conscious the whole time of Jeannie's steady, unforgiving gaze upon him. 'Something's happened, yes, but – but we don't know what. Yet.'

The young girl was crying now, clinging to her brother's arm. 'Oh no, not Dad. Not our dad.'

Robert's eyes, full of sympathy and contrition, turned towards her. 'I'm so sorry. So very sorry,' he whispered and, as the three pairs of eyes now looked upon him, he knew that they were all aware that he was not only apologizing for the tragedy which may have befallen the Lawrence family, but also for his part in the disgraceful incident on the night before his wedding.

He saw Tom Lawrence give a brief nod. 'Yes, sir, I do believe you are.' And Robert felt that the young man too was referring to both events. He felt himself relax a little, believing that his apology had been tacitly accepted, but when he turned to look directly at Jeannie he saw in her fine eyes that her understanding was not forthcoming.

Abruptly, he turned away, saying over his shoulder, 'I'll keep you informed. I promise,' before he strode away.

As he ran back up the steps and into the building, Robert Hayes-Gorton was still thinking about the girl with the fiery hair.

More than anything, he had wanted her forgiveness.

Eleven

'What are we to tell your mother?' Jeannie asked.

Tom hesitated and glanced at his sister. 'I don't think we should tell her anything. Not yet. What do you think, Grace?'

'Not tell her?' Jeannie was scandalized. 'You mean we're going to walk into that house and act as if – as if nothing's happened?'

Now Tom would not meet her eyes. 'There's no point in upsetting her. Not till we know for certain. We'll just say his boat isn't in yet.' He spread his hands. 'After all, we don't really know that anything has happened. Do we?'

'But you heard what *he* said?' Jeannie could not bring herself to refer to Robert by name. 'Something's going on.'

'Yes, I heard,' Tom said with quiet patience and resignation. 'And I heard him promise to let us know as soon as he knew more himself. And he will.'

Jeannie gave a snort of contempt. 'You think so?'

She made to turn away with an angry movement, but now Grace caught her arm. 'Please, Jeannie, don't say anything to Mam. Let's do what Tom says.'

Jeannie shrugged her shoulders, but her mouth was still tight. She hated deceit of any kind and what was happening now, to this family, was all too close to her own tragedy for her to think rationally. Had they all known back home that her father's ship was missing? Had they, too, all kept the secret from her, just leaving her to come gradually to the realization that he was not coming back? She hoped not. She didn't want to think that of her own people, her own kin. She knew herself well enough, her own strengths and weaknesses, to know that she would have dealt far better with the honest truth than this dreadful not knowing. Maybe never knowing.

Now, her words clipped by her anger, she lifted her shoulders as if shrugging off their problems. 'It isna my business, anyway. I'll be leaving soon. I'll be going home – to Scotland.'

And with that, she pulled free from Grace's hold and marched away.

'What do you mean, you can't find out?' Robert leant on his knuckles over the desk, towering over his brother.

Patiently, though with the anxiety evident in his voice, Edwin said, 'We'll find out when we've had time to talk to the men.'

'Who? Which men? Let me talk to them. I'll go. But tell me who?'

'Calm down, Robert,' Samuel Hayes-Gorton's voice boomed as the door to Edwin's office was flung open and their father, followed by Henry Hathersage and a languid, bored-looking Francis. 'We'll know soon enough if the news is bad. And if it isn't, I don't want you spreading fear amongst the crews unnecessarily.'

Robert straightened up and turned to face his father but the older man put out his hand, palm outwards, to stave off further argument. 'You know what might happen when we lose a ship. It makes no difference to the real fishermen, they're hardened to it. Accept it as part of the life, but the youngsters, well . . .' He glanced at his son's face and seeing the puzzlement there, added, 'A lot of them might not report for duty when the boats are ready to sail. They take fright or —'

'Or their dear mamas will try to keep them safely tied to their apron strings at home,' came Francis's sarcastic tone.

'What utter nonsense. Fishermen and their families have always accepted the hardships and dangers as part of the job. If you ask me, the women are every bit as courageous as their menfolk. More so, in a way. They have to sit at home waiting. Just waiting.'

Francis laughed sarcastically. 'Oho, all of a sudden we're the expert on women, are we?'

Robert felt himself colour at the innuendo in his brother's tone, but it was more from anger than embarrassment. He stepped towards the door, but passing Francis, he paused and thrust his face close to his, saying hotly, 'And even if they did try to keep their menfolk at home, can you blame them? I don't see you joining a ship, my dear brother, and learning what this trade – the trade that buys you all your luxury – is really all about.'

Francis smirked and raised his left eyebrow. 'Oh yes, and how many trips have you done, old boy?'

Robert clenched his teeth, 'None,' then he added ominously, '. . . yet.'

'Now, now . . .' came his father's voice, but Robert waited to hear no more and left the office slamming the door so hard behind him that the frosted glass in the upper panel of the door cracked.

He ran down the stairs and once outside stood again on top of the flight of steps, his glance taking in the busy fishdock in front of him. He must speak to the skippers of the vessels which had already docked. Surely someone must know something. For a moment, he paused. He didn't want to spread alarm through the community without just cause. It was a hard life for the fishermen and their families and whilst they all lived with the constant fear of disaster, he didn't want to be the one to make things worse. At least, not until he knew for sure.

He could not get the picture of the Lawrence family out of his mind: of the young girl's wide, fearful eyes, of the deep anxiety on the young man's face. And the other one, Jeannie, with her feisty spirit and her strength. He could see her so clearly; that glorious red hair flying freely in the breeze, wayward curls framing her face, her cheeks faintly pink from the cold and the tiny peppering of freckles across the bridge of her nose. He sighed as he thought about her. Such a lovely mouth, yet when she looked at him it was tight with disapproval and those wonderful green eyes held such contempt. Yet even though her look made him cringe in shame, he was sure he had seen sadness deep in those eyes.

He wanted to make it up to Grace Lawrence, but more than anything else, he wanted to see the look in Jeannie's eyes soften towards him. He wanted to see her smile.

Oh yes, more than anything else he wanted her to smile at him.

In their shared bed that night, Grace snuggled close to Jeannie and whispered, 'Don't go away, Jeannie. At least not yet. Not till we know – about Dad.'

In the darkness, Jeannie sighed thinking over the day's events.

Returning to work after leaving Tom and Grace standing on the quayside, Jeannie had regretted her sharpness. Her angry retort to them, saying that she intended to return home, had been said in the heat of the moment. The truth was, Jeannie acknowledged, that she didn't really want to go home. Who was there, back in Scotland, who really needed her now? Oh yes, kind friends and neighbours, but no kin. No one who would care for her and whom she could care for.

The brother and sister had looked so young and forlorn standing there on the bustling dockside as she had walked away from them. And lost. They needed someone, she told herself. Someone like her.

And you should know how that feels, Jeannie Buchanan, she reminded herself, if anyone does. She felt a shudder run through her, imagining the long hours the young brother and sister may stand, looking out to sea, watching the horizon in vain for the sight of their father's ship.

As long as she had watched until, at last, all hope was gone.

She had been unable to concentrate properly on her work and had incurred a reprimand from the foreman and now had a tiny cut on her little finger as a result of her own carelessness when allowing her mind to wander.

Arriving home had been the worst, seeing Nell bustling about her tiny scullery, red faced from a day's baking and cooking to welcome her man home from the sea.

'Hello, son,' had been her greeting to Tom as he had bent to kiss her cheek. Jeannie had watched as Nell had reached up and patted his muscled shoulder. 'How was your trip?'

'Good, Mam,' Tom replied and Jeannie marvelled that he was able to keep the anxiety from his tone. 'We had a good catch and there should be a fair pay out.'

'Aye well, you'll be needin' it if you're away to the Fisherman's tonight.' Nell's eyes twinkled mischievously behind her steel-rimmed spectacles as she had placed his meal before him. 'Or are you staying home?'

'Eh?' The young man looked up, startled. It was obvious to Jeannie that for one moment he thought his mother must have heard something and expected him to stay with the family until they heard news instead of joining his mates drinking and making merry. His tone was suddenly high-pitched as he asked, 'Why? Why, should I stay home?'

'No reason, son.' Nell shrugged her shoulders and winked at Jeannie. 'I just thought you might find something to keep you at home.'

'Such as?' he asked brusquely, picking up his knife and fork. He did not begin to eat but kept his questioning gaze upon his mother.

Careful, Jeannie wanted to say, you're going to give the game away yourself if you're not careful, and she found she was holding her breath.

'Well, I just thought . . .' Nell was saying and then suddenly Jeannie realized what the older woman was thinking. The last time Tom had come home from the sea, instead of going to the pub that first evening, he had taken her, Jeannie, for a walk. She remembered how Grace had teased her about it and she had understood that it was not Tom's usual behaviour.

Now she laughed aloud, trying to save Tom from falling into the trap that his mother was unwittingly setting. 'Och, I'll no keep a man from his drink, Mrs Lawrence.' She nodded towards Tom. 'You go, Tom.'

Tom looked at her and blinked and then, seeming suddenly to remember too, he gave her a quick, grateful smile.

'Och well now,' Nell was saying, 'I'm no' so sure I agree with you there, hen. It's all very well, these traditions, but when they've wives and families. Now, you take their dad, he's never gone out to the pub the minute he sets foot on land. The next day, well, maybe so, but he always liked to stay with his family . . .' Nell prattled on, busying herself between the back scullery and the range but Jeannie felt a cold spasm of fear clutch her heart. It was an unfortunate choice of words on Nell's part, in the past tense, and Jeannie prayed that they were not prophetic.

But she was very much afraid that perhaps already the sea had indeed taken George Lawrence.

Even with Tom gone from the house, the tension did not lessen. Not for Jeannie. She was aware all the time of Grace casting surreptitious, nervous glances at the clock above the fireplace. For a while Nell returned to her endless braiding against the wall, but by nine o'clock even she looked towards the clock and said, 'Well, it doesna look as if your dad will be home tonight. Away to your bed now, hen.' This to Grace, but her glance seemed to include Jeannie too.

'Are – are you going to bed, Mam?' To Jeannie's ear, Grace's voice seemed high-pitched with the anxiety she knew the girl was feeling.

'No, no, I'll sit by the fire a while longer, just in case.'

Oh no, Jeannie thought. The waiting's begun. Counting the hours, then the days and the weeks.

Oh no, not again.

She took a deep breath, rose from her chair and said as cheerfully as she could, 'Shall I make us all some cocoa?' And forcing a smile, she added, 'Even I can manage that.'

Minutes later as the three women sat sipping the hot liquid, the silence deepened between them until Grace sprang up from her chair, slopping the last of her cocoa over the side of the mug. 'I'm going up,' she said and Jeannie knew instinctively that the girl could not bear the suspense any longer, could not bear sitting there knowing that she was deceiving her mother and unable to shed the huge burden that was growing like a heavy weight in her chest.

'All right, hen,' Nell was saying calmly and lifting her face for her daughter's dutiful goodnight kiss.

As Grace left the room and they heard her footsteps mount the stairs, Jeannie too rose, but before she could move away, Nell's hand touched her arm. Softly she said, 'A moment, hen.' She waited, holding her head on one side, listening until her daughter's footsteps sounded in the room overhead.

With her right index finger, Nell pushed her spectacles higher up her nose and looked straight at Jeannie. 'I'm a wee bit concerned about George, but I don't want Grace to worry. And Tom, maybe tonight the pub was the best place for him. He'll think nothing of it, just that his father's boat is late. And even if he does, well, the drink'll dull his wits. But I know George. He always tries to beat the Hathersage boats back to Havelock. He should have been here on this morning's tide along with Tom's. Or at worst, tonight's.'

Jeannie said nothing but swallowed painfully, debating quickly within her mind whether or not she ought to tell Nell Lawrence what she knew. She felt caught in the middle now, between the family members each trying to keep their fears from the other.

She leant across and patted Nell's hand. 'If you've heard nothing by the morning I'll go to the offices mysel' and find out.'

'Thank you, Jeannie. I'd be grateful if you'd do that for me, hen. Very grateful.'

Jeannie stood and then she too bent and kissed the woman's cheek. A look of surprise crossed Nell's face and for a moment her keen glance searched Jeannie's face. She gave a slight nod of the head as if to indicate that she knew Jeannie understood what she was feeling only too well.

'Away to your bed, hen.'

As Jeannie opened the door leading to the stairs, she turned back once to look at the lonely figure sitting before the fire, gazing into its glowing depths, but every so often her glance would go to the clock on the mantelpiece. Without looking round, Nell said softly, 'You know, I canna believe the sea has taken him. Not my George. When he was a young deckie, he was washed overboard, but the next wave washed him back on board again. Twice that happened to him. They always say . . .' there was a catch in her voice now, 'that if that happens, the sea doesna want them.'

Jeannie could think of no reply and, quietly, she closed the door unable even to bring herself to say, 'Goodnight.'

Hours later, snuggled against her, Grace slept, but Jeannie found rest impossible. Through the long hours of the night, she waited, listening for the sound of Nell coming to bed or Tom returning home from the pub.

But the house was silent. Just waiting . . .

Twelve

Breakfast at the Hathersage mansion five miles beyond the outskirts of Havelock was a tense affair, at least between the two men, Robert and his father-in-law.

Louise, however, was in a frivolous mood, prattling endlessly about her plans for her nineteenth birthday the following week.

'I had such a marvellous time in London last year staying with Madeleine. She took me to all the smart balls and social events. Can I go back again this year, Mummy?'

Mrs Hathersage cast a coy glance at Robert. 'It's not up to us now, darling. You're a married woman. You must ask your husband.' But there was a sly insinuation in her tone that left Robert realizing that he really had no say in the matter.

Louise gave her tinkling laugh and leant towards Robert seated next to her. 'Can we go to London, Robert? For my birthday. We'd have such fun.'

Robert opened his mouth to say that he could not leave at present because of the uncertainty about the *Sea Spray*, but before he could speak, Mr Hathersage's voice came down the length of the table. 'Of course you can go, my princess. It would do you good . . .' He glanced at Robert as if suddenly remembering to include him and added quickly, 'Both of you.'

Louise clapped her hands in delight and cried, 'Oh thank you, Daddy.' She pushed back her chair and rushed to the end of the table to fling her arms about her father's neck.

How could they be thinking about such matters, Robert thought bitterly, when one of their trawlers may be lying at the bottom of the ocean with all hands? With a jerky, angry movement he stood up, turned and left the room, without dutifully kissing his wife's cheek, nodding to his father-in-law or giving a polite bow of his head and murmuring 'Mrs Hathersage'.

'Well, really!' he heard his mother-in-law say loudly as he marched across the hall towards the front door. 'That young man really has a lot to learn as a husband.'

And your daughter, Robert would liked to have said bitterly, has a lot to learn as a wife. As he drove down the wide sweeping driveway towards the wrought iron gates, Robert's anger cooled a little. He drove his own motor car into Havelock each morning. He had no intention of keeping the same office hours as Mr Hathersage who was chauffeured into his company offices at ten in the morning, took two hours for lunch and returned home to his mansion at three thirty each afternoon.

He sighed as he pulled the motor to a halt outside the Gorton offices and sat a moment. Perhaps, for once, the Hathersages were right. Perhaps a little time away together in London would be good for both Louise and him. Away from the influence of her parents, maybe he could talk gently to her and they could take time to get to know each other. Maybe . . .

As he walked towards the entrance to the building, other thoughts now pushed these plans aside. There were more urgent and important matters to be dealt with and as he ran lightly up the steps, Robert's mind was full of foreboding about the news this day might bring.

Jeannie awoke to the sound of frantic knocking on the back door. Slipping a shawl around her shoulders over her flannelette nightgown, she padded on bare feet down the stairs, through the kitchen and into the scullery in time to hear Nell's voice raised indignantly.

'And what right has the likes of you to come knocking on my door at this time of the morning? Or any morning, if it comes to that, Aggie Turnbull?'

Jeannie gasped aloud. Aggie Turnbull? Here? It couldn't be! But as she came to stand behind Nell and peer over her shoulder she could see at once that it was indeed the woman she had only before seen at a distance. Yet now she saw her close to, Aggie's appearance was not what she had expected. For one thing she was older than Jeannie had believed her to be. She was hatless and her coat looked as if she had pulled it on in a great hurry. Her blonde hair was dishevelled and though she wore bright lipstick, it seemed to have been applied with a shaky hand. The outline around her perfectly shaped mouth was smudged. Her skin, though smooth, was blotchy and when Jeannie looked into the woman's eyes, she saw why. Aggie's clear blue eyes were brimming with tears.

'Oh Nell. I'm sorry. I had to come. It's not true, is it? For God's sake tell me it's not true. They're saying – that George – that his boat is missing.'

'*My* George is a fine skipper. He'll no' be losin' his ship,' Nell said, her mouth prim and tight. Was it Jeannie's fancy or did Nell really emphasize the word 'my'?

'But it's all round the docks . . .'

'Well, I'll no' believe any tale you bring to ma door, Aggie Turnbull. Good-day.' And Nell made as if to close the door.

'Please, Nell.' The woman clasped her hands together

as if in prayer and Jeannie could see that her fingers were shaking. 'For pity's sake . . .'

But Nell shut the door and leant her back against it. She closed her eyes and let out a deep groan. Jeannie stood watching her.

'What was all that about?' she asked.

Nell opened her eyes, pushed her glasses up her nose with an irritated gesture. 'Dinna ask, hen. Just dinna ask.' But as Nell bustled away, Jeannie heard her mutter, 'The impudent begger, coming to ma house . . .'

'Are you sure? Are you absolutely sure?'

The bearded fisherman, standing before him, nodded gravely. Robert had come down to the fish dock to seek out the men from the other Gorton trawlers.

'As sure as I can be, sir,' the man was saying. 'The storm was dreadful. So bad that our skipper stopped trawlin'. And it takes a fair blow to do that. Before dark, the *Gorton Sea Spray* was alongside us, well, you know, fishing 'aside us.' He flung out his arm to the left as if indicating that the two vessels had been fishing parallel with each other. 'Then in the morning, she'd gone.'

'But maybe she'd moved. Maybe the storm had driven her away, out of your sight.'

The man shrugged. 'Possible, sir, I'll not deny it. But . . .' He hesitated and then shook his head. 'Not very likely.'

'Why?'

The fisherman looked kindly at the well-dressed young man and explained patiently. Son of a trawler owner, he might be, but Robert had little experience at sea. 'There were a lot of ships in the same area, sir. We'd found a good ground. And they,' he paused as if for dramatic effect, 'were all still there the following morning. All, except the *Sea Spray*.'

Robert felt his heart sink. 'I see,' he said heavily. 'Thank you for telling me what you know, but I still don't know if it's enough that we ought to – well – say the ship's missing.'

'There's one other skipper you ought to talk to, sir.' The man glanced around him, searching amongst the boats lining the quay. 'He's on a Hathersage ship, the *North Sea Spirit*. Hewson, they call him. There's a tale going about that he picked up a body from the water. Could be . . .' The man's voice faded away, as if he too didn't want to believe what might have happened.

Robert swallowed hard. 'But that still wouldn't mean the ship had gone down. It might be that he got washed overboard in the storm.' Robert was now like a drowning man clinging to the wreckage. And he knew it. And the skipper knew it too. Soberly, the man said, 'Could be, sir, could be.' But there was little hope in the wise old fisherman's tone.

It was Jeannie who opened the front door to find Robert Hayes-Gorton standing on the pavement outside. She knew at once, by the look on his face, that the news was bad.

Pulling the door wider, she said curtly, 'You'd better come in.'

Nell, standing before the net on the wall, her fingers never still, called, 'Who is it, hen?'

Receiving no immediate answer she looked up as Jeannie ushered the man into the kitchen. Then Nell's eyes widened, her glance flickering from one face to the other. And now, deep into her eyes, came the fear.

Robert stood, an awkward figure in the cluttered room. He was taller than Jeannie had remembered and, closer now, she could see that his slim build belied a strength in his shoulders. He removed his hat and smoothed back his dark wavy hair. In his brown eyes Jeannie could see there was a haunted expression. Twisting his hat round and round in his hands, he said, 'Mrs Lawrence . . .'

His voice too, was deeper, though perhaps that was because of the difficult news he was trying to impart. Jeannie could sense, though she was reluctant to acknowledge it, that there was sympathy and genuine concern for these people in his tone.

'Mrs Lawrence . . .' His glance went briefly towards Tom who was rising from his seat by the fireplace. 'I am so sorry to come with – with some bad news.'

For a fleeting moment, Jeannie felt a flash of sympathy for the young man, but remembering again the night she had first encountered him, her pity died and she stood, jaw clenched, as he dragged out each painful word.

Nell dropped the ball of sisal and the net flapped idly against the wall. She turned slowly to face Robert, her gaze now intent upon his face.

'The *Sea Spray* has not – not returned. Of course, there's still the chance that she's late. That . . .' He could add no further words, because he could think of none.

Tom spoke now. 'Have you asked around?'

Robert turned his glance towards him, with a sense of relief. He could deal better with another man, a fisherman. 'Yes, I've spoken to several of the other skippers from both our boats and those of the Hathersage company, and the last one, he – he had picked up a – a body from the sea

and it was ... I'm so sorry ...' Again his glance came
back momentarily to Nell. 'It was one of the crew from
the *Sea Spray*.'

For a moment there was silence in the room and then
Tom gave a groan, sat down heavily in his chair and
dropped his head into his hands, resting his elbows on his
knees.

With a slow, wooden movement, Nell turned back
towards the wall and picked up the half-finished net. Her
fingers grasped the braiding needle so tightly that her
knuckles showed white. It was left to Jeannie, the comparative stranger in their midst, to say, forcing politeness into
her tone, 'Thank you for coming, sir. I'll see you out ...'
and led the way to the door into the street.

Back on the pavement, he turned to face her. 'If there's
anything I can do – anything, you will let me know?'

She leant towards him, her eyes flashing, no longer
needing to hide her feelings. 'Go. Just leave them alone.
Havena you and yours done enough damage to this
family?'

He jerked backwards as if she had struck him physically. He stared at her for a moment and now she could see
the tightening of his mouth and the anger in his eyes.

He put on his hat, gave an exaggerated bow and said in
a low, tight voice, 'I'll bid you "Good day", Miss Buchanan.' Then he turned and walked swiftly away.

Turning back into the house, Jeannie closed the door,
leant against it for a moment and gave a low groan. She
shouldn't have spoken to him like that. Not now, not at a
time like this. He was the very person, probably the one
and only person, who could help this family in their hour
of need and now she had driven him away. She sighed
heavily and moved back into the kitchen to find the two
people there just as she had left them; Nell braiding the

net and Tom sitting with his head in his hands making no move to comfort his mother nor to go out and try to find out more news for himself.

Without stopping to think, Jeannie said as much. 'Are you going down to the dock to see what you can find out?' When there was no answer, no response of any kind from him, not even a movement, she said, more sharply, 'Tom?'

Slowly, like a man in a trance, Tom lifted his head and looked towards her, his eyes suspiciously wet. Jeannie gestured towards his mother. 'Tom, hadna you better do something?'

'What? What can I do?'

'Well, go out and ask around. Get more news. Anything.' She held her lower lip between her teeth, biting back the words, 'anything instead of sitting there looking sorry for yoursel''. 'You should be thinking of others,' she wanted to shout at him. 'Of your mam and Grace, who doesna ken yet.'

But all she said aloud was, 'I'll make a cup of tea,' and went into the tiny scullery to busy herself.

Minutes later she returned with a tin tray with three mugs on it. Nell was still braiding rapidly, her fingers steadier now and the net growing.

'Come on, let me finish that for you.' Jeannie tried to coax Nell away from the net. 'Sit by the fire and drink your tea.'

But Nell's fingers held fast on to the sisal like a drowning man clinging to a lifeline.

'Leave her be,' Tom said quietly. 'She's better keeping 'ersen busy.'

Jeannie moved away from Nell towards Tom to say softly, 'But she doesna seem to have taken the news in.'

He gave a shrug. 'It's just her way of coping, that's all. She's strong . . .' He glanced up at her. 'You women are a lot stronger than us men when it comes to coping with tragedy, you know.'

'Och now, I don't believe that for a minute.' It seemed ironic that she should be plunged into the midst of another family's tragedy. Perhaps, she thought, in staying to help them, she could come to terms with her own loss too.

As if reading her thoughts, Tom looked up at her and said softly, 'Jeannie, will you stay with us a while longer. Please?'

Jeannie did not answer at once but looked across the room at Nell, seeing the bent head and the busy fingers threading and twisting and knotting as if her life depended upon it.

Slowly, she nodded her head. 'Aye, Tom, I'll stay.'

He reached up and grasped her hand tightly, hanging on to it. 'Thank you,' he said hoarsely. 'I knew you would.'

Embarrassed by his display of emotion, she handed him a mug of tea and said brusquely, though not unkindly, 'Here, drink this and then go and see some of your mates. Maybe they've heard more.'

'He's gone,' Tom said brokenly, reaching out for the tea with a trembling hand. 'He's gone. I know he has. Oh how am I going to tell Grace?'

But Tom did not have to tell Grace anything for though he and Jeannie sat beside the fire far into the night and Nell refused to come away from her work at the wall, Grace did not come home.

And still, Nell's fingers twisted and knotted and the net grew longer.

Thirteen

Robert strode along the dock towards the company's offices. How dare that slip of a girl speak to him like that, he raged inwardly. Well, that was it, he wouldn't help that blasted family any more. He'd apologized for that other incident and, shameful though it had been, the young girl had not been hurt. Shocked and frightened, yes, but not physically harmed.

But even as he thought about that night again, guilt twisted at his stomach and his anger died. Sighing inwardly as he ran up the steps and into the building, he knew that despite Jeannie's rudeness, he would still do what he could to help the Lawrence family and that he would go on doing so.

One day, he promised himself, I'll make that red-haired firebrand smile at me.

As he opened the door to Edwin's office, his father came towards him. 'And where the hell have you been? Spreading the news, I suppose, to all and sundry.' He stepped closer to his son and thrust his face so close that Robert could smell the whisky on his breath. Eleven thirty in the morning and already he could smell it.

'Do you know what you're doing, boy? Losing us money, that's what. Half the crews won't turn up to sail tomorrow night, or if they do, they'll go on Hathersage boats. Just because you've married into the Hathersage family, don't forget your loyalty to this one.'

Robert stood unflinching as the older man's spittle rained upon his face. Three weeks away from his twenty-first birthday, it came to him now as he stood facing the blustering man that it was time he, Robert Hayes-Gorton, grew up. Time he took on the mantle of maturity, time he started acting like a man. And it was time too that he started to earn the respect of others. He was under this man's thumb, they all were, the whole family, even, to some degree, Francis. It was high time someone stood up to Samuel Hayes-Gorton.

How he wished with all his heart, that he had done this weeks, months ago. Then he would not be tied in marriage to a woman he did not love, nor she to him.

Thinking of his child-bride, he said with a calmness he was not feeling inside, lacing his words with sarcasm, 'I thought we were supposed to be in partnership with the Hathersage family since you so conveniently arranged a marriage between the two companies.'

'Arranged? Arranged? What are you talking about, boy?'

'Oh come on, Father. You know very well what I mean. You and old man Hathersage have planned a union between the companies for years and how better than by marriage.'

He was feeling slightly sick now, not only listening to the callous manner in which his father thought nothing of the loss of a ship and all its crew, save what it would mean to his company in lost revenue, but also realizing just to what depths he and his like would stoop. The two men, Hathersage and his father, had had no compunction in sacrificing the happiness of their own children for the sake of business.

From behind them, as if trying to break up the scene

that promised to grow ugly, Edwin's mild voice said, 'I have to say, Father, it seems definite now that the boat is lost. I think it behoves us to be open about the matter.'

Hayes-Gorton swung round, pointing his finger at his younger son. 'Don't you start. You just do as you're told . . .'

Slowly, Edwin rose from his chair behind the desk, leather topped and scratched with years of wear. 'I will do,' the young man said slowly, 'what I think is right. The same . . .' now every word was deliberate, 'as my brother obviously intends to do.'

For a moment, their father, standing between them, appeared stunned. Then he let out a loud bark of laughter, but there was no humour in it. 'Oho, the cubs are turning on the old fox, eh? Well, you're not too old for a whipping and this fox is not too old to give you one . . .' His glance went from one to the other. 'Either of you.' A malicious gleam came into his eyes. 'I can change my will, you know. Leave everything to Francis. If you're not careful, I'll cut the pair of you off without a penny. And you'll find yourself without a job too.' He glanced from first one to the other and back again watching what effect his words were having.

The two brothers exchanged a glance and Robert felt a warm glow spread through him as he read the support in Edwin's eyes.

'If that is what you want,' he said, 'so be it . . .' There was the slightest of pauses before he added, 'sir'.

There was silence and then with a swift unexpected movement Samuel Hayes-Gorton raised the ebony cane he carried and brought it down with a resounding crack upon the surface of the desk. His sons flinched but did not move.

'Damn and blast the pair of you then,' the older man

111

thundered. 'It's your own inheritance you're throwing away.' He paused and then barked, 'Where's Francis? Francis will handle this properly.'

Again the two younger brothers exchanged a glance and Robert said quietly, 'Try Aggie Turnbull's, Father.'

For a moment he thought he had gone too far, for Samuel's face grew bright purple and the veins on his forehead stood out.

'Damn you, boy,' he muttered, 'damn you to hell and back.' Then he strode to the door, wrenched it open, was through it and slamming it behind him so that the frame rattled leaving the two brothers staring at each other.

'Actually, he is right, you know,' Edwin said, leaning back in his chair. 'I don't agree with his attitude, mind you, but he is right when he says we might be short of crews tomorrow night.'

'Well, I don't go along with that. I'll grant you some of the young lads may use it as an excuse to stay ashore and miss a trip, but the older fishermen – well, sadly they're all too used to it.'

Edwin stood up. 'You're right, of course, but I'll have a quiet word with our ship's runner.' He tapped the side of his nose and winked at his brother. 'Jackson's just the man to round up the youngsters.'

'You see,' Samuel thumped his fist on the desk. 'I told you to keep your blasted mouth shut. We're short of crews. One ship can't sail.'

'It's affected our crews too.' Hathersage stood with his back to the coal fire burning brightly in Samuel Hayes-Gorton's office. 'What have you to say to that, young feller-me-lad?'

Robert glanced at Edwin and raised his eyebrows. The

other smiled and gave a slight nod and held out a hand-written list to his brother. They had both known that this confrontation would occur and were well prepared. Now Robert was able to face the two older men with equanimity.

He glanced down at the piece of paper between his fingers and began to reel of the list. 'There are precisely seven men whom our ship's runner has not been able to sign on. One has been ashore for three weeks with a broken arm, sustained, incidentally whilst at sea on a Hathersage boat. One is in hospital with pneumonia, another with a suspected appendicitis. That's three. Tom Lawrence will, of course, miss this trip—'

'Why "of course"? There's no "of course" about it.'

Robert glanced at his father-in-law and asked quietly, 'You really expect the man to put to sea for a three-week trip, leaving his mother and his sister . . .' to say nothing of Jeannie Buchanan, he added silently to himself, 'to cope alone?'

Mr Hathersage gave a grunt and twisted the tips of his moustache. But he made no answer.

Robert continued with the list of absentees and their reasons. 'That leaves three more. Abel Johnson, a cook, is retiring. It was his last trip anyway and we knew that. And lastly there are two brothers, aged fifteen and sixteen and, yes, it is their mother who is adamant that they shall not go to sea again.'

'Ah, there!' Samuel boomed with triumph. 'I told you so. Well, she needn't come running to me begging for shore jobs for them.'

Calmly, Robert went on as if the interruption had not occurred. His tone was deceptively soft. 'I don't think anyone with any feeling could possibly blame her. She lost her husband and her eldest son three years ago on the

Hathersage Evening Star when it went down in Arctic waters.'

There was silence in the room now as the two older men glanced at each other a little uncomfortably.

'Of course,' Robert went on smoothly, 'what is missing is a Gorton ship with all hands. The *Sea Spray* will never set sail again, nor will any of her crew.'

With that parting shot, he turned on his heel and left the office.

At breakfast the following morning in the Hathersage household, Mr Hathersage spread his newspaper and disappeared behind it, not even wishing his son-in-law 'Good morning'.

Robert stared down at the kipper on his plate, quite unable to eat a mouthful when he thought of the appalling price that men had paid with their lives to bring such fish ashore. He was about to ask the maid to fetch him something else when the door opened and Louise, her face more animated than he had seen it since their marriage and holding a letter in her hand, burst into the room.

'Oh listen everyone . . . Morning, Mummy . . . Daddy . . .' she added hastily but she was so excited and happy as she smiled at Robert and waved the letter towards him. 'You'll never guess. Madeleine has invited us to stay with her in London. I was so hoping she would. We can go the day after tomorrow. Oh Robert, isn't that wonderful?'

She was looking very pretty this morning, in the frilled morning dress and her hair neatly dressed. Her round cheeks were delicately pink with excitement and her blue eyes sparkled and, looking at her, Robert felt a wave of tenderness for her and hated to be the one to have to say that at present such a visit was out of the question.

'I'm sorry, my dear. I cannot possibly leave just now. The whole town will be in mourning for the loss of the *Sea Spray* and all its crew. And I must – I must see to the family . . .' Swiftly he added as a hurried afterthought, 'All the families.'

But in his mind was only one family: the Lawrence family and their visitor, Jeannie Buchanan.

Louise's pretty face crumpled and the ready tears spilled over. 'You don't love me,' she cried in a childish voice. 'Else you'd want to make me happy. What do I care about some silly boat?'

Appalled by her callousness, Robert rose from the table and went from the room, leaving his breakfast untouched.

'Have you heard any more news?' Grace came in at the back door, her hair awry, her clothes dishevelled.

'Where on earth have you been?' Jeannie flashed at once. 'And why didn't you come home last night? Where were you?'

Twenty-four hours had passed since Robert had brought the only news so far. Since then, they had heard no more. A steady stream of neighbours had knocked on the back-door, but when they saw Nell refusing to leave her net and Tom sitting gloomily by the fire, they patted Jeannie's hand and whispered, 'If there's owt we can do, lass, you just let us know.' But then they left, unsure how to deal with the strange reaction of each member of the Lawrence family.

Weeping, they could have handled, or even rage from the lost fisherman's son, but it was their silence they could not understand. A silence that seemed to rebuff their good intentions.

'Oh come on, Florrie,' Jeannie heard one woman mutter as she stepped out into the back-yard. Their voices drifted back to her as they waddled down the passageway between the neighbouring houses. 'Leave 'er be, if that's 'ow she wants it.'

'But I don't like to, Wyn,' her companion said, her voice high-pitched with distress. 'When my Charlie's ship were missing for a time, Nell were that good to me. I want to help her now, like.'

'Well, you can't,' Wyn said bluntly, 'if she dun't want your help.' She sniffed. 'Nor mine neither, it seems, and we've lived next door for years.'

'Seems she only wants that lass that's just come – the one that answered the door to us. What do they call 'er?'

'Jeannie summat.'

'She's a nice enough lass, but they hardly know her, do they?'

'She's a Scottie though, ain't she? Like Nell.'

'A relation, y'mean?'

'Don't think so.' The woman paused and then said, with an insight that was beyond Florrie's comprehension, 'Mebbe Nell finds it easier because the girl *is* a stranger.'

Jeannie sighed and closed the door as the voices faded and became indistinct. Returning to the kitchen, she said, 'Tom, I'll need to go to ma work to see the foreman. Will you take a walk?'

But Tom shook his head, not even looking up at her. He had sat before the fire during the whole of that time, moving only to answer the call of nature or to stoke up the fire and Nell had continued to work, non-stop, at her braiding.

So Jeannie had been the only one to leave the house.

'Take as long as you need, lass,' the foreman had said. 'We all know what's happened and we know Grace, and you too since you're staying with the family, will need a little time off. The other girls have said they'll cover for you.'

A lump came into Jeannie's throat. 'That's very kind of them. Please thank them for me, will you?'

'I will.' The man, usually so brusque, was showing a kindness Jeannie had not seen in him before. 'George Lawrence was a good skipper and a fine man. I feel for his family. Give Grace and her mam my best, will you?'

Jeannie looked at him, puzzled. 'You mean Grace isna here? At work?'

'No. She didn't come in this morning.'

'Oh.' Jeannie could not prevent the surprise from showing in her face. She had been worried enough when the girl had not come home the previous evening, but since neither Tom nor Nell had even mentioned it – in fact, they hardly seemed aware of it – Jeannie had waited until the morning to look for her. She had been so certain that Grace must have just stayed the night at a friend's but that she would be at work today. Now the young girl was missing from her workplace too.

Swiftly, Jeannie gave the foreman a weak smile. 'I expect she's gone down to the dockside. To – to watch . . .' Her voice faded away.

Poor Grace, she thought then. I must find her.

Excusing herself, Jeannie hurried away towards the docks. It was still early, yet the fish market was in full swing. Row upon row of kits of fish lined the pontoon and buyers, resplendent in black suits and bowler hats, moved amongst the freshly landed fish whilst the incessant drone of the auctioneers' voices could be heard above the general rabble. Men with barrows rushed backwards and forwards, carrying the sold fish ready to be transported to inland markets.

Jeannie pushed her way through the throng, past all the jetties where now the ships were making ready to set sail once more in a few hours' time. But there was no sign of Grace, no sign of a lonely figure far out at the end of one of the piers.

Jeannie searched everywhere she could think of, but she could not find the girl.

And now, standing facing Grace in the small back scullery, she felt both relief at seeing her safe but an overwhelming desire to shout at her for causing so much worry and at a time like this too.

The girl's face was suddenly mutinous. 'You sound like me dad.' The words were out before she thought and now Grace's eyes filled with tears as she stared at Jeannie. 'I – I'm sorry. I didn't mean to worry you, but – but I couldn't bear it here. I stayed the night with – with a friend . . .' She lifted her head again. 'Me mam didn't know, did she?'

'That you never came home at all? She must have done, but she's never said a word. Not all night.'

'What do you mean "all night"?'

'She never went to bed again. Grace,' Jeannie's tone softened, 'you should have been here to look after her. You're her daughter. It's you she needs. Not me. I'm a stranger.'

Grace shook her head. 'No, no, you can help her more than me. Really. Maybe it's because you're from her homeland and she still feels the pull. You know?'

Oh yes, Jeannie knew. She felt the pull of home even more strongly now, and yet something still held her here and even now she couldn't be sure that it was just because she wanted to stay and help these people who had befriended her.

'Where is she?' Grace whispered and Jeannie gestured with her head into the neighbouring room as she said grimly, 'Still braiding the net. She's been at it all night. Just standing facing the wall and braiding.'

Grace's mouth dropped open.

For the second time in two days, it was Jeannie who opened the door to Robert Hayes-Gorton.

'I presume you've heard the most recent news? That they've found some wreckage from the *Sea Spray*?' he asked gently.

Jeannie nodded and said shortly, 'One of the lumpers came to tell Tom.' She hesitated and then added, 'So it's definite then?'

'I'm so sorry, but yes.' He paused and then said, 'He – Tom – didn't go back to sea then?'

'No, but he's expecting to be ignored by the ship's runner for the Hathersage company because of it.'

Robert sighed, realizing that Henry Hathersage had more than likely already given instructions to his runner that 'that idle bugger, Tom Lawrence, is not to be given a berth on any of my ships again'. Aloud, Robert said, 'I'll make sure he doesn't suffer. That he finds a ship when he's ready to go back.'

Jeannie knew she ought to thank him, but the words stuck in her throat, so she merely gave a curt nod as if to say, 'That's no more than you owe this family.'

They stood there, an awkwardness between them for it was obvious that she had no intention of inviting him inside. His dark brown eyes troubled, Robert asked, 'How are things?'

Jeannie lifted her shoulders. 'How do you expect them to be?'

119

He sighed and said heavily, 'If you – they – need anything, please let me know?'

Again she nodded, then stepped back and closed the door.

Standing in the doorway leading into the kitchen, she watched Nell, still at her work on the net. Sadly, Jeannie shook her head. Just what were they to do with Nell? She clicked her tongue against her teeth in a noise of exasperation. Tom and Grace were little or no use.

After sitting by the fire for a full night and the following day, now Tom seemed to be out all the time, probably, she suspected, in the Fisherman's Rest. He'd no doubt be coming home the worse for the drink.

And Grace. Well, she was out again too and, at this moment, Jeannie did not like to begin to think where she might be.

Why am I bothering with them all? she asked herself. They're nothing to me. I should be on my way home, back to Scotland. But she knew exactly why she bothered. The Lawrence family reminded her of her own, the family she had lost.

No, she couldn't leave now. Not yet. Not till things were better.

She moved forward to say gently, 'Please, won't you rest?'

'I must finish this, hen. George will be home soon and wanting his tea.'

Jeannie's hand fluttered to her mouth to stifle a startled gasp. 'Oh no, Nell, no,' she breathed.

Fourteen

On the Sunday morning, Nell finally left her net and put on her black coat and hat. 'I'm away to the kirk.'

'I'll come with you,' Jeannie offered but Nell held up her hand.

'No, no, hen. I'll be fine. Sunday morning I always go to the kirk. George'll know where I am.'

Jeannie watched her go with a heavy heart. The little woman walked briskly along the street, nodding to her neighbours as she passed by. Jeannie bit her lip and hurried up the stairs.

'Grace, Grace . . .' She shook the sleeping girl by the shoulder. She had been very late home the previous evening, but at least she was now coming home each night and had not, since Jeannie had rebuked her, stayed away overnight again. Even so, Jeannie intended to question her about where she was going so often, but now she had a more urgent worry. 'Grace, wake up. You've got to get up. Your mother's gone out. To the kirk. You ought to go after her. See that she's all right. Grace, will you get up.'

But the girl shrugged her off, turned over and buried her head beneath the bedclothes. Exasperated, Jeannie dragged the covers off her. 'At least tell me where the kirk is and I'll go.'

Grace sat up and tugged at the blanket, but Jeannie held on and the two girls glared at each other. 'Just tell me where it is, then you can go back to sleep.'

'Two streets away, at the far end.' And Grace yanked the bedclothes from Jeannie's grasp and lay down again.

The church was almost full and when Jeannie arrived they were singing the first hymn but she slipped into a pew at the back, her glance darting around the congregation for sight of Nell Lawrence. Then her lips parted in a startled gasp for there, sitting in the third row from the front, his head bent solicitously towards Nell, was Robert Hayes-Gorton.

Jeannie could hardly believe what she was seeing, but there was no mistaking the slim build nor the dark brown hair that curled, just a little, over the edge of the stiff, white collar. Nor, as he turned and she saw his profile, the straight nose, the curve of his eyebrow just above those deep, dark brown eyes. His mouth was serious, yet when he bent towards the older woman, Jeannie could see the merest hint of a smile that uplifted the corner of his mouth and deepened the line running from nostril to chin.

Jeannie dragged her gaze away, picked up a hymn book from the ledge in front of her and rifled the pages to find the place. Glancing up towards the list of numbers on the hymn board, her glance again found the top of Robert's dark head and she allowed her gaze to rest upon it once more. Whatever was he doing here? Surely this was not the church where the Hayes-Gortons, nor the Hathersages, would normally worship? And he was alone too. She could see no other member of his family amongst the congregation.

She bent her head and tried to concentrate on the words, but the print danced before her eyes and her heart was still racing from having run all the way here.

The service continued, but Jeannie could not have told anyone what prayers were said, apart from the one that mentioned the *Sea Spray* and prayed for all those aboard, nor what the vicar said in his sermon.

Just before the end of the final hymn, Jeannie slipped from the pew and out of the church door. She walked swiftly across the grass between the gravestones and away from the main pathway to the gate. In the shadow of the yew tree she stood to watch the worshippers leaving the church and when Robert appeared, leading Nell on his arm, Jeannie shrank back even further beneath the low branches.

She could see now that Nell had a handkerchief to her face, a large, white, man's handkerchief. She was dabbing at her eyes and Robert was still leaning towards her speaking quietly and patting her hand that lay on his arm. As they passed among the other worshippers, Jeannie could see that it was Robert who nodded to them, or acknowledged their greetings, protecting Nell from their intrusive sympathy.

It should be Tom with his mother, or even Grace. Not him. Not Robert Hayes-Gorton. But then, the truthful, honest side of Jeannie's nature answered her. Neither Tom nor Grace were being a comfort or support to their mother. That had been left to comparative strangers, herself and now Robert.

When they reached the gate, Jeannie saw them stop and Robert gesture with his arm towards his motor car standing by the kerb, but Nell shook her head firmly. Jeannie guessed that he was trying to offer to take her home and Nell was, understandably, refusing.

Yet his action was a kind one, Jeannie admitted grudgingly as she watched them move off down the road, walking past the car as if intending to leave it and walk the distance to Nell's home.

Jeannie moved forward to the path and through the gate. She had almost reached them when she saw Robert look up and catch sight of her.

To her surprise, her smile as she went towards him was quite genuine. She had witnessed for herself his gentleness towards Nell. Whilst the cynical side of her nature, still smarting with resentment against him, might have said that it had been his guilty conscience making him act so attentively towards Nell, the more generous part of her character was, for once, willing to give Robert Hayes-Gorton the benefit of the doubt.

'I came to meet you, Mrs Lawrence,' she said as she came up to them. 'Grace told me where the kirk was.'

'Oh Jeannie . . .' Nell began and as she turned to glance at her, Jeannie could see that her eyes were red and that she still dabbed at them with the handkerchief, pushing the cloth beneath her glasses and almost dislodging them. 'Mr Robert has been so kind.'

Jeannie nodded towards him and smiled again. 'Thank you,' she said briefly, but now it was Jeannie who linked her arm through Nell's and drew her gently away.

Over her shoulder Nell called, 'Goodbye, Mr Robert – and thank you.'

They walked for some time in silence and then Nell said suddenly, 'You must have thought me a bit daft, hen. Going on about George as if – as if he was – well – still here.'

Involuntarily, Jeannie stiffened and she found she was holding her breath.

Nell's voice was low and flat, but quite steady as she went on. 'I know he's gone, Jeannie. I know that now, but I didna want to believe it – wouldna believe it until today.'

Jeannie said nothing. There was nothing she could say. For she knew exactly how Nell Lawrence was feeling

124

because it was how she had felt about her father. But Nell had accepted the truth more quickly than she had.

Jeannie took a deep breath. Well, it was time she did the same then. Angus Buchanan was never coming home from the sea again and neither was George Lawrence.

As they walked along, Jeannie hugged Nell's arm closer to her and feeling it, Nell tightened her hold on Jeannie in response. Together, they would come through this.

Watching them walk away from him, Robert was thinking, she smiled at me. And her eyes lit up until they sparkled. Jeannie Buchanan actually smiled at me. And, despite the sadness of the day, the thought made him smile too and for a brief moment he felt ridiculously light-hearted.

Fifteen

'Jeannie, I don't know what we would have done without you these past weeks. You – you've been marvellous.'

She was standing with Tom on the edge of the jetty, below the ladder leading up on to the boat on which he was about to sail. He had stayed at home for two weeks to be with his mother and sister, but now, he had to go to sea again. He had lost his place on the Hathersage boats, but Robert Hayes-Gorton had been as good as his word and had found him a berth on the *Gorton North Star*.

It had been a difficult time for all of them and Jeannie, keeping her own private battle just that – private – nevertheless found that helping the Lawrence family come to terms with their loss helped to ease her own heartache. It was strange, she reflected, standing once more on the quayside, the wind lifting her hair, how each of them dealt with their grief in a different way. After her visit to the kirk, Nell had at last accepted that her husband's ship had been lost at sea though she still turned to her work, standing before the wall in the kitchen, her fingers working automatically, her need to keep occupied an unconscious therapy.

Tom found his salvation in the Fisherman's amongst those who were, not hardened, but resilient to such tragedies. It had always been part of the fabric of their lives. As a miner lives with the knowledge that he may one day be entombed, as a steeplejack knows he may, sometime, fall, so a fisherman knows that one day the sea may take him. They live with the knowledge but rise above it, not allowing the might of the ocean to humble that inner core of courage that makes them men.

And Grace. Jeannie sighed whenever she thought of Grace, for the girl sought her comfort outside the family home with friends about whom Jeannie had serious misgivings. But when she tried, gently, to broach the subject with the girl's mother, Nell just lifted her shoulders in a shrug. 'Let her be, hen, for a while anyway. She'll come to no harm and if it helps her . . .'

She did not finish her sentence and Jeannie let the matter drop but it did not stop her worrying for now when Grace crept into their shared bed at night, Jeannie could smell the liquor on her breath. It seemed strange to her that Nell seemed unconcerned when, at their first meeting, she had been so strict with her daughter.

But since then, Jeannie reminded herself, the star by which Nell steered the course of her life had gone from her firmament.

So now Jeannie smiled up at him and said, 'Safe trip, Tom.'

His blue eyes were earnest as he looked down at her. 'Jeannie, you will stay? You will still be here when I get back?'

Jeannie sighed. Part of her longed to go home, back to Scotland and yet another part of her shrank from doing so. She nodded and said hoarsely, 'Yes, Tom. I'll be here. There's – there's nothing for me to go back home for. Not just now, anyway.'

Suddenly his huge hands reached for hers and he held them tightly. 'Jeannie, I want to know you're waiting for me to come back. I want to know you'll always be waiting for me. I need you. We all need you. Please, will you think about something while I'm away? Jeannie – will you marry me?'

'I hear your dear little wifey has gone to London to stay with her friend again.'

'How do you know so damned much about my life? You seem inordinately close to my father-in-law,' Robert growled.

Francis laughed aloud. 'Old man Hathersage and me . . .' he crossed two fingers and held them up to show his brother, 'we're like *that*.'

'Then maybe . . .' for once Robert resorted to the sarcasm that Francis so often employed with enjoyment, 'you should have married his daughter.'

Francis tweaked the sharp points of his fair moustache. 'My dear fellow,' he drawled, 'I am not the marrying kind. You know that. I prefer to love 'em and leave 'em.'

Robert stared at him. For many reasons he admired his elder brother. There was no denying his astute business acumen which, though perhaps a little too ruthless, far outstripped anything that Robert himself, or even Edwin, would ever attain. Francis always dressed elegantly; his suits were made of the finest materials and tailored expertly. He was a handsome devil. The trouble was, Robert thought, he knew it. He knew how attractive he was to women, yet he treated them with a callous disdain that seemed to have them hanging on his every word even more. Even amongst their parents' small circle of friends, Robert was certain there were one or two unmarried girls who had 'hopes' of winning Francis Hayes-Gorton.

'Even so,' Robert replied smoothly, 'I'd have thought

that it would have been much safer for the business if *you* had married her. I mean, as the elder brother, you stand to become head of the Gorton company. Who's to say whether I will even stay.'

For a brief moment there was an unguarded look of incredulity in Francis's eyes. Then the gleam of certainty was back. 'Oh you'll stay, Robert, my boy.' Maliciously, he added, 'You're trapped. There's no way out now. Besides, you'd be cut off with the proverbial shilling.' As he passed close beside Robert, heading for the door, he paused briefly to pat his younger brother's cheek. 'So be a good boy and let's have no more of such talk.'

He opened the door to leave, but then paused and said briefly, 'Oh, I'll be away for a few days. I've business in London. I'm sure you and Edwin can cope between you.'

When the door closed behind Francis, Robert stared at it for a moment and then moved towards the window of the office to look out across the docks that lay below. He could see the *Gorton North Star* nosing her way out of the harbour. Tom Lawrence would be on that ship – three weeks of backbreaking labour with little rest and icy, bone-freezing conditions. Three weeks of living every minute knowing that one freak wave, a storm or even an accident with the machinery could end a life in a second. Living with the knowledge that out there somewhere in the depths of the icy seas Tom's own father, George Lawrence, had lost his life.

Yet, despite all this, Robert Hayes-Gorton envied Tom his life. It seemed, to Robert, one of glorious freedom. And that was not the only reason he envied Tom. For as his gaze dropped and he watched the figures on the quayside, he saw her. Striding along, her hair blowing in the wind, her face lifted to the breeze, was Jeannie.

Robert leant against the window and watched her weaving her way amongst those thronging the quay, saw her turn and wave once more to the ship leaving the dock. Then she turned and hurried around a corner and was gone from his sight.

Even so, Robert stood staring at the place where she had disappeared for a full minute.

Jeannie Buchanan. The name seared itself into his heart and her image was indelibly imprinted upon his mind.

When she entered the house that evening, Jeannie was surprised to see the net hanging limply against the wall. She knew a moment's fear until she saw Nell sitting in the rocking chair at the side of the range, her head resting against the wooden back of the chair, her eyes closed, her hands idle in her lap.

Jeannie made to turn and tiptoe away, back into the scullery, but Nell opened her eyes. 'It's all right, hen. I'm no' asleep. But I just felt – all of a sudden, you know – so very weary.'

Jeannie came and sat down opposite her. 'It's time you had a good rest. Time – time you let go, Mrs Lawrence.'

'Aye.' Nell nodded slowly and her voice was heavy. 'Aye, you're right, hen. But I never thought the sea would take him, y'ken? Not after casting him back on board those times. I really though the sea didna want him. Ah well . . .' She paused and then asked softly, 'And have you "let go" too, Jeannie?'

The girl pressed her lips together tightly but nodded.

They sat in silence for a while, each with their own thoughts, but it was a companionable silence born out of a shared grief.

It was Nell who broke it at last. 'Has he asked you, then?'

Jeannie's eyes widened as she stared at her. 'You knew?' She felt suddenly cheated that Tom had discussed his proposal with his mother before even telling her of his feelings.

'I suppose,' Nell was saying slowly, her gaze on the flickering embers in the grate, 'a young man usually talks over such things with – with his father. But now . . .' She did not finish her sentence and Jeannie was a little ashamed of her spurt of anger against Tom and was thankful she had not voiced her feelings.

In answer to Nell's question, Jeannie now said slowly, 'Aye, he has.'

'And?' Nell prompted.

Jeannie sighed. 'I like Tom. Of course I do. He's a fine man and he's so like his own father but – but I've known him such a short time and in rather . . .' she allowed herself a small, rueful smile, 'strange circumstances.'

'I know, hen. But it's the same for all fishermen's sweethearts. And wives, if it comes to that. They're away so much that each time they come home, it can be like another honeymoon.' Nell's eyes misted over at her own memories and Jeannie was silent. 'And that's what makes it so difficult to accept what's happened now. You get so used to waiting for them to come home that you can't believe that this time they're not going to. That – that they're never going to come home again.'

Wordlessly, Jeannie reached out to lay her hand on Nell's arm. The silence lengthened between them; the only sounds the ticking of the clock on the mantelpiece and the settling of a log in the grate. For a moment, flames shot upwards, illuminating in its flickering light the pensive faces of the two women sitting close beside it.

'Think about it, Jeannie,' Nell said softly at last. 'Tom loves you, I know. And he needs someone like you. Someone steadfast and loyal and strong. We all do, Jeannie.'

Jeannie did think about it, long and hard. Though she loved her homeland and always would, there was really no one left for her to go back to in Scotland. Kind friends and neighbours certainly, but no family. No kin of her own. No house, for that had been rented. Not even any furniture that was worth very much. There were a few bits and pieces of sentimental value only to Jeannie to be packed and sent to her by carrier or rail. Mrs McTavish, who lived next door, would do that, Jeannie knew.

No, she decided, she wouldn't even go back at all.

There was no one there now who wanted and needed her like the Lawrence family did.

Sixteen

'It's been hard not to have a proper funeral for him,' Nell said, 'but George wouldna have wanted us to spend our life greetin' for him. He'd have wanted us to enjoy Hogmanay the same as ever. What do you think we should do, Jeannie?'

More and more Nell was leaning on Jeannie, deferring to her for decisions, almost as if she were now the wife of the house and Nell herself already the dowager.

'Whatever you would normally do.'

'We used to have Christmas when they were both home. Even if it's the middle of January, but we always keep Hogmanay. After all, you canna move that so easily, can you now?' She thought for a moment. 'We should get a dark man to first-foot for us. Do you know any dark-haired men, hen?'

Unbidden, the image of Robert Hayes-Gorton was in Jeannie's mind. Now why, she thought, angry with herself, should she think of him? And then jumped, almost guiltily, as Nell said, 'There's that nice young man, Mr Robert. He's got lovely dark wavy hair, hasn't he?'

Jeannie glanced at her sharply. Was Nell Lawrence a mind-reader? Deliberately casual Jeannie said, 'I can't say I'd noticed, but I doubt the likes of him would first-foot for us, do you?'

'No,' Nell said. 'But he's been very kind, coming to see us two or three times a week ever since George . . .' Her

133

voice trailed away but Jeannie was thinking, aye, he has, but it's more likely a guilty conscience. Then inwardly, she castigated herself. A young man of his position had no need to bother with a fisherman's family, even if that fisherman had been one of their company's skippers. He had been good, but no doubt that would soon end. To her surprise and chagrin, the thought that she would not see Robert Hayes-Gorton so often saddened her.

'There must be a dark-haired neighbour, surely?' she suggested, deliberately trying to steer the conversation, and her own unruly thoughts, away from Robert.

'Aye well,' Nell sighed, seeming to lose interest. 'We'll find someone.'

Christmas was quiet. With Tom away at sea and the very recent loss of the man of the house, the three women found the festive days very difficult. Once more, Grace disappeared on Christmas Eve.

'Let her go, Jeannie,' Nell said tiredly. 'There's no merry-making in this house this year, now is there?'

'She shouldna be merry-making so soon after . . .' Jeannie began to say, but stopped when she saw the tears in Nell's eyes.

'She's only young,' Nell murmured.

'But where's she going? Do you know?'

'She said she away to Jane's. An old school friend who lives three streets away. She'll be fine. And she's asked if she can stay the night.'

'And you've agreed?' Jeannie was startled. 'You mean, she'll no' be here in the morning? Christmas morning?'

Nell shrugged. 'She'll be home for Christmas dinner.'

Jeannie felt her mouth tighten. She could not help wondering if young Grace was being entirely truthful. It isna my business, she tried to tell herself. But it was. As long as she stayed here, she was, like it or not, involved.

During the week between Christmas and New Year, Nell seemed more like her old self. She bustled about baking, cleaning and dusting the tiny house, neglecting even the ever-present net on the wall. Every night when the two girls came home from work there was a tasty hot meal awaiting them. Although the outward signs were good, Jeannie began to be a little fearful that Nell had perhaps slipped back into thinking that George was coming home for Hogmanay.

But when Tom's ship docked on the morning tide on New Year's Eve, Nell said, 'Tom's the man of the house now.'

'Will he go first-footing to the neighbours?' Jeannie laughed. 'We'll have to black his hair with boot polish.'

Nell's sad expression lightened a little as she smiled and said, 'Like they black the bridegroom's feet at a Scottish wedding?' Then she actually gave a little chuckle as she said, 'Well, if I'm not mistaken, we might be blacking his feet soon anyway. Oh Jeannie, hen . . .' She reached out impulsively and caught hold of both Jeannie's hands. 'He'll be wanting his answer this time. Please, Jeannie, do say yes.'

'Oh Mrs Lawrence . . .' Jeannie began, but at that moment the back door flew open and Tom was home.

On the morning of New Year's Day 1925, Robert stood at the bedroom window and looked out across the smooth lawn. It was trying to snow; the sky, pearl grey, was laden with it. Behind him, Louise still slept on in their bed. Their virgin bed, he thought bitterly. He turned his head and watched her for a few moments. She was even pretty when she was asleep. Her lips curved in a gentle smile, her smooth blonde hair unruffled. Her skin, smooth and still shiny with cream, was flawless. How sad, he thought objectively, that such a lovely creature was so spoiled, so selfish, so – he searched for the word and found it – so unloving. He turned back to look out of the window, watching the birds pecking at the lawn, digging with their beaks to find a morsel, a worm, anything in this bleak, winter weather.

Dare he go? he asked himself for the hundredth time. Dare he take a bottle of whisky to the little terraced house in Baldock Street and ask them to 'tak a wee dram' with him? He didn't want to risk Jeannie's wrath again. He had deliberately not gone at Christmas for several reasons. One being that he felt it would be an intrusion on their grief at such a time and for another, he knew Tom to be at sea. He felt Hogmanay was different. All Scots celebrated the New Year with a fervour that the English sometimes found incomprehensible. But Robert thought he understood it. It was a new beginning; a time to look forward and hope for better things. And the Lawrence family, if anyone did, deserved better things in the coming year.

And now, too, Tom was home. It would look better if he visited when Tom Lawrence was there.

He washed and dressed quietly in his dressing room and slipped away without waking Louise. She would no doubt sleep until lunch time. She had not arrived home until almost three o'clock. He had feigned sleep and did not want a confrontation this morning.

He too planned a new beginning for a New Year.

The front door was opened to him by a surprised Nell. 'Why, Mr Robert. How did you know?'

Robert frowned for a moment, puzzled. Was there something he should have heard? Had something else happened to this benighted family that he should know about? Oh no, it wasn't Jeannie, was it? Oh pray God nothing had happened to her.

'Och no, I'm being silly,' Nell went on. 'How could you? Come away in.'

He stepped over the threshold straight into the best parlour, removing his hat and setting the unopened bottle on the table. Tom, Jeannie and Grace all rose from seats beside the fireplace and looked at him in surprise. Under their scrutiny, he felt a blush creeping up his neck and deliberately he kept his glance away from Jeannie.

'I just wanted to wish you – well – to hope that the New Year is better for you.' He touched the bottle. 'For you all, but . . .' His gaze rested upon Nell. 'Has something happened, I mean, what you said just now?'

Nell smiled. 'Och no, sir. It was just that I'd said to Jeannie that we should ask you to first-foot for us. You being so dark.' She gestured towards his brown hair. 'And then, when I opened the door and saw you standing there, well, I didna think what I was saying. But of course you couldn't have known about my wee joke.'

Robert too smiled. 'Oh I see.' He glanced at the others, his gaze coming to rest – as he had known it would eventually from the moment he had stepped into the house – upon Jeannie. 'Well, I would have come,' he said quietly, as if he were speaking to her alone, 'if you had asked me.'

She was returning his gaze steadily and for a moment there was no one else in the room, no one else in the world for him except her.

Tom's voice broke in harshly, breaking the spell. 'We first-foot for each other around here. My mother had no right to even think of asking anyone else. What would folks think? And besides, I'm sure,' he added and there was a hint of sarcasm in his voice now, 'that you had your own family celebrations . . .' There was a calculated pause before Tom added, '. . . sir.'

Robert looked at the young man, at the glowering face, the spots of angry colour against the tan of his skin and the blue eyes, icily polite yet unable to conceal resentment.

'Of course. I wouldn't dream of intruding,' Robert said tightly. 'I'll bid you "good day".' He gave a little bow to them all and turned towards the door. He replaced his hat carefully on his head and reached for the door knob. Then he hesitated and glanced back over his shoulder and looked now directly at Tom and only at Tom. 'I shall not be calling again, but if you need anything, just let me know.'

He raised an eyebrow and was rewarded by a quick, reluctant nod. He was gratified to see too that the young man's colour had deepened.

Robert stepped out into the street and as he pulled the door to close it behind him, he heard Nell say, 'There was no call to be so abrupt with him, Tom. He's been good to this family.'

'Well, there's no need,' Tom fired back, his voice raised so that Robert could hear him plainly. 'I'm the man in this family now. And I'll work to keep it. We're not a charity case.'

'Tom . . .' Robert heard Jeannie begin, but at that he had to pull the door shut and walk away up the street.

'Tom.' Jeannie laid her hand on his arm and said quietly, 'He was only trying to be kind.'

'I thought you didn't like him? Not after what he did.'

'I don't. But he has tried to be good to your mother. I watched him in the church that first Sunday after we heard about – about your father.'

Nell was shaking her head over the bottle of whisky.

'How kind of him. How very thoughtful . . .' But Tom's frown deepened.

Jeannie put her hand through his arm. 'Come, let's go for a walk. I could do with some fresh air.' She could feel the tension in the room rising and wanted to get him out for a while. Nell wanted to cook the dinner today, had insisted on doing it all. 'Just like I've always done.' So Jeannie was not needed. Misreading her words, Tom's face brightened. 'So could I, after that visit.' He sniffed the air. 'Phaw! What on earth had he got on? Perfume? Give me the stink of fish any day.'

'You coming with us, Grace?' Jeannie asked. 'The fresh air will do you good.'

Grace was looking peaky, Jeannie thought, but the girl merely huddled closer to the fire. 'No thanks. It looks like snow. I'll give me mam a hand.' She glanced at her brother and Jeannie intercepted a wink.

'Come on then, Jeannie,' Tom said. 'Get yar best bonnet on and let's be off.'

They walked a long way, skirting the docks and taking the coast road towards Farleston, a seaside town that was spreading so rapidly, its borders now adjoined Havelock. Here the sandy shore was a favourite place for holiday-makers and bathers.

Jeannie lifted her face to the breeze. Despite the cold and the threat of snow, she felt happier than she had done for many months. It was the start of another year and she was striding along in her smart new coat that would for ever remind her of George Lawrence. She was wearing, for the first time, the close-fitting matching cloche hat that Nell, Tom and Grace had joined together to give her as a Christmas gift.

Tom took her hand and pulled her arm through his as they walked. They didn't speak much, for the wind whipped their breath away and smarted their cheeks. But reaching the seafront at Farleston, Tom drew her into a sheltered spot and turned to face her.

'Well, Jeannie Buchanan. I'm waiting for my answer.'

Feigning ignorance, Jeannie teased him. Widening her eyes, she said, 'Answer, sir? And what answer might that be?'

'D'ya want me to go down on one knee in the snow, woman?'

Jeannie threw back her head and laughed. 'There's no snow yet.' But as if the heavens intended to defy her words, a delicate white snowflake drifted down and settled on her nose. Gently, Tom flicked it away with his fingertip. 'If you keep me waiting much longer,' he said softly, 'we'll be buried in a snowdrift. So, please, Jeannie Buchanan, will you marry me?'

She had thought about it constantly ever since he had first asked her and until this moment, she had still been unsure. Now, as she looked up into Tom's eyes that were suddenly serious, he said, 'I love you, Jeannie. It would be so wonderful knowing that you were here to come home to. I'll make you happy, I promise. Maybe one day, I could get a job ashore and then – and then you wouldn't have to spend your life watching and waiting.' He paused and then added, 'I'll look after you, Jeannie. We'll look after each other.'

She felt part of this family now, even whilst it was still coming to terms with a loss of its own. Perhaps that was the reason she felt such a kinship with the Lawrences.

She had a future to plan alongside this good man. He was offering her everything he had to give. What more could she ask?

Smiling, Jeannie said softly, 'Aye, Tom, I will marry you.'

Seventeen

'I hear that Scottish lass who's been staying with the Lawrences is to marry the son. Tom, is it?' Edwin said, not realizing what an effect the piece of news would have on his brother.

'What?' Robert stared at him and before he had thought to stop the words, he said, 'Jeannie is to marry Tom Lawrence?'

'Well, yes, if that's her name.' Edwin paused and then added, 'You seem to know her well?'

'Er – oh – I – er . . .' Robert stumbled and avoided his brother's shrewd glance. 'I got to know her – and the family – after George Lawrence's ship went down.'

Edwin nodded. 'I know. Tom explained how you'd found him a berth aboard one of our ships since he lost his place with the Hathersage boat. I presume you spoke to Jackson?'

John Jackson was the ship's runner employed by the Gorton Company. He was responsible for signing on the crews for each trip on every one of the fleet of fifteen vessels which the company now owned.

Robert nodded. 'He was amenable enough. He liked and respected George, but he did say . . .' He paused briefly, but then continued, 'He did say that the son was not the born fisherman his father was. He reckoned young Lawrence would jump at the chance to have an excuse to miss a trip.' He was thoughtful for a moment. 'Personally,

I thought Jackson was being a bit harsh. I mean it was natural, wasn't it, that Tom wanted to wait for news of his father?' Slowly Robert shook his head. 'I sometimes wonder where our humanity is, Edwin? I don't think our grandfather would have treated men like we sometimes treat them now? Do you?'

'No, Rob. And *we* won't, either.'

Robert smiled thinly, but without humour. 'Maybe. Maybe not. We're not going to be head of the company, are we?'

There was a happy, confident grin on Edwin's face. 'No, but there's two of us to keep Francis in line. We'll have a say. Don't you worry.'

'Mm.' Robert was only half listening.

'In fact,' Edwin was saying, 'I've already taken a managerial decision without asking either our dear brother, or father, if it comes to that. Tom Lawrence asked if he could miss the next trip to get married and have a bit of a honeymoon, so I said he could.'

Now Robert was all attention as he frowned at his brother. 'You did what?'

'I said he could have time off,' Edwin repeated patiently. 'To get married. It seemed only fair.'

'Well, you shouldn't have given him any more time off, whatever the reason,' Robert snapped, but even as he spoke he knew he was now guilty of being unreasonable. 'Not when we're short of crews as it is.'

'Hey, wait a minute. A moment ago you were saying you could understand him missing a trip when his father was feared lost and yet now—'

Robert interrupted harshly. 'Maybe Jackson was right after all. Maybe Tom Lawrence will jump at every opportunity to stay warm and cosy at home. No doubt he thinks that I'll intercede for him every time he condescends to go to sea again. Well, I won't.' He jabbed his forefinger in the air towards his brother. 'So just tell Jackson to watch him in future. He's to have no more time off. No more missed trips, else he'll find he hasn't a berth on a Gorton boat either.' With that, Robert turned on his heel and left the office slamming the door behind him.

The thought filled his mind and clouded his reason. Jeannie Buchanan – that lovely, red-haired, feisty girl, with green eyes and a wide, smiling mouth – was to marry Tom Lawrence.

He must talk to her. She couldn't marry Tom. She couldn't marry anyone. He must stop her.

'Can I be your bridesmaid then?'

Jeannie smiled at the excited young girl, pleased for once to see that Grace had something to interest her other than disappearing every night to be with her friends. Remembering an earlier conversation, she was now beginning to worry that Grace was meeting some boy. Someone of whom her mother would disapprove.

'Of course you can,' she said aloud, 'but we're not having a fancy white wedding. I thought you knew that. We've planned a very quiet affair. Just – just family. I mean, just you and your mother. It wouldn't be right, in the circumstances,' she said, referring to the fact that the Lawrence family were still within the expected period of mourning. Flatly she added, 'And there'll be no one from my side, anyway.'

'Yes, yes, but you'll have a pretty new dress surely and carry flowers? So, couldn't I too?'

'We'll see. We'll see what your mother thinks.'

But Nell agreed with her daughter. 'George wouldna have wanted us to spoil your day, hen,' she said and added wistfully, 'and he'd have been so pleased to see his son wedding a Scottish lassie.'

'Are you really sure, Jeannie? I mean, you haven't known him very long, have you?'

Jeannie stared up into the face of Robert Hayes-Gorton and her lips parted, the angry retort ready to spurt out. But she bit back the words, quite literally for she felt the sharpness of her teeth on the tip of her tongue. His dark brown eyes were looking into hers with such impassioned intensity that it was impossible for her to doubt that his concern was genuine.

Had she really misjudged this young man? Already, before today, she had seen his little acts of kindness but she had closed her mind and hardened her heart against him. Now, close to him, looking up into his face, she felt her resolve to hate him begin to crumble.

Before she had time to form a reply he was speaking again. The words came haltingly, as if he were voicing aloud, perhaps for the first time, his innermost feelings. And that he found it difficult and painful was obvious. 'Jeannie. I couldn't bear to see you make a terrible mistake. If – if I tell you something, it's just between the two of us?' He waited until she gave a slight nod in assent. Then she heard him let out a long deep sigh.

'I've made the most dreadful mistake in marrying Louise. It's not her fault,' he added hastily, 'or mine. But we've both allowed ourselves to be pushed into a marriage of – of convenience. A marriage our families wanted. I thought I did too. At least – what I mean is – oh this is dreadfully difficult . . .' He ran his hand distractedly through his hair. 'I don't even know if I should be saying this to you, but you see, from the moment I saw you . . . What I mean is, if I were still free, then – then I could speak, say all the things that are in my heart. But I'm not, and I – I can't. And now you're going to be married too.' Now his voice faded away and he just stood gazing at her helplessly.

And Jeannie just stood there too, looking back at him, for she could not think of a word to say.

Now, his voice hoarse with emotion, Robert just said, 'Please, Jeannie, just be sure. Very sure.'

And then he was gone, leaving her just staring after him.

Jeannie told no one of the incident. There was no one in whom she could confide such a thing. Maybe if Flora or Mary had still been here in Havelock, but they were long gone. They'd likely be back home in Scotland now. Aye, back home. Jeannie sighed at the thought. Was she really doing the right thing in marrying Tom? Mr Robert's strange, almost impassioned plea, had at least made her stop and think. His words had forced her to take stock.

She was sure that Tom loved her in his own bluff way, but he was not a demonstrative man. She didn't expect him to be. To Jeannie, men were like her father; strong, courageous and hardworking and they showed their love for their families in their actions. In going to sea and doing a very dangerous job to earn a living.

Jeannie was not used to the manners of a gentleman who, in her opinion, did little or nothing to earn his own living, but prospered on the toil of others. She had never encountered a man who made flowery speeches or showered a woman with expensive gifts. To her mind, Robert had no right to speak to her as he had done, though she did acknowledge that his words were genuine.

The thought that he felt something for her shocked her.

Not so much from a moral standpoint as that she could not believe that a man in his position should even notice someone like her.

He's just feeling guilty still, she told herself and tried to put the incident from her mind. But for many nights leading up to her wedding, her dreams were troubled by Robert's face, his dark eyes and his voice saying 'Are you really sure, Jeannie?'

On the eve of their wedding day, Jeannie was mystified by Nell and Grace.

Nell spent the early part of the evening forever glancing at the kitchen clock and then, on the stroke of seven, she said suddenly, 'Awa' to the Fisherman's, son, and give us women a bit o' peace. We've things to do for the morrow that you shouldna be seeing.'

Tom grumbled, but he got up, put on his jacket and left the house.

Jeannie eyed the two women suspiciously. They seemed to be sharing a secret, whispering and giggling and trying, yet failing, to stifle their amusement

'What's going on?' she said at last. 'I hope you're no' planning tricks on me. Sewing ma nightdress up or something.'

Mother and daughter exchanged a glance and then burst into laughter. 'We hadn't thought of that, Mam,' Grace said.

'We should ha' done, hen.' Again, they smiled at each other. 'Shall we tell her now he's gone?'

Grace nodded.

'The lads at the pub are going to have a wee bit of fun with your bridegroom. He'll no' be coming home in the state he went out.'

Jeannie groaned. 'Och, you dinna mean he's going to get drunk?'

'Aye well, a little merry, maybe. But no, they're going to wash his feet . . .'

'But first,' Grace gasped between peals of laughter and holding her side as if she had a stitch, 'they're going to smear his feet with shoe blackening, just to make it worth the washing.'

Nell chuckled. 'And if I know the lads round here, it won't stop at just his feet.'

'Oh, oh, stop it, Mam. Me side's aching wi' laughing so much.'

Jeannie felt the corners of her own mouth begin to twitch. Their laughter was infectious.

'Wait a while, till they bring him home,' Nell said. 'There'll be plenty to laugh at then.'

At ten thirty, they heard the commotion out in the street and hurried to fling open the front door and stand watching the merriment. Jeannie glanced at Grace, wondering if she were remembering the last occasion when they had witnessed the antics of a stag night, but the girl was convulsed with laughter watching her brother being borne down the street, plastered with black polish and covered from head to toe in flour. His tormentors had been thoughtful enough to remove his jacket and trousers, so Tom was being carried, shoulder high and amid much shouting and laughing, along the street in his shirt and long-johns.

'There you are, Jeannie lass.' A burly fisherman, who Jeannie knew was the third-hand on the same ship as Tom, came to stand in front of her. 'Here's your handsome bridegroom.'

Entering into the fun, Jeannie said, 'Thanks, but I'll no' be wanting him now. You can keep him.' Mischievously, she linked her arm through the big man's and said, 'Are you doing anything in the morning, Jack Brightman?'

The man's eyes twinkled and he laughed loudly. 'Don't temp' me, lass. Don't temp' me.' He winked at her. 'Shame, like, but I reckon the wife'd have summat to say about that, don't you?'

'Bring him in,' Nell was saying. 'We'll strip him down and wash him properly, now.'

'Oh,' Jeannie shrieked and, feigning coyness, she put her hands to her cheeks. 'Oh pray, spare my blushes.' She turned and hurried away into the house, the sound of their laughter following her.

It was all good, if not quite 'clean' in the literal meaning of the word, fun, and Jeannie was grateful to Tom's pals for helping to lighten what was, in part, going to be a poignant occasion for the Lawrence family. And for her too, she thought soberly, for on her wedding day there would be no father to give her away.

But he'll be there in spirit, she comforted herself. I know he will.

At the window of his office, Robert stood staring down into the bustling docks below him. To the west he could see the spire of the church where he knew, at this very moment, Jeannie was making her vows to love and to cherish Tom Lawrence and to remain his wife until death do us part.

He had realized, when Edwin had told him of their marriage plans, that he had fallen in love with Jeannie Buchanan and he had not been able to stop himself going to see her. Remembering his halting, puerile babblings, he groaned with embarrassment. How foolish and weak she must think him. Though she had said very little, in fact now he thought about it, she had said nothing at all, but he had read in the depths of those beautiful green eyes, her puzzled expression.

Perhaps she had even believed him to be drunk again. Perhaps she had not even understood what he had been trying to say. No doubt she had just dismissed him from her mind and thought no more about his near declaration of love. In fact now, standing here looking across at the church, he could not really remember what he had said. All he could remember was that he had wanted her to be absolutely sure that she wanted to marry Tom.

Tom Lawrence. How Robert envied him at this moment.

He sighed and turned away from the window and picked up his hat and cane. He would walk to the church in time to see them come out. He patted the inside pocket of his jacket, feeling the rustle of the white envelope that contained a cheque. It was his wedding present to Jeannie. He could neither write nor say the words that were in his heart but with this gift would go all his loving wishes that at least she would be happy.

Sadly, he knew now that he would never find happiness in his own marriage.

As Tom and Jeannie emerged from the dim interior of the church, they both blinked in the brightness of the January sunlight.

Nell and Grace came to stand on either side. 'Ha' you some coppers in your pocket, Tom, ready for the bairns?' Jeannie heard Nell ask her son.

Tom looked about him. 'I don't see any . . .' he began and then stopped.

'Not here, maybe, but back at the house, the bairns in our street'll be waiting. You can be sure of that.'

But Tom was not listening to her now, 'Look,' he said quietly, 'there's Mr Robert standing at the gate.'

Jeannie's lips parted in a little gasp of surprise as she watched Robert walk up the path towards them. Stretching out his hand towards Tom, he shook it warmly.

'Congratulations, Tom. You're a very lucky man.' His voice was firm and he was smiling as he wished them both well. From his pocket he took out an envelope and pressed it into Tom's hands. 'Please – just a little personal gift. And I hope you have a lovely honeymoon. Where are you going?'

'Across the river, Mr Robert. On this afternoon's ferry and then on to Scarborough.'

Robert nodded and there was a moment's awkward pause before he said, 'Well, then. I'll – er – not keep you . . .' He nodded at Tom and then turning to look at Jeannie said, his voice deep and low, 'May I be the first to kiss the bride?'

'Of course, sir,' came Tom's dutiful, though reluctant, reply.

He was standing before her, looking down at her once more and now he leant forward and his lips touched her cheek in the most gentle, almost reverent kiss, that Jeannie could ever have imagined. Close to her ear, he whispered so softly that even she scarcely heard the words, 'Be happy, my dearest Jeannie.'

Then Robert straightened up and stepped back from her, smiling and raising his hat to them both. He turned and, with long strides, walked swiftly away from them.

Eighteen

They were walking along the seafront at Scarborough. Jeannie paused to watch the breakers far out to sea.

'Do you wish you were back at sea?' Jeannie asked him.

Tom laughed, the wind whipping away the sound. 'Fancy asking me that, Mrs Lawrence. On our honeymoon.'

He put his arm about her waist and they walked on in companionable silence, until at last Tom broke it by saying, 'Why did you ask me that question?'

'I remember ma father,' she said quietly. 'Whenever he was ashore you could see it in his eyes, a faraway look whenever he looked out to sea. He could hardly wait to get back aboard his ship.'

'Huh, more fool him, then.'

'Tom!'

'Oh, I'm sorry, Jeannie, but I've never been able to understand it. Me dad was just the same. Me . . .' he shrugged, 'I'd as leave be ashore.'

Jeannie was silent but she watched him now and saw that he hardly glanced out across the water, nor took any notice when the grey shape of a ship appeared on the distant horizon.

She thought back to the previous night, their first as man and wife. She had known what to expect. Her aunt, God rest her, Jeannie thought, had been a sensible, down-to-earth woman, who had, at what she considered an appropriate age, explained the facts of life to her niece. A no-nonsense, practical explanation of the workings of a woman's body, and of a man's, it might have been, but it had left Jeannie with a well-balanced view, with no fears born out of ignorance and certainly no romantic expectations that were unlikely to be fulfilled.

She had been surprised to find, however, that Tom was a gentle and considerate lover, and a practised one too. Tom Lawrence knew exactly what to do and how to do it, and even when he entered her for the first time and she felt the pain of the breaking of her maidenhead – as her doughty aunt had warned – he was thoughtful for her.

If she had expected the inexperienced fumbling of a boy, then Jeannie was either pleasantly surprised or acutely disappointed to think that for him, it was not his first time.

At this moment, she was not quite sure what she did feel. The matter, she decided rationally, was best left unspoken of, at least for the moment. Later in their marriage, perhaps.

What had surprised and definitely pleased her was that Tom had not – as her aunt had also led her to expect once the lovemaking was over – turned over and fallen sleep. He had held her gently in his arms and he had talked to her, telling her of his life at sea.

'I suppose there are some good things about it. The comradeship and the sight of a net coming up over the side, fair bursting with fish. And in the Icelandic waters, the views are magnificent. You feel as if everything's so clean and pure, the icebergs sparkling and the blue of the sea and the sky. It's as if no man has ever seen that part of the world before. As if you're the very first to ever see it. But that's about all that's good. For the rest, it's hard labour. Eighteen hours non-stop when we're fishing.

Longer, if the skipper's a greedy bastard and the hauls are good . . .'

She had nestled against him listening to his voice rumbling in his chest as he spoke. She was drowsy, scarcely taking in what he was actually saying. She drifted into semi-consciousness and imagined that it was her father once more telling her stories of his voyages. The same stories that George must have told his son, Tom. And now Tom was a fisherman too and experiencing all the wonderful sights for himself. Tom was like his father and her father. She believed that he, too, was a fisherman, born and bred.

So her question this morning had seemed quite a natural one to ask. 'Do you wish you were back at sea?'

But his answer had shocked her and left her with a disconcerting feeling of disappointment.

'Louise. My dear, I've booked a room for us at your favourite London hotel. I'm so sorry I couldn't go when you wanted me to, but there were problems at work. You know—'

'Oh, I don't want to go now, Robert.' Louise waved her slim hand, with its perfectly manicured nails and its soft skin that never saw a moment's drudgery. 'I've only just come back from Madeleine's. I don't want to go again.'

'I've booked theatre tickets and I thought you might like to go shopping for a new spring outfit.' He paused then added pointedly, 'But if you're too busy . . .'

He watched as the gleam came into her blue eyes.

'Well, I suppose,' she said slowly, but he could see that in her butterfly brain she was already in the Knightsbridge stores, 'I could re-arrange my plans, seeing as you've gone to so much trouble.'

What, Robert thought to himself, did his wife ever have in her life that would prevent her accepting the chance of shopping in the London stores and the round of social parties they would soon find themselves caught up in once they arrived there? He was quite prepared, before he had even made the suggestion, that their weekend would become a week-long holiday.

But Robert stretched a smile. It would be worth it if he could salvage their marriage. He was determined now to do everything he could to make it work. He was in it for better or worse. And it couldn't get much worse, he told himself wryly. So there was only the 'better' to hope for. And he really meant to try. He had resolved to put all thoughts of Jeannie out of his mind. He was married and, now, so was she. He almost wished that she had gone back to Scotland, that she could have become just a distant memory of a girl he had once seen.

Now, however, he was going to be faced with the prospect of seeing her, of knowing what went on in her life and her family. Yet part of him longed for that very thing; to know that he could see her, that he could, in a way, look after her from a distance – and without her knowing it.

Pushing thoughts of the beautiful firebrand to the back of his mind, he smiled at his wife and said, 'When shall we go then?'

To his surprise, Louise jumped up, threw her arms about his neck and kissed him on the cheek. 'Tomorrow. I can be ready tomorrow.'

*

Jeannie had never in her life known such idleness, at least not for so long a stretch at any one time. From quite an early age, she had to do household chores to help her invalid mother. After her mother's death Jeannie had, with the help of her aunt, kept the house always in readiness, waiting for her father coming home from the sea. The only holidays she could remember were the occasional trips with her father; each an idyllic time that she held in her memory amidst a lifetime of waiting.

And now she had let herself in for another life of waiting for her man to come home. But it was a life she was quite happy to accept. She would be proud of Tom, she knew, whatever he did. So she tucked her hand through his arm, and smiled, determined to store the memories of her honeymoon that she could live and relive in her mind. The beach in winter and, further up the coast, quaint villages and coves. Inland, the moors seeming to stretch for ever, broken by streams and vales with water-falls tumbling over craggy rock faces.

'It reminds me of home,' she murmured once, without thinking.

'Lincolnshire's your home now, Jeannie,' Tom reminded her and then laughed. 'All flat land and sea and sky. That's your home now.'

Maybe it was, Jeannie thought, for now. But one day I'll go back, she promised herself. One day I'll see my homeland again.

'Not more parcels, Louise.' Robert smiled as he teased his wife. Louise glanced at him and seeing that his expression belied the words, gave her tinkling, joyous laugh.

'Oh darling, I've bought the perfect dress for tonight's

party at Madeleine's. It's the very latest fashion. It's blue silk with a low waist and a tiered skirt. Just wait till you see it.'

'You're pretty to me whatever you wear,' he said and moved closer to her.

'Oh sweetie, you say the nicest things.' She patted his cheek and made a kiss in the air at the side of his face, but moved away before he could reach out for her and draw her to him. Stifling a sigh, he said, 'Shall we have a look round St Paul's or the Abbey after lunch?'

Louise made a little moue with her perfectly painted mouth. 'I want to rest this afternoon, Robert, if I'm to look my best. And then I want to have a long lovely bath in that gorgeous bathroom.' She waved her elegant hand towards the adjoining bathroom with its deep bath and gold taps in the shape of dolphins. 'But don't let me stop you, darling. You go, if you want to, but you will be back in time to be ready for eight o'clock, won't you?'

'Of course,' Robert said, hiding his disappointment. Dutifully, he held out his arm to her. 'Shall we go down for lunch.'

'In a minute, I must just renew my lipstick.'

'Jeannie, it's such a pretty hat. Let me buy it for you?'

'Oh no, Tom, it's far too expensive and frivolous. When would I wear a hat like that?'

The item under discussion was displayed in the centre of a shop window; a broad brimmed straw hat decorated with pink silk roses.

'Well, I don't know,' Tom said, wrinkling his forehead. 'Does it matter? Can't you wear a hat like that any time? On a Sunday?'

Jeannie laughed. 'To the kirk? Oh Tom, really. It's

more the sort of hat . . .' She bit back the words swiftly, for she had been about to say, it's the sort of hat that Aggie Turnbull would wear, but she turned the moment into a joke and hugged his arm to her side, and said, 'To wear at a wedding. Now, if you'd bought me it last week, then I could have worn it on my wedding day.'

'Well, I'm sorry I didn't see it in time. But won't you let me buy it for you now?'

'It's sweet of you, Tom, but really it isn't practical. It would be a waste of your hard-earned money.'

'You let me dad buy you that coat.'

'Yes, and the three of you bought me this hat for Christmas to go with it, didn't you?'

Tom's mouth turned down at the corners petulantly. 'I bet it's the sort that Mr Robert would buy *his* wife.'

Then his face brightened as he thrust his hand into the inside pocket of his jacket. 'Of course! I was forgetting. Mr Robert's cheque.'

He waved the envelope in the air. 'We'll need most of this to pay the guest house at the end of the week, but there should be enough left over. I'll get it cashed and then we'll buy that hat. You'll look a treat in it, Jeannie.'

She sighed inwardly. She didn't want to upset him by throwing his generosity back in his face and this was, after all, their honeymoon. 'Well, if you're really sure you can afford it . . .' she began and before she had finished speaking, she saw that his face had brightened and all sign of little-boy surliness had gone.

Tom grasped her hand and pulled her towards the shop. 'Come on, Jeannie. By, you'll be grand in it.'

Alone in the echoing vastness of a city church, Robert stood looking at the sweet face of the Madonna. In his imagination, the carved figure became not his own wife, but Jeannie.

The trip to London had not been entirely unsuccessful, he told himself. At least he and Louise were now friendly and she did not entirely rebuff his gentle advances in their bed at night. But she would only allow him to hold her in his arms and cuddle her and talk about the theatre play they had just seen or the party they'd just been to and what everyone had been wearing. If he tried a bolder move, she would move away, out of his arms and say, 'I'm tired now. Good night, darling.'

As he looked now at the mother figure, saw the love and devotion etched even into those carved features, he knew that it was very unlikely he and Louise would ever have children. But now, Jeannie, he could see her as a mother, an earth mother devoted to her husband and his children.

Swiftly, Robert turned on his heel and walked the length of the aisle, his footsteps echoing eerily in the silence. He hurried from the holy place, feeling guilty that he could have had such irreverent thoughts in this place. That he had dared, in the Lord's House, to covet another man's wife.

Nineteen

'Just where is it you're going, Grace, nearly every night?'

They had been married a month and Tom was away at sea on his first trip since their honeymoon. He'd had to go. There had no longer been any choice. He had no money left to give Jeannie during her first weeks as a housewife.

With her mouth set in a grim line, Jeannie had wrapped the pretty straw hat in tissue paper and placed it in a box on top of the wardrobe. She no longer wanted to set eyes on it, for it was a reminder that, until Tom came home from the sea again, the only money coming into the household would be earned by the three women in it.

With Tom away and Nell still mourning, Jeannie felt she should find out just where it was that Grace was going night after night. Besides, it was what Tom wanted of her.

She had been a little hurt by his parting words. She had gone to the dockside to see him off. 'You will take care of yourself, Tom, won't you?' she had said, sudden fear gripping her.

'Don't you worry about me, Jeannie. I'll be fine. Now I've got something – or rather someone – to come home to.' The smile had begun on Jeannie's mouth but it froze as Tom spoilt the loving words by adding, 'And knowing you're there to take care of Mam and Grace, well, I shan't worry so much when I'm at sea.'

So now, Jeannie told herself, she had every right to question Grace.

'It's none of your business,' the girl snapped back.

'Well, I'm making it my business. You're not being fair to your poor mother. Nor Tom either, now he's head of the family.' She knew it was cruel to make a reference, even a veiled one, to George Lawrence's death, but desperate situations required desperate measures. 'He feels responsible for you. You're still only sixteen.'

'I'm not doing anything wrong. I'm just going to a friend's, that's all.'

'Who? Who is this friend?'

'It's none of your business,' Grace said again.

'Is it Jane?'

There was a guarded look in the girl's eyes and she avoided meeting Jeannie's gaze. 'It might be.'

'Oh well, if that's how you feel, you'd better get on with it.' Exasperated, Jeannie turned away. Deliberately, feigning disinterest now, she made up her mind to follow the girl the very next time she left the house. She was worried about Grace and now it was more than just Tom's request that she should look after his sister. Just lately the girl had seemed thin and pale.

'Are you sure you're not sickening for something?' she'd asked her countless times, but each time Grace shrugged off her concern.

'I'm just tired, Jeannie. I feel the cold so at work, you know.'

Jeannie did know. For anyone not as healthy as herself, she could well understand how the cold seeped through the fingers until there was no feeling left and the slicing and filleting became merely a series of repetitive movements that they could do in their sleep.

That evening when Grace went out, Jeannie waited a few moments and then followed her. Pulling her shawl around her head and shoulders, Jeannie bent her head against the wind whipping down the wet street and hurried after the figure ahead of her, yet minding to keep her distance.

At the end of their street, Grace turned to the right and then, passing by the next turning, turned right again. Jeannie hovered on the corner. This was the street where she had first encountered Grace, where the attack had taken place.

This was Harbour Road where Aggie Turnbull lived. Surely . . .? In the darkness, Jeannie squinted to see where Grace went. She saw the girl hesitate about half-way down and glance around her as if to make sure no one was watching. Jeannie drew further back into the shadows of the house on the corner. Then, as she watched, she saw Grace bend her head and scuttle into a passageway between two houses. Leaving her hiding place, Jeannie walked swiftly down the street in time to hear, in the stillness of the damp night, voices and laughter coming from the back-yard of the house as the door was opened to let Grace in.

Jeannie stood in the darkness, biting her lower lip, uncertain, now, as to what to do next. She was sure that this was Aggie Turnbull's house. What could she do? What ought she to do? Should she knock on the door right now and demand Grace to come home? Should she go back and tell Nell just where her foolish, wayward daughter was? But her mind shied away from that. Nell was still mourning the loss of her beloved husband. Jeannie could not bear to bring further trouble to her unless it became absolutely necessary. And with Tom now away at sea again, the burden of responsibility fell upon her.

As she stood debating, Jeannie heard the sounds of a motor car in the distance, but for a moment she took little notice. Then she realized that the sound was coming closer, that the vehicle was turning into this street. Anxious not to be thought loitering, especially outside the house of Aggie Turnbull, Jeannie bent her head and hurried back to the corner where once again she paused in the shadows and peered round the end house to watch.

The motor drew to a halt outside Aggie's house and the noise died away. As the man stepped from it, Jeannie inched forward, but she could not see him clearly, only his shape. Tall, with a slim build, the man was dressed in an evening cape and top hat. He went towards the front door of the house and rapped smartly on it with his cane, the sound echoing along the street.

Has he no shame, she thought, to be seen knocking at the door of that house? Obviously not, she answered herself, as she crept closer. The door opened and light and laughter from the house flooded into the street. Nearer now, and with his features illuminated in the seconds before he stepped into the house and the door closed behind him, Jeannie recognized him.

Francis Hayes-Gorton.

That did it! Now, without a moment's hesitation, Jeannie marched up to the front door and banged on it with her fist. 'Open this door. Open this door at once, d'you hear me.'

The door was flung back and Jeannie, her arm raised to knock upon it again, almost fell forward. She clutched at the door frame to steady herself and blinked in the sudden light. Before her stood Francis in the action of taking off his cloak and hat. He turned and a smile twisted his mouth. 'Oho, Mrs Jeannie Lawrence, if I'm not mistaken. Come to join the fun whilst your man is away at sea. Come in, my dear, come in . . .' He made a motion towards her with his hand inviting her to step inside but Jeannie stood resolutely on the doorstep. Then her glance went beyond him to where the staircase rose behind him. At the top, dressed in a shiny, red satin evening gown, with diamonds glittering at her throat, stood Grace. She was descending the stairs, her gaze upon Francis Hayes-Gorton and seeing the look on the girl's face, Jeannie gasped.

Grace had the rapturous look of a young girl hopelessly and helplessly besotted by the young man standing at the foot of the stairs.

Francis shrugged. 'Oh well, if you won't join in the fun, then . . .' He turned towards Grace and took her outstretched hand in his. Raising her fingers to his lips, he kissed them and then glanced, with a sly, triumphant look, over his shoulder at Jeannie. 'See what you're missing.'

Then Jeannie lunged forward. 'I see what I'm missing, all right,' she muttered and grasped Grace's arm, dragging her away from Francis. Because her move had been so swift and unexpected, she managed to pull the girl towards the door and almost had her across the threshold and out into the night, before anyone realized what was happening. But then, Grace resisted, pulling against Jeannie's grasp and at the same moment Francis stepped forward and gripped Jeannie's wrist so fiercely that the feeling went from her hand and her hold on Grace slackened.

'Trying to play the avenging angel again, are we, Mrs Lawrence?' he said through thin, tight lips. 'I think you should let Grace decide whether she wants to go or stay, don't you?'

In the red heat of anger, Jeannie faced him boldly. 'No, I don't. She's only a girl. Scarcely more than a bairn.' She became aware that others had appeared at the top of the stairs, and behind them, emerging from the front room, was Aggie herself. Now, Jeannie turned on her. She opened her mouth to scream a tirade of abuse at the woman, but instead she found herself forestalled as Aggie smiled and, stepping forward, put her arm about Grace's shoulder. In a husky voice, she said, 'I think you should go home with your sister-in-law, my dear.'

But Grace interrupted. 'No,' she shouted, pulling herself free. She stepped close to Francis, putting her cheek against his chest and her arms about his waist. 'No, I want to stay here.' She stared boldly at Jeannie and added defiantly, 'All night.'

Jeannie knew her mouth dropped open. She was shocked and, suddenly, very afraid.

Now she tried the softer approach, making her tone a gentle appeal. 'Grace, please. Just come home. Your mother will be worried.'

For a moment there was a haunted look of doubt in the girl's eyes. And guilt. Yes, Jeannie could see it. Guilt. Suddenly, with a woman's intuition, Jeannie knew there was something very wrong. Her voice low, she held out her hand towards Grace and said, 'Grace, we'll help you. We'll stand by you.'

The girl's eyes widened and she whispered, 'How – how did you know?'

Jeannie's heart was heavy within her chest. She hadn't known, not really. But she had guessed and sadly, it seemed, she was right.

She saw Francis stiffen as he looked down at the girl snuggling so close to him. 'What? What do you mean?'

Grace looked up into his face and Jeannie saw again the look of adoration and she groaned inwardly. Grace idolized this man. Her face was shining with happiness now as she said, 'I'm to have your child, Francis. Isn't it wonderful?'

All around them there was a silence, as if everyone

listening were holding their breath. Although her gaze was upon Grace and Francis, Jeannie was aware that Aggie gave a little gasp and her hand fluttered to cover her mouth. She, too, was staring at the couple and Jeannie was sure she heard the woman breathe, 'No, oh no.'

Well, at least we're in agreement on that, Jeannie thought grimly.

Francis's eyes narrowed and his mouth was hard. Suddenly, his handsome face was ugly. He pushed Grace from him and then gripped her wrists savagely, shaking her and bending towards her, hissing in her face, 'Don't you try to pull that one with me, you little whore.'

Grace's eyes were wide, her mouth dropping open. 'But – but Francis . . .'

With a vicious movement, he flung her away from him so that she fell backwards, losing her balance, and before anyone could move to help her, she had fallen heavily against the wall, cracking her head. Slowly, she slithered down into an ungainly heap on the floor. Her head lolled forward and she tipped to one side.

At once, Jeannie and Aggie rushed forward and knelt either side of the girl. Aggie ran her fingers over the girl's scalp. 'There's no cut,' she said, 'but she'll have a nasty bruise.'

Grace moaned and her eyelids fluttered.

'Let me help you up—' Jeannie began, but Aggie said at once, 'No, don't move her for a moment.'

Suddenly, they felt a draught of cold air and heard the front door slam behind them. The two women glanced at each other.

'Good riddance,' Aggie muttered and bent over Grace, stroking the girl's face with such a gesture of tenderness that Jeannie was mystified.

'Here,' a voice spoke behind them and Jeannie turned to see that one of the other girls was holding out a glass of water.

'Thank you.' Gently Aggie raised the girl's head and shoulders. Cradling her against her breast, Aggie took the glass and held it to Grace's lips. The girl's face was deathly pale, the bright red lipstick a smudged gash across her mouth.

As consciousness returned, she drank the water and then she pressed her face into Aggie's bosom and wept.

Twenty

'Tom . . .' She put her hand out towards him.

'Jeannie!' The smile spread across his face to see her standing there, waiting for him, and he dropped his bag to the ground and held out both his arms. Jeannie went into them, but, whilst submitting to his kiss of greeting, she held herself back a little from him. Feeling her reserve he looked down at her and said at once, 'What is it? Is something wrong?'

'Tom, I'm sorry to greet you with bad news . . .'

His eyes darkened with anguish. 'What is it? Not Mam? Oh she isn't . . . She hasn't done something silly?'

Jeannie blinked and looked up at him in astonishment. 'Do something silly? Your mother?' she countered sharply. 'Never! She's a Scot, Tom Lawrence, and dinna you forget it.'

For a moment a wry smile twitched his mouth and he made a fair impression of the Scottish brogue. 'Och, Ah'm no' likely to, the noo.' But then his face sobered again as he asked again, 'Then what is it?'

'Two pieces of news, really. One is, I'm sorry to say, bad news. The other – well – I hope you'll think it good.'

Tom sighed. 'Don't keep me in suspense, woman. Let's have the bad first then.'

'It's – it's Grace. She's expecting.'

Tom's mouth dropped open and he stared at his wife without saying a word. When he did speak his voice was a

167

hoarse, strangulated whisper. 'Pregnant? Our Grace has got 'ersen pregnant? Oh, no . . .' He shook his head violently now, as if the very idea was unthinkable. He pulled away from Jeannie. 'No, no, I don't believe it.' He paused a moment and then said viciously, 'I bet it's him again, isn't it? She's been attacked, raped. That's what'll have happened. By God, if only me dad was still here, he'd . . .' He turned and took a few steps forward and then stopped, swaying for a moment as did most fishermen when they stepped on to firm land after weeks at sea. Then Jeannie saw his shoulders slump as if in defeat. The drive to do something, to take some action, lasted only seconds with Tom Lawrence.

He half-turned back towards her. 'Who is it?' He asked flatly. 'Do you know who the father is? Will he marry her?'

'I do know who he is, but no, he won't marry her.'

His haunted eyes met her steady gaze. 'Who is it? Is it him? Hayes-Gorton?'

Jeannie swallowed. 'Not the one you're thinking. It's the other one, Francis.'

He stared at her and then repeated incredulously, 'Francis? Francis Hayes-Gorton. You mean he – he attacked her?'

'No – no.' Swiftly, Jeannie shook her head and then looked down at the ground. This part was even more difficult than the first, awful news. 'Grace fancies herself in love with him. She's been meeting him secretly.'

'Meeting him? How? Where?' And then before Jeannie could speak, Tom answered his own question. He gave a nod of his head and said flatly, 'Of course. Aggie's.'

Mutely, Jeannie nodded and they stood staring at each other for several moments oblivious to the hustle and bustle of the dockside going on all around them.

Wearily, Tom held out his hand towards her. 'Come on, we'd best go home.'

'Don't you want to hear the other piece of news?' she asked, a trace of sadness in her tone now that the bad news had obliterated any chance of joy and excitement at her own.

'Of course,' Tom said, but she could sense that whatever it was, he was scarcely interested.

'Tom, we're going to have a baby. I'm expecting too.'

In the intimacy of their bed that night, Tom took Jeannie in his arms and held her close. 'I'm so sorry,' he whispered against her hair, 'that your wonderful news was spoilt by – by Grace.'

Jeannie snuggled closer but said nothing. She was not about to say, 'It's all right' because it wasn't. Her happy surprise had been spoilt and she felt cheated.

'What are we going to do?' came Tom's deep voice.

Jeannie lay perfectly still, wondering, for a moment, if she had misunderstood. He, Tom, the man of the house, was asking her what they should do. The realization came slowly, creeping into her being like icy water, then flooding through her like a tidal wave of disappointment.

The man she had married was not the man she had thought him to be. His father, yes, now George Lawrence had been a strong, steadfast man. Mistakenly she knew now, she had thought that his son would take after him.

But Tom's outbursts were not those of a strong character, determined and sure, but the bluster of a man who had perhaps always lived in the shadow of a more dominant man. And even though that man was gone now, the son had not the personality to step into his shoes. Yet Tom was a good man, she would not deny. And that he loved her, she was sure. But she knew that it was she who was the rock to which they all clung. Even Nell, since George's going, had floundered helplessly in the raging torrent of her loss and had turned to Jeannie for strength and fortitude. It was odd, Jeannie pondered, how the whole family had so readily leant on her, the girl who had come as a stranger into their midst. Why did Nell have no friends amongst her neighbours? Was it merely because she was the wife of a skipper and perhaps set slightly apart from them? Or was there something more?

And now Grace. Jeannie sighed. Silly, foolish, gullible Grace. Now she would have to see to Grace too.

With her cheek still against his chest, she let out a long sigh. 'We'll take care of her, of course. And the child.'

His arms tightened about her in unspoken gratitude, but again his voice rumbled deep in his chest against her cheek. 'But ought we to do something? I mean, about the father?'

'What can we do? A Hayes-Gorton will never the marry the likes of us . . .' As the words came out of her mouth, in her imagination it was not her husband lying by her side, holding her, but Robert Hayes-Gorton, with his gentle smile and his dark, brown eyes and his deep voice whispering in her ear. The feeling was so overwhelming that Jeannie pulled back, frightened by the power of her emotions and the wickedness of her imagination.

'Jeannie? What is it? What's the matter?'

Overcome with a sudden rush of affection and guilt that she should even think of being unfaithful to this good man, she reached for him and pulled him into her arms. 'Let's forget Grace,' she whispered softly. 'Just for tonight, the one night you're home.'

*

When Tom went back to sea, anxious, for once, to be gone and away from all the trouble at home, Jeannie marched to the house two streets away and rapped sharply on Aggie Turnbull's door.

'Jeannie—'

'Dinna you "Jeannie" me,' she snapped as the woman she had come to see opened the door herself. 'How could you let her do it? How could you encourage her to come here? She's no more than a bairn. Sixteen—'

'Seventeen next month,' Aggie countered swiftly.

'Och aye. Old enough to become one of your whores, I suppose?'

'She came here for one thing only—'

'Aye, and we know what that was.'

Aggie, two pink blotches of anger showing in her cheeks, took a step towards Jeannie. 'She came here for a little fun. To dress up in pretty clothes and escape from the stink of fish. Just for a few hours. And she came to escape from the endless cod net on the wall and Nell always working—'

'Good, honest work.'

Aggie continued as if Jeannie had not spoken. 'And to try – just for a while – to forget about her dad.'

For a moment, Jeannie was silent and then it appeared that Aggie had taken in exactly what Jeannie had just said, for she went on, 'And as for Nell being a good, honest woman. Well, I could tell you a thing or two about Nell Lawrence. Oh yes, indeed I could.'

'There's nothing that you could tell me about that family that I'd want to hear.'

Aggie shook her head. 'No, Jeannie, I don't suppose you would want to hear anything that I might have to say. I don't think you would like it.'

'My name's Mrs Lawrence to you,' was Jeannie's only reply as she began to turn away.

'Mrs Lawrence,' Aggie said softly, seeming to almost savour the name on her lips. 'Mrs Lawrence.'

Glancing back, Jeannie was shocked to see sudden tears in the woman's eyes. All her anger had evaporated, leaving only a pensive, wistful expression. 'I am sorry about Grace,' Aggie said gently now. 'More sorry than you'll ever know. I tried to warn her, but she wouldn't listen.'

Jeannie stopped and twisted round to face her again. 'Tried to warn her? Well, you didna try very hard. You could have stopped her coming to your house very easily. Stopped her meeting him here.'

'I could, yes.' Surprisingly, Aggie agreed. 'But she would only have met him some other way. She loves him, really loves him.' She paused and then added, 'Watch over her, Jeannie. Please. I'm so afraid of what she might do now he has deserted her.'

'Och, the Lawrences wouldna let the likes of him bring them down.'

'Are you sure, Jeannie?' Aggie said softly.

But as Jeannie now turned away finally, she was not so sure herself of her own vehement statement.

It was not the first time she had been to the offices of the Hayes-Gorton Trawler Company. She had come to collect pay due to Tom, lining up with all the other fishermen's wives to be sure that they had enough money to feed their family before it all disappeared behind the bar at the Fisherman's Rest. She would not so easily forget the incident over the hat and, in future, she intended to hold the purse strings.

But it was the first time she had ventured beyond the

pay window and further into the building to find the offices of the partners. Her heart beat a little faster and her hands felt clammy.

The woman in the outer office was middle-aged and spinsterish. Small, round, steel-framed spectacles and straight, grey hair cut short with a heavy fringe did nothing to enhance her appearance. Her thin-lipped mouth did not even stretch itself into the pretence of a smile.

'I would like to see Mr Hayes-Gorton, if you please? Mr Francis Hayes-Gorton.'

The woman looked up and then slowly her gaze travelled down to Jeannie's shoes and then up again, assessing her from head to toe. 'Do you have an appointment?' The voice affected superiority but far from intimidating Jeannie, it only made her more determined and icily polite.

'No, I dinna have an appointment, but if that is the way things are done, then I would like you to make one for me.' She paused ever so slightly and added again, 'If you please.'

Languidly the woman flickered over the pages of a diary. 'He's very busy just now. I really don't know when he would be able . . .'

Jeannie heard the door open behind her and without needing to turn round, she knew who had entered the room. She could feel his presence, feel him close to her. Resolutely, she licked her dry lips and continued to stare at the woman in front of her.

'Jeannie?' Robert began as he closed the door and came around her to stand to the side of the secretary's desk. Then, hastily, he corrected himself. 'Mrs Lawrence? What brings you here? Is there anything wrong?'

Jeannie opened her mouth to reply but the woman forestalled her. 'She's requesting an appointment to see Mr Francis, sir, but I really don't think . . .'

Robert held up his hand. 'It's all right, Miss Forbes, I will attend to this. Please . . .' He turned towards Jeannie and spread his hand in a gesture of invitation to precede him from the room. 'Won't you come into my office? Maybe I can help?'

'But I dinna think . . .' she began and then, glancing briefly at the tight-lipped expression of disapproval on the secretary's face, with a spark of devilment Jeannie nodded agreement and turned in the direction he indicated.

Closing the door of his office behind them, he gestured towards a chair. 'Please, sit down. May I get you a cup of tea – or anything?'

Jeannie shook her head but took the seat he offered whilst Robert went around the desk and sat down in the swivel chair on the opposite side. He leant his arms on the edge of the desk and bent forward a little towards her.

She's here, he was thinking, she's really here, in my office, sitting opposite me and I can't think of a sensible thing to say to this woman who has become the object of my every waking moment and even most of my sleep too. It is her I think of when I wake in the morning and she is the last face I see in my mind's eye in the darkness of the night before I sleep, hoping to dream about her too.

Now here she is. Sitting in front of me and I am like a tongue-tied schoolboy. And she looks so calm, so dignified, so in control. But then, he reminded himself sadly, why shouldn't she? She dislikes me, perhaps even hates me. The thought saddened him so that when he spoke, his voice was devoid of all emotion, flat and almost unfriendly.

'How may I help you?'

Jeannie tried to still the rapid beating of her heart, tried to sit facing him calmly and without a trace of the tumult of emotion inside her from showing on her face. How could she be so foolish as to even allow herself to feel like this when she was married to another man and expecting that man's child? How could she let herself think such wild, wicked thoughts? Why did she keep wondering just what it would be like to be held in this man's arms, to feel the touch of those lips on her mouth, to dig her fingers deep into that thick, dark brown hair and pull his head down on to her breast and hold him close . . .

Aloud, her voice harsh, she said, 'It's Mr Francis I need to see.' She licked her lips and added deliberately, 'Sir.' His smooth forehead puckered in a frown and his brown eyes were unfathomable depths.

Robert felt his heart plummet and there was a pain in his chest. There was a cold edge to his voice as he said, curtly, 'I see. Then I can't be of assistance?'

Jeannie swallowed. Now she had made him angry. She could see it on his face. 'I'm sorry. It's a delicate, personal matter. I must see him.'

He could hear the urgency that was almost a desperation in her voice. And deep in her eyes was a haunted look that tore at his heart. What the hell had his dear brother been up to now to make Jeannie look like that?

Robert stood up suddenly. 'Please – stay here a moment. I'll see if he's in the building.'

'Oh – I . . .' She made as if to rise when he did, but at his bidding she sank back into her chair.

Whilst he was out of the room, Jeannie looked about her. Though her mind was occupied with the problem and she thought that she hardly took in her surroundings, later she was to find that she had remembered Robert's office in minute detail. An antique mahogany desk with polished brass handles and a green leather top. The walls were lined with mahogany bookcases and over the fireplace hung a portrait of an elderly man dressed as the skipper of a trawler. Jeannie guessed he was Robert's grandfather and supposed he must have dressed up like that for the painting. But then she remembered Flora's story of the Gortons. This was the man who had started out with one boat, which he had skippered himself. She looked again at the picture. He wore the clothes with a comfortable familiarity. This was no upper-class gent dressing up. The man in the painting was a genuine, born and bred fisherman.

The door opened and Robert appeared. 'He's in his office. Come along, I'll show you the way.' Now she rose and followed him along a corridor and passed into a similar office as he held open the door for her, though here the furnishings were modern, sleek lines of wood and metal that, for Jeannie, had neither warmth nor soul.

Francis was sitting behind the desk, leaning backwards, his hands linked behind his head. 'Well, well, well, if it isn't Mrs Lawrence. Protector of the young and innocent.' He laughed, a cruel sound. 'Though they're not so innocent as she'd like to believe. Eh, my dear Jeannie?'

Robert had closed the door but had remained in the room. Now he came and stood between them, to one side of the desk so that he glanced first at one and then at the other.

Jeannie took her gaze away from Francis for a brief moment and said, 'This is between me and Mr Francis, sir.'

At once Robert made as if to leave. 'I'm sorry—' he began but Francis interrupted. 'There's nothing you can have to say to me that my brother shouldn't hear.'

For a brief moment, Robert and Jeannie stared at each other, the one mystified, the other embarrassed by what she was being forced to say in front of him.

Tight-lipped, she turned her bold, green gaze upon Francis Hayes-Gorton. 'Very well,' she said in a voice that was deceptively quiet. 'You must ken why I'm here. What are you going to do about Grace Lawrence?'

For a moment there was complete stillness in the room until Francis, still rocking gently back and forth on two legs of his chair, said with a calculated indifference and a glitter of malice in his eyes, 'Absolutely nothing.'

'But you are the father. We all heard her say so.'

Now Francis let his chair drop forward with a crash and at the same moment brought his fists down on to the desk in front of him with a thump that startled both Jeannie and Robert. 'How dare you! How dare you come into this office with your malicious tales! Just because one of Aggie Turnbull's trollops gets herself . . .'

Now Jeannie was angry too and she leant across the desk, bending her face close to his, forgetting now in the white heat of her ire, that this man held the Lawrence family's livelihood in his hands. But at this moment, even if she had thought about it, she did not care. Right now, this was about a young girl brought low by this man.

'She's no' one of Aggie's girls, and you know it. She's a silly, naive, yes, foolish, girl, but she is not – not a whore.' Her voice dropped. 'She imagines herself in love with you, and in her stupidity, believes you love her.'

'Ha!' Francis threw back his head and laughed aloud, but the sound had no humour. It was cruel, mirthless laughter. 'Then you are right about one thing, Mrs Lawrence. She is stupid and deserves all she has brought upon herself.' He leant closer again. 'And whilst I make no secret of the fact that I visit Aggie and her – er – friends, I most certainly make no admission as to fathering the girl's bastard. It could,' he said with slow deliberate malice, 'be any one of a number of men.'

Jeannie's lips parted in a gasp and slowly she straightened up. 'I see. So that's how it is, is it?'

Francis rose to his feet and leant on his knuckles across the desk. 'That is exactly how it is. I'll bid you "Good day", Mrs Lawrence.'

Jeannie wagged her forefinger in his face. 'You,' she said slowly and with emphasis on every word, 'have no' heard the last of this, Mr High n' Mighty Hayes-Gorton.'

Smiling sarcastically, he said smoothly, 'Oh, I think I have. I think you will find, dear lady, that your husband will not approve of today's little visit, never mind any further trouble-making on your part.'

'Are you threatening me? Threatening that Tom will lose his job if I—'

'That's enough.' For the first time, Robert spoke, his deep voice breaking into the quarrel.

Jeannie tore her gaze away from the man before her, gave one swift, furious glance at Robert then turned and in one quick movement dragged open the door and marched from the room.

'Jeannie – Jeannie, wait . . .'

She heard him clattering down the steps behind her, but he did not catch up with her until they stood side by side on the steps outside the building.

She stood a moment, gulping fresh air into her lungs, almost as if to clear herself of the putrid air of Francis's presence.

Giving full vent to her anger, she turned on Robert, spewing out her wrath, yet even as she did so, she knew she was being unfair. He was not to blame and yet she could not stop herself. 'Leave me be. You and your family have caused us enough grief. She's no' what he says. There've been no other men. I'd stake my life on it. It's him. Just him.'

'I believe you.' Touching her arm briefly, Robert spoke with a quietness that was such a direct contrast to her

178

angry words, that she immediately felt ashamed. Then the anger that had carried her here, buoyed her up to confront one of their 'masters', died and she felt suddenly exhausted.

'I'm sorry,' she said at once. 'It's no' your fault.' She could not resist a fleeting, wry smile as she added, 'At least, no' this time.'

Robert too gave a slight smile of regret. 'I've wanted to tell you so often, Jeannie, to explain about that night.'

She gave a gesture of dismissal with her hand but he went on, haltingly at first and then with greater assurance as he realized that for the first time she was ready to listen to his side of the story. 'I remember very little of what happened. Please believe me. I'd been drinking, and yes, I admit it a little too much. But not *that* much. Not enough to make me so paralytic that I didn't know what I was doing. I found out later,' he added grimly, 'that my dear, caring . . .' here the word was heavy with sarcasm, 'brother Francis had mixed my drinks with rum. It always makes me ill and he knows that. And it was certainly he who led our party to Aggie's house. What I don't understand . . .' his brown gaze was now searching Jeannie's face for her side of the story, 'is what a nice girl like Grace Lawrence was even doing at Aggie's.'

Jeannie sighed, seeing for the first time how the events of that night had really been. Young men out on a stag night, intent on causing the greatest embarrassment to the young bridegroom that they could. And the ringleader had been his own brother.

Jeannie sighed. 'She shouldna have been there. I know that now. But still, she's not what your brother calls her. She's just young and silly and gullible, bowled over by fancy clothes and parties.' She shook her head slowly. 'I suppose, in a way, you can't blame her either. She just wanted a bit of fun and didn't realize what it would lead to.' Now she looked at him full in the face. 'She does love him, you know.'

'Oh Jeannie.' Her name was a whisper on his lips as they stood on the steps together just looking at each other.

Then becoming aware that they were standing in full view of passers-by, of the whole dockside area if it came to that, Jeannie said, 'I must go.'

'Just one more thing . . .' he said softly. 'Would you please not – this time – take it as an insult if I say that I will try to see what I can do for Grace? In – in the way of money, I mean.'

Jeannie stared at him for a moment, reading so many emotions deep in his eyes. Shame, regret, concern, even . . . She turned away, shutting out the one feeling she could see there that threatened to overwhelm them both.

Nodding, she said heavily, 'Aye, I'll no' refuse you this time, Mr Robert. For she'll be needin' all the help she can get.'

She walked down the steps and, though she was aware of him standing watching her, she did not look back.

Twenty-One

Jeannie sailed through her pregnancy hardly noticing her condition. She was lucky that she had good health, but wryly she admitted to herself that there was precious little time for her to indulge herself.

In contrast, Grace was ill throughout the following months. Whilst her stomach swelled, the rest of the girl's body grew thinner, until her face was pinched and her skin, devoid of colour, was stretched tightly over the bone structure of her features. Unable to face the gossip, she gave in her notice at work and sat all day hunched in the chair at the side of the fire. Whilst Nell continued to work at her net on the wall, not a word, as far as Jeannie could hear, passed between mother and daughter. Shattered by the loss of her husband, her daughter's downfall seemed to have robbed Nell of her last ounce of strength. She turned to the only comfort she knew: work. As the weather improved, Nell took her net into the back-yard and hung it from the rail fastened across the kitchen window. During the summer days the back-yards were filled with the sound of laughter and chatter as neighbours, their hands busy with the braiding, called to each other. Only this year, Nell worked in silence whilst Grace stayed indoors, even on the warmest days.

'You must eat, Grace, for the sake of the baby. You're no' eating enough to keep a bird alive.' Jeannie tried to coax her gently.

But Grace would not answer.

'Will you talk to her?' Jeannie asked Nell.

Tight-lipped, Nell said, 'There's nothing I can say to her, Jeannie. I never thought my Grace would shame us in this way.'

Jeannie pleaded the girl's cause. 'She's no' the first and she willna be the last. She loved the man, worthless though he is.'

Nell glared at Jeannie, stung to anger. 'You might be married into this family now, Jeannie, but you dinna ken everything about us. Grace knew that she shouldna go to Aggie's and not only for the obvious reason. There are other reasons too.'

'What?' Jeannie demanded, but Nell turned away and though she said no more, her action spoke loud and clear: 'Mind your own business'.

Annoyed, Jeannie turned and marched along the alley-way running between the back-yards of the houses. Tom's ship was due in on the next tide.

He would help her, she told herself, he would talk to Grace.

'She's a little whore and a bloody liar and if you so much as breathe a word of this to Father, I'll kill you.'

Robert watched the face of his elder brother contorted with rage, his blue eyes bulging, his face white.

Calmly, Robert murmured, ' "The lady doth protest too much, methinks".'

'What? What are you burbling on about?'

'I should have thought you, of all people, would have known your Shakespeare. You, with your public school education. Edwin and I were not so – er – fortunate.' The sarcasm was evident in Robert's tone. 'But perhaps the local Grammar School was not so bad after all.'

'Huh, you think a good education is being able to spout the Bard?'

'Oh no.' Robert shook his head. 'I think a good education is learning how to lead a good, honest, decent life. And that . . .' he paused for emphasis, 'includes standing by your mistakes.'

Francis's eyes glittered and his lips curled. 'Just like the Honourable Robert in his farce of a marriage.'

Robert felt the colour begin to creep up his neck, but he kept his tone level. 'My marriage is nothing to do with you.'

'Ah,' Francis said slowly. 'You think not, eh?'

The brothers stared at each other for a long moment before Robert said once more, 'What are you going to do about Grace Lawrence?'

'I've told you. Nothing. Absolutely nothing. I shall deny everything. I might even, if you don't stop meddling in my affairs, start a few rumours that the child is yours. So I should be very careful what you do, dear brother.'

'Your threats don't bother me,' Robert snapped.

'Really? Well, I don't think Father or your father-in-law would be too pleased to hear that you have a bastard child by a little whore when you can't even provide the company with a legitimate son and heir.'

Robert opened his mouth to retaliate, but anything he said would be disloyal to Louise. And despite everything, he could not descend to that.

'Oh go to hell, Francis,' he muttered, but his brother only laughed. 'Since you're so fond of quotations and sayings, dear boy, how about this one: "The Devil takes care of his own".'

*

183

Jeannie stood on the jetty, pulling her coat around her. The buttons would scarcely meet now over the bulge of her stomach and the wind, whipping along the quay, found its way inside her coat and made her shiver. It was a blustery day and cold for July.

'Come on, Tom, for goodness sake!' she muttered, her gaze on the distant gates for sight of his ship nosing its way into the dock. She walked up and down, more to keep herself warm than searching for sight of his ship, but when she came near to the end of the jetty, she saw the *Gorton North Star*, its nose tight against the wall and the lumpers already unloading the kits of fish. She went nearer. 'How long has she been in?' she asked one of the workers.

'Two hours, missis. One of the first in when they opened the gates.'

'Do you know Tom Lawrence? Did you see him come ashore?'

The man shook his head and, as a yell from the boat caught his attention, he turned back to continue his work.

Jeannie hurried away down the length of the quay, annoyed with herself. Here she was standing in the cold and all the time Tom was already ashore at home or in the Fisherman's.

She went home first but he was not there.

'No,' Nell said. 'He's no' been home.'

'But his ship came in two hours ago.'

The two women stared at each other, fear for a moment in their eyes.

'Oh no.' Jeannie shook her head. 'We'd have heard by now if . . .' She left the sentence unfinished and Nell turned away, back to her braiding.

'I'll go to the Fisherman's,' Jeannie said, 'but he'd best not be in there, else I'll skite his lugs for him.'

Tom was not in the pub on the corner nor had he been to the pay office to collect his money. She was turning away from the narrow window when she heard someone call her name. Looking round, she saw Robert striding towards her.

'How are you?' he said and she could see at once that he was trying hard not to glance down at her stomach.

'I'm well, but at this moment, rather angry.'

'Oh? Can I help?'

'Only if you can tell me where my husband is. His ship's docked, but I can't find him anywhere.'

For a moment, Robert looked uncomfortable.

'You know where he is, don't you?' Then as a thought struck her, she shook her head. 'Och no, he wouldna . . .'

Misunderstanding her, Robert said swiftly, 'He's all right. Nothing's happened to him, I promise you.'

'I wasna thinking it had,' she said wryly. 'I was thinking he might have gone to Aggie's.'

'Tom?' The surprise on Robert's face was genuine. 'Go there?' He could not believe that the man lucky enough to be married to Jeannie could even look at another woman, let alone frequent the house of Aggie Turnbull.

Jeannie sniffed and before she had stopped to think, she said, 'Well, it was no' the first time for him on our wedding night . . .' Then she clapped her hand over her mouth in horror. 'Och, what am I saying.' She could not believe that she had confided such a thing to anyone, especially to a man and, more especially, to Robert. 'I'm sorry,' she said at once. 'I shouldna have said that.'

She had seen the spark of anger in his eyes and had misinterpreted its meaning for Robert was by no means offended by her confidence, but he was angry on her behalf. 'No, *I'm* sorry, Jeannie. The man's a fool if . . .'

In her confusion, Jeannie reached out and touched his arm. 'Please, don't say any more. Just – just tell me if you know where he is.'

Robert sighed. 'Jackson said he came off the *North Star* and went straight out again on the *Arctic Queen*. She was just waiting to sail and they were a deck-hand short. Jackson said that Tom jumped at the chance.'

Jeannie stared at him. 'Tom? Tom went straight out again on another boat?' She couldn't believe what she was hearing.

Robert nodded. 'Yes, I have to admit, it surprised me a little. He's not exactly got the name for being a "born fisherman". Not like his father.' He paused and then added, 'You'll be all right, won't you? I mean, the office will let you have his money.'

Jeannie nodded. 'Och aye. I suppose,' she added with wry amusement, 'there's one good thing about it. Half his pay won't disappear across the bar at the Fisherman's.'

As Jeannie walked home she realized that far from being the courageous act it appeared on the surface, Tom would rather brave the perils of the ocean than face the problems at home.

Robert called at the Lawrences' house in Baldock Street the following day and thereafter, regularly every week, running the gauntlet of the gossips in the street and the tales that would be told.

'It must be him, that's the father of Grace's bairn.'

'No, no. It's the other one. Mr Francis. One of the girls from Aggie's told me. She used to meet him there. Daft over him, she was. But, of course, he denies it.'

'Mebbe she ain't sure which of 'em it is.' And the

raucous laughter would echo around the fishdocks, tearing Grace's reputation into shreds.

Now, Jeannie did not refuse Robert's help and, whilst it went against her proud nature to accept money from him, this time she took it and spent it on titbits to tempt Grace's appetite or things for the coming baby.

When he stepped into the tiny, stuffy kitchen on his first visit and sat down on the opposite side of the fireplace to Grace, Robert was appalled by the change in the girl.

Later, outside, he said, 'Oh Jeannie, I can't tell you how sorry I am about this.'

She looked at him keenly and could read the haunted look in his eyes. There was more there, she thought shrewdly, in those brown depths than just sorrow at the downfall of a fisherman's daughter. In that moment she was sure, now, that there was some truth in the servants' gossip that his marriage was not all that it might, or should, be. And he had told her as much himself.

Overwhelmed by a sudden feeling of pity for him, she reached out towards him and touched his arm. 'We appreciate your kindness, Mr Robert, all of us. But even I, this time, have to say that the fault is as much Grace's as – as the man concerned.'

He gazed long into her eyes and murmured, simply, 'She loves him, Jeannie.' His voice dropped to a whisper as he added, 'You – you should know how that feels.'

It was as if a gigantic wave had hit her, carrying her on its crest in a flood of emotion. The blood was pounding in her ears and she felt suddenly giddy. She felt an over-whelming desire to reach up, to cup his face between her hands and to kiss his mouth.

'What is it?' she heard his concerned voice say as if from a great distance.

Swiftly, her voice hoarse, she managed to say, 'Nothing – nothing. I . . .' But she could say no more, for there was such a tumult of emotions going on inside her that she was robbed of her power of speech.

'Jeannie, what is it? Are you unwell? Here, let me take you back into the house.'

Solicitously, he took hold of her arm and made as if to lead her back indoors, but she resisted. 'No, no. I'm fine. I'm better out here. In the fresh air.'

'Let me fetch you a chair, then?'

'No, no, really. Thank you. You go. Dinna let me keep you. I'll be all right.'

She didn't want him to go and yet she couldn't bear him to stay. She needed to be alone. To control her riotous emotions and castigate herself sternly for them.

'I don't like to leave you like this.'

'Please, I'll be fine. It's just the heat, I expect.' The July weather was capricious and today was hot and oppressive.

'Well, if you're sure?' She nodded and he stepped back from her but he did not turn away and leave her immediately. He saw her glance about her as if looking to see who of their neighbours in the street might be watching. He followed her glance and saw that there were two or three women further down the road who had found it imperative that their front steps needed scrubbing at this very moment.

'You're right,' he said, giving her a quick, understanding smile. 'I'd better be going.' Then glancing down briefly towards the now-obvious mound of her stomach, he said huskily, 'Take care of yourself, Jeannie, won't you?'

She watched him go, walking up the street away from her towards his motor car.

I love him, she thought and the knowledge made her ridiculously happy. I've fallen in love with him. But then as realization of her true situation crept into her mind, she felt plunged into the depths of despair.

But I shall never, she told herself, know what it is to be loved by him.

Twenty-Two

Jeannie's baby was due about a month after Grace's, but when the expected date of the younger girl's confinement came and passed by, Jeannie became concerned.

'I wish Tom was home.' A tiny vestige of hope still remained that he would help her shoulder the burden of worry. But, more than that, Jeannie needed to see her husband, needed his reassurance that he loved her and to prove to herself that she still loved him.

'The men are best out of the way, hen,' Nell was saying. 'This is women's work.' It was the first time during the long months of waiting that Nell had shown any concern for her daughter.

At once Jeannie decided to try to encourage Nell's involvement. 'Was your husband away at sea when your two were born?'

Nell's expression softened. 'My George was different. Very different.' She glanced at Jeannie and then away again, almost apologetically. 'He was a fine man. One you could lean on, lass. But I'm afraid, Tom, though I love him dearly, mind, well, he's not quite got the strength of character his father had.'

Jeannie stared at her mother-in-law. She had never thought to hear such words from a mother's lips. But she could not think about that now. Grace was more important. 'Do you think we should get the midwife?'

Nell pushed her spectacles up her nose. 'Aye, you could.'

'Please, won't you go up and look at her. She hasna even got out of her bed all day.'

'We'd soon know if it was coming, hen,' Nell said. 'We'd hear her down here.'

Jeannie sighed and levered herself up from the chair by the range and reached up to the lamp to turn down the light.

'Leave it, hen. I must stay a while and do a little more braiding.'

Jeannie glanced over her shoulder at the older woman and shook her head. 'You shouldna be staying up half the night at the nets. It isna right.'

Nell sighed heavily. 'I've got to do something, hen. It's not fair to expect Tom to keep the lot of us.'

'Then I'll stay and help you.'

'No, no . . .' Nell now rose stiffly from the chair. 'No, you away to your bed. I promise I'll only bide an hour or so.'

'We-ell . . .' Jeannie said slowly. 'Mind you do.' And she wagged her forefinger in mock admonishment.

At half past two in the morning Jeannie awoke to find Grace sitting up in bed beside her and moaning. When Tom was away, they shared the double bed in the front bedroom, Nell sleeping in the back room.

'Is it the bairn, hen?'

'I – think so.' The girl leant back against the pillows, her face, in the low night-light they had kept burning through the dark hours for the past few nights, was wet with sweat.

Jeannie heaved her bulk from the bed and began to dress hurriedly.

'Don't leave me, Jeannie,' Grace gasped.

'I must fetch the midwife. Mrs Jackson, isn't it? The ship's runner's wife? I'll wake your mother before I go.'

'No, no, don't. She only came up half an hour ago.'

Jeannie clicked her tongue against her teeth in annoyance. 'So much for her promise, eh?'

'What?'

'Ne'er you mind, hen. Lie back and try to keep calm.'

Ten minutes later she was banging on the door of number twenty at the bottom of the road. The window above opened and Mr Jackson, his bald head shining in the moonlight, his mouth shrunken in, squinted down into the street below.

'Who's that?'

'Jeannie Lawrence, Mr Jackson. Could you ask Mrs Jackson to come to Grace, please? It's her time.'

'She ain't here.' He jerked his thumb over his shoulder. 'Gone t'other side town. Midwife there's ill and she's 'ad to tek her place.'

'Then who can I get?'

The man shrugged. 'Dunno. The doctor, I suppose.'

Jeannie bit her lip. It would be costly, but they'd have to have someone. She had no idea what should be done. And by the look of Grace already, the birth was not going to be easy.

But the doctor, too, was out on a call and when she returned home, she found Grace in a distressed state. Her cries had awakened Nell, who was standing beside her daughter's bed, wringing her hands.

'Jeannie, get help. We must have help.'

Swiftly, Jeannie explained and added firmly, 'There's no one. We'll just have to help her ourselves.'

'If only George was here,' Nell wailed and she pushed her fingers behind her glasses to wipe away the tears.

'We can do it,' Jeannie said. 'You must tell me what to do . . .'

The woman looked up with startled eyes. 'Me? I don't know what to do.'

'But you've had two children of your own.'

'Yes, but . . .' She watched helplessly as Grace writhed in agony now. 'But George was here. He fetched the midwife and stayed with me.' The tears flowed afresh. 'All the time.'

Then the two women standing either side of the bed looked down at the girl in surprise as Grace gasped, 'Aggie. Fetch Aggie. She'll help me. She'll know what to do.'

Jeannie looked across at Nell, the question in her eyes.

Nell was shaking her head vehemently. 'I'll no' have that woman in ma hoose.'

'But there is no one else and we need help,' Jeannie argued.

Nell leant across the bed. 'If you fetch that woman in here, I'll no' speak to you again, Jeannie Lawrence, as long as I live.'

Jeannie's lips parted in a gasp of surprise. She had not realized that Nell's hatred of the woman and all that she was supposed to be went so deep that she would put her own daughter's life at risk. For, as Jeannie looked down at Grace, at the sweat running down her face, at the dark shadows of suffering beneath her eyes and the gaunt hollows of her cheeks, she knew it was exactly that. If they didn't do something quickly, Grace's life was ebbing away.

Jeannie made her decision. 'I'm sorry, but I must think of Grace. If Aggie Turnbull is the only hope we have, then . . .' She said no more but turned swiftly away and hurried down the stairs again as quickly as her own cumbersome bulk would allow.

Dawn was breaking as Jeannie hammered on the door of the notorious house two streets away from the Lawrence home. It took some minutes before the door was opened by a bleary-eyed Aggie herself.

'Heavens!' the woman uttered. 'What on earth brings you to my door?'

'It's Grace. She's come to her time and – and there's something wrong. The midwife and the doctor are both out and – and—'

'I'll come at once,' Aggie said and was already turning back towards the stairs.

'I'll go back now, but please, hurry.'

The woman turned, resting her hand for a brief moment on the newel post at the foot of the stairs. 'Does Nell know you've come for me?'

Jeannie nodded. 'Aye, but she doesna like it.'

Again, the small smile. 'No,' she said softly, 'I don't expect she does.' Briskly then, she said, 'You go back, I'll be as quick as I can.'

'Thank you,' Jeannie said simply.

To Jeannie's horror when she reached home again, Nell was standing in front of the net on the wall, seemingly calmly braiding and completely ignoring the desperate cries of the girl in the room above.

Jeannie shook her head in disbelief but said, 'She's coming. I'll get clean sheets ready and towels. What else do we need?'

Nell made no sign of having heard. Her mouth tight, her shoulders rigid, her fingers worked faster and faster, only pausing to push her spectacles up the bridge of her nose every so often.

Jeannie set the kettle to boil and a large pan of water too. Somewhere she'd heard about boiling water at such a time, but she didn't know exactly what it was for. Back upstairs, she sponged Grace's brow and stood helplessly whilst the girl gasped and groaned.

Suddenly, Aggie was beside them, bending over Grace and saying gently, 'Now then, my dear. Let me look at you.' Swiftly, and to Jeannie's inexperienced eye, Aggie examined the girl knowledgeably. Then she looked up at Jeannie and said quietly, 'It's not coming normally. You'll have to get a doctor. I think it's breech and with her being so small, it could be dangerous. She's already weak.'

Jeannie waited to hear no more but was already lumbering down the stairs again. Nell had drawn back the curtains and now Jeannie saw that it was full daylight.

'I must find a doctor,' she told Nell. 'Something's wrong. Please, go up to her, Mother.' It was the first time Jeannie had used the name to Nell and she did it deliberately, trying to force Nell to overcome her prejudice and help her daughter. 'She needs you.'

But Nell continued to move between pantry and kitchen setting the table for breakfast as if everything within the household was just as normal. Exasperated and fearful of wasting any more time, Jeannie pulled on her coat and rushed into the street.

The midwife was still not home, nor was the doctor.

'Do you know of another doctor?' she asked the maid who answered the surgery door, but the girl shook her head.

Jeannie was almost frantic with worry and as she hurried down the steps and on to the pavement to cross the road, she almost stepped in front of a motor car. There was a squeal of tyres as the driver swerved to miss her. She stepped back and lifted her hand in apology, but the driver had drawn his motor to the side of the road and the noise of the engine died as he leapt down and came towards her.

Oh no, Jeannie thought abstractedly. This is all I need.

Some man giving me a telling off for not looking where I was going.

But as she lifted her eyes and looked at the man coming towards her, her heart leapt with thankfulness. It was as if her prayers of the last few hours had been miraculously answered. Striding towards her was Robert.

'Jeannie – are you all right. I didn't hit you, did I?'

'No, no.' She managed to smile tremorously. Without consciously thinking what she was doing, she reached out with both her hands towards him and he took hold of them in his.

'What is it?' he said at once. 'Something's wrong, isn't it?'

'It's Grace. She's been in labour half the night and – and the baby's the wrong way round. The midwife's away and so's our doctor. Oh Mr Robert . . .' Unaccustomed tears threatened to overwhelm her. She was exhausted and frightened.

'I'll find you a doctor.'

As Jeannie opened her mouth to protest, Robert said quickly, 'Please, at least let me do this. I can find one for you much quicker in the motor. And besides, it is my nephew or niece who's about to be born, you know.'

Jeannie closed her mouth and nodded swiftly. 'Thank you. That would be kind of you.'

For a brief moment they stared at each other and then he was running back towards his car.

So, thought Jeannie, as she stood watching as Robert steered the car away from the pavement and sped down the road, at least one member of the Hayes-Gorton family is willing to acknowledge that the child is Francis's.

Twenty-Three

It was while she was still bending over poor Grace, mopping the beads of sweat from the girl's forehead, noticing how the girl's face was now grey with fatigue, how the dark shadows beneath her eyes deepened to black rings, that Jeannie felt the first pain low in her groin.

'Oh not now, please, not now.'

She said nothing to anyone else and the pains, whilst persisting, were only at half-hourly intervals. For the moment her whole attention was upon Grace. The girl, weak with exhaustion, could no longer help Aggie and the doctor – the Gorton family's own – bring her child into the world.

'There's nothing else for it,' Jeannie heard the doctor mutter. 'She's slipping away from us.'

Dimly, she was aware that the doctor had flung his instruments aside, rolled up his sleeve and – though she couldn't quite be sure afterwards – seemed to delve into Grace and pull the infant from her with his bare hand. The young mother, now almost unconscious, gave only the faintest of gasps, though Jeannie imagined that the pain must have torn her apart.

In contrast, four hours later, in Nell's bed, Jeannie gave birth to a fine, lusty squalling boy who slipped into the world with the minimum of fuss and trouble. The doctor,

197

Margaret Dickinson

returning on Robert's insistence, examined her and pronounced Jeannie 'as strong as an ox' before shaking his head sadly and returning to the other bedroom that was strangely and ominously silent. There was not even the sound of a newborn baby's wails.

As Jeannie put her son to her breast for the first time, Aggie, standing watching, said, 'It's a good thing you've plenty of milk already, Jeannie. I'm very much afraid . . .' her voice broke as she added, 'that you're going to have to feed two now.'

Tired and triumphant, but certainly not exhausted, Jeannie looked up at her noticing, for the first time, that Aggie's face was distraught.

'What is it?' Jeannie whispered, suddenly afraid. 'Tell me?'

'It's Grace . . .' The older woman's face crumpled and tears welled in her eyes and trickled down her cheeks. 'She's gone, my dear. Too weak to fight any more. And I don't think she had the will.'

Jeannie closed her eyes and bent her head over her tiny son, who, oblivious to his mother's tears falling on to his downy head, sucked noisily at her breast. Then Jeannie raised her head and said, 'Bring the child to me. Bring me Grace's son.'

A smile flickered briefly on Aggie's face. 'I knew you'd do it. I told Nell, you would. Salt of the earth, I told her. Jeannie'll cope with the two of them.'

'You've spoken to Nell?' Jeannie asked in surprise. 'How is she? Is she – all right?'

Aggie lifted her shoulders. 'I've tried to talk to her, but she won't speak to me. Won't leave that net on the wall to look at the babies.' Harshly, she added, 'Who knows what Nell Lawrence is thinking. She's a hard woman.'

But Jeannie was shaking her head. 'No, no. It's just her

way of coping.' And privately she thought, once Aggie was gone, out of the house, Nell would come up the stairs to see her two grandsons.

But Nell did not mount the stairs, did not even come to see if there was anything Jeannie needed. She did not even come to see her still and silent daughter.

Tom did not arrive home in time for his sister's funeral though Jeannie waited as long as she could before arranging the ceremony. Robert came with the news. 'The *North Star* has put into a small fishing port on the Scottish coast for urgent repairs. They're all safe,' he added hastily, reaching out in his concern to touch Nell's hand, 'I promise you, but they're landing their catch there so they'll be going straight back to sea. We have an agent in that area who's arranging everything, so Tom won't be home for a while. Although I could . . .' he appeared to be thinking quickly, 'send word for him to come home by train.'

Quickly Nell shook her head. 'No, no, sir. You've been very kind, but it would leave the crew short.' Even amidst her own troubles, a small smile touched her lips. 'And I know what trouble that causes. My – my George used to tell me that if they could stand, they had to be on deck.' It was the first time Nell had spoken in the two days since Grace's death.

Robert smiled gently down at the woman who, over the past few months, had had so much tragedy to bear.

And Jeannie. His Jeannie, as he thought of her within the secrecy of his own mind. She was still so young and yet womanhood had been thrust upon her. His glance went to her now as she bent over the two cradles, her beautiful hair falling around her face as she tucked the coverlet gently around her sleeping son. As she straightened up, her gaze met his and she gestured towards the other crib.

'Would – would you like to see him?' she asked quietly and Robert knew she was pointing to the child that was his brother's son.

Robert nodded and moved forward to look down upon the tiny sleeping form. 'Is he all right?' he murmured. 'I mean – I know the birth was very difficult and in the circumstances . . .' His voice trailed away as he felt himself on delicate ground.

'He's fine. A little small, especially considering he was overdue, but poor Grace had been . . .' She sighed. 'Well, she didn't look after herself properly. She was thin and ill even before the birth.'

'I am so sorry.'

Gently, she said, 'It's no' your fault, nor ours either. We – her mother and me . . .' Deliberately, she glanced at Nell not wanting the older woman to be excluded, trying to convey to her that she bore no grudge towards her mother-in-law for what had passed in this house on the day of Grace's death or during all the months preceding it. She could understand how Nell had felt even though she did not condone her behaviour towards Grace. 'We did all we could,' Jeannie said, firmly including Nell and deliberately sharing in whatever emotions Nell must now be feeling. 'But we both feel guilty for all that . . .' She left the words hanging in the air. As Aggie had said, the poor girl had not had the will to go on living, not even for the sake of her child.

Robert bent over the cradle and reached out with a gentle finger to touch the baby's head. Wordlessly, he straightened up but stood looking down at the tiny scrap of humanity for a long time. Then he cleared his throat, turned to Jeannie and asked, 'May – may I see your son?'

'Of course.' She gestured towards the other cradle

where the infant also lay sleeping. Robert felt a moment's surprise. Despite the fact that they had been born on the same day, this child looked much bigger than the other one. The fair, downy hair that covered his scalp already had a touch of ginger in it. Robert felt a fond smile twitch his mouth in spite of the sadness that was in this house. Already, he could tell which was Jeannie's child.

How he wished with all his heart that this child were his. He glanced back at the other cradle. But he did have a connection now to this family. A genuine reason for involving himself in their welfare. From his pocket, he took out two small silver coins and placed one on each pillow beside the sleeping baby boys.

'Thank you,' he heard Jeannie whisper, and knew that the gratitude in her eyes was more than for the money itself. He knew it was a Scottish custom and guessed that it was one Jeannie would hold dear.

He turned to face both women and said, 'I hope you will allow me to – to see my nephew from time to time and I hope also that if there is anything – anything at all you need – you will let me know. I can only once more express my sorrow that my family has treated yours so – so shabbily.'

There was nothing more to be said, nothing more he could say, but he would have been gratified if he had heard the conversation in the kitchen after his departure.

'He's a kind young man,' Nell said, speaking to Jeannie directly for the first time since her stony-faced rage at Aggie Turnbull being asked into her home.

'Yes,' Jeannie said slowly. 'I think, perhaps, in the past, I have misjudged him.'

'Sit you down, hen. I'll get us a bite of dinner. You must rest, y'ken, if you're to feed both bairns.'

Jeannie, with a small smile on her mouth, did as Nell said. It had taken Robert Hayes-Gorton's visit to melt the ice around Nell's heart and Jeannie was more than ever grateful to him for his visit.

'And what, pray, is the attraction in Baldock Street?' Louise asked and Robert looked up to see his wife's lip curl with distaste on the last two words of her question.

They were seated at the Hathersage family breakfast table and it seemed to Robert that if Louise wanted to pick a quarrel – as indeed she so often did these days – she always chose a time when she had the support of her doting papa. And meal times were an ideal opportunity.

Robert felt the muscles in the back of his neck tighten with tension as he decided prevarication was not the answer. Boldly, and without even glancing towards his father-in-law yet knowing both Louise's parents were listening intently, Robert said, 'It's where the Lawrence family live and – as you may recall . . .' he bit back the sarcasm that threatened to line his words, 'they've had more than their fair share of trouble just lately.'

Louise cut her bacon and slanted her glance across the table as she did so. 'Most of it brought on by themselves, I don't doubt. But, if what I hear is true, I understand you are not entirely blameless.'

Robert swallowed. Surely Mr Hathersage had not betrayed his confidence and told his daughter? he thought, but at her next words it was obvious that was exactly the case, particularly as Hathersage himself began to bluster. 'Now, now, my dear, this is hardly the sort of talk for the breakfast table and in front of your mother too.'

Louise's blue eyes flashed towards her father and her lips pouted petulantly. 'If what you said to me last night is true, then it's all my mother's fault that my husband seeks his comfort elsewhere.'

To Robert's consternation, tears brimmed her eyes. He leant across the table towards her and started to say quietly, 'Louise, we should talk about this in private—' but he was interrupted by Mrs Hathersage's voice from the other end of the table rising shrilly. 'What? Henry, what on earth have you been saying?'

Now, even her father cast a half-despairing, half-exasperated glance at Louise. He rose from the table, leaving his half-eaten breakfast, flinging his morning paper to the floor. 'I'm going to the office. I won't be in for lunch and probably not dinner either. I, too . . .' Now he wagged his forefinger down the length of the table towards his wife. 'I, too, will find my *comforts* elsewhere, though I make no secret of the fact.'

'Well, really,' Mrs Hathersage said as the door slammed behind her husband. 'What is the world coming to when a man speaks like that to his wife.' With delicate fastidiousness, she pressed her napkin to her lips.

Robert stood up. 'I must go. I have a funeral to attend this morning.'

'In Baldock Street, I take it?' was Louise's parting shot.

There were two people who stood apart from the family members at Grace's funeral, though they did not stand together. A little way off, but in no way trying to hide his presence there, stood Robert. Beneath the trees and deliberately trying to keep herself from being seen was Aggie Turnbull.

But Jeannie spotted her. Jeannie saw them both, though she hoped that Nell had not seen Aggie. It was a pathetically small gathering around the grave side, Jeannie thought. Just Nell and herself and one or two neighbours. It seemed so few for a young girl whose loss should have been mourned by many.

As the committal ended and the mourners moved away, leaving only Nell and Jeannie looking down into the grave to take their last sight of the coffin, Robert moved forward.

'Mrs Lawrence,' he said softly. 'I'm so very sorry.'

Nell, her arm tightly through Jeannie's and leaning against her, looked up at him. Her face was drawn, pinched with sorrow, but her eyes behind her steel-rimmed spectacles were dry. It seemed, however, that she could not speak, for she just nodded in answer to his condolence and Jeannie felt her arm squeezed even more fiercely.

'Would you allow me to take you home in the car—' he began but Jeannie cut in sharply.

'No . . .' Then realizing her brusqueness she added, 'No, thank you. It's kind of you, but it's not far and . . .' She glanced around at the neighbours who were still lingering in the churchyard, still watching.

'I understand,' Robert said at once. 'I'll be going then, but I just thought you might like to know,' his brown eyes were full of sympathy as they turned back to Nell, 'we've had word that your son's ship is at sea again and all is well, but – I am sorry – it's as I thought. They're going back to the fishing grounds again before they come home.'

Wordlessly, Nell nodded again but it was Jeannie who said, 'Thank you for letting us know.'

Robert gave a slight bow, put on his black hat and said, 'I'll call to see you in a day or two, if I may.'

Now it was Jeannie who merely nodded and did not speak.

As the funeral party dispersed, Robert to his motor car, Nell and Jeannie to walk back home to offer tea and sandwiches to those neighbours who cared to call in, only Aggie Turnbull still stood beneath the shadows of the trees, watching everything that went on.

Twenty-Four

When Tom first saw his son, the child was almost a month old. It was a difficult moment, Jeannie realized, for although he had already been told of his sister's death and knew her funeral had taken place, the joy in the birth of his son was marred by his sorrow. As he stood looking down at the sleeping boy, he said, 'He's like me dad.' A slow smile spread across his face. 'I'm glad about that.'

'Grace's bairn is fair too,' Jeannie said softly. 'They're very alike. At least, at the moment.' She gestured towards the other cradle where the baby made snuffling, whimpering noises.

'Aren't you going to move it away? It'll wake *him*.' There was a harshness, a strange belligerence in Tom's tone.

'They don't wake each other. Not often, anyway.' She watched Tom's face as his gaze remained firmly fixed upon his own child.

'Aren't you going to look at your nephew?'

She saw him stiffen and glance up at her. 'I aren't interested in it.'

Jeannie stared at him. 'What on earth do you mean?'

He shrugged his huge shoulders. 'What I say,' he said curtly. 'It's nowt to do wi' me. Anyway, what's going to happen to it? Mr Francis Hayes-Gorton going to look after his bastard, is he?'

'No,' Jeannie said sharply. 'We're going to look after it – him.' She altered her words quickly.

'Oh no, we're not.'

Jeannie stood facing him, anger welling up inside her. 'What on earth do you mean?' She leant closer to him, her glance raking his face, trying to read the meaning behind his words. 'If you think the Hayes-Gortons are going to do anything, then you're mistaken. Mr Robert's been very kind, but even he . . .'

'Oh aye. Mr Robert. Mr bloody Robert Hayes-Gorton's nearly worn a path in the road leading to this door whilst I've been away, by what I've heard.'

Jeannie stepped back suddenly, as if he had physically hit her. She found, to her surprise, that she was defending Robert. 'He was genuinely sorry. He's been trying to do something to help Grace's bairn.'

'Trying to help himself, more like.'

She shook her head, bewildered. She did not think herself naive or stupid, but she could not guess what Tom meant. 'What *are* you talking about?'

'He's been coming here, hasn't he?'

'Yes, but I've told you—'

'To see *you*.' Whilst she knew herself innocent of his accusation, Jeannie could not help a quiver of embarrassment. Perhaps, she thought suddenly, perhaps Robert was visiting a little too often. In the dark recess of her mind she remembered her wedding day and almost felt again the touch of his lips on her cheek. Because she had secretly acknowledged the change in her own feelings towards Robert, now she could feel the colour creeping into her face.

Tom jabbed his finger into her chest. 'Aggie ses—'

'Aggie? You've been to see Aggie before you even came home to see your wife and your bairn for the first time?'

'No, no, of course, I didn't.' Now Tom was on the defensive and Jeannie knew intuitively that in his temper he had said more than he had intended. 'She – she was on the dockside when the boats came in.' He spread his hands in a gesture of appeal. 'Jeannie – you know she always is.'

In this Jeannie knew he was speaking the truth. Mollified a little, she said, 'Aye well, maybe so. But you shouldna have listened to her gossip. For all that she helped us at the births, she's still a blether.'

'Eh?' Now it was Tom's turn to look mystified. 'Here? She was here? I don't believe it. Me mam would never let her across that threshold.' He flung out his hand towards the door to emphasize his words.

'She had no choice,' Jeannie said and told him all that had happened, ending by adding, 'and she came to Grace's funeral, though she kept well out of sight. But I saw her there, standing beneath the trees.'

Tom said, his voice quieter now, 'I think she was very fond of our Grace.'

'Aye well,' Jeannie sighed. 'Maybe so, but it was at her place that Grace's troubles started. Aggie condoned what was going on. Encouraged it even. Never forget that.'

Now Tom looked a little sheepish. As if wanting to change the subject he glanced again towards the other cradle. 'So, you want to keep him, eh?'

Jeannie's anger flared. 'You sound as if you're talking about a kitten or a puppy, Tom. The wee man is your nephew and your mother's grandchild. Her first grandchild, as a matter of fact, for he was born a few hours before our own son.'

For a long moment, there was a heavy silence between them, then the man turned away with an angry, defeated movement. 'Have it your own way then, but don't expect me to treat him like I'll treat me own.'

He slammed out of the house, leaving Jeannie staring after him wondering how a man could be so callous towards the tiny mite.

She had thought Tom like his own father, and so consequently, like her own.

But the man she was seeing now was nothing like the kind-hearted Angus Buchanan.

'We're going to have to decide on names,' Jeannie said, forcing a brightness into her tone. 'We really can't go on calling them Grace's bairn and young Tom, can we?'

'What does Tom say?' Nell asked.

Jeannie sighed. 'He's leaving it to us.'

Nell glanced at her over the top of her spectacles. 'Don't let him worry you, Jeannie. We'll take him at his word. Now then . . .' Nell came and sat down at the table. 'Make us a cup of tea, hen, and let's think.'

Jeannie set the kettle to boil and laid the cups out. 'Well, of course, our way . . .' she began, referring to the Scottish custom, 'would be to call Grace's bairn Samuel and ours, George.'

Nell nodded. 'After their paternal grandfathers.' She was thoughtful for a moment. 'I wonder what Grace would have wanted,' she murmured sadly.

'Probably "Francis" but I don't think we should do that. It would look a bit pointed, wouldn't it?'

Nell sighed. 'Aye, I dinna want any more trouble or bad feeling. Tom's got to keep his livelihood.'

Jeannie felt the older woman's sharp eyes on her. 'Not happy about Grace's bairn, is he?'

'No,' Jeannie said shortly, 'but I told him, the wee man bides here.'

'Thank you, hen,' Nell said simply. Jeannie said nothing but marvelled at the change in the woman since Grace's death and the birth of her two grandsons. Nell bore none of the resentment towards Grace's child that she had shown to his mother in the final months of her life. Jeannie thought the saying that 'they bring their love with them' was very true in this case. How she wished Tom could feel the same. And now, the poor woman must be feeling overwhelmed with remorse for the way she had treated her daughter.

Jeannie reached out and touched the wrinkled hands, lying, idly for once, on the table. 'So,' she asked softly, 'what are we going to call them?'

'We-ell,' Nell said slowly. 'I rather like Samuel and . . .' She pushed her spectacles up her nose. 'And my George's second name was Joseph, and it was my father's name too, but do you like it?'

Jeannie's smile widened. 'We'll christen him George Joseph then, just like his grandfather, but call him Joe. And yes, we'll call Grace's boy, Samuel, after old man Hayes-Gorton.' She laughed, her green eyes glinting with mischief. 'You never know, he might inherit a fortune.'

Now Nell laughed too. 'I shouldna hold your breath, hen. That'll no' happen as long as there's fish in the sea.'

So, on Tom's next time ashore the two little boys were christened in the church where Jeannie and Tom had been married and this time, Jeannie was relieved to see, Robert Hayes-Gorton did not put in an appearance.

Robert was restless and he knew why. He was aware that at this very moment his nephew and Jeannie's son were being christened and he was finding it difficult to resist the urge to go to the church.

Instead, he went in search of his wife. 'Louise, are you busy?'

Considering she was lying on a sofa, a box of chocolates at her elbow and a book lying open on her knee, it was a silly question, but he had learnt not to presume. Amused, he watched her glance up at him with a mixed expression of coyness and suspicion. 'That depends,' she said archly. She, too, had learnt not to be too hasty with her replies. Whatever it was he wanted, it might of course be something distasteful to Louise, but on the other hand, her husband was capable of nice surprises now and again. Robert hid his smile, realizing that his wife had learnt caution.

'My dear, I'd like to take you for a drive. I have something I'd like to show you. Something I'd like your opinion about.'

'Really?' At once, Louise's interest was aroused. She flung aside her book and swung her shapely legs to the floor. 'Is it something nice?'

'I'm hoping you'll think so,' he replied mysteriously.

'Oh, you tease.' Louise pecked him on the cheek before running from the room. 'I'll just get my coat.'

Half an hour later when Louise had not only 'got her coat' but had renewed her lipstick, powdered her face and changed her dress three times before she found one that suited an outing in the motor car, they were driving from the Hathersage mansion towards the town.

'Are we going shopping?' Louise leant against his shoulder and twisted her head to look up at him.

'Sort of,' he laughed, 'but not quite the sort of shopping you mean.'

Louise pouted prettily, but for once it was deliberate pretence. She was still intrigued.

Just before they reached the outskirts of the town,

Robert turned to the left down a country road for a distance of about half a mile and drew to a halt outside a square Georgian house set in an acre of gardens bordered by trees. It was nowhere near the proportions of the Hathersage home but it was an elegant country house.

'Now,' Robert said, leaning forward, his arms resting on the driving wheel. 'What do you think to that?'

'It's nice, but . . .' Louise looked at him and her eyes widened. 'Oh! For us, you mean?'

'Well, only if you like it?'

'But we're all right at home, aren't we?'

He thought he detected a little note of fear in her voice, as if she were afraid to leave the protection of her parents' home. As if, once in their own home, she was afraid of what her husband might demand of her.

Carefully, Robert took her hand in his. 'Louise, my dear, I know certain aspects of being married are – well – difficult for you.'

'Robert, please, I . . .' She made to pull her hand away but he held it firmly.

'No, my dear, listen to me, please, because we need to talk about this.'

Reluctantly, she left her hand in his, but her pout was no longer a teasing pretence.

Quietly, as if talking to a child, he said, 'And I do understand, really I do. It's – not altogether your fault. But we are married and even if – if, well, we can't be man and wife in that way, there's no reason why we can't have a home of our own. Louise, we can be friends with each other, can't we?'

Her blue eyes were large in her perfect doll's face. 'You mean, you mean you're not going to ask me to . . .? You know?'

He looked down at her, their faces, for a moment, close

211

together. 'My dear, I'd like nothing better than for us to be man and wife in every sense, but I am not going to force myself on you. I – I'm not that kind of man.' As he spoke the words he blotted out the shameful memory and yet he knew he spoke the truth, for that dreadful night had not been of his making.

He was startled to see tears well in Louise's eyes. 'Oh Robert, you are perfectly sweet and you make me feel so awful.'

Now he felt pity for her overriding his own disappointment. He patted her hand tenderly. 'I don't want you to feel awful. I just want us both to make the best out of this marriage that we find ourselves in.'

She nodded and with a sudden flash of wisdom that he had never before credited her with, Louise said, 'Yes, we were rather pushed into it, weren't we? I – I am sorry if you feel, well, let down. I – I am very fond of you, Robert.'

His only answer was to lay his lips gently against her forehead, trying to blot out thoughts of a red-haired girl with sparkling green eyes. Then, forcing gaiety, he said, 'I've got the key to the house. Shall we go inside and take a look?'

Like an excited child, Louise clapped her hands. 'Oh yes.'

Half an hour later, when they had gone from room to room, Louise running ahead, exclaiming each time, 'Oh yes, yes. Oh Robert, it could be such a beautiful house. It needs redecorating throughout, but it's got such promise. Just look at these lovely French windows leading out on to the terrace. What summer parties we could have out there. Oh darling, it's perfect. Do let's buy it. Daddy will help us, I know he will.'

Robert smiled. 'There's no need, my dear. On my twenty-first birthday, I inherited a legacy from my maternal grandfather. It was divided equally between the three of us and my share should be enough to buy this house and for you to be able to have it decorated and refurbished just as you wish.'

Louise stood perfectly still for a moment. 'Oh Robert,' she whispered, 'you do spoil me. I – I don't deserve it.' She came towards him and put the flat of her palms on his chest. Looking up into his eyes, she stood on tiptoe and gently kissed his mouth. 'I'll try to be a – a good wife to you, Robert. Truly I will.'

Automatically, he returned her kiss gently, but he felt no stirrings of passion. All he could think of was the little christening party that would be coming out of the church about now.

'Weren't they good? No' a peep out of either of them all the time.' Back in the terraced house, Nell was bustling about her kitchen more like her old self than at any time since the death of her husband.

Jeannie smiled as she sat down before the fire and opened her blouse to feed the two babies. 'I thought they were supposed to bawl lustily to drive out the devil,' she laughed and Nell joined in.

As Jeannie put Sammy to her breast she glanced up to see Tom watching her with bitter resentment. Harshly he said, 'Shouldn't you feed Joe first?'

Anger flashed in Jeannie's eyes but she managed to keep her voice calm as she said, 'I haven't enough milk for both now, so they take it in turns and the other one has the bottle.'

Tom gave a grunt. She saw his gaze on her breasts and saw the desire leap into his eyes. And there was something else there too. Jealousy, she supposed. Abruptly, he turned away and blundered towards the door. Sighing, she watched him go and, as the door slammed behind him, she wondered briefly whether it was the pub he was heading for – or Aggie Turnbull's.

Twenty-Five

Robert came rarely to Baldock Street now and, whilst part of her was pleased that Aggie no longer had reason to spread vicious rumours, Jeannie found she missed him.

It was from Nell that she learnt the possible reason. 'Have you heard, hen, about the big house that Mr Robert has bought?' Nell was sitting in the wooden rocking chair, nursing Sammy, gently moving backwards and forwards. 'They say he's letting his wife have a free hand in all the renovations.'

Jeannie lowered her head over Joe, whose sturdy legs were kicking so strongly that she found changing his nappy difficult. 'My, who's a strong boy then.' Keeping her voice level and making it deliberately disinterested, she said, 'No, I hadna heard.'

'That'll be why he's not been down to see the bairn.' Nell glanced down at the sleeping infant in her arms. 'But he's still sending the money every month, just like he promised. He's as good as his word, I'll say that for him. And it was kind of him to send that big pram so that you can wheel them both out together. Do you think he chose it himself?'

Now Jeannie laughed. 'No. He'd send one of their employees. Someone from the office, I expect.'

Nell was quiet for a moment, then she said slowly. 'At least he's taking more of an interest than the bairn's father.

You – you dinna think that . . .?' She stopped and Jeannie prompted, 'What?'

'Well, that Grace might have been protecting him. That it was Mr Robert after all and not the other one?'

'No,' Jeannie said sharply and when Nell glanced at her in surprise she realized that her denial had been too swift. 'No. Dinna forget, I saw them together. I was there when she told Mr Francis. If you could have seen the way she looked at him, there was no mistake that it was him she was in love with.' Jeannie sighed and muttered, 'Poor Grace.'

Now there was silence between the two women, each busy with her own thoughts, and the only sounds in the kitchen came from the two babies.

'We must have a party to celebrate your twenty-first birthday, Robert and the completion of all the renovations to the house. Mr Portus,' Louise referred to the builder, 'says we can move in as soon as we like. Everything's finished.' She linked her arm through his. 'You must come and see it. I'm dying to show you everything. I just hope you like it.' She pulled a face like a little girl pretending to be fearful of his displeasure.

He patted her hand. 'Of course I shall like it, my dear, if you're happy with everything.'

When he saw the house, Robert was hard pressed not to blurt out his disappointment. He could see at once that his wife had been heavily influenced by her London friend and everywhere he could see Madeleine's hand in the choice of decor.

Louise led the way across the new parquet flooring in the hall. 'I wanted to achieve a feeling of spaciousness and elegance,' she said.

Robert glanced wryly at the only furniture in the large hall; a small table set against the wall with a mirror above it. For 'madam' to check her appearance just before going out, he presumed. Two chairs on either side were the only other items.

'Where's the hat-stand?' he murmured.

'Oh darling! There's a teeny cloakroom through that door. I don't want hats and coats cluttering the place.'

She threw open a door to the left. 'This is the morning room, and this . . .' the door to the right of the hall, '. . . the dining room. And this, next to the dining room, is the sitting room.'

As Robert stepped into it, he imagined for a moment that the store had not yet delivered the furniture. But then he realized. This was all there was. A large sofa and two armchairs, a small table and a cocktail cabinet.

'I thought we might have a baby grand piano in that corner, darling.'

'But neither of us play.'

'I know, but they look so elegant with silver framed photos on the top, don't you think? Besides,' she waved her hand, 'when we have parties, *someone* will play.' Louise fluttered her eyelashes and added, 'Your brother, Francis, plays, doesn't he?'

'Mm.' Robert was only half listening, his glance still roaming around the room.

He said nothing more until he had toured the whole house, even the kitchen.

'You don't like it, do you? I can see you don't.' Louise's voice was high-pitched.

Setting a smile on his mouth, Robert turned to face her. 'Of course, I do. It's wonderful. Very – tasteful.' But try as he might, he could not feign the enthusiastic praise she wanted to hear. Her voice rose hysterically,

217

'You don't like it. Oh, you've spoiled everything. *Everything.*'

Louise burst into tears and rushed from the room whilst Robert stood helplessly listening to the sound of her wild crying as she ran up the stairs. Then he heard the slam of the door of the master bedroom and heard the key turn in the lock leaving him standing alone amidst the cold, stark emptiness of the newly decorated house.

Unbidden, came the picture of the tiny terraced house in Baldock Street; overcrowded and never free of the reek of fish from the nearby docks and the ever-present net on the wall to remind them of the constant need for work. But that house, Robert thought, was more of a home than this palace would ever be.

'I'm just taking the boys for a walk. They'll soon be too big to go out in the pram together.' Winter had given way to spring and summer once more and the two boys, at nearly eight months old, were growing rapidly.

'Aye. They'll be walking before ye ken.' Nell nodded fondly towards her two grandsons. 'Then we'll be needin' eyes in the back o' our heeds! But I have to say, Jeannie, you've been a grand lass rearing them both. It's been like having twins for you.'

'It's perhaps a little unfair to say so,' she said, thinking of Grace. 'But to be honest, I do think of them both as my own now. Perhaps I shouldn't.'

'Aye well,' Nell said. 'Grace wouldna have minded. And the bairn needs a mother's love.'

'And a grandmother's. I couldna cope without you, you know,' Jeannie said softly.

Nell flapped her hand as if to dismiss the compliment

but Jeannie saw the pink flush of pleasure on the woman's face. 'Och, awa' with you and have your walk.'

It was a bright blustery June day and Jeannie walked through the streets scarcely noticing the distance she was covering until she came to the outskirts of the town and found herself in a country road.

The two boys, their heads at either end of the pram, were fast asleep. Jeannie smiled down at the round little faces, soft in repose. She was wandering aimlessly, enjoying the fresh air of the countryside away from the ever-present stink of fish, feeling the warmth of the sun on her back. It seemed so quiet, so peaceful out here and reminded her sharply of the fields behind the village back home.

As she heard the sound of a motor car approaching from behind she pushed the pram on to the grass verge and waited until the vehicle should pass her. But it did not. The motor stopped and the engine died. When she turned to look over her shoulder, she saw Robert emerging from behind the wheel. She felt the colour pink in her cheeks and glanced away from him, suddenly shy as if she had been caught in a place she should not be.

He came close and said simply, 'Jeannie.'

Then she looked at him, screwing up her eyes against the sunlight behind him.

'Mr Robert. I . . .' There was so much she could say, so much she wanted to say and yet, now, the words would not come.

It seemed as if he felt the same; for a long moment they just stood staring at each other. Then he removed his hat and swept his hand through his hair.

'How are you?' His voice was deep and gentle. 'And how is Samuel?'

It seemed strange to hear the child called by his proper Christian name.

'He – he's fine.'

'And your boy? Joseph, isn't it?'

Now she smiled but there was a tinge of sadness in her tone as she said, 'They are both my boys, Mr Robert. I never think of them as being anything else. Not now.' Silently, she thought, I just wish Tom would feel the same.

'Of course not,' Robert said swiftly. 'I'm sorry.' He smiled ruefully. 'It's a word I often seem to be saying to you, isn't it, Jeannie? Sorry.'

'There's no need, not now,' she said gently. 'That's long forgotten.'

'And,' he said, his voice suddenly so deep and quiet that she scarcely heard, 'and forgiven?'

Her throat was suddenly strangely constricted and all she could do was nod.

'You don't know how very happy that makes me, Jeannie.'

There was an awkward pause and then he cleared his throat and said, more briskly, 'Would you like to come up to the house? The gates are just here . . .'

She turned to look over her shoulder at two huge black wrought-iron gates and the sweeping drive that led up to a house nestling against a background of trees.

Startled, she said, 'Is this your house? Och no, I couldna. I mean . . .' In the shaded lane, with the sun beating down, she was suddenly hot. 'It wouldna be right.'

'My wife's away in London and there are no servants here today.'

'Then it certainly wouldna be right,' Jeannie said crisply. Though her heart was traitor to her words and beat faster at the very thought of being alone with him.

'I didn't mean to offend you. I'm sorry . . .' he began

and then laughed at himself. 'There I go again.' And the tension between them lightened.

From the pram there came a whimper as Sammy stirred and began to wake.

'I must be getting back. It's quite a walk.'

'Let me drive you.'

'No, no.' Now her voice was sharp again at the thought of the Hayes-Gorton motor car pulling up outside the house in Baldock Street and all the gossip that would cause. 'It's kind of you, but I'd rather not.'

He nodded. 'I understand,' he said and she knew that he did.

They talked for a few moments longer and then, when she turned the pram around and said again, 'I really must go,' he turned back to his motor, swung the starting handle, climbed up and in a moment was driving through the gates and up the driveway towards the house.

Jeannie stood at the gates watching him go. Then she turned and began to push the heavy pram back towards the town feeling suddenly lonelier than she could ever remember feeling in her life before this moment.

Part Two

Twenty-Six

'Those two lads are always fighting. Can't you handle them, Jeannie?' Tom complained irritably.

'Well, you're their father. You do something.'

He glared at her. 'I'm Joe's father,' he said pointedly.

'Canna you spare a mite of affection for the wee man? Sammy is your nephew, whether you like it or no',' Jeannie snapped, weary of his attitude that had never softened in the thirteen years since the birth of the two boys.

Tom leant back in his chair, put his feet on the brass fender and wriggled his toes. 'Ah,' he said with satisfaction. He opened his newspaper. 'Maybe so,' he said, grudging to acknowledge even that much. 'But I don't see enough of my own son when I'm hardly ever here, never mind me sister's bastard.'

'You're ashore more than most.' The words were out of her mouth before she could stop them.

The paper was crumpled to his lap in a fierce, angry movement. 'And what's that supposed to mean?'

Jeannie sighed, wishing sometimes that she could hold her runaway mouth in check. Now they were heading for yet another row.

'You should try it on a bloody boat out in the Arctic ocean in a force nine gale and still expected to gut fish on deck. You don't know you're born, woman. Nice, cosy little house you've got here with only two lads to look after . . .'

And your mother, she wanted to retort, whose mind's beginning to wander now. But she held her tongue. She had not yet told him that she was worried about Nell's health. The woman was not old and yet some days she acted like an old lady, just sitting staring into the fire, her hands lying idly in her lap.

Nell was no longer the bustling little woman Jeannie had known when she had first arrived. Now it was Jeannie who stood hour after long hour braiding the nets against the kitchen wall.

Tom leant towards her, his mouth twisting. 'I s'pect you dream about living in a fancy house just outside town, eh? Still coming here, is he?'

Jeannie's heart lurched, but she managed to return his glare calmly and steadily. 'Who?'

But as Tom opened his mouth again, she realized that it would look more suspicious than ever if she made out that she did not understand that he was referring to Robert. Jeannie gave a wry laugh and said, 'Oh Mr Robert, you mean. We never see hide nor hair of him these days.' Now she deliberately laced her own voice with sarcasm for she still felt bitter towards the Hayes-Gorton family, if not so much at Robert himself now. 'I expect he feels he's discharged his duty towards his nephew.'

For a moment Tom looked nonplussed. It was not the calm reply he had expected – nor probably wanted – from her. 'What? What do you mean?'

'I told you that he'd set up a monthly payment into a post office account for me . . .' She altered her words swiftly. 'For us. Just as a gesture. He didn't have to. Mr Francis has never even acknowledged the boy as his.'

Tom gave a grunt and his scowl deepened. 'I've always had me doubts as to that anyway. I reckon it's him –

Robert. I've always thought it was him. It was him that attacked her that time, weren't it?'

No, no, no, she wanted to shout at him. I know the truth now, but you'd never listen, would you, Tom Lawrence? You're so tied up with bitterness and hatred that you can't bring yourself to hear the truth. So twisted that you take it out on a young innocent lad for the circumstances of his birth. But the words, reeling around her mind, remained unspoken. She said nothing but was glad that his train of thought had at least moved away from accusing her. But she was mistaken. 'So you haven't seen him lately?'

Her heart was thumping as she said casually, 'I canna remember when I did last see him.' She hated telling Tom a deliberate lie for she could remember very well exactly when she had last seen Robert. The day she had told him not to visit Baldock Street again.

The back door crashed open and both Tom and Jeannie looked up, startled. Tom opened his mouth to bawl at Sammy who stood in the doorway but when he saw the boy's face, even he, for once, held his anger in check.

Jeannie rushed forward. 'Oh whatever's happened, son?' Sammy's face was covered in blood from a cut on his left eyebrow. His right eye was so swollen that it was completely closed and blood and mucus oozed from his nose.

'Is it true?' He was breathing heavily through his mouth, pulling in great gasps of air. His injuries seemed not to concern him; there was something far more important on the boy's mind.

Jeannie leant down towards him and put out her hand towards his face. But he leant backwards away from her. 'What is it, Sammy?'

'Is it true?' he said again, 'that he's . . .' he flung out an arm towards Tom, 'not me dad and you're – you're . . .' the young boy's voice faltered a little, 'not me real mam?'

'Who's been saying such things?' Jeannie began angrily. 'Just you tell me . . .'

But from the hearth came Tom's voice. 'Oh tell him the truth, Jeannie, and let's be done with it. He's old enough now to know.' He turned away back to his newspaper, dismissing the whole thing as being none of his concern.

Jeannie rounded on him. 'You don't care, do you? You don't care that someone's been opening their mouth and . . . Just wait till I get ma hands on whoever . . .' She turned back again to look down at the boy who was staring up at her with his bright blue eyes. His fair curling hair was rumpled and speckled with dirt and blood. His knees were scraped and there was a tear in the elbow of his jacket. 'Who told you?' she demanded.

'Is it true?' he said doggedly, yet again ignoring her question. His voice was calmer now but there was a quiet determination in his tone that demanded to be told the truth

Jeannie put her arm about his shoulders and urged him towards the kitchen sink. 'Let me sort that cut and then we'll sit down quietly and I'll explain.'

'Oh, for God's sake,' Tom exploded. 'Just tell him. Tell him the truth. That he's my sister's bastard and that she was no better than a whore and that we're not quite sure who his father is. Mebbe it is one of the Hayes-Gorton brothers, but which one . . .' He shot a venomous look at his wife. 'Well, your guess is as good as mine.'

Tom stood up from his chair, flung the paper to the floor and marched out of the back door. 'I'm away to the Fisherman's,' he said, quite unnecessarily, and slammed the door behind him leaving a stricken young boy and an angry woman staring at each other.

Sammy stood stoically silent whilst Jeannie bathed his cuts and bruises and then allowed her to lead him towards the fire. Still he said nothing as she sat down and pulled him close to her so that he was standing beside her knee, their eyes on a level. She left her arms draped loosely around his waist. The boy made no protest but stood waiting patiently for her to explain.

First, Jeannie had a question of her own. 'Who were you fighting with? Who was it who told you?'

His voice was scarcely above a whisper. 'Joe.'

'Joe!' She was shocked. They had always squabbled and she knew that now they were older, they resorted to fisticuffs now and then. But she had still thought that it was just boyish quarrelling between two brothers. She had not realized that feelings went much deeper than that. For they were not brothers, but cousins, and now, they both knew it.

She sighed. 'Your father's . . .' she began and then stopped. Even this was not true. She began again. 'Tom had a sister called Grace. She was your mother, but she died giving birth to you and later the very same day, Joe was born.'

'So you and Dad . . .' there was the slightest hesitation over his reference to the man he had always believed to be his father, 'are Joe's Mam and Dad?'

Jeannie nodded. 'Yes, but to me, you've aye been my son too. I suckled you as a bairn and I've never treated you any differently to Joe. I've always thought of you both as my sons. My twin sons, really.'

He appeared to be thinking for a moment, then Sammy shook his head. 'Yeah, I know you have. But . . .' His blue eyes gazed earnestly into hers. 'He hasn't.'

Her arms tightened around him. 'I know,' she said softly. 'And it's never been fair. It wasn't your fault you were born, but you're the only one left for him to take it out on.'

There was silence again. Jeannie didn't need to ask how Joe had found out. People round here had long memories. Children overheard adults gossiping and so . . .

'Joe said I ain't got a dad,' Sammy's voice was small, barely audible even standing so close to her.

Jeannie almost smiled despite the emotion of the moment. 'Of course you've got a dad. Everyone has. But – well – because your mam and dad weren't married, he doesna acknowledge you as his. See?'

The boy thought for a moment and then nodded. 'I think so. But – but who is he? Do you know?'

'Mr Francis Hayes-Gorton.'

'The man who used to come here sometimes?'

Jeannie winced. Another piece of common knowledge that had obviously found its way to the boys' ears as it had to Tom's.

'No, that's his brother, Mr Robert. He's aye shown an interest in you.'

'But he doesn't come now.' The boy's voice was accusing, suggesting that the man's interest had waned.

Jeannie sighed. 'No. But that wasna his fault. I had to stop him coming.'

'Why?'

Her mouth was tight. 'Same reason that's caused today's trouble, son. Bloody neighbours blethering.'

The boy blinked. Jeannie never swore and the fact that she did so now, underlined her bitterness.

Sammy was silent for a moment and then gently he pulled away from her embrace. 'Thank you for telling me,' he said, with an unusual adult courtesy. Then he turned and walked towards the door, a defiant bearing in the set of his shoulders and a dignified carriage of his head that had not been there before. Sammy, Jeannie realized, had in the last hour, grown up. The shock he had just received would not defeat him. It would be the making of him.

Twenty-Seven

Robert stood at the long window of the drawing room and looked out upon the neat garden realizing that he was a lonely, unhappy man with little to look forward to in a desolate future. Even his visits to Baldock Street had ceased long ago.

He thought back to the last time Jeannie had opened the door to him. It was the little boys' fifth birthday and he had come loaded with presents. A new blazer for each of them for school, a pencil case and a satchel. All well-meaning gifts, yet he had learnt, many years later, that they had never been used. His middle-class offerings would have set the children apart from their peers, and Jeannie, swift to protect them, had waited to see if the boys themselves chose to use them. They never had.

But Robert remembered that day. If he closed his eyes he could still see her so clearly. Her unruly red hair twisted up onto the top of her head, her green eyes troubled and a dab of flour smudging her nose. He had longed to reach out and brush it away with a tender, loving action. But as he had taken his leave, he had stood on the doorstep listening to her words that would extinguish the only bright spot in his life.

'I'm sorry, Mr Robert,' she had said. Had it been fanciful imagination on his part, or had there been a tearful catch in her voice? 'But I'll have to ask you not to come here any more. There's been gossip.' She had given an exasperated toss of her head towards the street outside her home. 'You ken what they're like . . .'

She had not needed to say more. He could guess the rest. And now, eight years later, standing alone in the empty house, he still remembered the moment with regret for his own reaction to her words. To hide his disappointment, he had behaved like a pompous oaf, he told himself. He had raised his hat to her, given a stiff little bow, and said, 'As you wish,' then turned and walked out of her life.

As she had watched him walk away, Jeannie had thought her heart would break. But she had had no choice. After Tom's last time ashore, when he had made snide remarks about Robert's continuing visits, she had known that she would have to stop him coming to the house.

'Aggie ses Mr Robert still comes here on a Thursday afternoon, even though the lads have started school now. And that's the afternoon me mam goes out. That right?'

'No, it isna,' Jeannie had replied shortly. 'And Aggie Turnbull'd do better to mind her own business.'

'But he does come here?' Tom had refused to let the matter drop.

'He comes to see Sammy,' Jeannie had said, trying to keep her voice level, though she was fast losing patience.

'What, when he's at school? Pull the other one, Jeannie. It's you he comes to see.' He jabbed a finger towards her. 'Well, I aren't havin' it! He might let his wife mek a cuckold out of him, but I aren't. Not even if he is me boss.'

Jeannie swung round, her temper flaring now. 'How dare you accuse me of any such thing!' She advanced towards him, her own finger now wagging in his face, only inches away. 'He comes here to see the boy. Let's face it, he's the only man who does take any interest in the wee man. His father doesna and neither do you.'

For a moment Tom had looked ashamed. 'I can't help it if I can't feel the same about him as I do about our Joe.'

'Well, you could at least act it,' she had snapped back, but even as she had said the words she had known it was useless. Tom would never change in his attitude towards Sammy, nor in his jealousy over Robert Hayes-Gorton.

It was not until later, after she had spoken to Robert and told him not to visit any more, that Jeannie remembered Tom's words again and wondered what he had meant about Robert being made a cuckold. Well, she wasn't going to be able to solve that little bit of gossip and besides, it wasn't really any of her business.

She had thought her action would stop the chatter but no, even eight years after that day, it was still going on. And now wagging tongues had rocked young Sammy's world.

Well, this was her business and there was something she could do. There was only one person to blame: Aggie Turnbull.

In the years since she had come to Havelock that woman had seemed to intrude upon Jeannie's life in all sorts of ways; ways that she did not fully understand. Mention of the woman's name would upset Nell for the rest of the day and yet Tom had no compunction in talking freely about her.

It was time, Jeannie decided, that she had words with Aggie Turnbull herself.

When the door opened, Jeannie felt a smug satisfaction at the surprise on the woman's face.

'Well, well.' Aggie smiled and held the door wider, tacitly inviting Jeannie inside. 'Who'd have thought I'd ever see you on my doorstep again, Mrs Lawrence. Not requiring my midwifery services again, are you?'

'No,' Jeannie said shortly, feeling the familiar stab of disappointment that there had been no more bairns for her and Tom. 'But there is something you can do for me.'

'Do come into my drawing room.' Aggie led the way and Jeannie found herself sitting down on a silk brocade covered sofa. Aggie sat down in a matching easy chair, crossed her slim, white-stockinged legs and said, 'Now, my dear, what can I possibly do for you?'

Jeannie stared at her. It was thirteen years since she had seen Aggie close to. Not since the night the two boys had been born when, she had to admit, she had been thankful for Aggie's help. Remembering, some of the anger that had carried her here faded.

She was still much as Jeannie remembered her except that now the cosmetics could not cover the passage of the intervening years. Beneath the blonde hair, the bright lipstick and the silk dress, Aggie was growing old. She must be nearly as old as Nell, Jeannie thought, as Aggie serenely submitted herself to Jeannie's scrutiny without a trace of embarrassment, a small smile on her mouth.

Jeannie said bluntly, 'I dinna like you blethering about me. It's no' true and every time Tom comes home, he still—'

'Ah yes, Tom,' Aggie said smoothly. 'Poor Tom. Such a dear, but a little, what shall we say, weak, don't you find?'

'Weak?' Jeannie was startled.

'Mm. Isn't that what you would call it? He goes to sea for one or two trips and then suddenly there's some excuse for him to miss the next one and languish ashore for the following three weeks. Then back to sea he'll go, one or two trips and then . . .' She leant forward. 'Don't tell me in all these years, you hadn't realized?'

Jeannie was silent, staring at the woman. Oh yes, of course she'd realized it. But to hear it from someone else's mouth, particularly from the likes of Aggie Turnbull, shocked her.

Aggie leant back amongst the brocade cushions and sighed, waving a slim, elegant hand in the air. 'Of course, he's not the man his father was. Now, there was a man.'

Jeannie levered herself to her feet. What on earth had possessed her to come here and why was she sitting here allowing this woman to talk about the Lawrence menfolk as if she knew them both – intimately?

Well, if she did, then Jeannie had no wish to hear about it.

'Going already?' Aggie looked up, amusement in her eyes. 'So soon?' She stood up too and now her face was suddenly serious. 'Jeannie, I know what everyone round here thinks about me and I expect you share their opinions. Well, some of it's probably true, but a lot of it isn't. One thing I will tell you, I do not spread gossip. Oh, I hear a lot. I know just about everything that goes on around here. But it wasn't me who spread the rumours about Mr Robert Hayes-Gorton and his visits to see his nephew when Tom was at sea. Nor did I tell young Joe about young Sammy's – er – origins.'

Jeannie gasped and her eyes widened. So, Aggie knew even this.

'Your gossip-monger, Jeannie, is closer to home. Someone in your own street whose lace curtains twitch every time someone sneezes.'

'Who?' Jeannie said, disbelieving.

'Well now, I'd be gossiping too if I were to tell you, now wouldn't I?

'Och, dinna be so aggravating, Aggie Turnbull.'

At this the woman threw back her head and laughed. 'Oh Jeannie, I like you. I really like you. How I wish I had a friend like you.'

As Jeannie opened her mouth to make a sharp retort, Aggie held up her hand. 'Don't worry,' she said and, suddenly, Jeannie detected a note of wistfulness in her voice. 'I know it can never be. Just, my dear,' her tone was softer, gentler, 'as there can never be anything between you and Mr Robert.'

'There is nothing between us,' Jeannie retorted hotly, her face fiery red.

'I know, I know. But you'd both like there to be, wouldn't you?'

'No!' The denial was like the crack of a sail, yet both women knew it to be false.

'Why else,' Aggie asked quietly, 'would you bother to come here, to risk visiting a woman with my reputation, if there was absolutely nothing to feel the tiniest bit guilty about?'

Jeannie blundered from the room and out of the house, knowing that she had made a dreadful mistake in coming. Aggie Turnbull was nothing like the woman she had imagined her to be. She was intelligent and sharp and she had neatly turned the tables upon Jeannie.

Robert turned away from the window as he heard the rattle that heralded the arrival of the evening newspaper. Automatically, his mind still preoccupied, he walked across the tiled floor of the hall and pulled the paper from the jaws of the brass letterbox. He unfolded it and stood in the middle of the hall, staring down at the paper. The newsprint blurred before his eyes and then suddenly, it sharpened as he read the headline. A headline so dramatic that at once his thoughts were pulled back with a jolt from the events of eight years ago to the present.

'HITLER MARCHES INTO CZECHOSLOVAKIA'.

The answer to his boredom was staring up at him. With more energy and enthusiasm than he had felt for years, he flung the newspaper to the floor where it lay in a crumpled heap on the otherwise immaculate and sterile floor. Robert picked up his hat from the table and left the house, pulling the door closed behind him with the satisfied air of a decision made.

Twenty-Eight

'You are going to do what?' Samuel Hayes-Gorton rose from his swivel chair and leant on his desk towards his son standing on the opposite side.

'I said,' Robert repeated calmly, 'I am going to join the Royal Navy Volunteer Reserves.'

'Edwin,' the older man roared. 'Get in here this instant.'

A moment later the communicating door between two offices opened and Edwin poked his head round it. 'Hullo, old chap,' he beamed at his brother. 'Nice to see you back. Feeling better?'

Robert felt the colour rising in his neck and felt guilty about the small lie he had told for his absence from the family business during the past week. 'I've got the bost dreadful co'd,' he had said into the telephone five days earlier, holding his nose as he did so. 'I can't bossibly come in.' He remembered sniffing loudly and had even manufactured a sneeze.

'Of course not, Mr Robert,' Miss Jenkins, secretary to all the senior partners, had gushed. 'I do hope you'll soon be feeling better.'

And now he was back with not so much as a red nose to lend credence to his pretence. 'Fine. Didn't last long, as it happens.'

'Fine? Fine, he says?' their father boomed. 'The boy's taken leave of his senses.' He snorted derisively. 'If he ever had any.'

239

Edwin's puzzled glance went from one to the other. Then Samuel Hayes-Gorton flung out his arm. 'Only says he wants to join the Royal Navy. That's all.'

'The . . .?' Edwin began and then said, 'Whatever for?'

'Exactly!' Samuel bellowed again. 'Whatever for?'

'The Volunteer Reserves,' Robert corrected. 'And I shan't be going away. There'll just be training sessions once or twice a week, I expect.'

It had all seemed so easy, that spur of the moment decision standing in the empty loneliness of his house – and he used the word 'house' deliberately for it never had been and never would be a home. Not without a woman who . . . He sighed again. Not without Jeannie there. And that was another reason. Maybe if he could find some direction for his energies, he might be able to stop thinking about her every waking moment.

'Robert?' Robert heard Edwin's gentle voice interrupting his thoughts. 'Why, old chap?'

Robert lifted his shoulders. 'I just need something positive to do with my life."

'Something positive?' their father roared again. 'You don't regard running the Gorton-Hathersage Trawler Company as something positive?'

Since the alliance of the two companies through marriage, the ties had become even stronger and following the death of Henry Hathersage the two companies had merged and become the Gorton-Hathersage Trawler Company Limited. Samuel Hayes-Gorton took the Chairman's position and Francis, Managing Director. With Edwin as Company Secretary, Robert had only a seat on the Board as a Director. There was no useful position and little for him to do in the day-to-day running of the business. His role, he thought bitterly, was, and always had been, merely a means to an end.

Well, they all had the 'end' they had wanted now.

Even Louise was quite happy with the money she received as a major shareholder, though she had never bothered to attend so much as one meeting of the Board.

'Of course, Mummy's got an annuity for life but everything else comes to me,' Louise had informed Samuel Hayes-Gorton and his three sons after the reading of her father's will. 'But I don't want anything to do with the business.' She had fluttered her eyelashes and looked at each of the men in turn. 'What does silly little me know about boats and the price of fish. So, Robert is to have – what did the solicitor man call it, darling?'

'Power of attorney.'

'Oh yes. It means Robert can sign anything on my behalf. All I want,' she giggled prettily, 'is the money.'

'My dear Louise,' Francis had risen from his chair behind his desk and come round it to take her slim hand in his and raise her fingers to his lips, 'your business could not be in safer hands than your husband's and his fellow board members.' He waved his hand to encompass himself, Edwin and their father. 'You leave everything to us, my dear, and you just enjoy yourself spending the money we make for you.'

'Oh Francis, you say the sweetest things. You must come to dinner on Friday. Mustn't he, Robert?'

'Of course,' Robert murmured dutifully.

'That's settled then,' Francis said as he opened the door for her. Louise, clad in a suit with a fur stole around her shoulders and a hat with a pheasant's feather, kissed the air beside her brother-in-law's cheek.

'See you Friday,' she trilled as she left the office, but Robert had the distinct feeling that Francis had not been referring to her invitation to dine, but to the official amalgamation of the two companies which had long been his ambition.

Since then, Francis had set about systematically acquiring not only all the other small shipping companies in Havelock, but he had begun also to buy out the service industries including engineering and ship repairing, coaling and even cod liver oil production and net making.

Net making, Robert thought, immediately reminded him of Jeannie. If his brother had his way, all the nets would be made in one of his factory units and the women who worked in their own homes would lose a valuable source of a little extra income for their families.

'By God, the ingratitude.' Samuel was still shouting, bringing Robert's wandering thoughts back to the present and the bombshell he had just dropped. 'After all I've done for you, this is the thanks I get. Your duty is here with the family business and even more so if there is going to be a damned war.' He paused, waiting for some response from his son. When none came, he threatened, 'Well, if you go, boy, you go without my blessing. You'll have no part in this company ever again. I'll have you voted off the Board and I'll cut you out of my will.'

'Father, I'm superfluous in this company and you know it.' Robert's mouth tightened. 'The only useful purpose I have ever served was to be the means of an alliance between the Gorton and the Hathersage companies.'

Samuel's face turned purple. 'You make it sound like a business transaction, boy, instead of a marriage between two people, who—'

'It was,' Robert said curtly. 'You and old man Hathersage concocted the idea between you. She was his only daughter, his only child, and more than anything he wanted a grandson. You saw your chance to build your empire. But why me? Why the second son? Why not Francis?'

His father glanced away now, suddenly embarrassed

under the scrutiny of his two sons. He cleared his throat and said gruffly, 'Francis would have broken the poor girl's heart in a fortnight. The – er – kind of life he leads. You knew that at the time.'

Robert nodded slowly. 'The only trouble is, we weren't in love with each other. Not then, not now. You know she spends nearly all her time in London. Has done for years. She's there now, has been for the past week. That so-called home I bought was a last-ditch effort to try to make the marriage work. Well, I failed.'

Samuel, still belligerent, wagged his finger towards his son. 'You should have given her a child, boy. That'd've made her stay at home instead of gallivanting to the city every five minutes. You should have—'

'I tried, oh I tried, believe you me. But she wouldn't let me near her. Never has. Why do you think we came back from honeymoon early? Why do you think I spent the whole of my inheritance from my grandmother on a house for her? Why do you think I indulge her every whim?' Robert leant towards his father and slowly and deliberately, said, 'The marriage has never been consummated.'

Now Samuel's mouth dropped open. 'What?'

'You heard,' Robert said bluntly. 'And now it never will be, because I've no taste for it either.'

'Really?' Now there was sarcasm in his father's tone. 'Maybe not with your wife, but from what I've heard you're not above trips to a terraced house in Baldock Street.'

It felt as if a knife had been driven in just below his ribcage and Robert almost gasped aloud at the force of it. He stood rigidly still for a moment and then let out a long breath. So, he thought, Jeannie had had good reason to stop him going to her home. If the rumours had even reached his father, then they must certainly be rife around the docks. He pulled in a breath now and then sighed heavily. 'Like I said, I'm not much use around here anyway. You're still head of the company. Francis, for all his dissolute ways, has a superb business sense. He's proved that over the last few years. He just about controls the whole of the fish docks. And Edwin here, well, he runs the office side of things like clockwork. So what exactly is my role? Tell me, because I'd really like to know.'

For a moment Samuel blustered, refuting Robert's words, but then his voice trailed away leaving unfinished sentences.

'Precisely,' Robert said quietly and calmly now. 'Even you can't define my usefulness, can you? Look, Father, I don't want to quarrel with you. That's the last thing I want, but I want to do something useful with my life. And if,' he added sadly, 'you don't want me to be a part of the family business in the future, well,' he paused before saying, 'then so be it.'

'That's not going to happen,' Edwin's quiet voice put in now, with such a firmness in his tone that both Samuel and Robert looked at him in surprise.

'Now, don't you start—' Samuel began, but Edwin said, 'Father, the company, one day, will come to the three of us. The three Hayes-Gorton brothers. Nothing is going to change that. Francis and I wouldn't want it any different.'

'Don't you try to tell me how to arrange my own affairs.'

'I'm not,' Edwin said. He remained unruffled and there was even a small smile on his lips. 'I'm just saying that whatever happens, whatever Robert decides to do . . .' He lifted his shoulders. 'Whatever you leave in your will, Robert will always be a part of this company. Francis and I will see to it.'

'Well, I'll be damned,' Samuel sat down suddenly and heavily in his chair and rocked backwards. 'The young cubs ousting the old fox, eh?'

Edwin laughed. 'Oh, I think there's plenty of bark still left in the wily old fox yet, don't you?'

Robert looked on in amazement. His younger brother was really showing his mettle these days. Edwin turned and laid a hand on Robert's shoulder. 'I don't want you to leave the company, old chap, but you must do what you want to do. And – and I'm sorry if I've taken the role that should rightly be yours.'

Robert shook his head. 'You haven't. You're brilliant at the administration side. You've a head for figures and accountancy that I've never had. I couldn't do it anyway. Any more than I could wheel and deal like Francis does. I haven't got his – er – business acumen.' The two brothers exchanged a glance and smiled slightly at one another.

'Have you told Francis?' their father put in, glaring at Edwin. 'Are you sure he feels the same way?'

'Not yet,' Edwin said and added confidently, 'but he will.'

Samuel grunted. 'Where is he, anyway?'

Again the two brothers exchanged a glance.

'In London,' Robert said and he could not keep the edge of bitterness from his tone as he added pointedly, 'he's been there the past week.' Then, with the deliberate intention of giving his father food for thought, food that might well give him indigestion, he said slowly, 'Perhaps Francis should have been your chosen bridegroom for Louise, after all.'

'So, your fancy man's running away to sea, is he?'

Jeannie glanced quickly at her husband and then away

again. 'What are you talking about?' Then deliberately she added, '*Who* are you talking about?'

'As if you didn't know,' Tom sneered.

She turned to face him now. 'Aye, I ken. And I'm tired of it. You shouldna listen to the neighbours' blether. Mr Robert used to come here to see his nephew or to bring money for his keep. But he hasna been for years. You know that, yet still you accuse me of all sorts of dreadful things that are . . .' she stepped towards him and thrust her face close to his, 'that are not going on. D'you hear me?' She tossed her head and added, 'And whilst we're on the subject, why is your first port of call when you come ashore always to see *her*? Not quite the actions of a devoted husband, is it?'

Tom was visibly flustered. 'I don't. I mean, it isn't.'

'Really?' Now it was Jeannie's turn for sarcasm.

'I do see her. Now and again . . .' he blustered and as Jeannie's eyes flashed resentment he put out his hand as if to fend off an expected attack. 'Not for that, Jeannie. I promise you. Never for that. I never have. But – but . . .'

'But what then?'

'There's things about Aggie Turnbull and this family – our family – that you don't understand.'

'Eh?' Now Jeannie was surprised. 'What things?'

'I can't tell you. Maybe some day, but not now.'

'Huh,' Jeannie snorted. 'Well, I've heard some excuses in my time, but that's a new one. I'll ask your mother.'

'No,' Tom was shouting now. 'No, you won't. I forbid you to.'

'Forbid me?' Jeannie retorted. 'How dare you say such a thing to me?'

'Jeannie, please, don't say anything to me mam. It'll hurt her too much.'

Slowly, Jeannie nodded. 'Very well then, but only for that. And one day you'll tell me what you're on about.'

He shrugged. 'Maybe.'

'Och there's no "maybe" about it, Tom Lawrence. You will.' She paused and then asked, feeling in control now, 'So, what was it you were saying about Mr Robert?'

'He's joined the Royal Navy, they reckon. Gone away to sea. Though why he didn't just ship aboard one of his own trawlers, beats me. He could have pulled rank, as they say, and skippered a Gorton boat if he'd been so desperate to go to sea. More fool him, I say.'

Jeannie turned away hardly listening to Tom now. He didn't even come to say goodbye, was all she could think.

Twenty-Nine

A few months later, at the beginning of 1939, Tom startled
Jeannie by announcing that he, too, was going to join the
RNVR.

'You?' she said unable to keep the surprise from her
tone. 'But if war is declared, you'd be one of the first to
have to go.'

'I know.' Tom, now approaching his mid-thirties, ran
his hand through his hair. He had never achieved pro-
motion, not even to third-hand status never mind mate or
skipper, but had remained a deckie all his working life. It
was, Jeannie knew, because he was unreliable.

'But why?'

'All the lads are joining. You know, a sort of "Pals
Battalion". A bit like they did in the last lot. And it's the
obvious choice for fishermen. They reckon if the balloon
does go up, the Navy will be commandeering our ships
anyway. I s'pose it makes sense,' Tom shrugged. 'There
won't be much point in us trying to fish in the North Sea
when it's alive with enemy submarines. And there's no
point in the trawlers lying idle if there's a useful job for
them to do.'

'Tom,' she said, placing her hand on his arm and
looking up into his face, 'don't – don't let yourself be
pushed into doing something you don't really want do. I
mean, just for the sake of – of how it looks.'

He stared down at her, his blue eyes troubled, his

mouth tight. And then he put his arms about her and drew her to him, resting his chin on the top of her head. 'Oh Jeannie. You know, don't you? Have you always known, how I fear the sea?'

She moved her head against his chest in a tiny movement of denial. 'No,' she said, her voice muffled against him. 'Not at first, but I began to realize.'

'When I missed a trip at the slightest opportunity, you mean?'

'Aye, something like that.'

Close to him she heard the sigh deep within his chest. Then he pulled away from her and held her at arm's length looking down into her face. 'I just wanted to be like me dad,' he said simply.

'And you went to sea because of him?'

Tom nodded. 'And now,' he said slowly, 'I'm going to get involved in this blasted war just because I still want him to be proud of me.'

'Your father would be proud of you whatever you did, Tom.'

'You think so?'

'I know so. You dinna have to keep proving yourself over and over again.'

Quietly he said, 'Maybe I do, Jeannie. Maybe I do, even if only for myself.'

'Oh Tom.' She shook her head and there were sudden tears in her eyes. 'I dinna want anything to happen to you.'

He touched her cheek with calloused fingers. 'You mean that? You really mean that?'

'Of course I do,' she said, now with a trace of impatience. Then, more gently, she added, 'But you do what you want to do for yourself. I'm not going to stand in your way, but please, Tom Lawrence, just come home safely.'

As he drew her against him and wrapped his arms about her again, now with a fierce intensity, Jeannie buried her head against his chest and closed her eyes, knowing a sudden fear for her husband.

Robert'd be safe, she told herself. With his connections, Robert would get a desk job. With his father's influence, he'd be bound to be in a safe, shore job. He wouldn't be sent to sea. At least Robert would be safe, Jeannie told herself.

But what about Tom?

On 26 August 1939, Robert, in London on business, received a telephone call. The voice on the other end of the telephone said, 'You're to report to Lieutenant-Commander Walsh at Lowestoft, Gorton, at 0.700 hours tomorrow. That's where the Royal Naval Patrol Service has been set up. Bit of a hotch-potch at the moment, but the chaps down there will soon sort it all out. Walsh asked for you personally. He'll be mustering his crew and wants you as his first lieutenant aboard a minesweeper . . .' The man went on with travel details and finished by saying, 'Walsh says you have particular knowledge of trawlers. A fisherman, are you? I know a lot have volunteered.'

'Not exactly,' Robert replied, not wanting to explain fully. 'But I do have a knowledge of trawlers, sir, yes.' He wanted, in this war in which he was obviously going to be involved now, to be treated on his own merits. Without deliberately lying, he intended to conceal the fact that he was a trawler owner with the distinction of the name Hayes-Gorton. He had considered using the name Hayes only, and dropping the Gorton, but instead had decided to drop the double-barrelled bit and become plain Robert Gorton. It was doubtful now that the Gorton-Hathersage

Trawler Company would have many ships left by the end of the conflict. He wondered what would happen to his family's business and if there would be any company left for his father to cut him out of.

He listened as the voice crackled down the wire giving him further instructions ending with the words, 'You'll be going to a place called Havelock. Ever heard of it?'

'Oh yes, sir.'

'Oh good. Can't say I have, but there you are. A chap can't know of all these little fishing villages round the coast.'

As Robert replaced the receiver, he was smiling to himself, and murmured, 'What a pity my father couldn't have heard that last remark.'

'Jeannie, I'm to report to Lowestoft along with a lot of the other lads.'

'Oh Tom. So this is it, then?'

'Looks like it.'

She watched him. There was apprehension in his eyes but something else too. Was it, could it possibly be, excitement? At his next words, Jeannie began to understand a little of what Tom was feeling.

'Me dad never went to war. He didn't serve in the last lot. I'm doing something me dad never did.'

Was that it? Was that what Tom had needed all along? The chance to emerge from the shadow of the big man and be himself? Smiling, Jeannie went to him and put her arms about his waist, saying again what she knew he needed to hear. 'We're all proud of you, Tom, and your dad would be too. Just take care of yoursel' and get home whenever you can.'

He was back in a few days and the exhilaration was gone already from his eyes. 'You'll never believe it. I've not only got drafted back to me own home town but on bloody trawlers turned into minesweepers. I'll be serving on the same bloody boats I've been on all me life. I thought at least I'd get chance to go on a proper warship or summat. But a bloody trawler . . .'

'Will you be minding your language, Tom Lawrence,' Jeannie snapped, disappointed that the first tentative signs of a change in Tom had already been swept away.

'And that's not all.' His expression was resentful, full of loathing. 'Jimmy the One on my ship is none other than Mr bloody Robert Hayes-Gorton. Lieutenant Gorton, as he wants to be known now.'

'Jimmy the Who?' Jeannie asked.

Tom clicked his tongue against his teeth with exasperation and waved his hand. 'Oh, it's the nickname they give to the first lieutenant on board ship. And do you know what I'm to be called? Sparks.'

'Sparks?' Jeannie repeated and then started to laugh. 'What on earth does that mean?'

With a sudden change of mood, Tom puffed out his chest proudly. 'I took a course to be a wireless operator when I joined the RNVR. And after the war, I could become a sparks aboard a trawler. No more eighteen hours – and longer – on deck guttin' for me, Jeannie.' He rubbed his hands together. 'Nice cosy little room for me from now on. The most important people on a trawler, is the sparks. A skipper relies on his wireless operator, he does.'

Jeannie glanced at him and then looked away. He was forgetting she was a fisherman's daughter and knew that every man aboard a trawler was just as important as the next, from skipper to galley boy. Poor Tom, she thought with sudden sympathy, always trying to prove himself and never quite managing it.

Aloud, she laughed, wanting to hold on to his sunnier

temper. 'Well, sit down to your dinner, laddie, else there'll be sparks flying in this hoose if you let this meal go to waste.'

'So, dear boy,' Francis said languidly, 'you're going to play the hero at last, are you? Well, just mind you take care of our ship and don't let her get blown up by the enemy.'

Robert grinned. 'Thanks, Francis, for your concern about *my* safety.'

They were all gathered together to dine at Samuel Hayes-Gorton's home, Louise and her widowed mother being present too.

'I must say, you look awfully handsome in your uniform, darling, doesn't he, Mummy?'

Conscious that she was a guest, she smiled politely, but, Robert noticed, the smile never reached her eyes which remained as cold as they had always been when turned upon him.

'We'll go to London when you come home on leave, darling, and I can show you off to all Madeleine's friends. Her husband's joined the RAF and they all make such a fuss about the glamorous boys in blue, but I think the Royal Navy uniform is even smarter.'

'Louise, it won't be safe in London from now on. You really shouldn't go there any more.'

'Not go? Not go to London?' Louise was plainly horrified. 'Oh Robert, you know I couldn't stay and stagnate in this place for months on end.'

'She'll be safe enough,' Francis said. 'It'll not last long and I doubt even Herr Hitler would dare to bomb London . . .'

*

Robert and Tom had been going to sea for almost two months, four or five days at a stretch then returning to Havelock for thirty-six hours or so, out of which they were allowed about eight hours ashore. On 13 November, the first bombs were dropped on British soil: the Shetlands. Jeannie read the news with horror, at once imagining part of her beloved homeland to be laid waste. People dead or dying and beginning interminable days and nights of living with constant fear. Later that same month, specially designed enemy U-boats began to lay a devastating new type of mine, the magnetic mine, around the coast of Britain. And so began a game of cat and mouse between the scientists on both sides. The one to invent newer and deadlier mechanisms, the other to find ways of destroying the mines before they blew up the convoy ships.

Already the war was a devastating reality and the two men were now engaged in trawling the icy waters of the North Sea for a far more deadly fish.

Thirty

'Why can't we go and join up like Dad?' Joe asked mutinously.

She could not remember ever having seen the two boys so united, standing shoulder to shoulder to argue with her, the common enemy. Though she had to admit that since the time Sammy had found out the circumstances of his birth, he had not allowed Joe to dominate him. The realization that Joe was his cousin, and not his brother, had strengthened the boy's character rather than weakened it. Sammy's new stance had for a time resulted in some bloody-nosed battles between the two of them. But Jeannie thought that the best way was to allow them to sort it out between themselves. Now, as they stood before her, she knew she had been right, but, she thought wryly, maybe to her own detriment.

'You're no' old enough,' she said firmly. 'You have to be eighteen at least.' She wasn't sure if that was exactly right but she was relying upon them not knowing either. 'You're only just sixteen.'

'We could sign on as cabin boys, couldn't we?' Sammy stood beside Joe. 'We're old enough for that, aren't we?'

She glanced at each of them in turn, deliberately making sure that her glance did not rest longer upon Sammy than it did upon her own son. Why was it, she thought, fight it though she did, she could never stop feeling more for the boy that was not flesh of her flesh, bone of her bone, than she did for the one who was? Just the same, her conscience pricked her, as she worried more about Robert Hayes-Gorton than she did about her own husband.

'Well, I'm signing no papers to let you go anywhere. Either of you.'

'But we look old enough.' It was Sammy who was persisting.

They did. She had to admit that. They both had fair hair and blue eyes, but there the similarity ended. Joe was the taller; he was going to be a big man like both his grandfathers as he matured and broadened out. Even now, his shoulders were muscular and his slim hips belied his strength. Already he had been at sea for a year as a deckie on one of the few battered old trawlers that still ventured into the mine-ridden waters of the North Sea. Sammy, too, was a deck-hand on a Gorton-Hathersage ship that was too old and dilapidated to be of interest to the authorities.

'Dad'll clear the channels for us,' he'd say jokingly, but Jeannie knew he was only trying to reassure her. 'He'll know where we're going.'

For the most part Joe was jovial and outgoing. The life and soul of the party, Jeannie heard him described by his pals in the Fisherman's. But his temperament was volatile; he could switch from laughter to rage in a second. And, to Jeannie's disappointment, though he was more of a born fisherman than Tom, he seemed to have inherited his father's streak of jealousy and resentment. Throughout their childhood it had always been Joe who had started the fights with Sammy, rather than, as one might have expected, the other way about.

Sammy was smaller, but stockily built. He was the quieter of the two with a placidity that belied his strength of character. He would never begin a quarrel, but once challenged he would defend himself ferociously and usually, to everyone's surprise, emerge the victor. A deep thinker, Jeannie judged him, who would weigh up the pros and cons of a situation before making his decision. Yet once that decision was made, he would not waver, despite whatever pressures were put upon him.

Jeannie suspected that this trait was inherited from his natural father. She was thankful, though, that whilst the boy vaguely resembled Francis Hayes-Gorton in looks, she was sure he had none of the man's cold, ruthless streak. When Sammy smiled, his eyes twinkled with warmth and merriment and his face creased disarmingly. A fact that had not escaped the notice of the young girls in the neighbourhood.

So she still found herself turning towards Sammy, for she knew instinctively that whereas Joe would be caught up in the glamour of being a hero, Sammy would have been the one to think it out carefully.

'We won't be in that much more danger than we are now, Mam,' he said quietly and she knew he could read the anxiety in her face.

Jeannie sighed inwardly and tried another tack. 'How would I manage Grandma without your help? At least you're home fairly regularly now.'

Nell needed constant supervision, for though she was physically well, her mind wandered so badly now that she scarcely seemed to know where she was, what time of day it was or even that there was a war going on all around them. Getting her to the Anderson shelter which the boys had constructed in the back-yard was as big a battle as any fought in the front line and without Sammy's patient coaxing and wheedling the old lady when he was home, Jeannie thought, she'd never get Tom's mother to safety.

The boys said nothing now but exchanged a glance that

spoke more than words could. 'And dinna you go planning to run away to sea together . . .' Jeannie began and as they both glanced at her with the same guilty look, she knew she had been shrewd in her guess.

But they went anyway. Four days later she found a note on the kitchen table saying that they had done just that.

'We're sorry, Mam,' the note said in Joe's untidy scrawl, 'but me and Sam have got to go.' And in Sammy's neat handwriting were the words, 'Take care of yourself and Gran. Please don't be cross. Love Sammy.'

She crumpled the note. She wasn't cross, she thought as she bit her lip to try to stop the tears from flooding her eyes and spilling down her cheeks.

Just so terribly alone.

'I wouldn't have believed it possible,' Tom was still complaining. 'After two years sweeping the bloody North Sea, we're still on the same ship. I thought at least when that mine blew our ship up we might get drafted to different ships then. But no, here we are still the same happy little band. We even got into the same lifeboat.' His voice dropped to a low growl. 'Given half a chance, I'd have let the bugger drown.'

'What on earth are you talking about?' Jeannie was exasperated now and only half-listening. Nell had wandered out in the street and had gone missing and all Tom could do was rant on about how badly life was treating him.

'Mr flaming Robert Hayes-Gorton. That's who I'm talking about. Only he's a bloody lieutenant now, ain't he? I'm still taking orders from him.' He punched one fist into the palm of his other hand. 'If there'd been any justice in

world, *I'd* have been over *him*. Bloody trawler owners!
:kon they rule the bloody world.'

Calmly Jeannie said, 'I expect it's because he joined the
R sometime before the war started.'

'How do you know that?' Tom rounded on her and, at
:e, Jeannie realized her mistake. Luckily she remem-
ed how she had come by the information.

'You told me.'

'Oh. Did I?' Tom was fazed for a moment and mut-
:d, 'Mebbe I did, but I still think he's done it on
pose.' He glowered at Jeannie as if the whole thing
:e her fault. 'Mebbe he's going to pick his moment
en no one's looking and toss me overboard.'

'Never mind all that just now and do stop swearing.
lp me find your mother. If she gets into the town, we'll
er find her.'

'Then you should look after her better. You've nowt
: to do all day now me and the boys have gone.'

'I'm doing a bit of war work like all the other women
nd here.'

Tom gave a humourless laugh. 'Oh aye. I've heard that
: before. Supplying comforts for the troops. Aye . . .'
face darkened. 'Comforts for the troops billeted in the
n, I don't doubt. Setting up in opposition to Aggie
nbull, are ya?'

Her hand flew threw the air of its own volition and her
m met the side of his face with a loud smack. He
pped her wrists and for a moment they stood glaring at
h other, breathing heavily, their faces only inches apart.

'What the hell did you do that for?'

'I'm sick of your snide remarks, Tom Lawrence. I
ena done anything – you hear me – anything to deserve
m.'

He stared at her and then his face seemed to crum
and he flung his arms about her and pulled her to him i
fierce embrace that was more like a child clinging to
mother than the embrace of a husband for his wife. I
cheek was against her hair. 'Jeannie, oh Jeannie. I'm so
It's just . . .' His voice dropped to a whisper. 'I'm so bloo
scared, that's all.'

Jeannie did not answer him but just held him tigh
Knowing what he must be feeling, she tried to comf
him, tried to give him strength and courage. But who v
there to comfort her? Who was there to help her c
alone with Nell and the worry of the men of her fam
who were in the front line of the war.

And then there was her secret worry. Always, ir
special corner of her heart, there was Robert.

It was more than eleven years since he had last stood
this doorstep. And now he felt like a nervous schoolb
or a young bashful cadet instead of a lieutenant in
smart uniform with the wavy rings around his sleeves.
found he was holding his breath as she opened the doo

At once he could see the changes. There were a f
strands of white amongst the still thick and luxuriant h
Though there were tiny lines around her eyes and d
shadows of strain and tiredness beneath them, they w
still bright and sharp as they widened at the sight of h
She was as slim and lithe as ever and the smile that Rob
had so longed to see for him alone was on her mouth. A
now, after all this time, it was for him.

'Robert . . .' She said the name by which she alw
thought of him before she could stop herself. Swiftly, :
said, 'I'm sorry, Mr Robert . . .'

He was smiling down at her, saying softly in the d

voice she remembered so well, 'I prefer it without the Mr.'

Her smile faded and anxiety clouded her eyes. Her joy at seeing him – private joy though that must be – was obliterated by the thought that he was the bearer of bad news.

'What is it? Is it Tom?' It dawned on her, swiftly now, that whilst Robert was obviously on leave, Tom had not arrived home at the same time. 'Has something happened to him?'

'No, no,' Robert said quickly, suddenly realizing what she must be thinking. 'He's fine. I've been granted compassionate leave because my father's ill. He's dying, Jeannie.'

'Och, I'm sorry. Please, won't you come in.' She opened the door wider.

In the front parlour, he perched awkwardly on the old couch.

'Can I get you anything? A drink or . . .?' she began, but he shook his head.

'No, no, thank you.' He cleared his throat in embarrassment. 'Jeannie, this is very difficult, but I've come to ask a favour of you. At least, if it's possible.'

She said nothing but her gaze was on his face and he was having trouble remaining in his seat, when what he really wanted to do was to take her in his arms and tell her just what he felt about her. He cleared his throat and said, 'Does Sammy know the truth? About his birth and – and who his father is?'

'Aye,' she nodded. 'He found out when he was about thirteen.' Her tone hardened slightly. 'Joe told him.'

'Really? But he's never – I mean – doesn't he want to meet us? His family. I mean, the other side of his family?' he amended swiftly.

Jeannie shook her head. 'No. He's adamant he wants nothing to do with the Hayes-Gortons.'

'Oh,' Robert said and his tone was flat with disappointment.

'Why, does it matter?' she asked and then allowed herself a wry smile. 'I'd have thought you'd've all been quite relieved that you weren't facing a paternity suit or that he was trying to lay claim to the Hayes-Gorton millions.'

Now Robert smiled too. 'Scarcely millions. But in fairness, he ought to have a share in the company. If only Francis would acknowledge him.' He sighed heavily.

'I dinna think he ever will,' Jeannie said bitterly.

'But young Samuel's his all right. Oh, you haven't known, Jeannie, but even though I had to stop coming here, I've still watched the boy grow up. I used to make some excuse to visit the school where he was, just so that I could see him. He never knew,' he added hastily. 'I'd make a point of talking to all the children so that it never looked as if I was singling out Samuel – Sammy you call him, don't you?'

He even knew that, she thought, as she nodded in answer.

'I never wanted to be the cause of him learning the truth.'

There was silence between them for a moment as they sat gazing at each other. Only a few feet lay between them and yet the gulf that separated them was as wide and as deep as the Humber and the currents were as treacherous as those of the river.

'So why,' she said softly at last, breaking the spell their silence was casting around them, 'are you here?'

'My father always wanted a grandson. More than anything he wanted to know that there was another generation for his company to pass on to.' Robert sighed. 'He doesn't see that perhaps at the end of this war there might be precious little company left for anyone to inherit.'

Surprised, Jeannie asked, 'Do you mean he knows about Sammy?'

Robert nodded. 'Over the years he's heard rumours that the boy you're bringing up as your own could be his grandson.'

There was a tense silence before Jeannie said, 'And?'

'He's asked to see him.'

Now her mouth dropped open in a gasp of surprise. 'You're not serious?'

Solemnly, he nodded. 'Very.'

Bluntly, she said, 'I don't think Sammy'll agree. Besides, he's not here. They're at sea. Both of them.'

'I know. Their ship docks in Hull the day after tomorrow and I could arrange for Sammy to be granted compassionate leave.'

'Is there anything you don't know about this family?' she asked tartly.

'Not much,' he admitted and grinned with such disarming boyishness that Jeannie found herself smiling too.

'Well, you can try,' she said slowly, but the doubt was evident in her tone. 'Just so long as you make sure he knows straightaway that his compassionate leave has nothing to do with this family. You see,' she added, glancing towards the ceiling indicating the bedroom above where they were sitting, 'Mrs Lawrence is not well now and he would immediately think . . .'

Robert stood up. 'Of course. I'll go myself to meet him off the ship and I'll mind I'm the one to explain everything to him.'

'He might not want to come even then.'

'That's a risk I'll have to take. My father has set his

heart on seeing the boy. In fact, he seems to be hanging on to life just for that. I must do what I can.'

'Be sure to tell Sammy that,' Jeannie said quietly. 'He's a good boy at heart.'

'I'm sure he is, if you've had the raising of him, Jeannie. But I have to remember that he has Francis's blood in his veins too. And my dear brother can be quite ruthless when he's a mind. As we all know to our cost.'

To this remark, Jeannie had no answer.

Thirty-One

Robert had waited a long time whilst the ship went through its docking procedure and the crew were allowed to step ashore. But at last he was standing on the quayside as the young sailors ran down the gangway, hit the solid ground, staggered for a moment, and then rushed forward to greet their loved ones waiting to meet them.

Then he saw them, almost the last to leave the ship, coming down the gangway, Joe in the front, leading the way.

Robert stepped forward. 'Excuse me. Might I have a word?'

The two young men stopped and, recognizing him at once, Joe said, 'What's wrong? Is it me dad?'

'No, no,' Robert said swiftly. 'All your family are well.'

Mystified now, Joe and Sammy glanced at each other and then both turned their gaze back upon Robert, who took a deep breath and said, 'I have a favour to ask of Sammy.'

'A favour? Of me?' His surprise was evident and again he glanced at Joe.

'Look, would you allow me to take you to lunch? Both of you.'

'If it's Sammy you want to talk to, you don't want me along.' There was a hint of belligerence in Joe's tone.

'Perhaps you should be involved, Joe. I can see how close you are to each other.'

'Close!' The two laughed aloud and Joe punched Sammy playfully on the shoulder, and added, 'We fight like cat and dog. We were both in trouble last week for fighting.'

Sammy, too, grinned and pointed to his chin. 'See. I've still got the bruise to prove it.'

But Robert was smiling too. 'Maybe so. But just tell me one thing. Just suppose your ship was torpedoed and sinking and you could save only one other person from the whole ship. Tell me,' he asked quietly, 'who would it be?'

The boys' faces sobered now and with one accord they both jerked their thumbs towards the other and said in unison, 'Him.'

'I thought as much,' Robert murmured and then, more briskly, he said, 'Now will you *both* have lunch with me? Please?'

Seated in the restaurant, Robert could see that both boys were ill at ease. Not only were they sitting with a superior officer, but also with the man who had been and still was, in a way, their employer. Only because of the war did they all three find themselves in the same service.

Robert did his best to put them at their ease, but until the food was served the conversation was stilted, the older man trying to open lines of communication only to be met by monosyllabic answers.

It was when they picked up their soup spoons and took the first mouthful that, suddenly, the atmosphere changed.

'By heck, this is like me mam's Tattie Soup,' Joe said. 'I ain't tasted anything as good as this since I was last home.'

Robert chuckled. 'The chef here is a Scotsman, a kinsman of your mother's.' He saw the young men glance at each other again and thought, for two who are supposed not to get along together they have a remarkable affinity between them.

Robert cleared his throat. 'Talking of your mother . . .'

An identical closed look was immediately on both their faces. 'My mother, ya mean,' Joe said and jerked his head sideways towards Sammy. 'She in't his.'

'I know,' Robert said at once and now he looked straight at Sammy. 'I know all about your parentage, Sammy. That's the reason I'm here. You're my nephew. The son of my elder brother, Francis.' When the boy made no answer, though his face was stiff with resentment, Robert went on. 'I believe you did know that, didn't you?'

Sammy gave a quick nod as if he were loath even to acknowledge the fact. Joe was smirking. 'I told him years ago.'

Robert pushed away his empty soup bowl and leant his elbows on the table. 'I'll come straight to the point. My father is dying.'

The boys looked uncomfortable, not knowing quite what they should say, but Robert continued, not expecting any reply from them, 'He has no other grandchildren except you, Sammy. And he wishes to see you before he dies.' He paused a moment to allow this to sink in and then added softly, 'That is the favour I have come to ask of you.'

'You want me to come to see him?' Sammy blurted out. 'To meet him? Me?'

Robert nodded.

'Don't go, Sam,' Joe put in at once. 'They're up to summat.'

Robert spread his hands, palms upwards. 'No catch, I promise you. No strings – nothing. I'll even arrange it so that you don't run into Francis, if that's what you're afraid of.'

'He ain't afraid of nothing, mister,' Joe shot back. 'You tell 'im, Sam.'

'Shut up, Joe. I'm thinkin'.'

Piercing blue eyes that were so like Francis's were regarding Robert, who felt a shiver like a cold dousing of water run down his spine. There it was, the likeness he had been looking for. There was that same calculating reasoning going on in the boy's mind as he had witnessed so often in his brother. Yet, he was thankful to see, it stopped short of ruthless cruelty.

'He's not wanting to have me become part of the family, is he?' Sammy asked, putting his head on one side. 'Not wanting me to come into the company?'

Robert gave a wry laugh. 'There's little of the company left at the moment for you to come into. We won't know until after the war whether we'll still have a fleet of trawlers. We're only fishing the North Sea now with the few ancient ships we have left and the crews are made up of old men and young boys. No, I promise you I'm just asking you to come and see him before – before it's too late. Obviously, it's more for his sake than for yours. Nevertheless . . .' He paused and then added, 'You never know, there might come a time when you'll be glad you at least met your grandfather.'

There was silence now around the table as Sammy considered. 'All right,' he said at last. 'I'll come.'

'Fine.' Robert stood up. 'I think I've got enough petrol to get us back via Goole. I'll drop you off at home if you like, Joe?'

'Thanks, but I can walk from your place.'

'My parents are at my house. Their own was bombed two months back.' He sighed. 'I think that's what brought on my father's heart attack.'

'Well, just drop me in the town then, please,' Joe said, and Robert had the feeling that the young man was doing everything he could to prevent Robert having any reason to visit Baldock Street.

Driving to the outskirts of the town, having left Joe in Main Street, Robert asked carefully, 'Are you concerned about running into Francis?'

Sammy pulled his mouth down at the corners and shook his head. 'Not really. In a way, I suppose, I'd quite like to see him. It might be quite funny to come face to face with him.'

The boy even had the same sarcastic sense of humour, almost the same turn of phrase. Whilst he didn't speak in the same way, didn't use such lofty wordage – Francis would have said something like, 'it would be most amusing to encounter him' – nevertheless the sentiment expressed was exactly the same.

There was certainly no doubt in Robert's mind now – if there ever had been – that Samuel Lawrence was indeed his brother's son.

As he swung into the driveway, he said, 'Here we are, then,' and drew the vehicle to a halt.

As he opened the front door and ushered Sammy inside, Louise's high heels came tapping across the hall floor. Even in wartime, Louise managed to dress in the latest fashion: a knee-length tan wool dress with padded shoulders. However did she do it, Robert thought, and couldn't help feeling a pang of guilt for all those women who were having to 'make do and mend', including, he suspected, Jeannie.

Her high-pitched, affected voice echoed shrilly through

the hall. 'There you are, Robert. I've sent for Francis and Edwin. Your father's worse. Your mother's with him now. Who's this?' she said, without seeming to pause for breath.

'This, my dear, is Samuel Lawrence. My father's only grandson.'

Louise's face was scandalized. 'You've brought him here? Now? You're not thinking of taking him upstairs to see your father, are you? Oh surely not.'

'I am about to do exactly that, my dear. At my father's express wish.'

'But you can't. What about Francis? He'll be here at any moment.'

'Francis can go to hell for all I care,' Robert muttered and then, looking her straight in the eyes, added, 'and probably will.'

He saw the colour suffuse her face as her glance darted from him to the young man at his side and back again.

'If you'll excuse us, Louise . . .' and Robert gestured towards the staircase.

He led the way into the bedroom realizing that the moment for the boy must be very difficult. Even he was unsure of what his mother's reaction towards Sammy would be. But the woman who was sitting on the far side of the bed as they entered rose with difficulty from her chair and came round the end of the bed to meet them. 'Robert, oh my dear. You've brought him. Thank goodness. He's been making himself worse with fretting.'

She turned then to Sammy and studied him intently for a moment before stepping in front of him and putting her hands on his shoulders. She did not, Robert was relieved to see, make any attempt to kiss the young man, but contented herself with smiling at him and saying softly, 'I am your grandmother, my dear. I am very pleased to meet you.'

For a moment Sammy's cool composure seemed to crumble and Robert caught sight of a side of his nature that came from the Lawrence genes. After all, poor Grace had been a gentle creature and his other grandparents were George Lawrence and Nell. Robert almost smiled at the thought of his maternal grandmother. Why, there was even a drop or two of Scottish blood in young Sammy's veins. How could he have believed that Sammy would be just like Francis, as ruthless and selfish and . . .

But there was a likeness for his mother was commenting upon it now.

'You're just like Francis was at the same age. Come.' She laid her hand on Sammy's arm and urged him to step closer to the bed. 'Come and meet your grandfather. He has been waiting for this moment.'

Thirty-Two

'Did you know about it, Mam?' Joe demanded as soon as he set foot across the threshold. 'About Sammy going to see old man Gorton?'

Jeannie answered him with another question. 'Where is he?'

'I've just said, gone to see the old man. He's dying. Did you know?'

'Aye. Robert – Mr Robert came here to ask me if Sammy knew about . . .' She gestured with her hand. 'Well, everything.'

'He met us in Hull.' Joe put on an affected tone. 'Took us to a fancy posh restaurant for lunch.' Then he relaxed into his normal way of speaking, adding, as if reluctant to give praise even when it was deserved, 'Mind you, it were good.' Jeannie felt his glance upon her. 'He's been here again then?'

'Och now, dinna you start. I've had enough all these years with your father seeing things that aren't there.'

'Oh well, you know what they say? There's no smoke without fire.'

'The only fire that's here is the one in the grate there and it's nearly out, so you'd best be fetching the coal in,' she snapped and turned away, afraid lest he should see the flames that smouldered within her, so deeply banked down that they were not even allowed to smoke. She picked up the tray to take it upstairs to Nell, who, more often than not these days, stayed in bed. But her thoughts were a couple of miles away inside another bedroom, unknown to her, but where she imagined old Samuel Hayes-Gorton lay dying.

Robert watched as Sammy approached the bedside to stand looking down at the old man. His namesake was a shadow of the rotund, bewhiskered gentleman he had once been; the proud owner of the Gorton Trawler Company of Havelock. Since his illness, he had shrunk to a skeleton. Coming home each time on leave, Robert noticed the difference more markedly than those who were with him every day.

He knew, before anyone else, that his father would not live much longer and the thought had prompted him to broach the subject of young Sammy's existence. The day they had first spoken of it, the old man was still able to sit out of bed for part of the day near the window with a rug over his knees. Robert had broached the matter carefully, sensitive to his father's feelings.

'You know, I'm sorry, Father, that I have not given you the grandson you wanted.'

Samuel Hayes-Gorton had grunted, his eyes watery, still bright and certainly sharp and knowing. He'd smoothed his white moustache and then squinted up at Robert.

The words had come haltingly. 'Not altogether your fault, m'boy.' There had been a long pause whilst Samuel had gone back to gazing out of the window. Then, very quietly, he had said, 'I do have a grandson though, don't I?'

'Yes, Father. You do.'

Another long silence before the old man had said, 'I have a mind, Robert, to see the boy before . . .' He'd looked up then, straight into his son's eyes, and Robert had seen the knowledge there. Much was said in that exchange of a long look even though no words were spoken. Samuel had let out a long sigh and said, 'Well, soon.'

Robert had touched his shoulder. 'I'll see what I can do.'

And now they were here, standing in the room, almost too late for the sick old man to know. Already his breathing was laboured and every few moments it seemed to stop and everyone held their own breath, fearing they had heard the last of his. But then the stubbornness to hang on would return and he would pull in a breath once more.

As he stood watching, Robert saw his father, propped up against several pillows, open his eyes. The voice issuing from the shrunken form was still remarkably strong. 'Has he come? Is he here? My grandson?'

Mrs Hayes-Gorton bent closer. 'Yes, yes, my dear. Robert has brought him. Young Samuel is here.'

The tired eyes focused and the mouth sagged and then old Samuel gasped, 'My – God!'

'Yes, my dear.' His wife took the words from him, saving him the labour. 'I thought just the same. He's so like Francis was at the same age, but not quite so tall, don't you think?'

She turned then and whispered to Sammy, who was standing rigidly beside the bed, not knowing quite what was expected of him. 'Say something to him. Speak to him.'

Sammy half turned towards Robert as if seeking reassurance of some kind. Robert nodded and the boy turned back towards the old man again. 'Good afternoon, sir. I'm – I'm sorry to see you ill. Mr Robert, he came to meet the ship. He said – he said you'd like to see me.'

A great sigh escaped the old man's lips and his whole body seemed to relax and sink into the pillows. 'I am glad see you – Samuel.' The struggle to speak was supreme t no one present thought to tell him to rest. They knew at although this effort may well be his final one, it was portant to him. For what else was there for him to serve his energies now? 'You've – been to – sea?'

'I'm in the Navy, sir.'

The watery eyes squinted up at him. 'Ah, I see now – ur uniform.'

His breathing rasped again for a minute as he gathered ength to ask, 'You love the sea?'

'Yes, sir,' Samuel said and added with unmistakable ide, 'When we've won the war, I'll still go back to sea. a trawler, more n' like.'

'Gorton trawlers, my boy. Make sure – it's on a Gorton wler. One day – one day they'll be yours . . .'

The eyes closed and the hands on the coverlet were otionless now. Mrs Gorton knelt by the bedside and wed her head. Clutching at her husband's hand, she pt quietly whilst Robert touched Sammy's shoulder and l him from the room.

'Is he – did he . . .?' the boy began.

'No, no, he isn't dead, but I fear it cannot be much nger. He's been drifting in and out of consciousness for couple of days now.'

They had reached the hallway, when the front door w open and Francis marched into the house, for all the rld as if he owned the place. Robert saw him stop in prise as he saw the young boy standing there.

'What the hell . . .?' he began and then his cold eyes rrowed. 'So, dear brother, you thought to bring your stard into the family fold, did you?'

Beside him, Robert felt Sammy stiffen, yet he held head proudly and returned Francis's disdain with a stead composed look.

Robert cleared his throat. 'Father wished to see grandson.'

'Only because you . . .' Francis jabbed his cane at Ro ert, 'put him up to it.' The smirk on his face was malicio now. 'Still afraid he's cut you out of his will as threatened? Thought you'd get back in favour by the ba door, eh? Well, no bastard's going to inherit the Gort company, let me tell you . . .'

'I want nowt to do with your company.' Sammy's voi rang out, cool and calm. 'Except perhaps to work aboa one of your ships after the war.'

Robert watched in a kind of horrified fascination father and son stared at each other, the nearest they h ever been. He could see now that each was assessing t other, each searching for – and finding at once – t likeness to one another.

Quietly Robert said, 'He's your son, Francis. You kno full well he is.'

Francis let out a bark of laughter. 'Ha! Never. F mother was nothing but a slut, a whore. One of Agg Turnbull's trollops. I doubt she even knew who this bra father was. But she saw a chance to lay the blame at door and you . . .' again he jabbed his ebony cane towar Robert, 'were fool enough, besotted by that red-hair bitch, to believe their tales. Been paying for it all the years. Well, I hope you got your money's worth wh Lawrence was away at sea.'

Robert heard Sammy make a funny noise in his thro and then the boy ran towards the door, pulled it ope leapt down the steps and flew down the driveway.

Through clenched teeth, Robert spat, 'You're the ba

tard, Francis . . .' With two strides he came close to his brother, drew back his arm and punched Francis on his chin. The man fell backwards, sprawling on the floor and as Robert left the house it was to the sounds of Louise running across the hall, crying, 'Oh Francis, oh darling, what has he done to you?'

Thirty-Three

Though Robert climbed at once into his motor car and drove after him, he was unable to find Sammy. And once he reached the town, he knew his search was fruitless. He could be in any one of a dozen pubs. At last he turned towards Baldock Street and knocked upon Jeannie's door.

'He's not here, is he?' he asked, without explanation, when she opened it.

'Who? Sammy?' Jeannie said and then shook her head. 'What happened?'

Robert ran his hand through his hair and said, 'Everything was fine, well, as fine as it could be in the circumstances, if you know what I mean?'

Jeannie nodded and then, swiftly, he recounted the events. 'He just ran out and by the time I'd thumped Francis on the jaw and gone after him, he'd just disappeared. Jeannie, I am sorry.'

'You hit your brother?' she asked, scarcely able to conceal her laughter.

'Oh yes.' He grinned at her. 'We used to fight as kids. I suppose sometimes the feeling never goes away, not even when you're grown up.'

'Just like Joe and Sammy,' she chuckled.

Robert put on his hat. 'Well, I'd better go, seeing as you're obviously not going to invite me in.'

Jeannie grimaced and said, 'I can't. I'm sorry. Nell is having a bad morning. I daren't leave her.'

'She's ill?' Robert frowned in concern.

'Not physically. It's her mind. She seems to live in a little world of her own these days. I daren't leave her for a minute. If she wanders off, I'm searching the streets for her.'

Robert nodded in sympathy. 'I've just found out what that's like.'

'Och, dinna worry about Sammy. He'll come rolling home, drunk as a lord, when he's ready.'

As he turned to go, she called after him, 'I'm sorry about your father. It's – it's a difficult time for you.'

He glanced back at her, taking the picture of her into his memory. 'Thank you, Jeannie.' Very softly, he added, 'Goodbye, my dear.'

Samuel Hayes-Gorton lived another week after meeting his grandson for the first, and only, time. The news of his death soon spread around the local community and the subject of his will was general speculation for days though only the family were, at first, aware of its detailed contents.

He had not, as he had threatened, cut his middle son off with the proverbial shilling, but had left his company to his three sons, although Francis Hayes-Gorton had a 49 per cent share. He had, of course, made generous provision for his wife for her lifetime, but the codicil to the will, made only six days before his death and the day after his meeting with his grandson, altered the share of his two younger sons. Instead of the remaining 51 per cent being divided equally between Robert and Edwin, it was split into three parts of 17 per cent each to the two brothers and to '*Samuel Lawrence, of Baldock Street, Havelock, being my eldest son's natural son and, therefore, my grandson.*'

'This is outrageous!' Francis jumped to his feet as the lawyer read out the will to the family gathered together after the funeral. 'I shall contest it. He wasn't of sound mind. This is your doing, Robert.' He pointed his finger towards his brother, who sat calmly with a slight smile on his mouth. 'I won't have it. I won't be outvoted by the two of you and some slut's bastard who imagines he's a claim on this family. I've never acknowledged him as mine and I never will. If he's anybody's, then he's yours.'

Again he jabbed his finger towards Robert, who said calmly, 'Then in that case, he still has a right to his inheritance. He's still Father's grandson.'

For a brief moment Francis's handsome face twisted into ugliness. He picked up the chair he had been sitting on and hurled it against the wall, causing a picture to fall, shattering the glass. 'You'll pay for this, Robert. I'll ruin you, I'll . . .'

'Francis, control yourself,' came their mother's imperious tones. 'Robert had nothing to do with your father changing his will. He knew no more about it than you until this moment. If anyone's to blame, then it is me. I witnessed the codicil and approved its terms. But the suggestion came from your father. It was what he wanted, and, I'll have you know, he was in complete charge of his senses almost until the end. Physically, yes, he was very weak but his mind was clear and . . .' her gaze upon her eldest son was unflinching as she added, 'I would be prepared to stand up in court and say as much.'

Now Edwin, who had not spoken, rose. 'There will be no need for that, Mother. We shall resolve this between the three of us. The young man in question is not old enough yet, I believe, to take an active part on the Board anyway. His shares – if I understand the terms of the will correctly – are to be administered by Robert until young Samuel attains the age of twenty-one. Is that correct, Mr Paige?'

The lawyer nodded.

'I don't care for all the legalities,' Francis spat. 'I won't have any of it. You'll be hearing from *my* lawyer on the matter.'

With that parting shot, he strode from the room leaving his mother shaking her head sadly and murmuring, 'Oh dear.'

'Don't worry, Mother,' Edwin said. 'We all know Francis. He has a brilliant mind and has every right, not only as the eldest son but also because of his business acumen, to the major share of the company. But that doesn't mean we're going to let him ride roughshod over us. Does it, Robert?'

Robert smiled. 'Well, at the moment I'm reeling from hearing that I am still a part of the business. I thought I was to be – er – cut off.'

Mrs Hayes-Gorton chuckled. 'Your father thought he could bring you to heel by his threats.' She leant forward across the polished surface of the mahogany dining table. 'But I'll tell you something now. He was secretly rather proud of you for having the courage to decide your own future. Even I knew he never meant to cut you off.'

'Didn't I tell you so, Robert old chap.' Edwin, too, was smiling as he put his hand on Robert's shoulder. 'And Francis will come around too. Just give him time.'

To that, Robert made no reply.

The legal-looking letter arrived for Sammy long after he had returned to his ship. Jeannie put it on the mantelpiece, unopened, but often over the following weeks her glance would go to the long, white envelope wondering what lay inside it.

But then other matters demanded her attention and she forgot all about the letter addressed to Mr Samuel Lawrence.

Thirty-Four

Lieutenant Robert Gorton stood on the bridge. They were nearing the end of a sweep and his eyes were sore, red-rimmed with tiredness from gazing out across the grey waters. They had completed four days at sea and were returning to Havelock for replenishment and a few brief hours ashore before coming out again to sweep the same area of sea again and again and again to clear a safe channel for the convoys.

They were searching for acoustic mines now as well as the magnetic type.

Would it never end? Robert asked himself. Almost four years already and still the war raged on. At least now, he thought, the Americans were in too. Surely with their might, the end could not be in doubt. Yet, when would it come? And how many more young men would lose their lives before it was all over?

Robert blinked, trying to focus his attention once more upon the water. It was so cold that he couldn't imagine ever feeling warm again. Not for the first time, did his thoughts turn to the trawler men who spent most of their lives at sea. And he had been one of the privileged few – an owner – who had sent those men out here. Well, now he was one of them and no longer an owner of very much.

Since the Gorton trawlers had been commandeered, half of that number had already been blown up by the very mines they were attempting to clear or had been attacked and destroyed by enemy fighter planes. Two had succumbed to U-boats.

Now he and the men the Hayes-Gortons had once employed were – quite literally – in the same boat. Fighting not only a common foe, but the wind and the sea and the terrible cold.

And what, he wondered, would there be for any of them who did manage to survive to go back to?

Some fishing in the coastal waters still went on and if he knew his elder brother – his scheming, devious, yet clever brother – Francis would already have transferred his business interests to war work of some sort. But it would undoubtedly be an effort for the war that would be profitable for him too. Oh yes, thanks to Francis, there would be something for Robert to go back to. But for what?

Here on this ship, a battered old trawler turned minesweeper it might be, he had earned the respect the men gave him. He had earned his place as 'Jimmy the One'. Now, when they called him 'sir', it was more than because he was the son of their employer.

Maybe, Robert thought, as he passed his hand over his tired eyes once more and squinted at the clouds above, raking the sky for the tell-tale signs of enemy aircraft, maybe, he mused, if he survived, he'd stay on in the Royal Navy.

His brothers would run the company, or what was left of it. His wife would spend most of her time in London with her smart friends as she still did, despite the dangers.

And Jeannie? His heart contracted at the thought of her. She would be waiting for her Tom to come home from the sea.

Thinking of her, as he often allowed himself to do

through the long cold hours, Robert promised himself that after the war, he'd see what he could do for Tom.

During their time together aboard this ship, the man had never once let his animosity for his former employer show, had never let slip to the ship's company just who and what Robert Gorton had been before the war. He had kept the pact they had made.

When Robert and Tom had come face to face for the first time aboard the minesweeper, he had seen the surprise in the other man's face, not only for the ironic twist of fate that out of all the ships on the ocean they should end up serving on the same one, but also when he first heard his superior officer addressed without the 'Hayes' to his name. And Robert had seen something else in the man's eyes: a wariness that he himself was feeling too. Later, Robert had come to Tom's radio operator's room.

He'd come straight to the point of his visit. 'I suggest we leave any differences we have ashore, Lawrence, don't you? And the circumstances of our backgrounds. It's known I had some connection with trawlers before the war, as I'm sure that's the case for you too. But no one knows exactly what. I prefer it that way.'

There was a note of command in Robert's voice. 'Are we agreed?' he prompted when Tom made no reply.

When Tom had looked at him, he had seen the insolence in the man's eyes, but all Tom had said was 'Aye, aye,' and had added, with the slightest hesitation, 'Sir.'

Robert stretched his face and blinked again, forcing himself to concentrate. It was one thing to let his thoughts wander when on watch, but not for one moment must he relax his vigil even though they were on their way home.

They passed Spurn Head and entered the mouth of the Humber, anchoring until the high tide made their passage through the dock gates possible. With the outline of the buildings on the fishdock clearly visible against the skyline, the whole atmosphere aboard the ship seemed to relax.

Robert watched Tom Lawrence walking along the deck, the slip of white paper he was holding fluttering in the breeze. The man seemed to be hesitating about what to do and now Robert saw him glance up and look directly at him. For a moment their glances met and held, then Tom moved forward and began to climb the ladder to the bridge.

As the captain half-turned and held out his hand for the piece of paper, Tom saluted and said, 'Message for Lieutenant Gorton, sir. Of a personal nature, sir.'

The senior officer's eyebrows rose and he glanced at Robert with a slight frown of disapproval on his forehead. At sea, such an occurrence was strictly against regulations, but here, almost home, even the skipper relaxed a little too. When he said nothing, Tom persisted, 'With your permission, sir?'

The sub-lieutenant due to take over the watch from Robert, had arrived on the bridge a few moments before Tom and so, released from his duties, Robert turned towards Tom and saw at once that in the man's eyes now was a mixture of anxiety and sympathy.

'Sir . . .' Even his voice was hesitant. 'I am very sorry, but I have some bad news for you.'

Robert swallowed but said nothing. He was glad that Tom Lawrence could not read his thoughts, wild and irrational as they were. All he could think of at this moment was, it can't be Jeannie else he would be the one receiving the bad news, not me.

Tom was speaking again and Robert forced himself to listen. 'It's your – your wife, sir. She's been killed in an air raid in London.'

Poor Louise, poor little girl, was Robert's first thought.

The pretty, bright, pleasure-seeking child, who had not been able to resist London even when the Blitz had been at its height, was gone, her butterfly life crushed. He felt a deep sorrow, not so much because he loved her, for he did not and never had, not in the same way that he loved . . . No, no, he must not think of her, not now. Poor Louise, he thought again, she hadn't deserved to die in that way and so young too.

Tom Lawrence was still standing before him, making no move to leave him alone with his supposed grief. 'I'm sorry, sir, but there's something else. Your brother, Mr Francis . . .'

Robert's eyes bored into the other man's, his voice harsh and abrupt. 'What about him?'

'He was killed too, sir. In – in the same air raid.'

Now Robert turned away abruptly before Tom could read anything in his face. Robert knew that Tom Lawrence was editing the truth. He could have said, so easily, that they were together, maybe even in the same bed. For without being told, Robert knew, instinctively, that was the case. He had felt for some time, though he had no proof, that he was being cuckolded by his own brother.

What a shame, he thought dispassionately, that Francis had not been the chosen one to unite the two companies by marrying Louise Hathersage.

Then he realized and the sudden knowledge hit him like a forty-foot wave.

He, Robert Gorton, was now not only the senior partner and head of the Gorton-Hathersage Trawler Company, but he was also Louise's next of kin and consequently would inherit her shares too. It was an awesome responsibility.

Now briefly, he turned back to face Tom. Quietly, he said, 'Thank you for taking it upon yourself to be the one to tell me. It can't have been easy for you.'

Tom gave a quick nod, saluted and turned away. As Robert watched him go he thought, I wonder if he realizes just how very lucky he is to have Jeannie as his wife.

'So, your fancy man is free now and head of a giant company.'

Two days later on a brief shore leave, Tom faced Jeannie across the kitchen table, a sneer in his tone and bitter resentment in his eyes.

Calmly Jeannie continued kneading the dough for the bread she was making, though deep inside she sighed. She glanced at him and, her mouth tight, said, 'I've more things on my mind than listening to your jealous imagination running riot. What are you going to do about the boys running away to sea? Can't you do anything to get them brought home?'

Tom shrugged. 'They're eighteen in a few months. Hardly worth it now, anyway. I still haven't worked out how they could have got away with it. Didn't you ask *him* to pull a few strings to get them out?' When Jeannie did not answer, he added, resentfully, 'I bet it was Sammy's fault. He'll have shamed our Joe into going. Made him feel a coward if he didn't.' Tom fell silent and Jeannie glanced at him, wondering, fleetingly, if that was what had made Tom volunteer for the Reserves. He wouldn't have wanted to be branded a coward when all the other fishermen were joining up.

'They went together,' Jeannie said aloud. 'I think it was mutual agreement.'

Tom gave a snort of derision. 'Huh, pull the other one, Jeannie. They don't get on. You can't tell me they've gone together. They were always fighting.'

'Well, they have and now they're fighting side by side

288

instead of each other.' Her fear for their safety lent a bitter sharpness to her tone. 'War makes strange bedfellows of folk.' She looked at him meaningfully now.

Tom sat down in the chair by the fire. 'It does that,' he said heavily. Softly, he added, 'It was me told him, y'know?'

The time for pretence was over. There was no point in feigning ignorance for Jeannie knew full well who Tom was talking about.

'About his wife and his brother?'

'Yeah.' He paused and then added, 'First time I've ever felt sorry for him, y'know? Fancy being told that your wife's been killed in bed with your brother.'

Jeannie gasped. 'You told him that?'

'Not in so many words, but he knew. Oh he knew all right.' He looked up at her then. 'Jeannie, just tell me. Please. Is there anything going on between you and him?'

Jeannie set the bowl of dough beside the warm fire to prove and knelt down on the hearthrug. Leaning her elbows on his knees she looked into his face and said, 'Tom, there is nothing between us. Never has been and never will be. I was brought up a good, God-fearing Scottish lassie and the vows I made in the kirk to you I have kept and I always will.'

There was silence for a moment. 'Till death us do part, eh Jeannie?'

Jeannie swallowed the lump in her throat for every day death was very close to both of them. She reached up and touched his cheek. 'You're a good husband, Tom Lawrence, and a good father, I'll never say otherwise. But I just wish you'd stop imagining things that aren't true.'

He leant down and gathered her into his arms, holding her tightly and burying his face in her hair. Hoarsely he said, 'I'll try, Jeannie, I promise I'll try. But you're everything to me. I love you so much, I just couldn't bear it if . . .'

'And I love you, Tom,' she said and stroked his hair.

She closed her eyes tightly and pressed her face against his shoulder and prayed silently, may God forgive me for this lie.

Thirty-Five

Another legal-looking letter arrived addressed to Mr Samuel Lawrence and joined the first behind the clock on the mantelpiece to await his next leave. And whilst speculation ran rife, no one, this time, seemed to have definite knowledge as to the contents of Mr Francis Hayes-Gorton's will.

'They'll have to pay a lot of death duties, won't they?' went the gossip. 'Two of 'em dying so close together like that.'

'Dunno. Shouldn't think the company's worth all that much just now. More'n half the trawlers have been converted to minesweepers and fishing's difficult even in the near-waters.'

'Aye, ya could be right.'

But the person who could have told them what was in Francis's will, was far out at sea, serving on a destroyer. On his eighteenth birthday, Samuel Lawrence had no idea that he was now a major shareholder in the Gorton-Hathersage Trawler Company.

Aboard the minesweeper, the alarm bell shrilled and the order 'Action Stations' was given. Immediately, they heard the whine of enemy aircraft overhead and Robert looked up to see six screaming down towards the ship. The seven guns on board were given leave to fire independently and the splatter of bullets arced skywards.

Two bombs hurtled from the bellies of the planes swooping low across the deck. They splashed into the sea on the starboard side, sending a plume of water into the air. The ship rocked under the turbulence.

Robert, standing beside the skipper, dispatched a rating to report any damage. The young lad was running along the deck when it took a direct hit. Helplessly, Robert watched as the blast blew the youngster off his feet and over the side of the ship. Several others were lying injured on the deck now, but the guns above the bridge swung to follow the path of the plane, the rapid fire never faltering.

'Fire!' The cry went up as flames erupted from the hole in the deck and, with growing horror, Robert realized that just below where the bomb had fallen was not only a crew room, but the radio operator's room too.

Jeannie's husband could be dead or dying, but though Robert's whole being cried out to scramble down the ladder and run in search of Tom, duty kept him on the bridge, calmly carrying out the orders of his commanding officer.

The next few chaotic minutes seemed to take an eternity to live through until, with the ship burning fiercely and listing badly to port, the captain was forced to give the order to abandon ship.

Only then, when it was an 'every man for himself situation', could Robert go in search of Tom. The heat almost defeated him, singed his hair and scorched his arms as he held them up to shield his face. But desperation drove him on. Jeannie, Jeannie, was all he could think. He must find Tom for Jeannie's sake.

He was slumped over his radio, his fingers still grasping the dials as if he had been trying to send a last urgent message. Robert hauled the inert figure on to his shoulder in an ungainly kind of fireman's lift and, finding a strength he hadn't known he possessed, staggered towards the hole in the side of the ship. Then he pushed Tom through it and followed him into the water below.

For a moment, he thought Tom had sunk beneath the waves, but suddenly, there he was, bobbing up beside him. Robert grabbed at him and began to swim, dragging Tom away from the ship that looked as if it would go to the bottom at any second.

At what he considered a reasonably safe distance, Robert trod water, holding Tom's chin up. 'Hold on, man,' he kept saying. 'Think of your family. Think of Jeannie. For God's sake, hold on.'

At last, with the help of some of the crew, Robert managed to have Tom hauled out of the water before willing hands pulled him into the life-raft too.

They were in range of the coastal lifeboat, but it was four hours before they were found and picked up. Four hours in which Robert held Tom to him, trying to keep him warm, trying to keep him alive.

As the lifeboat man climbed down into the life-raft to help the cold, oil-covered men aboard, one said, 'Let him go, sir. He's dead.'

But Robert clung on to Tom's still form, whispering hoarsely through cracked lips, 'No, oh no. How will I tell her?'

'Come along, sir. We'll have to leave him.'

'We must take him back. We must take his body . . .'

'We can't, sir. The lifeboat's already overloaded. We must think of the living.'

Robert's reason, for a moment, had deserted him, but the calm, rational tones of the lifeboat man brought him to his senses.

'You're right, of course. I'm sorry. I don't know what I'm thinking of.'

Still with reluctance, Robert and the lifeboat man gently tipped Tom's body into the waves. Robert crossed himself, bowed his head and muttered a short prayer.

'Friend of yours, was he, sir?' the man asked kindly.

'Sort of,' was all Robert could say, for all he could think of was, how am I to tell Jeannie?

As Robert stood outside the door of the Lawrence home, part of him wanted so much to see her again and yet his heart quailed at the news he must bring her. He glanced briefly over his shoulder up and down the street and saw a lace curtain fall back into place.

Within minutes, all the neighbours would be aware of his visit. He knew that. But this time, it was different. This time only he could be the bearer of this news, painful though it was.

The door opened and she was standing before him and as he said swiftly, 'May I come in . . .' she pulled the door wider and gestured for him to step inside.

Almost before she had closed the door, shutting out the inquisitive gaze of the neighbours, he turned to face her and said, 'I'm sorry to come with bad news.'

Her hand was still on the door knob and now she leant against the door, staring at him. 'It's Tom, isn't it?'

He nodded. 'I'm afraid so. We were attacked by enemy aircraft and the ship took a direct hit just above where he worked. It caught fire and he was badly burnt even before I got to him. We began to take water fast and we had to abandon ship. I kept him with me, tried to keep his spirits up, but his injuries and then being so long in the water, well, I'm so sorry, Jeannie. He died in my arms.'

She moved woodenly to sit in a chair and rest her arms on the table. Robert followed her. He did not sit down but went towards the range where he reached up for the tea caddy on the mantelpiece above, catching sight as he did so of the two unopened letters. He spooned tea into the pot and poured boiling water into it from the kettle which always stood on the hob. Then he took two cups and saucers down from the dresser and set them on the table.

'Milk?' he enquired gently and Jeannie gestured towards a pantry where the milk stood on a cold stone slab.

Moments later he pushed a steaming cup of strong tea towards her and ordered gently, 'Drink it.'

Automatically, she obeyed him. He noticed, as she put the cup back on the saucer with a clatter, that her hands were trembling. 'You – you tried to save him?'

He said nothing, merely nodded.

Her eyes filled with tears. 'Thank you. Whatever you did, thank you.'

He looked at her directly then, stared at her for a long moment before he said, 'Anyone would have done the same.'

She nodded, but hoarsely she whispered, 'Oh yes, I know that. But only *I* know what it must have cost you.'

He closed his eyes and shook his head slowly. 'Oh Jeannie. I would do anything to spare you pain. I would even – even have sacrificed my own life if it would have brought back the man you love.'

She could not tell him, she could not say the words, for it would have felt so wrong, would have been wicked at this moment. But never before had she loved him quite as much as she did now, sitting opposite him, watching the lines of sadness etched deeply upon his face knowing that he had fought with a desperate bravery to save Tom, risking his own life, not so much for the man himself, but to bring her husband back to her.

How very much at this moment she loved Robert

Gorton. But her mouth remained closed and the words unspoken.

The boys were given compassionate leave and they stood either side of Jeannie and Nell during the memorial service in the church where she had married Tom and where too, years before, Nell had married George. Jeannie mourned her husband deeply and sincerely. He had been a good man and she had loved him, perhaps in the way that one loves a brother or a good friend, but not, she knew now, as a lover with a searing, consuming passion. She had never felt the trembling of her knees nor the pounding of her heart nor the sudden dryness in her throat for Tom as she felt when she saw Robert.

He was standing behind her now. A little way back from the family mourners, keeping a respectful distance. As they came out of the church and into the grey November day, Jeannie made as if to move towards him, but Joe, his arm firmly through hers, steered her towards the curving pathway leading to the gate.

'What's he doing here?' Sammy, on her other side, muttered.

'He has a right to be here,' Jeannie said. 'He tried to save your father and he was his employer. He's just come to pay his respects. And another thing. That medal they've awarded Tom, well, who do you think put in the recommendation, eh?'

Joe, from his lanky height, looked down at her. 'Well, it wouldn't be him. If you believe that, Mam, then you've not the sense you were born with.'

'Joe!' She looked up at him and despite herself, angry tears filled her eyes.

'Don't talk to Mam like that,' Sammy put in. He was

still smaller than Joe and always would be, but he had taken up boxing and now iron muscles rippled beneath his uniform. Jeannie had the feeling that in the future Joe would not be so ready to pick a fight with his cousin and wondered if that was the very reason that Sammy had taken up the sport.

But Joe was not awed by Sammy's new-found strength. 'I'll talk to *my* mam any way I want, thank you very much.'

Suddenly Jeannie was angry with the pair of them. 'Don't start. Not here. Not now. Look to your Gran, both of you.' She glanced at them, leaving neither in any doubt as to her feelings as she said pointedly, 'She is grandmother to you both, after all.'

Then she pulled her arm from Joe's, turned deliberately around and marched back towards Robert. Defiantly, she held out her hand towards him and said clearly, 'I want to thank you for all you did to try to save my husband. Please excuse my boys. They are too distressed today to know their duty.'

Then before giving him chance to reply Jeannie turned away again, back towards her family. She took hold of Nell's arm and said kindly, but firmly, 'Come, Gran, it's time we were away home.'

As they left the churchyard, she did not look back towards Robert, but beneath the trees near the wall she suddenly spotted another figure, dressed from head to toe in black, a veil over her face.

Aggie Turnbull.

Thirty-Six

'So, are you going to open your letters, then?'

Sammy scowled towards the mantelpiece. 'There'll be nowt I want to read in them,' he muttered.

'Aw, go on, Sam. At least see what they say,' Joe encouraged, but Sammy's scowl only deepened.

'Oh well, in that case . . .' Jeannie said, stepping towards the hearth and reaching up for the two envelopes. 'I left them for you because they're addressed to you and even though you are still underage legally and I have every right, I thought . . .' She held the letters in her hands now, turned one over and made as if to open it. 'Seeing as you're doing a man's work now, you'd a right to handle your own affairs. Seems I was wrong.'

As she slid her finger under the flap to tear it open, Sammy lunged forward and snatched the letters from her hands. 'I'll open them mesen when I'm good an' ready.'

Jeannie shrugged. 'Well, they've been sat there for weeks now. You'd best get on with it.'

Glowering, Sammy slit open the envelopes and unfolded the letters, smoothing them out on the table. Then, reading the dates, he picked up the first one. Jeannie and Joe watched the expression on his face alter as he read. First there was surprise and disbelief, then a brief delight. Then as he scanned the second letter, his face grew red with anger. Suddenly, he picked up both letters and tore them into shreds.

'Wait a minute . . .' Jeannie reached out. 'Whatever are you doing?'

'I want none of it,' Sammy muttered through clenched teeth. 'I want nowt to do with any of them. You're me family. Not them. I don't want to be a – a Hayes-Gorton.'

He stepped towards the range as if to throw the pieces of paper on to the fire, but Joe barred his way. 'Oh no, you don't. Not till you've told us properly what's in them letters.'

They began to struggle, gripping each other's shoulders, wrestling to gain supremacy, whilst the fragments of the paper fluttered to the floor.

'Stop it, both of you, else I'll bang your heads together . . .' And when they didn't stop at her bidding, Jeannie did just that, their two skulls coming together with a crack.

'Ow!'

'What did ya do that for, Mam?' Joe said ruefully, rubbing his head.

'If you behave like bairns, then I'll treat you like bairns. Now then, son . . .' She turned to Sammy. 'You just sit down at that table and piece those letters together and tell us what's in them that's made you so angry.'

Grudgingly, Sammy picked up the scraps of paper and began, like tackling a jigsaw puzzle, to sort out the pieces.

'The first letter said that old man Hayes-Gorton . . .' he still refused, Jeannie noticed, to refer to Samuel as his grandfather 'left me 17 per cent of the shares in the Gorton-Hathersage Trawler Company.'

Joe whistled. 'Blimey, Sam, you're rich.'

Sammy's mouth tightened. 'Huh, that's not all. The second letter, would you believe, ses that Francis Hayes-Gorton left the whole of his fortune divided equally between Louise Hayes-Gorton and his natural son . . .'

Jeannie saw Sammy raise his eyes and look straight at her. 'Samuel Lawrence.'

Now Jeannie felt her legs give way beneath her and she sat down heavily on a chair, resting her arms on the table. 'He acknowledged you? After all this time of denying your existence, he actually says that – that you're his son?'

'Seems like it.' Sammy was still tight-lipped.

'Why did he leave the other half to her?' Joe put in, puzzled. 'She's Mr Robert's wife, ain't she?'

Jeannie saw Sammy look up at Joe. Now there was a smirk on his face. 'Bit of gossip that's missed those flapping ears of yours, our Joe? Mr Francis and Mr Robert's wife were . . .' He glanced swiftly at Jeannie. 'Well, y'know.'

Joe blinked for a moment or two and then his face cleared. 'Oh, I get yer. My God! Were they really?' He thought for a moment and then with a sly glance towards his mother said, 'Well, suppose you can't blame her if her husband went visiting elsewhere . . .'

It did not go unnoticed by Jeannie, but for once she chose to let the innuendo pass.

'So, Sammy,' she said instead, 'you're a man of means now, are you?'

He stood up, shoving all the pieces of paper into a heap again, though this time he made no effort to burn them. 'No, I aren't. I don't want none of it. You hear me? Not one penny.'

He left the room and they heard the back-door slam.

'Silly bugger!' Joe muttered. For once Jeannie did not reprimand him.

Robert came to see her later the same afternoon, knocking on the door and standing hesitantly outside on the street, until she persuaded him to step across the threshold. She ushered him into the front parlour and invited him to sit down. He declined and instead stood awkwardly in the centre of the room twirling his cap between restless fingers.

'I'm not going back to sea yet. I have what they call survivors' leave.' He paused and she guessed that he was feeling guilty because he was a survivor and Tom was not. He cleared his throat and went on. 'I just came to see if there was anything I could do. If there was anything you need.'

'We're fine. At least,' Jeannie smiled sadly, 'as fine as we can be.'

'I know. It must be very hard for you, especially with the boys away too. Very hard. And the old lady?'

His words were like a jolt. Old lady! Was that how he thought of Nell Lawrence? Perhaps it was how everyone thought of her now? Well, she supposed with a shock, Nell was old now and she probably looked older than her years anyway.

Jeannie sighed and shrugged. 'I'm not even sure she understands what's happened. That Tom has gone.'

Robert nodded and said again, 'It must be very difficult for you.'

There was an awkward silence between them and a tension too. Jeannie felt it and knew he must feel it also. She had the overwhelming desire to fling herself into his arms, knowing that he would hold her and comfort her and take care of her.

But she could not. He would be going back to sea. He was leaving and there was always the possibility that he would not return. In that moment, she knew that she had to tell him. She could not let him leave her not knowing how she felt about him.

'Please, won't you sit down a moment.'

'I must go, I . . .' Then she saw him hesitate and knew

that there was something in her face that made him move to a chair and perch uncomfortably on the edge of it. She sat down opposite him and clasped her hands so tightly in front of her that her knuckles were white.

'I'm going to say something to you now. I should not be saying it. Not now. Not so soon after Tom's death and on the very day we've held a service for him. I'll probably be condemned to eternal damnation for it.' She gave a wry smile and hurried on. 'And I don't want you to say – or do anything – when I've said it. I just want you to go. But it has to be said. I – I can't let you go back without you knowing – how – how I feel about you.'

She saw him start physically, saw the flame of hope leap into his eyes. He breathed her name, 'Jeannie.' Just that. Just her name. 'Jeannie.'

'I was very fond of Tom,' she went on. 'He was a good man. A good husband and father and I – I thought I could love him.'

She thought back now in her own mind, but not saying the words aloud, how she had believed that Tom Lawrence would be like his father who had reminded her so much of her own beloved father. She had been disillusioned and yet she was still able to say quite truthfully that Tom had been a good man.

'I loved him but I was never *in love* with him. I never knew what it was to fall in love until . . .' She licked her lips nervously. 'Until I met you.'

'Jeannie . . .' He was up and out of his chair and taking the two strides that it took to reach her.

'No, no,' she cried and held up her hands, palms outwards, to fend him off. 'Please, don't. Don't say or do anything. It wouldn't – wouldn't be right. It's bad enough that – that I'm even saying this at all. Please . . . don't.'

Reluctantly he sank back into the chair.

Flatly now, she said, 'I just had to say something. I couldn't let you go back without – without telling you. I mean, Havelock could be bombed or you could . . .' The words stuck in her throat.

His face was serious but there was more life and hope in his eyes than she could ever remember seeing. 'I'll come back to you, Jeannie. I promise you. And you – you take care of yourself.'

He rose from his chair. 'And now I must go or I shall be guilty of an action that I might well feel ashamed of.' They looked at each other, their eyes meeting as they both remembered. He smiled and said softly, 'And I wouldn't want that to happen. Not again.'

As he passed close to her on his way to the door, he touched her shoulder gently. 'Remember I love you, Jeannie, as I have never loved another woman in my life. It feels as if I have loved you for ever.'

And then he was gone, closing the door behind him. As she heard the back-door close too, Jeannie picked up a cushion from the sofa and buried her face against it to stifle the sobs that would no longer be held in check.

Robert felt guilty at feeling so happy. It didn't seem right that he should be so full of hope and actually, for the first time for as long as he could remember, looking forward to the future. Not when that future was only going to happen because of the death of two people: his wife Louise and Tom Lawrence. And yet, he couldn't help it. But for a while he must keep his happiness in check. He was still supposed to be mourning his wife and paying respectful tribute to a man who had been his employee and a shipmate in wartime.

But privately Robert dreamt of a future with Jeannie

and he couldn't stop himself from making plans. After the war was over – and it must be soon – he would return home. He would pay court to Jeannie properly and openly and after a decent interval they would be married. He would sell the house Louise had furnished and decorated with her own individual taste. It had never, for a moment, been his and he would buy Jeannie another home. No, no, he corrected himself, this time they would buy one together.

So it was with a happy heart and bounce in his step that Robert strode up the gangway of the minesweeper with an air of 'Let's get this damned war finished and get home again'.

Thirty-Seven

Now why, Jeannie questioned over the following days, had Aggie attended Tom's funeral? She was deliberately trying to keep her thoughts from straying to Robert and at least the puzzle gave her something else to concentrate her mind on. The boys had returned to sea and the house, with just her and Nell in it, was lonely. Nell was no company now for she spent her days lost in a little world of her own. Jeannie wondered if she even realized that she had now lost every member of her family except her grandsons.

So, with the figure of the black-clad woman still in her thoughts, the day Jeannie opened the back-door to find Aggie standing there was no surprise.

'May I come in?'

Jeannie hesitated, glancing over her shoulder. Nell was in the front room, asleep on the couch. There could be no harm, Jeannie thought, in Aggie stepping into their kitchen. Just for a moment.

She nodded and held the door open.

Aggie stood in the centre of the homely kitchen and looked about her, as if drinking in the scene and committing it to memory. Slowly she pulled her gloves from her hands and moved towards the wooden chair near the fireplace and ran her fingers over its smooth high back.

'Was this George's chair?' she asked and as she turned

305

to look at her, Jeannie was shocked to see tears shimmering in her eyes.

Jeannie nodded and then said, 'Won't you sit down? Would you like a cup of tea?'

But Aggie seemed not to be listening. She was still standing looking down at the time-worn chair and then, very slowly, she moved round and sat down in it.

Jeannie set the kettle to boil and a few moments later she held out a cup of tea to the woman without even asking further if she would like it.

Taking it, Aggie said, 'You must be wondering why I've come?'

'Aye, well. I suppose I am.'

Jeannie sat down in the chair opposite and waited.

'Where's Nell? I don't want to upset her.'

Jeannie gestured with her head towards the next room. 'Asleep. Besides, I shouldna worry. Her mind's . . . Well, let's just say she might not even remember who you are.'

'Poor Nell,' Aggie murmured. 'To come to this. I wouldn't have wished this on her, not even though I've detested her for years.' She smiled wryly. 'Though not, I suspect, as much as she has hated me.'

Once more, as she had been on the few occasions she had come into contact with Aggie Turnbull, Jeannie was surprised at the cultured tones of this woman.

'And I don't hate her now. Not any more,' Aggie was saying. 'She hasn't deserved all the tragedy that has befallen her. To lose her husband . . .' the voice quavered a little, 'and both her children.'

Jeannie said nothing but she was thinking, the nerve of this woman! To sit here in Nell's kitchen and talk of her loss as if they had been bosom friends, when in fact Aggie had played a part in Grace's downfall. The very nerve . . .

The blue eyes were now regarding Jeannie steadily. 'I'm not as black as I'm painted, you know. I loved Grace like my own daughter.' The smile on her mouth was wistful now. 'If things had been different, she might well have been *my* daughter. She should have been my daughter. Not Nell McDonald's.'

'What – what do you mean?'

Aggie leant her head back against the chair. 'George Lawrence and me. We were walking out together. We'd talked about getting engaged to be married. A proper engagement, you know. For a year or so. Not like now when they're rushing to the altar. Living for today because they don't know if there's even going to be a tomorrow.'

Jeannie stiffened and gripped the arms of her chair. But she did not interrupt Aggie.

'Yes, we were going to be married. Me and George.' There was a pause and then a bitter note crept into her tone as she said, 'And then the herring girls came and with them, Nell McDonald.'

For a long moment there was silence and as Jeannie opened her mouth to prompt Aggie in her story, there was a sudden noise and both women in the kitchen jumped as the door opened and Nell stood there, as if on cue.

Nell glanced from one to the other and then her gaze rested on Aggie. Jeannie watched in amazement as recognition flared in Nell's eyes. Gone, in an instant, was the vacant look of the past months. Nell's eyes flashed and her mouth tightened.

'What is she doing in *my* kitchen?' she asked and her tone spat venom. Already Aggie was rising from the chair, setting her cup on the table and reaching for her gloves. 'I'll be going, Jeannie. I don't want to upset her.'

'Her? *Her?* I have a name.'

'I know your name. Only too well.' Now Jeannie could see that Aggie's patience was at an end. 'Oh yes, I know your name all right, Nell McDonald.'

'Lawrence,' Nell screeched. 'And dinna you be forgetting it.'

'I'm not likely to do that, Nell. Since you're the one who wrecked my life.'

'Oho, so it's ma fault you became a whore, is it? But you took revenge right enough, didn't you? Taking my daughter down the way you did.'

Softly now and sadly, Aggie said, 'I would never have harmed a hair of her head. Grace was the daughter I never had. The daughter I should have had. *His* daughter.'

Nell seemed about to speak, but Aggie had control now and held up her hand. 'No, Nell, you shall hear me out. After all these years, you shall know the truth. When George fell in love with you and left me, it broke my heart. And my heart never mended. Oh, I was foolish, I admit that. I went a little mad for a while. I thought I could fill my life with fun and laughter and – and other men. By the time I came to my senses, it was too late. All too late. My reputation was in shreds.' She nodded towards Nell. 'Aye and you did your share in spreading the gossip. So, I did become what everyone said I was. But there was no one, not any man, who could ever fill George's shoes. And then Grace came into my life. A little piece of the man I loved. I had watched her grow, and Tom, too, from a distance, and then suddenly, she came to my house one day. She came for a little fun. To dress up and look pretty for while.' She leant forward. 'For a few hours she wanted to get away from the stink of fish and the net on the wall and the worry of wondering whether her father and her brother were going to come home again from the sea. She just wanted a little harmless fun, Nell. That was all.'

'All? All, you say? To become a – a whore, like you? To – to . . .' Nell spluttered, her mouth unable to form the dreadful words.

Aggie was shaking her head. 'Now that is where you're wrong, Nell. Grace never lay with any other man than Francis Hayes-Gorton. And that only because she loved him and believed he loved her.'

Nell advanced towards Aggie threateningly. 'How dare you even speak of my daughter in that way!'

'Oh I dare, Nell, because it's the truth. I've only come here today because I wanted Jeannie to know the truth. I no longer hate you, Nell. I feel sorry for you . . .'

'I'm no' needin' your pity,' Nell spat, but Aggie carried on as if she had not spoken. 'I feel sorry that you have lost them all now. You don't deserve that. And no mother should go to her grave believing her daughter a bad woman. She wasn't, Nell, truly she wasn't.'

For a moment Nell stared at the woman and then suddenly her features crumpled and she covered her face with her hands. Swiftly, Jeannie moved to her and put her arms about her, holding her close. Over her shoulder, she said, 'I think you'd better leave,' but the words of dismissal were not spoken harshly but with more understanding than Jeannie had ever thought she would be able to use towards Aggie Turnbull.

'I'm sorry,' Aggie whispered and she made to leave. 'I didn't mean to upset her.'

With head bowed, Aggie passed through the back door and closed it quietly behind her.

Thirty-Eight

They spent a restless night. Jeannie lay awake listening
to Nell tossing and turning in the next room, anxious
lest Aggie's visit would tip the elderly woman completely
into the realms of confusion. In the morning she was
surprised to find that Nell was up early and downstairs
in the kitchen, singing. When Jeannie descended the
stairs, her head aching behind her eyes after only brief
snatches of sleep throughout the night, she was startled
to find Nell standing at the kitchen wall, braiding the
net.

For a moment, time took a tilt and she thought she was
back in the early days when she had first come to this
house.

'The porridge is on the hob, hen,' Nell said and glanced
up briefly. She turned back to her work, but not before
Jeannie had noticed that her eyes were unnaturally large
and bright, though her fingers were working with the easy
rhythm of old.

'Right,' Jeannie said, moving forward, glancing at Nell
warily for she did not know quite what to make of this
sudden change, this recapturing of her old vigour. Then
Jeannie shrugged. Oh well, she told herself. Perhaps it had
needed a shock to jolt Nell from her lethargy.

Jeannie fervently hoped so.

The day continued as it had begun. Nell even hummed
softly to herself as she worked.

'You should rest now,' Jeannie said in the middle of the afternoon. 'It's lovely to see you back to your old self, but don't try to overdo it.'

Nell cast her a puzzled glance. 'My old self? Why, haven't I been?'

'Well.' Jeannie cast about in her mind for words that were not a lie, but would not tell the whole truth. 'We've both been a bit under the weather recently, haven't we?'

Again, a quick glance and a smile, but Nell's fingers never stopped.

Jeannie longed to question Nell about Aggie's visit and the meaning behind all that had been said. But she dared not take the risk.

Maybe I'll go and see Aggie myself sometime and find out, Jeannie promised herself. Maybe tomorrow, when I've seen Nell up and about, I can slip out. But today, I don't want to leave her.

Jeannie's glance rested again upon the woman who was her mother-in-law, her son's grandmother and Sammy's too. How good it was to see her back to her old self.

The following morning Jeannie was first down to the kitchen, half an ear listening for signs of Nell moving about upstairs. When eight thirty came and she had not appeared, Jeannie went up the stairs and tapped on the bedroom door. 'May I come in?'

There was no reply, so Jeannie opened the door. 'Gran?'

In the half light shining through the drawn curtains, it seemed as if Nell was still asleep, lying on her back, her arms resting above the covers. Jeannie moved across the room, opened the curtains and then came back to stand beside the bed. She touched Nell's shoulder and bent over her. 'Gran?' she said again, but already she knew.

Nell had died, quite peacefully, in her sleep.

The boys got compassionate leave once more only a few weeks after Tom's death.

'I got a bit of flak from my skipper.' Joe grimaced. 'Asked me how many more relatives I'd got who were likely to pop off so that I could wangle more leave. I told him, there's only me mam and even Hitler wouldn't dare to bomb her.' He tried to grin, but it was an effort. Both boys had been very fond of their grandmother and she had never been a cause of animosity between them.

'I've only got forty-eight hours,' Sammy said quietly. 'Mine was quite good about it, surprisingly, 'cos he can be a right bastard about everything else.' They were serving on different ships now and saw little of each other.

'Sammy . . .' Jeannie said warningly.

'Sorry, Mam, but he is. Anyway, I explained about Dad and told him I thought probably the shock had affected Gran worse than we knew. I mean, when we came home for his funeral service, I thought it was all sort of – well – passing her by.'

Jeannie smiled sadly. 'I wish you could have seen her that last day. She was just like her old self. Giving Aggie Turnbull a piece of her mind . . .'

'Aggie Turnbull?' Both young men spoke at once. Then Joe said, 'She was here? In this house?' and Sammy asked, 'Why?'

Jeannie shrugged and said slowly, 'There's a mystery somewhere. Something to do with years ago and George –

your grandfather. But whatever it was, it certainly roused Nell out of her – well – whatever it was she was in.'

Joe glowered. 'More than likely that's what killed her.'

Jeannie stared at him. 'Oh no, dinna say that. It's no' fair. She died of a stroke.'

'Exactly,' Joe said grimly. 'Brought on by the likes of Aggie Turnbull daring to set foot in this house. I'm surprised at you, Mam, even letting her across the threshold.'

Jeannie stared at him. Standing there, a scowl on his handsome features, she had never seen Joe look so very like his father. It was almost as if Tom had come back to life.

And then Sammy spoke in his gentle voice in a tone so reminiscent of his Uncle Robert, that Jeannie was forced to reach out to the nearest chair for support. 'Aggie's not so bad. She . . .'

Joe turned on him viciously. 'Oh aye. Know her well, do ya? Been visiting her whorehouse?' Then he turned and slammed out of the room, leaving Jeannie and a red-faced Sammy staring at each other.

'I've come to see Sammy, really,' Robert said, as he removed his hat and stepped into the house by the front door. His voice dropped to a whisper as he added, 'But it's a good excuse to see you.'

'Ssh, they'll hear you,' Jeannie said and felt herself blushing.

She led him through the front room and into the kitchen, raising her voice to say, 'They're both in here. You've only just caught them. They're away in an hour.'

Both young men rose to their feet as Jeannie said, 'Mr Robert's come to see you, Sammy.'

Jeannie beckoned Joe to follow her from the room, leaving Robert and Sammy alone, but Robert held up his hand. 'No, no, please don't go. That is unless Sammy has any objections?'

He looked towards the young man whose face was set in mutiny. 'I've nowt to say that they don't know already, mister.'

'I see,' Robert said slowly and cast a look at Jeannie, raising his eyebrows slightly in a question. But Jeannie lowered her gaze.

There was a tension in the room already as Robert sat himself at the table opposite Sammy. 'It seems I've left it a little late if you're leaving shortly, but Edwin and I would like you to come to the office to discuss the future of the company. As you know . . .'

Sammy stood up with such a sudden, jerky movement that his chair fell backwards. 'I aren't coming anywhere, mister. Not now, not ever. I want nowt to do wi' you or your company.'

'Sammy,' Jeannie said, 'think what you're saying.'

'You keep out of this, Mam.'

'That's right,' Joe agreed, moving nearer Sammy. 'He's a right to choose what he wants to do.'

'Not until he's at least twenty-one, he hasn't,' Jeannie snapped.

Sammy was quick on the uptake. 'Then I can't be involved in decision-making either.' There was a sneer on his face as he spoke directly to Robert. 'I aren't old enough.'

Carefully, Robert said, 'No, we realize that, but we want you to feel involved. We want you to be involved.'

'Why?' Joe demanded. 'Why should you want him – a bastard who's only just been acknowledged by his own father *after he's dead* – to have a hand in running your company?'

Robert spread his hands. 'It was his grandfather's wish. I admit, Francis's turn-about has surprised us just as much as it has you, but we all know that this is what old Samuel wanted.'

'Oh aye, an' he took his time acknowledging him too, didn't he?' Joe was vociferous. 'Eighteen years, to be exact.' He paused, his eyes narrowing. 'If you ask me, you only want *him* . . .' Joe jabbed his finger first into Sammy's shoulder and then towards Jeannie, 'because it'll give you an excuse to keep seeing *her*.'

'Joe, how dare you? Apologize at once.'

'I won't, 'cos it's true, ain't it, mister?'

Calmly, Robert said, 'Actually, no, it isn't. This has nothing to do with Jeannie . . . your mother and me.'

Careful, Jeannie wanted to say, careful what you say.

Quietly, in his own way, Robert was trying to explain, trying to win the two young men over, but Jeannie knew it was a hopeless task. 'Our two families have been inter-twined for many years. Your Grandfather Lawrence worked for the Gorton Trawler Company all his life, first as a deckie-learner, then as a deck-hand, mate and lastly, for many years, as a skipper. Don't you think he would have been proud to know that you, Sammy, were an important part of that company now?'

'No, 'cos he wouldn't have been proud of his birth. He wouldn't have been proud of the likes of you bringing his daughter down and causing her death, if it comes to that.' It was surprising how Joe was suddenly Sammy's mouth-piece and even more surprising that Sammy himself seemed content to let his cousin speak for him.

'George was a good man who would have stood by

Grace and would have brought up Sammy and loved him. Just as we have done,' Jeannie put in.

'Oh aye,' Joe flashed at her, the bitterness of years suddenly surfacing. 'You've certainly done that. You treat him more like a son than you do me.'

Still Sammy said nothing, but a slow, burning redness crept up his neck.

'So, Sammy,' Robert said, trying to steer the conversation away from dangerous currents. 'Do I take it that you want nothing to do with the company and that, when you're old enough, you intend to sell your shares?'

'Ah, now I see. You want his shares.' Still, it was Joe speaking.

'No,' Robert said quietly, holding on to his temper. But only just, Jeannie thought, as she saw the impatience flicker in his eyes. 'What I want, is for Sammy to take a full and active part in the running of the Company in any way he wants.'

'How generous,' Joe said sarcastically.

'Shut up, Joe,' Sammy muttered at last. 'I'll say what I'm going to do – or not do.'

'Well, get on an' say it then, instead of standing there like a piece of wet fish.'

'I don't want the shares,' Sammy said. 'I don't want anything to do with the Gortons or their ships. When I come back from the war – if I do – I'll get a berth with another line. Mebbe the Hathersage Company or . . .'

Joe gave a bark of wry laughter. 'Don't be daft. They're all one now.'

Sammy's mouth dropped open and he turned back to Robert. 'Is that true?' and when Robert nodded, he said, 'Oh well, that's it then. There'll be no job for me here after the war.'

'Now don't be so hasty,' Robert tried one last time.

'Think it over. None of us can do anything until after the war anyway. My brother's keeping things going as best he can, but with more than half the fleet requisitioned by the Navy, well, there's not a lot of fishing being done anyway. Will you at least promise me, Sammy, that after the war's over you'll see how you feel then?'

'All right,' the young man said stiffly. 'But I aren't going to change me mind.'

Thirty-Nine

'If you marry that man, I'll – I'll never speak to you again, as long as I live. Oh I saw him lookin' at you.' His lip curled. 'And you at him.'

Jeannie stared at Joe and her mouth tightened. 'And who are you to tell me what I should or shouldna do?'

'I'm your son, that's who. Though you seem to have a job remembering which of us is.'

Robert had left and now the three of them stood facing each other in the cramped kitchen.

Jeannie stared at Joe and shook her head sadly. 'So, you'd condemn me to a life of loneliness? And for why? What have you got against him?'

'Me dad hated him and that's good enough for me. He made Sammy the excuse to keep coming here, didn't he?' He glanced at Sammy and then away again. 'It were him, Mr Robert, who attacked me dad's sister. And isn't *he* the result?' He flung his hand out towards Sammy.

Aghast, Jeannie said, 'No, no, you've got it wrong. Mr Francis is – was – his father. Grace loved him.'

'If you believe that, Mam, then you're daft,' Joe sneered. 'After she died, I 'spect Mr Robert thought he'd have a go at you, did he?'

Jeannie was incensed. 'How dare you speak to me like that! Or say such things about your brother . . .'

'He's not my brother. He's my cousin.'

'Well . . .' For a moment Jeannie was confounded.

'Well, yes, that's true, but I still won't have you saying, or believing, such things.'

'If I'm old enough to fight in a war, I'm old enough to say what I like in my own house. And yes, it is my house. I am head of it.'

'Not while there's breath in my body, you're not,' Jeannie retaliated.

'Then,' he said slowly. 'I'll leave.'

'No,' Sammy spoke up. 'If anyone should go, it ought to be me.'

He stood between them, looking at each of them in turn. 'We've never got on, have we, Joe? So, we'd best be going our separate ways. And Mam – for I shall always think of you as me mam, even though I know the truth now—'

'Don't be silly, Sammy,' Jeannie said sharply. 'There's no need to be talking of leaving. This is your home and always will be. All brothers fight.'

'I tell you, he's not my brother,' Joe roared. 'He's a Gorton bastard. And he's too stupid to take what's handed to him on a plate.' Now he turned to face him. 'God, Sam, you are stupid. Turning down all that money.'

'Oh aye, I'm stupid all right. Stupid to stand here and let you be me mouthpiece. But me mind's made up. I'll make me own way in the world. But one thing I do know. I'm not the result of a rape, nor am I Mr Robert's bastard. Like Mam has always said, I'm Francis Hayes-Gorton's son, 'cos there's no way a man like him would have left his will the way he did, if I weren't. Besides, I asked someone who really knows the truth.'

'Oh yes, there is,' Joe said maliciously, referring to the will and ignoring the last part of Sammy's remark. 'He left it like that to get back at his brother, Mr Robert.'

'What do you mean?' Both Jeannie and Sammy spoke at once.

Joe smirked triumphantly. 'Stands to reason, dun't it? We all know – now – that Mr Francis was having an affair with Mr Robert's wife. So, he left his shares in the business between her, what was her name . . .?'

'Louise,' Jeannie murmured, without stopping to think.

Joe cast her a glance but went on, 'Aye, Louise and Sammy. Sammy already had 17 per cent of the shares from the old man, so together him and Louise owned 66 per cent of the company. Between 'em, they had enough to outvote both Robert and Edwin every time, if they wanted.'

Jeannie gasped. 'How do you know all this? How do you know such exact figures?'

Joe grinned. 'It was all set out in Sammy's letters. I pieced 'em together again and read 'em.'

'But that's not the case now, is it?' Sammy said. 'She's dead so Mr Robert's got all her shares too.'

'I know that. I'm just saying that I reckon that was the only reason Mr Francis left *you* anything. Because he wanted to get back at his brother.'

'You could be right, I suppose,' Sammy said, and Jeannie was sure she detected a note of disappointment in his voice. 'But why bother leaving me anything at all? Why not leave the whole lot to her?'

'Because he wanted to get back at 'em all. At Mr Robert by proving all the rumours true. That he had been having an affair with her and also making it that the Hayes-Gorton family had to accept you. You still own forty-one and a half per cent of the company. You could make life difficult for them if you wanted. By heck, I wish it were me. I'd mek 'em all sit up and take notice of me.' He thumped his chest as he said it.

'Well,' Sammy said again. 'I still don't want any part of it. Though he's right about one thing. I'll make up me mind when the war's over. A lot can happen 'afore then.'

'Sammy,' Jeannie was frantic now. 'You didna mean what you said? You will come back here. This is your home.'

The two young men glanced at each other and suddenly Joe grinned and put his arm about Sammy's shoulder. 'Course he will, Mam. Don't worry. I'll see we both come back safe and sound.' He stepped forward and suddenly kissed her cheek. 'You'd not know what to do with yarsen, if you hadn't us to keep sortin' out and getting between us when we start scrapping.'

She hugged them both swiftly. It was time they were leaving now, but before she let go of Sammy she said, 'What did you mean when you said you'd been to see someone who knew the truth about your birth?'

For a moment Sammy looked embarrassed. 'I went to see Aggie Turnbull.'

Now Joe let out a huge guffaw. 'Find you a girl, did she? Or do you fancy an older woman?'

He glanced briefly at Joe. 'Don't be disgusting, Joe. She's old enough to be me grandmother. And no, she didn't find me a girl. I can do that well enough for mesen.' Then he turned back to Jeannie again. 'Mam, she's very ill. She took bad the day after she'd been here. The day Gran died. She told me everything. Even about her and me grandad and then about me own mam and Mr Francis. I know the truth now, but I still don't want anything to do with that family. The Hayes-Gortons. I'll earn me own living.'

'I still bet you'll go to sea on one of his boats, though,' Joe put in slyly. 'Ne'er mind what you say now. Work'll be hard to find after the war. You'll be glad to take what you can then, I bet.'

'Mebbe I will,' Sammy said quietly. 'But if I do, it'll be honest labour and I'll be paid for the job I do.'

'Aye, an' they earn plenty of the sweat off our backs,' Joe said. 'You don't see them going out on them trawlers, putting themselves at the mercy of the North Sea. Oh no, but they're quite happy to buy their fancy houses and live like lords on the money we earn for them. And I suppose that's what you want now, is it, Mam? Living out of town with Mr Robert in his fancy house and dressed in furs and dripping jewellery. Well, if ya do, you won't see me any more, I'm telling you.'

'Joe—' she began but then Sammy cut in, saying, 'Mam, I'm sorry, but I'm with Joe on this. If you have owt to do with Mr Robert, then you won't see me either.'

She was stunned into silence.

'Well, I'll be damned.' Joe was beaming and he slapped Sammy on the back.

'And there's another thing.' Sammy was going on as if she had nothing to say nor comment to make on their organization of her life. 'Aggie was asking for you.'

Wordlessly, Jeannie nodded and sat down heavily in the chair. For the first time in the whole of her life she was speechless. She could say nothing.

There was nothing to be said.

Forty

She sat beside Aggie's bed and took the frail, wrinkled hand into her own.

'Aggie, it's me. It's Jeannie.'

She could hardly believe that the woman lying in the bed was indeed Aggie. In just a few days, the woman looked as if she had aged twenty years. The meeting with Nell had taken its toll on Aggie too.

'Jeannie?' Even the voice was different. 'Oh yes, Jeannie. I'm glad you've come. I'm not long for this world and . . .'

'Oh now, don't say that, Aggie.'

The smile was wistful. 'I'm tired and I'm ready to go. There's no one left now to even mourn me.'

Jeannie felt the tears smart her eyes.

'So many memories. So many regrets . . .'

Now Jeannie was silent as Aggie continued, her voice a little stronger as she did so. 'I wanted to see you. There's something I need to tell you, Jeannie. I suppose I'm looking for a kind of absolution.'

'You want to see a priest?'

'No, no . . .' Now the smile was almost mischievous again and yet there was still a tinge of regret. 'No, I'm afraid me and priests haven't had much to do with one another for a long time.' She paused and then went on quietly. 'I'm sorry for what happened to Nell. Sorry if I caused it.'

'Nobody could ken that, Aggie. There's no point in taking the blame.'

Aggie cast her a glance of wry amusement. 'One more burden of guilt won't make much extra weight for me.'

She sighed and nestled back against the pillows, glancing away from Jeannie, out of the window at the grey clouds scudding by, though she let her hand lie in Jeannie's.

'I wanted to tell you about myself. Do you know, Jeannie, out of all the folks around here, you were the only one I ever wished could be my friend?' Her smile was wistful as she added quietly, 'I knew it was impossible, of course. Not only were you married into the Lawrence family but you were, by nature, a good woman. Not the kind who could ever consort with me and my sort.'

Jeannie desperately wanted to deny that she had ever judged Aggie, but her innate honesty kept her silent. She knew, to her shame, that she had played her part in shunning Aggie and her like, had physically dragged Grace from her 'house of ill repute' without knowing either what really went on there or anything about the woman everyone was so eager to malign. Unable to say anything, Jeannie merely patted Aggie's hand and settled back to listen. That was the very least she could do for the dying woman.

'I was born in this house, you know,' the frail voice began, but as she talked, Aggie became more animated, almost as if she were reliving her early years and some of the youthful vigour crept into her tone just once more. 'My father was a fisherman, a hard worker, I'll give him that, for it's a tough life.' She paused. 'But that's about all I can say good about him. He was a brute of a man. When he came home from sea he was straight to collect his settlings and into the Fisherman's Rest. If my mother didn't waylay him somewhere between the two, there'd be no money till the next trip. Then he'd come home roaring drunk, knock Mam about – and us kids, too, if we got in his way – and then he was off to sea on the evening tide the next day. We used to dread him coming back.'

'How did your mother manage? Were there many of you? Bairns, I mean?'

'Six. Well, eight really, but two died in infancy and I think she had a miscarriage somewhere in amongst us all. And she worked. Braided the nets and took work on the docks if she could find it. I tell you, Jeannie, if it hadn't been for her, we'd have starved. We damn well nearly did as it was.' Now there was a bitter twist to her mouth. 'But she was a hard woman. Understandable, I suppose, when you think what she had to put up with, but she never showed us any affection. Never hugged us or praised us. She loved us in her way, I suppose. Certainly, she worked hard for us, but . . .' Aggie sighed. 'Kids need to feel affection, don't you think? They need to be told they're loved.' Again there was a pause before she said softly, 'I never knew what it was to be loved or what a good man was until I started courting George Lawrence. I'd always known him, of course. We'd been kids at school together, though he was a couple of years older than me. I'd adored him then. Ever since the age of seven. You know how little girls talk, well, I was always going to marry George Lawrence when I grew up and have two children, a girl and a boy.' Her voice faltered a little.

'When did you start courting?'

'George went to sea as soon as he could. I think he even stowed away his first trip, he was that mad keen to be a fisherman. He was eighteen and I was sixteen when he first asked me out. When I got home, my mother leathered me with Dad's belt. I couldn't understand what I'd done wrong. We'd only gone for a stroll around the docks. He loved looking out to sea, watching for the boats to come in on the evening tide. "I won't have you hanging round the docks like a woman of the streets," she yelled at me.' Aggie chuckled. 'Do you know, Jeannie, I didn't even know what she meant? Well, the next time George was home, I met him in secret and we went on meeting like that for months, almost a year. That was the happiest time of my whole life. I loved George and I knew he loved me. At least, he did then. Just for a year . . .' The voice faded away as she remembered. She closed her eyes and Jeannie thought she had dropped to sleep but then her eyelids fluttered. She sighed heavily and began to speak again but now her tone was flat with sorrow. 'It was the middle of August and that was when the Scottish fisher lasses arrived every year. It's more than forty years ago now, Jeannie, but I remember it as if it was yesterday. George was a young deckie then. On the day his boat was due in, I'd dress in my prettiest dress and go down to the docks. Of course the girls working on the fish docks called me names. Names that weren't true. Not then. I was just prettying myself up for my feller. You know?'

'I know,' Jeannie said softly.

'They were hard workers those fisher lasses, all of them, and it wasn't an easy life, not by any means, and I suppose when they stood there day after day with the stink of fish on their clothes and in their hair, well, the sight of a girl with time to dress up and stand idly on a corner waiting for her man, it riled 'em I suppose.'

'Aye, I suppose I could understand that,' Jeannie said softly. 'They'd be jealous of you, with time to spare and nice clothes to wear.'

'When he came ashore, George came straight to me, of course, and we went off together, but they called after us, shouting things. He just turned and waved good-naturedly at them. Just a lark, he said, that was all it was.' She paused again and now a note of bitterness crept into her tone. 'But the next day, it wasn't a lark. I went to the quay to see him off, but before he came a group of the girls surrounded me, dragged me into an empty warehouse and kept me there until his ship had sailed.'

She was silent for so long, that Jeannie said, 'What happened?'

'I was upset, of course. I cried a bit that I'd missed seeing George off, but I daren't say anything to my family. They still didn't know I was even meeting him. I was only seventeen, remember. And I think, at that stage, if I'm honest, the fisher lasses didn't mean any real harm. They were only having a bit of fun, y'know, taking me down a peg or two for showing off.'

'But surely, it was all right the next time he came home, wasn't it? The fisher girls would have moved on by then.'

'That's what I thought, but it wasn't to be, Jeannie. Yes, they had moved on, but the boat that George was on had engine trouble and put into Yarmouth for repairs. And that's where that same team of girls had gone. And of course, when they recognized him . . .'

Jeannie was beginning to piece the story together now. 'You mean that Nell was one of those girls? That she was one who locked you in the warehouse?'

'No, no,' Aggie said swiftly. 'I'll not accuse her of that, because I don't think she was. No, she was a young lass, only a year older than me and down here on her first trip with the herring girls. Some of the older girls teased her a bit about George, told her he'd followed her down the coast. Come looking for her especially. He felt a bit sorry for her, all those miles from home, learning the trade. It is hard work, I know that. And she'd cut her finger badly.

He told me years later that he'd said, straight up, that he had a girlfriend back in Havelock but then – then . . .'

Her voice broke and tears threatened. Though she longed to hear the end of the tale, Jeannie said at once, 'Aggie, dinna say any more.'

She drew in a shuddering breath. 'No, no, I want to tell you. I need to tell you, Jeannie.'

'Then the girls told him that the time I'd not gone to see him off, they'd seen me go off with another feller whose boat'd just come in. They implied, you see, that I was there waiting for the fishermen to come ashore, collect their pay and then – then I'd go off with them.'

'And George believed them?' Jeannie was scandalized.

Aggie sighed. 'You couldn't blame him, Jeannie. He was only eighteen. We were both so young, so innocent. And I mean that, Jeannie, 'cos we were.' She paused and added meaningfully, 'Then.'

'Do you mean to tell me that Nell made up that story about you?'

The white head moved from side to side on the pillow. 'No, I don't think so. I think the girls – the older girls, that is – were just having a bit of sport with the two of them. Maybe they didn't even mean to cause the trouble they did, though the story about me was unkind.'

'To say the least,' Jeannie murmured.

'George's boat repairs took a week. In the life of a fisherman, Jeannie, a week is a long time. He was far away from home with nothing to do. And so was Nell. Not able to work for a few days because of her cut finger.'

'So, they spent a lot of time together?'

'Yes. And they fell in love.'

From the recesses of Jeannie's memory, into her mind came Nell's words when she had been telling Jeannie a little about herself. 'I just never went home,' she had said.

'But – but when George came home from Yarmouth, didna you tell him what had happened? What they'd done?'

'I tried, but I could see it was too late. Nell had hooked him and he was as helpless as a fish on the end of a line. I suppose in that week, they'd spent more time together than George and I had managed in almost a year.'

'Oh Aggie, I'm sorry.'

'Ah well, it's all a long time ago now,' Aggie said, but Jeannie could detect that the hurt and the loss were as keen as ever they had been. 'And then, I suppose, you can guess the rest. I left home to escape my domineering mother. I just wanted to be loved by a strong, kind man. A man like George Lawrence. But, I never found him, Jeannie . . .' The voice was fading now as Aggie drifted into sleep. 'I never found another George.'

For a long time, Jeannie sat there, imagining how it must have been. Imagining how the practical joke a group of young girls had played had led to the ruining of this poor woman's life. And yes, she was a 'poor' woman, for she had been misunderstood and maligned the whole of her life.

Over the next few weeks until the day that Aggie Turnbull slipped into unconsciousness from which she never recovered, Jeannie visited her daily, even sitting with her throughout that long, last night.

And Aggie's last words were to remain with her. 'If you find happiness, Jeannie, take it. Grasp it with both hands and never let it go.'

Forty-One

He was going home. The war was over, in fact it had been over for almost five months. Whilst there would be work for the minesweepers for some time to come, Robert was no longer needed. He could go home. And now there was something – or rather someone – to go home to. A new year – 1946 – and a new life.

Of course, there was still the company, such as it was now. He and Edwin would run the family firm together and one day Sammy would inherit it from them. Robert was sure Edwin wouldn't mind. Maybe even Tom's boy, Joe, would come into the company too. Jeannie would like that. Her son and the boy whom she had always looked upon as her own, running the Gorton-Hathersage Trawler Company. Then he could retire and he and Jeannie could travel the world. He could take her to all the most beautiful places. Oh, they were going to be so happy, he and his Jeannie . . .

When she opened the door to him, he saw at once the anxiety in her face. That she was pleased to see him, he could not doubt, for even on the doorstep in full view of the whole street, she flung her arms about him crying. 'You're safe. Oh thank God, you're safe.'

But as she drew him into the house and closed the door upon the world and they sat together, their arms about each other, Robert said gently. 'Something's happened. What is it?'

They had not written to each other, nor had he come to see her again, since the day of Nell's funeral service. Deliberately, he had stayed away, confident in the thought that when the war was over, she would be waiting for him. Then, he had promised himself, there would be nothing and no one to stand in the way of their happiness.

She told him of Aggie's death, not sure whether he had heard the news. When she fell silent, he said, 'But there's something else, isn't there? Something to do with us?'

She looked at him then and, as she did so, Robert felt a stab of fear, for her eyes were brimming with unshed tears. 'What is it?'

'I'm sorry, Robert, but I can't marry you.'

For a moment he could not speak. He just sat there, staring at her and gripping her hands tightly. At last, he said hoarsely, 'Why?'

She dropped her gaze, shook her head and then rested her forehead against his chest. His arms were about her. 'Just tell me why, Jeannie?'

'It's the boys. They – they're both so – against the idea. I could understand Joe, but not Sammy. I mean, you're his uncle. But even he . . .' Her voice trailed away.

'I'll talk to them . . .'

'No!' She pulled away from him then. 'Please, let me handle it.'

'Jeannie, I love you. I want you to be my wife.'

She was shaking her head slowly. 'I know, but . . . I'm not sure myself. Now.'

'You mean – you're not sure if you love me?'

'Oh no, not that. I love you. Please don't ever think that. Maybe it's because I do love you so very much that –

that I'm not sure. I'm so afraid. I mean, you live in such a different world. You're from a different class . . .'

Robert shook his head, his voice a gentle whisper. 'Don't talk like that. Not about me. Not about us.'

'But it matters. I wouldna fit into your world.'

'We'll make our own world.'

'But your family. It's not true what they say, you know.'

'What do *they* say?' He traced the outline of her face gently with the tip of his finger. He wasn't taking her seriously. He couldn't believe that she could say she loved him and yet allow her boys to dominate the rest of her life. His life too. Their life together.

'That you don't marry a person's family. You do. You marry into the whole family.'

Suddenly, he felt cold, colder than he had ever been out in the North Sea. She was serious. She did mean it. She was afraid of losing her own son and Sammy too. Trying, still, to make light of it, he said, 'But there's only Edwin left now and he's the most easy-going chap in the world. A good business man, mind you, but . . .'

'But there are friends, the circles you move in. Even the world of business. Your wife would be expected to be a – a hostess.'

He laughed. 'Louise never once hosted a business dinner for me.'

'Really?'

'Really.'

'Oh.'

'So, you've not a thing to worry about with my world, as you put it. The problem,' he sighed heavily, 'seems to be with your boys. What is it? Just that they don't like me or . . .?'

'I think it goes deeper than that. I think Joe is carrying on Tom's resentment against you and your family.' She glanced at him apologetically. 'Tom never made a secret of it.'

'Because of Grace you mean?'

Jeannie said nothing. She didn't want to tell him the full extent of Tom's bitterness that concerned not only Grace but Jeannie herself. Robert sighed. 'And I suppose Sammy's resentful for the very same reason.' He was quiet for a moment then asked, 'And do they blame me for Tom's death?'

Carefully she said, 'I think that comes into it.'

'Oh.' Now his tone was flat with despair. 'Well, there's going to be no way I can win them over then. Not if their reasons are as deeply rooted as that.'

'No.'

'So, you're going to have to choose, aren't you? Me – or your boys.'

Again tears filled her eyes and she nodded wordlessly, unable to speak.

He closed his eyes and gave a deep-throated groan. 'I can see you've already decided. But, oh my darling, please be sure you're doing the right thing. They'll marry, have families of their own. Are you really sure that you'll be content to live your life through them? Don't throw away the rest of your own life, Jeannie.'

She shook her head. 'I'm sorry. So sorry. But I love them both as my own sons. I couldn't bear to lose them. Not now, when they've come through so much.'

Robert picked up her hand, traced the tiny scars on her fingers, the hardened callouses. Then he pressed it to his lips and murmured against her palm, 'I thought you were made of stronger stuff, Jeannie.'

That hurt. Oh, how that hurt her. She snatched her hand away, angry now, and pulled herself free of his embrace. She stood up. 'How would you know what it feels like to be a mother? Or even a father? You've never had children of your own.'

She saw at once by his bleak expression, how much she had now hurt him. But there was no taking back the words. They were said and could not be unsaid. He rose and gave a stiff little courteous bow towards her. 'If that is your final answer,' he said, his words clipped, 'I will take my leave of you.'

'Robert, please, try to understand. I'm sorry, I didn't mean to hurt you.'

'But you are hurting me, Jeannie. And, worse still, you're hurting yourself just for the sake of two selfish young men who don't know the meaning of love yet.'

He turned away then and left the house without another word, leaving her bereft and empty, with a pain inside her too deep for tears.

Three days later, she received a letter from him. '*My darling, I can't bear to part with you in anger. I just want you to know that I will always love you and always be here for you. If ever you should need me, you know where I am . . .*'

The loving, forgiving words brought tears to her eyes, tears that now spilled over and ran down her cheeks. Impatiently, she brushed them away. He was right, she thought. She was made of sterner stuff than this. She had never been the weepie sort and yet here she was, allowing others to dictate her life.

I will go to him, she decided. I will marry Robert. Joe and Sammy will come around to it in time. Without stopping to think any more – she had done enough thinking over the past weeks, she told herself – she hurried to put on her hat and coat.

She caught the bus to the outskirts of town and then marched purposefully along the road until the houses petered out and she was in the countryside, heading for the lane where she remembered Robert's fine house lay. Frost lay on the hedgerows and the February wind was bitter, but Jeannie scarcely felt the cold.

She couldn't wait to see him now, couldn't wait to tell him . . .

She came to the gate. A wooden, five-barred gate had replaced the fancy wrought-iron one she remembered seeing on the last occasion she had come here. The war effort, she supposed, had taken them. It seemed so long ago now, since she had last stood on this spot. The two boys had been but bairns. She paused, her hand resting on the top of the gate. She was staring at the house set against a backdrop of trees, the long windows leading out on to the front terrace, the heavy oak front door, yet she was not really seeing it or the beautiful, well-kept gardens or the surrounding countryside with its flat, panoramic views.

She was remembering Joe and Sammy as babies and reliving the feel of their chubby arms clasped tightly about her neck or a sticky kiss planted on her cheek. She remembered the day they walked for the first time, those first faltering steps, the wide grin on their faces at the sense of achievement. Joe had been first and a week later, not to be outdone, Sammy had followed suit. In those first few years they had grown together believing themselves to be brothers. Oh, they had squabbled like any siblings, but not until the day Joe had told Sammy about the circumstances of his birth, had the resentment between them begun to fester.

Yet now, they were the closest they had ever been, united in their hatred of the Gorton family and so fervently opposed to her involvement with Robert.

They were so passionately set against him with the sureness of youth that they were right, that she knew they would never come around.

If she were to marry Robert Gorton and come to live in this grand house, she would lose her boys for sure.

There was a lump constricting her throat as she let her gaze wander over the house for the last time. She knew now that she would never live there. Much as she loved Robert, the heartbreak marrying him would bring would blight their love and cast a shadow over their lives. In time, it would eat into their love like a canker. Of course, she was sensible enough to realize that in time, resentment might creep into her relationship with the boys for they were forcing her to make the most difficult decision of her entire life. But now, at this moment, she could not guess to what extent that might happen.

Tears blurring her vision, she turned away. As she did so, she thought she caught sight of a figure standing at one of the first-floor windows. This time she made no effort to wipe away her tears.

This time she had good reason to weep.

Forty-Two

'Mam, this is Thelma.'

Jeannie rubbed her hands down the front of her overall, held out her hand and smiled a welcome towards the girl who was standing nervously in the doorway. She was tall and thin, so thin that Jeannie could have believed the girl hadn't eaten for days. And she stooped slightly, her shoulders rounded. Her dress was faded, the type a smart woman might have worn before the war and Jeannie guessed it was either a hand-me-down from a better-off relative or maybe even from the second-hand clothes shop. But her eyes were bright and sharp and her long fair hair curled around her face.

'I'm pleased to meet you,' Jeannie said kindly. 'Come in, hen.'

The girl's eyes widened and she giggled at the unfamiliar endearment. 'Oh, you're Scotch.'

Jeannie bridled at the misnomer but let it go. 'And you're a local lass?' she said instead.

'Oh yeah. Born an' bred in Havelock. Me dad's a fisherman, just like Joe.' The girl's eyes turned towards Joe and Jeannie could see at once the adoration in her expression. 'He's a skipper, just like Joe's going to be one day. Aren't you, Joe?'

Joe grinned, his arm about the girl's shoulders. 'I reckon.'

Jeannie smiled at the young man's confidence.

'The sea's me life,' he was saying, 'Always will be. Thelma understands that, bein' brought up in a fisherman's family. She won't mind being a fisherman's wife.'

'Wife?' Jeannie was surprised.

'We're getting engaged, Mam. There's a little house come up for rent at the end of Wessex Street. Just ideal. We don't want to miss it. If we get it, we'll be getting married straight away.'

'This is a bit sudden, isn't it?' She felt aggrieved. It was only five weeks since she had turned her back on Robert. Then, Joe had been ecstatic, picking her up bodily and dancing around the kitchen with her. 'We'll look after you, Mam. Me an' Sammy,' he had said. 'You've done the right thing. It'll be just the three of us. You'll not regret it, I promise.'

She was regretting it already. He had the audacity, she thought, only weeks later to waltz into her kitchen and calmly announce that he was leaving home to get married.

She looked at him keenly. 'Is that the only reason or is there something else you should be telling me?'

Joe's brow met in an angry frown. 'No, Mam. She's not expecting, if that's what you're meaning.'

Beside him the girl gasped and turned bright red.

'I'm sorry, hen,' Jeannie said swiftly, gesturing towards the girl. 'But you've got to admit that it all seems a bit of a rush. How long have you been walking out together?'

The couple glanced at one another.

'A month?' Joe muttered.

'A month!' Now Jeannie was scandalized. 'And you've been away at sea for the past three weeks.'

'But we've known each other a lot longer than that,' the girl put in. ''Aven't we, Joe? I'm a barmaid at the Fisherman's and—'

'A barmaid?' This was getting worse by the minute.

Once upon a time, Aggie's girls had worked behind the bar at the Fisherman's.

'What's wrong with that?' The girl bridled. 'It's hard work there and long hours.'

Jeannie pursed her lips and said nothing, but she knew her expression would give away her disapproval. Then she realized she was being unfair. She should not judge this girl by what had happened years ago. She turned away, shrugging her shoulders. 'Well, there doesna seem to be anything I can say. You seem to have made up your minds, but I hope . . .' she turned back briefly to face Joe once more and knew that he would understand the meaning behind her words, 'I hope *you* know what you're doing.'

It all happened so fast that Jeannie hardly had time to draw breath. Joe and Thelma got the house and were married on Joe's very next shore leave. And, as if not to be outdone, Sammy produced a girlfriend and, whilst he made no announcements of engagements or impending marriage, when he was home from the sea he was hardly ever in Jeannie's home.

In the once bustling, over-crowded Lawrence household, Jeannie was now alone and all the days of the rest of her life stretched before her, empty and meaningless.

Oh she had neighbours, and soon, she would no doubt be a grandmother, but was that all she could hope to look forward to?

It wasn't enough. Not for Jeannie.

On a fine spring morning, Jeannie locked the door of the terraced, back-to-back house in Baldock Street and walked away from it. In her handbag was more money than she had ever carried before. From the wooden box under her bed she had taken her life savings. Shillings and sixpences scrimped and saved over the years. Saved for a rainy day or for that promised trip back to her homeland.

Well, the rainy day had never come nor had the trip to Scotland. Today was a bright, glorious morning and she was going to spend the lot on herself. What was that saying she'd heard someone say once? 'Today is the first day of the rest of your life.'

Oh yes, indeed it was. And from now on, this was how it was going to be.

'Are you sure, madam?' The sales assistant sounded very doubtful. 'I mean, are you going to a wedding? That's the sort of dress and coat and hat that you'd wear as – well – the mother of the bride.' The woman's face cleared. 'Is your daughter getting married, madam?'

'No,' Jeannie said shortly and offered no further explanation but inside she was laughing, hugging the secret to herself. 'No, I just thought I'd spoil mysel'.'

The woman eyed Jeannie's own sober, serviceable coat and hat lying across the chair in the fitting room. 'Come up on the pools, have we, madam?' There was an edge of sarcasm to the woman's tone, almost of jealousy. But nothing could ruffle Jeannie's feathers today.

'No, it's my savings.'

Now the woman looked worried and eyed Jeannie suspiciously.

Maybe she thinks I've been to the Fisherman's, Jeannie thought. She'll be sniffing my breath next. Then she almost laughed out loud as another thought struck her. Maybe she thinks I've stolen the money. But the woman merely said, 'And I thought the Scots were supposed to be mean.'

'No' mean, hen, just canny,' Jeannie countered, still not offended. She twisted this way and that, eyeing the new Jeannie Lawrence reflected in the long mirror. 'Aye, I'll take it.'

Now the woman brightened. It would be, Jeannie surmised, her best sale of the week.

'Thank you, madam. Shall I wrap everything for you?'

'No, no. I'll keep it on. If you'd just remove the labels.'

'Then shall I – er – wrap your own garments?' There was a distinct look of distaste on the assistant's face now.

Jeannie chuckled. 'No, hen, you can throw them away.'

And with them, she thought, would go the aroma of fish that she had lived with for the whole of her life until this moment.

'But you can do one more thing for me?'

'Yes, madam?'

'Where is the underwear department?'

Jeannie spent the rest of the morning and half the afternoon in the store. In the hairdresser's, she had her hair restyled, curled and wound up on to the top of her head. It was the most sophisticated style she had ever had and, though she doubted she could repeat it herself in front of her own bedroom mirror, just for today she felt as if she had stepped off the front cover of a fashion magazine.

As she left the store, Jeannie's step was light. Clad in new clothes from the silk underwear that felt deliciously smooth against her skin to the new dress and coat that fitted snugly against her still slim figure, and her new hat set at a jaunty angle, she walked the full length of Main Street with a smile on her mouth. She could still turn a few heads, she thought.

She caught the bus heading out of town and within half an hour she was walking down the lane towards Robert's house. As the sun dropped behind the far horizon, she approached the gate once more. Her heart was beating rapidly. She stood again with her hand resting on the top bar and let her gaze roam slowly over the house. Twice before she had stood here and then turned away, back to her life near the dockside.

But this time was different. Now she took a deep breath, pushed open the gate and walked through it.

Forty-Three

'We'll buy another house, my darling. I'll put this on the market and . . .'

But Jeannie was standing in the centre of the huge drawing room, her hands clasped in front of her, turning slowly, taking in everything around her. Then she walked to the long French windows and stood looking out across the smooth stretch of lawn to the copse at the end of the garden. He came and stood beside her, putting her arms about her waist and resting his chin on her shoulder.

She leant back against him and sighed dreamily. 'But it's a beautiful house. Surely you don't want to leave it. It's your home, Robert.'

'It's never been a home, Jeannie. Louise decorated and furnished it in her own ultra-modern style. And then, she hardly ever lived here.'

Jeannie turned in his arms to face him. 'So what are you saying? That you don't want to live here because it has unhappy memories for you?'

'No, no,' he said swiftly. 'The house is right enough. I just thought that – well – you wouldn't want to live where I'd lived with Louise.'

Jeannie wrinkled her nose. 'Well, I dinna like some of her choice of decor.' Then she laughed impishly. 'Well, to be truthful, I dinna like any of it.'

'Nor me,' Robert put in with heartfelt fervour.

'But,' Jeannie was more serious now, 'I'm not jealous of

Louise so I'm not afraid of her ghostly memories in this house.'

'My darling, you have no need to be. I have only ever loved one woman in the whole of my life and she is now here in my arms.' He sighed as he added, 'But I have to admit to being jealous of your Tom.'

Jeannie blushed a little. Even now she was not quite ready to lay open her soul to Robert about the truth of her own marriage. It seemed to her that she would be dishonouring Tom's memory if she did so. And she would never want to do that for he was the father of her son and the closest to a father that Sammy had known.

They were married very quietly with Edwin the only family member present.

Neither Joe nor Sammy came to her wedding.

The day she had returned to the house in Baldock Street to meet the two boys, due home for a day and a half, had been very painful. She stood at the open front door and watched them walking down the street. Her heart contracted at the sight of them. Two good-looking young men, laughing and joking and pushing each other. They were arguing already, she thought, even though they'd stepped off different boats and hadn't seen each other for three weeks. Then they saw her standing there, dropped their bags and ran towards her.

'Mam! You look smart. Been into town?' Joe gave her a bear hug, lifting her and swinging her round. Sammy, as always, kissed her cheek and asked, 'You been all right, Mam?'

'I can't stop,' Joe went on, without giving her chance to speak. 'I must get home to Thelma. She'll be waiting for me.' He gave a suggestive chuckle and nudged Sammy. 'I'll see you in the Fisherman's later – if I've still got the strength.'

Trying to keep her voice calm, Jeannie said, 'There's something I must tell you.'

Joe grinned. 'Well, make it snappy, Mam. I ain't seen my lovely wife for three weeks, y'know.'

No, she thought, you're impatient to see your wife and that's only natural, but you think nothing of condemning me to a life of loneliness. 'Come in, just for a moment.'

The house was cold for she had not lived there for a week now and as soon as the two men stepped into the kitchen, she saw them glance at the cheerless grate and then at the wall, empty now of a half-braided net. Eyebrows raised, they looked at each other and then, with one accord, turned towards her.

Jeannie stood facing them, the kitchen table that had once been the hub of the crowded family home, between them.

'Joe,' she began, 'you're married and have a home of your own. Sammy, although you dump your washing here, you dinna sleep here even when you're ashore. You're with Sally or Sarah or whoever the girl of the moment is—'

'Helen, as a matter of fact.'

'With Helen, then,' she went on calmly, though she was aware of the fluttering just below her ribs. She clasped her hands tightly together to stop them trembling. 'I've thought things over very carefully and decided that I'm not prepared to spend the rest of my life alone.'

Joe was frowning, as if half-guessing already what she was about to say. 'You're not alone. We always come to see you. We come here *first*,' he added belligerently, as if they were bestowing a great favour upon her.

'Yes,' Jeannie agreed, 'And how long do you stay? Five minutes? Ten minutes? Long enough,' she glanced at Sammy, 'to drop your washing off?'

There was a moment's silence and then as she opened her mouth, Joe took the words from her lips. Pointing his finger at her, he burst out, 'I get it. You're going to him, aren't you?'

Silently, she nodded.

'Aw Mam, no,' Sammy said. 'No, don't do it. Please.'

'She already has,' Joe snarled. 'Just look at her fancy clothes. She didn't buy them hersen'.'

Resolutely, though her insides had turned to jelly, Jeannie said, 'You can apply for the tenancy of this house, Sammy, and you can have everything that's in it, apart from any bits and pieces that Joe might want. I'm sure,' she added with a hint of sarcasm, 'it won't be long before you follow Joe's example and get married.' She paused and then, mentioning his name for the first time, she said, 'Robert and I are getting married in three weeks' time to coincide with the next time you are both due ashore. We hope you will come to the service. It's at—'

'Never! Never in a million years. In fact . . .' Joe leant towards her, all the resentment and bitterness that had been his father's as well as his own, clearly etched into his twisted features, 'I don't want to see you again. Not ever!'

With that, her son turned and left the house slamming the door behind him so hard that the window next to it rattled.

'Oh Mam,' Sammy was saying sadly, shaking his head. 'How could you? How could you do this to us? I thought you loved us.'

That, more than Joe's anger, had been the cruellest shaft of all.

Forty-Four

'Where are you going, Jeannie?'

Robert came up behind her as she pinned her hat on to her head. 'To see Thelma.'

'Thelma?' Robert repeated, surprised.

'Aye, ma daughter-in-law.' Her mouth was tight, her words clipped with disapproval. 'If what I've been hearing is true, she's about to get a piece of ma mind.'

Robert put up his hands, palms outwards. 'Oho, I wouldn't be in her shoes, not for all the fish in the sea.'

Jeannie turned and gave him a wide smile, but her eyes still sparkled with the light of battle.

She and Robert had been married for three months and during all of that time she had not seen, nor heard, from her boys. Instead, she had heard gossip about Thelma.

Intrigued now, Robert leant towards her. 'What exactly have you been hearing?'

But Jeannie only tapped him on the nose and said, 'Never you mind. This is women's business.'

'Ah.' He asked no more but offered, 'I'll drive you, if you like.'

'You can take me into the town, but not to her door. I'll walk from the end of their road.'

He smiled knowingly. Jeannie didn't want to be seen by the neighbours drawing up in the fancy motor car. He glanced down at the grey coat and hat she was wearing. Although of good material and fine cut, they would not attract the attention that some of the items now in her wardrobe would.

'Shall I wait for you?' he asked half an hour later as he opened the car door for her and helped her to alight.

'Are you going to the office?'

'Yes.'

'Then I'll walk from their house to the dockside and meet you there.' The corners of her mouth lifted slightly. 'It'll be nice to see Edwin. We should ask him to dinner soon. Do you think he'd come?'

'Of course, he would. He likes you, you know.' He closed the door as he added, 'See you soon, then. Good luck!'

Jeannie's smile broadened. 'It'll be her needing the good luck.'

Chuckling to himself, Robert got back into his car and drove away as Jeannie set off to walk the length of Wessex Street until she came to the terraced house where Joe and his wife lived.

Rapping smartly on the door she stood and looked about her, tapping the toe of her shoe whilst she waited. Across the street, she saw the net curtains twitch. Further along the road, two women stood, their arms folded beneath their ample bosoms, their hair tied up, turban-style, in headscarves. They watched her, their heads bent towards each other as they gossiped.

Thelma opened the door. She was still in her dressing gown though it was gone eleven in the morning. 'Oh, it's you,' was her only greeting.

'Well, are you no' going to ask your mother-in-law in?'

The young woman pulled the corners of her mouth down, but left the door open and led the way, scuffing along on worn-down slippers, through to the back kitchen. Jeannie wrinkled her nose in disgust as she entered the stuffy room. There was a stale smell of cabbage water. The floor did not appear to have been swept for a fortnight, nor the windows cleaned.

Jeannie flicked the chair with her glove before sitting down. Turning to look at the girl, she asked, not unkindly, 'Are you ill, hen?'

Thelma looked up in surprise. 'Ill? No, course I aren't. Why d'you ask that?'

Jeannie's glance around the room spoke volumes and the girl reddened though more from anger than embarrassment. 'Oh I see. Not posh enough for you, now?' Her lips curled.

Jeannie's own mouth was tight. 'I've never lived in fancy houses, not until now,' she admitted. 'But I've always kept my home clean and tidy. There's no excuse for this.' She waved her hand to encompass the whole room. 'It's not what Joe's used to.' Thelma opened her mouth again, but Jeannie forestalled her. 'But that's not what I've come about. If you want to live in a pigsty then that's up to the pair of you.' She leant forward. 'But what I don't like, is hearing gossip about you while my son's away at sea.'

'Eh?' The girl looked startled.

'Aye.' Jeannie nodded slowly. 'From what I hear, you're fast taking over from where Aggie Turnbull left off.'

Thelma sprang up out of her chair so suddenly that Jeannie jumped, her spine coming up hard against the back of the wooden chair. Thelma leant over her, raining spittle on Jeannie's face. 'How dare you? How dare you come into my house and say such things?'

Jeannie rose slowly and stood facing the younger woman. 'I dare because I care about my son.'

'Well, he dun't care about you. Not since you married *him*. He dun't want anything more to do with you. So, you can get out of this house and stay out.'

'Very well. But I shall be on the dockside the next time his ship comes home.'

A look of sudden fear passed over Thelma's face. 'He won't believe you,' she said, though now there was a tiny sliver of doubt in her tone. 'He'll not believe anything *you* tell him.'

Jeannie made to turn away towards the door, but glanced back to say calmly, 'He'll believe me, because he's the jealous type. Just like his dad. He believed the gossip about Mr Robert calling at the house when he was away. Never mind that Sammy was his nephew and he was trying to help him. Never mind that he was the one who kept Tom at sea when other ships' runners would have passed him over for the times he missed a trip. Oh no, Joe's just like his dad in that. He believes what he wants to believe.' She shrugged. 'And even if I don't tell him, you can bet someone from around here will. I've heard the gossip about you as far away as my posh house.' She raised her eyebrows and put her head on one side. 'Haven't I?'

Before her eyes the girl's bravado crumpled. 'Oh please, don't tell him. Please. He'll kill me.'

As she burst into noisy tears, Jeannie stepped forward and put her arms about the girl. 'There, there, hen. Whatever's been going on, must stop. I'll say nothing, but I canna promise he won't hear from others.'

The sobbing only increased as, muffled against Jeannie's shoulder, Thelma said, 'It has stopped already. It was – it was only the one time. There was this sailor. Swedish, he was. He kept coming into the Fisherman's. I know it was stupid of me, wrong of me, but he was so handsome and charming and Joe'd been away at sea so long, longer than usual.'

She drew back and looked up into Jeannie's face now. 'I swear it was only him used to come to the house, but there was one time when some of his mates called round here for him. I suppose that was when the neighbours . . .'

'Och aye, the neighbours,' Jeannie said with a sudden, heart-felt sympathy. 'What they don't know they'll make up, hen. That's why you've got to be so careful. But if it's over, then we'll say no more about it. And, as I say, Joe will hear nothing from me. Forget all about it. Put it behind you and get yourself prettied up for when he comes home.'

The tears were still flowing down Thelma's face. 'I – can't forget all about it. I'm – I'm pregnant. And – and I don't know whose it is. Joe's or – or Olaf's.'

'Och no,' Jeannie whispered. 'No, hen.'

'I canna be pregnant. I'm forty-one. It's no' decent at my age.' Jeannie, wide eyed, faced the doctor. She was appalled at the very thought of becoming a mother again and a grandmother almost within the same month.

'Well you are, Mrs Gorton. A good three months gone, I'd say. Had you really not thought that could be the case?'

Jeannie shook her head. 'After my son was born I thought there might be another bairn or two, but it just never happened. I only came to see you because I thought – I thought maybe it was the change starting early.'

The doctor smiled. 'No. A late baby, my dear, not the menopause.'

Jeannie was silent, just staring at him.

'I'd have thought you would be pleased. An heir for the Gortons, eh? If it's a boy, of course.'

A legitimate heir she was thinking. Would he oust Sammy? She didn't know the law well enough to know. But he would be a threat to Sammy. Maybe when he was old enough, he would fight Sammy in court and win.

Maybe Sammy would just hand everything over to him without a fight. He had never shown any sign of even wanting the share of the company that he already had, let alone one day playing an active part in the running of it. He had climbed down far enough to work on a Gorton trawler, but, Robert had told her, Sammy left the money that came from his shares just sitting in the bank account into which it was paid twice a year.

'He's never even touched it,' Robert had said. 'Not even when there's been a bad trip and he must be short of cash. It's as if he denies, even to himself, that it's even there.'

'Does he know about it?'

'Oh, yes, statements are sent to him regularly.'

Remembering the previous times, Jeannie said, 'Perhaps he doesna even open the letters.'

Robert had laughed, unable to believe such a suggestion. 'Oh, he'll come around one day.' And then referring more to her than to the company or to money, he had added, 'They both will.'

'I don't want it,' she heard a voice saying now and realized it was she who had spoken.

'Oh come, my dear,' the doctor said. 'It's a shock, I've no doubt but . . .'

'I'm too old. It – it could be born, well, no' right.'

The doctor spread his hands. 'The risk is higher when you're older, but really there is no reason to talk like that. You must talk to your husband. Robert, I'm sure, will be delighted.' Suddenly the kindly doctor was disapproving. 'I do hope you're not contemplating doing something very silly.'

Mutely, Jeannie shook her head and stood up suddenly. She needed to get out of this stuffy consulting room. She needed to think.

She walked the length of Main Street and found herself

at the docks. She did not stop but kept on walking right out past the dock master's office, right out to the end of the pier. The very place where she had stood that first night in Havelock watching for her father's boat. The night she had met Robert and Grace and all the people who were to change her life for ever.

All at once she was very homesick. Homesick for Scotland. For years she had promised she would go back. Visit the cottage where she had lived as a child, see if there was anyone still left in the village who remembered her or her father.

The wind whipped at her hat and tore it from her head. She watched it whirling high, born on the wind, tossed and blown then dropped lower and skimming the surface of the river below her until it flopped into the water and lay there for a few minutes bobbing like a tiny craft. Then, as the water soaked the fabric it slowly sank beneath the surface and disappeared from her view. It was like watching a boat sink. Her father's boat had been just as helpless against the might of the ocean as her smart hat. She missed him still. She wished Joe had been more like him, but Joe was like Tom, given to bitterness and resentment, though he was, Jeannie admitted, more courageous than his father.

How would he feel when he heard that he was to have a half-brother or sister? And what would Sammy say if she were to produce a legitimate heir to the Gorton inheritance? Would he change his mind about becoming part of the company?

Jeannie gazed down at the water lapping against the pier and then she turned away.

As she walked back, she was aware of the glances. She was out of place here now, dressed in her fine clothes. She knew most of the men must recognize her; some as the 'Mester's Missis', others as Tom Lawrence's widow. A few

touched their caps to her, some turned away, deliberately
ignoring her. That didn't worry her. Inwardly she smiled
to think of the days when they would call after her, trying
their chance with a pretty girl. Now, their deference was
to an older woman of position. Yet her mature body was
still trying to act like that of a young woman, allowing
itself to become pregnant.

When she told him, Robert was ecstatic.

'Jeannie, oh Jeannie, that's the most wonderful news
I've ever had in the whole of my life – except,' he smiled
broadly, 'the day you walked through that gate.' His gaze
searched her face. 'Aren't you happy about it?'

'I can't help worrying that, at my age, something might
go wrong.' She avoided looking directly at him. She was
afraid to look into his happy face, afraid that he would
read the truth in her eyes.

She did not want this child.

'I'll take you to London,' Robert was saying. 'You shall
have the best doctors . . .'

Jeannie was shaking her head. 'No, no, I don't want
that. Dr Walker is quite capable.' And besides, she was
thinking in the secret recesses of her own mind, if something were to go wrong then . . .

'Are you thinking of the boys and how they might react
to the news?' Robert was probing gently.

Jeannie shrugged. 'I don't see them anyway.' She sighed
heavily and she knew she could not hide the hurt from
showing in her eyes. 'I don't think they'll care one way or
the other, to be honest.'

'They will. They'll come around. They'll both be related
to him.' Hastily, Robert added, 'Or her,' but Jeannie knew
how much he was hoping for a son. 'They won't be able

to resist seeing him,' he went on. 'He'll be Joe's half-brother and cousin to Sammy, just in the same way that Joe is.'

Jeannie wrinkled her brow, working it all out. 'Yes, you're right about that, but I don't think you're right about them coming around. I don't think . . .' she said and there was no mistaking the catch in her voice, 'that they ever will.'

'One day, they will,' Robert said, 'and besides, Joe's wife is expecting a baby too, isn't she?'

Jeannie's heart felt as if it skipped a beat. So, that news was out too. She hoped not every secret surrounding Thelma's child was common knowledge. She nodded, wordlessly.

'That'll bring you closer together. They'll come around, I promise.'

But it was a promise – the only one – that Robert was not able to fulfil for his beloved Jeannie.

Forty-Five

'Have you told Joe the truth?'

Jeannie was once again sitting in the kitchen in Wessex Street, but this time the atmosphere was much different. The room was clean and warm, the net curtains freshly washed and the windows sparkling. A fire burned in the grate and the kettle sang on the hob. On the table lay Thelma's knitting: a white matinée jacket. So, Jeannie thought, at least she's making preparations for the coming baby. That's more than I am doing.

'Oh Mam,' Thelma began and Jeannie realized with a shock that it was the first time her daughter-in-law had ever addressed her that way. 'I couldn't. I just couldn't. He was that pleased, I couldn't spoil it for him. And besides . . .' she bit her lip and glanced at Jeannie, 'it could be his. So what's the point in telling him something that might not be true.'

Jeannie was silent, wrestling with her own conscience. She was remembering how differently Tom had always treated Sammy, who was not his own son, even though Jeannie had always been able to treat the boy as if he had been her own. She thought, too, about how Joe had seemed to carry on that resentment, one moment fighting with Sammy, the next defending him against outsiders. She shook her head slightly. Joe was a funny mixture, just as Tom had been. But there was one thing she did know.

Joe would never accept another man's child as his own.

As the weeks passed, Robert became desperately anxious about Jeannie. She seemed tired all the time and uninterested in the coming child. She refused to buy baby clothes or a new pram or even to redecorate one of the bedrooms as a nursery.

'It might not live,' she blurted out one day to a horrified Robert.

'Oh, my darling.' At once he put his arms about her and drew her to him. 'Is that what's troubling you?'

She clung to him, afraid that now he would guess the truth. That it was not what she believed would happen. It was what she hoped.

'What does Dr Walker say? You're in good health, aren't you?' He held her from him, searching her face. She shrugged listlessly and avoided looking at him.

'I'm fine, Robert.' But as Jeannie turned away from him, he stared after her, hurt and puzzled.

'Come in, Mr Gorton. What can I do for you?'

Sitting down, Robert said, 'It's about my wife.'

'Ah.'

He looked straight at the doctor. 'I do realize there are questions you may not be able to answer, but I'm worried about Jeannie. It's – it's . . .' Helplessly, he cast around in his mind for the right phrase. 'It's almost as if she doesn't want the baby.'

When the doctor did not answer, but picked up his pen and played with it, turning it end over end and tapping his desk with it at each turn, Robert felt a cold fear run through him. 'Is that it?' he asked hoarsely, unable to believe that Jeannie, his Jeannie, would be even capable of such feelings. Why, she was a devoted mother to Joe and to Sammy too.

'Ah,' he said slowly, thinking aloud. 'Could it be because of the two older boys? Joe and Sammy? They've cut her off, you know, because she married me.'

The doctor wrinkled his forehead and pulled down the corners of his mouth. 'Could be, I suppose. Physically, she's very well. Remarkably so, considering her age.'

'That's another thing. She keeps on about her age. That the baby might not – survive. She won't even discuss names.'

'Women of her age are often – well – embarrassed about being a mother again in their forties. And of course that feeling may be compounded because she's going to become a grandmother around the same time.'

The doctor paused and glanced at Robert, who nodded.

'Of course,' Dr Walker went on, 'you understand that I must insist that she goes into the hospital for the birth but I'm afraid that will only add to her feelings of being, well, something of an oddity. All the other mothers there will probably be young enough themselves to be her daughters.'

Robert winced. 'Oh dear.'

The doctor spread his hands. 'The only advice I can give you is that you should just bear with her moods. It's not long now, only another two months and once the child is born . . .'

'But what if she rejects it then? I've heard of that happening.'

'It can, yes, but all you can do now is be supportive towards her. And don't keep questioning her. The last thing she wants is for you to know what she's feeling about the baby.' Dr Walker smiled sympathetically. 'For the next few weeks, Mr Gorton, you are going to have to be a very good actor.'

Jeannie knew nothing of Robert's visit to the doctor's, she was just so thankful that he had stopped fussing over her and asking her questions. He was still as loving as ever, kind and concerned for her welfare. And that he was joyfully anticipating being a father was never in any doubt.

But it only added to her feelings of guilt.

'Jeannie! Jeannie, where are you?'

She heard him calling from the hallway and then his feet pounding up the wide, sweeping staircase.

'In the bedroom,' she called and as he came in, she stood up and turned to face him. He was breathing heavily and she could see at once by his expression that something was wrong.

Her hand flew to her throat. 'What is it? Is it the boys?' Joe and Sammy now sailed in the same Gorton ship.

'No, no, it's Thelma. One of her neighbours came to the office today. It's the baby . . .'

'Oh no. It can't be. It's too early . . .' Already she was rushing to the wardrobe for her coat.

'I'll take you there, Jeannie.'

This time he took her right to the door and even stepped into the house with her, though he waited below whilst she rushed up the stairs.

As Jeannie stepped in through the bedroom door, she stopped in horror to see the blood-soaked sheets and the white face of the girl against the pillows. Her eyes were closed and she seemed scarcely to be breathing. The midwife, a stranger to her as Mrs Jackson had long since retired, was bending over her patient. 'The doctor will be here presently. You may have to go into the hospital, dear.' She looked up as Jeannie tiptoed to the bedside. 'You are Mrs Lawrence's mother?'

Jeannie shook her head. 'Mother-in-law. What's happened?'

'She's lost the baby, I'm afraid,' the midwife said in low tones. 'Stillborn.'

'Will – will she be all right?'

'I think so. She's young, but . . .' She paused, glanced at Thelma and added, 'It's not for me to say more than that. The doctor, or the hospital if he sends her there, will tell you more.'

Jeannie sat by Thelma's bedside until the doctor arrived half an hour later. Whilst he examined Thelma, she went downstairs to sit with Robert who was still pacing the kitchen.

'How is she? Do you want me to radio Joe's ship?'

'Not at the moment. Let's wait until the doctor comes down.'

They spent an uncomfortable, worrying twenty minutes until they heard him descending the narrow, dark staircase.

'She should go into hospital. There's still some bleeding. A surgeon should take a look at her. I'll call the ambulance. It shouldn't be long. Perhaps,' he glanced at Jeannie, 'you could get a few things ready for her to take. The midwife was unable to stay. She had another urgent confinement.'

Robert repeated his question to the doctor. 'Should I let her husband know?'

'Fisherman, is he?' When Robert nodded, the doctor asked, 'When's he due back?'

'Two days' time.'

'Leave it until then. She's not going to die, if that's what you're worried about. Better to tell him when he's safely back on dry land than have him worried to death out at sea where he can't do anything about it.'

There was reasoning and good common sense in his words and both Robert and Jeannie knew he was used to dealing with this community and its particular problems.

As he left the house, Jeannie went back upstairs to sit by Thelma's bedside once more and hold her hand. A tumult of emotions was going on inside her and she was glad that the girl was sleeping and she didn't have to speak. Not at this moment. Not now when she was trying to quell the overwhelming guilt she was feeling.

She had wished to lose the child she was carrying and instead, in a cruel twist of fate, poor Thelma had lost hers. Yet perhaps, in the circumstances, it was a blessing. Joe might, some day, have heard ugly rumours. She looked at Thelma's white face, at the blue smudges beneath her eyes and the colourless lips, her hair spread over the pillow and wondered briefly if the girl had done something to herself to bring this about. As, she reminded herself sternly, she had contemplated.

Much later, Jeannie asked Robert to drive her to the church where in the quiet, deserted sanctuary, she knelt and begged forgiveness for her own wickedness and for the soul of her still-born granddaughter.

'I'll come with you, if you like, to meet his ship,' Robert offered, but Jeannie shook her head.

'No, no. I must do this alone.'

And so, as the *Arctic Queen* nosed her way to the jetty

and the gangway from ship to quay clattered into place, the deckies were the first ashore. Jeannie stepped forward and put out her hand towards one of the men. 'Please, would you fetch Joe Lawrence for me. Tell him, it's urgent.'

The man looked at her for a moment and then as if reading something in her face, he nodded, 'Right, Missis.' He turned and ran lightly back up the gangway and she heard him calling as he went, 'Joe, Joe . . .'

She glanced up and saw Joe looking down at her standing there on the quayside. She could not read his expression from this distance, but she knew he would not be pleased to see her.

She saw the deckie climb aboard again, saw the exchange of conversation between him and Joe, saw the deckie gesture towards her. Then Joe was standing at the top of the gangway and coming down towards her.

He nodded in greeting but said nothing as he stepped, a little unsteadily, on to firm ground.

'Joe, it's Thelma. She's in hospital, son. I'm sorry, but she's lost the bairn.'

He stood staring at her for a moment. Then, she saw him glance down at the mound beneath her own coat and his mouth twisted with bitterness. Still without a word, he turned and walked unsteadily away from her.

'Joe,' she called after him, but he did not look back.

She turned and glanced up at the ship to see Sammy standing at the top of the gangway, but instead of coming down to speak to her he, too, turned away and disappeared from her sight.

Jeannie, her eyes blurring with tears, walked back along the quay to the Gorton offices where she knew Robert was waiting for her.

*

When the child – the boy that Robert so wanted – was born Jeannie was surprised how quick and easy it was. She had expected a difficult confinement considering her age and the fact that it had been twenty-two years since she had given birth to Joe.

She was given a room on her own in the hospital with the child in a cradle at the side of her bed. When Robert came to visit her and she saw him standing in the doorway, his arms full of flowers beaming like a Cheshire cat, Jeannie burst into tears.

'Oh darling . . .' He flung the flowers down and sat on the edge of the bed and drew her to him.

'You're not – supposed to sit on the – bed,' she hiccupped, her words muffled against his chest. 'Sister will have a fit.'

'Never mind the sister. I'll buy her a whole new bed if I have to. Now, come, dry your tears. Show me my son, Jeannie.'

Still leaning against him, she glanced down towards the cradle, saying nothing.

'He – he is all right, isn't he?' Robert asked anxiously.

She nodded. 'He's perfect. Just perfect. He's even . . .' her voice became high-pitched as fresh tears threatened, '. . . got my red hair. That's why I feel so guilty.'

'Eh?' Robert said, trying to make light of what she was saying, trying to sound as if he did not already understand what meaning lay behind her words. 'You feel guilty because he's got your red hair?'

'Oh Robert . . .' She clung to him then, fiercely like a drowning person. 'You're going to hate me. I didn't want him. I kept wishing that . . . that . . . Oh it was so wicked of me. I'll never forgive myself. And then when poor Thelma lost hers . . .' She was babbling, the words pouring out in a tumult of pent-up emotion. 'And now, I love him so much if anything were to happen to him . . .'

'Nothing's going to happen to him. I promise you.'

A shudder ran through her. He meant it, she knew he did, but that was something outside the power even of Robert Gorton.

He had not been able to fulfil that other promise he had made her. That one day she would be reunited with Joe and Sammy.

Forty-Six

'You spoil him.'

'So do you.'

They laughed and then put their arms about each other standing looking down into the cot and the sweet face of their child. Jeannie and her son had been home from the hospital a week and every day Robert had returned from the office with yet another toy or a tiny new outfit for the little chap. But he never omitted, too, to bring flowers or perfume or chocolates for the new mother. During that first week, Jeannie had barely left the nursery, even though Robert had employed a capable nursemaid. She even hovered close by whilst the child slept.

'He's perfect,' she murmured. 'I just canna believe I've been so lucky. I dinna deserve to be . . .'

'Now, now, stop that,' Robert remonstrated gently and tactfully changed the subject. 'Edwin has asked if he can come and see him tomorrow.'

'Of course he can.'

He thought for a moment and then said, 'I was thinking that we should ask Edwin to be godfather, but we could ask Joe and Sammy instead, if you like. If you think it would help?'

'It's sweet of you to suggest it, Robert. But I don't really think it would. Besides, I want to ask your brother to be his godfather. I like Edwin.'

'But you could ask Joe and Sammy as well, you know.'

'I'll see. I'll think about it.'

'So, are we decided on his name then?'

Jeannie smiled as she looked up at him. 'If you're really sure you dinna mind?'

'Of course, I don't. Angus Buchanan Gorton, it is.'

Since the birth of her own child, in robust health, Jeannie had found it difficult to bring herself to go to see Thelma. But when she had been home three weeks, she realized she could not put the moment off any longer. Taking fruit and flowers, she knocked once more on the door of the house in Wessex Street.

Thelma's eyes widened when she saw Jeannie. 'You can't come in,' she said bluntly. 'He's home. At least, he's at the Fisherman's. He could come back at any minute.'

'That's all right,' Jeannie said calmly, stepping over the threshold. 'I want a word with Joe anyway. How are you feeling, hen?'

The girl shrugged listlessly. 'All right.' She paused and then glanced keenly at Jeannie. 'You aren't going to tell him, are you?' Her eyes were brimming with tears as she whispered, 'He must never know. Never. I was a fool. I love Joe. I couldn't bear to lose him.'

Jeannie swallowed the huge lump that rose in her throat. No more can I, she wanted to say, but it looks as if I already have. Instead she said aloud, 'No. I gave you my word. I won't break it, whatever happens.'

The girl seemed to relax. 'Would you like a cuppa?'

'I'd love one, but I thought you didna want me to stay?'

Thelma smiled suddenly and her young face lost some of its misery. 'Oh sod 'im, for once,' she said. 'You've been good to me, Mam. He's a fool, the way he's acting, if you ask me.'

'Well, I dinna want to cause trouble between the two of you.'

Again she shrugged. 'Oh I can handle Joe,' she said, more confident now that she had extracted Jeannie's promise. 'Dun't you worry.'

Jeannie placed her gifts on the table, wondering at the sudden change in the girl's attitude towards her. Wondering if it would last.

As she set a cup of tea in front of Jeannie, Thelma said, 'You'd better have all the baby clothes I'd got ready. I shan't be wanting them.'

'Of course you will,' Jeannie tried to say briskly. 'You're young. There'll be more bairns.'

Thelma shook her head. 'The doctor seemed to think I didn't ought to have any more. It might be dangerous.'

'Och, what do they know?' Jeannie tried to reassure her, but in her heart she knew that the medical advice would not have been given lightly. 'Give yourself time to heal and then see, eh?'

There was silence between them before Thelma said suddenly, 'I told Joe you'd been here. I told him how good you'd been to me. Stayin' with me an' that and getting me to the hospital.'

'But – he still doesna want to see me?'

Thelma pressed her lips together and shook her head. 'He . . .' she began, but at that moment they both heard the back door open. There was only a chance for the two women to exchange a glance before Joe lurched into the room.

He stood in the doorway, swaying slightly and blinking as if to focus his gaze. 'What the hell is *she* doing in my house? I thought I told you . . .'

Before the girl could speak, Jeannie rose. 'I'm going. I came to ask you to be godfather to your brother, but it seems I'm wasting ma breath.'

'You are,' her son said. 'I want nowt to do wi' any of that family. Nor you, now you're a part of it. Far as I'm concerned, I have no brother.'

'I'm sorry you feel that way, son. I'll no' be coming here again. But if ever you need me . . .' she paused fractionally as her glance flickered briefly towards Thelma to include her too, 'you know where to find me.'

'Not afore the North Sea freezes over,' Joe muttered through clenched teeth as he moved away from the door to allow her to leave.

As she walked up Wessex Street, Jeannie felt the tears burn behind her eyelids and the lump grow and grow in her throat. She longed to rush home to Robert, to feel his arms around her and to stand with him and look down upon their child. But there was one more place she must visit first.

'Mam!'

She saw the surprise in Sammy's eyes as he opened the door and the fleeting pleasure, but it was gone so swiftly that she wondered if she had fondly imagined it. Now the veil of disapproval had come down once more. He seemed edgy, too, for he glanced over his shoulder and made no move to invite her into her old home.

Then she understood as a girlish voice called out, 'Who is it, Sammy?'

Jeannie's mouth twitched with amusement. 'Och I'm sorry, I wouldna want to spoil your homecoming.'

He gave a swift grin and for a moment his eyes danced with mischief. 'Just me girlfriend. That's all.'

'Aye.'

They stood in awkward silence for a moment and then both spoke at once.

'What was it . . .?'

'Sammy, I just wanted . . .'

They both stopped and then Sammy gestured that she should continue.

'I've been to see Joe. He's still adamant. I just wondered. Are you?'

The young man sighed heavily and closed his eyes a moment. 'I don't want it to be like this, Mam. I never did. If only you hadn't married *him*. If it'd've been anyone but him, we'd have understood. I don't think even Joe, in time, would have expected you to spend the rest of your life alone, you know? But to marry that man, after all that's happened. Well, we just can't handle it.'

'Oh Sammy.' Her heart was heavy. 'I'm sorry too.' There was another pause before she said sadly, 'If that's all you've got to say, then I'd best be on ma way. But I'll always be there for you, son. If you need me. Whatever you feel about me now, I'll always be your "Mam".'

For a moment, she thought she had broken his resolve. Sammy's face crumpled and, for one heart-stopping moment, she thought he was going to fling his arms about her and bury his head against her shoulder.

But in that instance the plaintive voice from inside the house came again. 'Sammy . . .?'

He turned away and quietly closed the door in her face.

Forty-Seven

So Joe and Sammy never saw Angus grow up. They were not around to witness the surprise on the child's face the first time he found he could roll over, nor the delight when he fathomed out how to crawl and reach the things he wanted. They were not there to teach him his first words nor to hold out their hands to him as he tottered to his feet, for all the world like a fisherman coming ashore. They were missing from his christening and his first birthday party.

In the early years of his life, Angus, knowing no different, was unaware of the lack of their presence in his life. His father doted on him and his mother, compensating for the guilt she felt, idolized him. She channelled all the love that she could no longer show towards the two older boys into this one tiny infant. That he grew into a sunny-natured, unspoilt child, was nothing short of a miracle. Anything he wanted, he got; anything he wanted to do – within reason on the grounds of safety – he did. Even his uncle was bowled over by the red-haired, mischievous little rascal.

'Wouldn't old Samuel have been tickled pink by him,' Edwin would say, sitting on the lawn with Robert and Jeannie watching the boy's first faltering steps. As he sat down with a thump, each one of the grown-ups made a start forward, hands outstretched towards him. But the child merely chuckled, turned a beatific smile upon them and hauled himself upright to try again. 'He's a real charmer with that smile of his,' Edwin murmured, never taking his eyes off his nephew and godson.

At a year old Angus was walking sturdily. At two, he was saying several words clearly and once he learnt how to string words together, he never stopped talking. From morning until he fell asleep at night, he chattered.

'He's so clever,' Jeannie would say, her fond gaze following him everywhere. And then, briefly, her eyes would cloud. 'I do so wish Joe and Sammy could see him.'

'I saw them last week,' Robert told her gently and, when the hope flared in her eyes, he wondered if he had been wrong to mention it. Quickly he said, 'My dear, I'm sorry, but they're still resolute.'

'You talked to them? How are they? Are they well? Is Joe a father yet?'

'They're fine,' Robert said carefully. 'Rumour has it . . .' he paused and Jeannie held her breath, 'that poor Thelma can't have children now. It's a shame, not only for them, but for you too. Perhaps, if Joe were to become a father, he might soften in his attitude a little. Towards you, I mean, if he knew what it was like to have children of his own.'

She sighed and then asked, 'And Sammy? Is he married yet?'

'No. He's still living in the house in Baldock Street. He has some lodgers, I believe, so that the house is occupied whilst he's at sea.'

'And Helen? Is he still with Helen?'

Robert shook his head. 'Lord, no. By all accounts, he has a different girlfriend every shore leave.'

'Huh, just like his father,' Jeannie said bitterly. 'I hope he's not as cruel and unfeeling as Francis was, Robert. I hope there's a little of you and Edwin in him.'

'And Grace,' Robert murmured. 'Don't forget Grace.'

'No, no,' Jeannie said. 'I willna forget Grace.' But guiltily she realized that she often did forget that poor Grace had been Sammy's mother and not her.

'Take me to see the ships, Dad.' Every weekend when his father was not at the Company's office, Angus would make the same request. He was besotted by the sea and everything to do with it. All the toys he asked for were boats, all the picture books and later, reading books, were about the sea or ships. When his parents took him on a day trip to the nearby seaside town, he would smile and say, 'But can we go to the docks on the way back home? Please?'

When he started school and began to read and write, the teachers despaired. 'Can he think about nothing else, Mrs Gorton, other than trawlers and fish? I know we're a major port and justifiably proud of our fishing industry here, but there are other things that Angus should be learning.'

But neither Jeannie nor Robert could do anything.

'Where is he? Robert, I canna find Angus.' As he grew older and learnt to ride a bicycle, the boy would go missing. In the school holidays Jeannie's anxious telephone calls to the office punctuated Robert's working day.

'My darling, you know where he'll be. But I'll find him.' And Robert would leave his desk to walk along the jetties until he saw his son watching the latest catch being landed. Some mornings Angus even crept out of the house before dawn to be in time to see the first fish sold in the auction on the dockside.

He would still be there late at night when the trawlers were being coaled up and supplies taken aboard for the ship to go out with the next tide.

'One of these days he'll really go missing. He'll stow away. I know he will,' Jeannie would say distractedly, but Robert would only smile.

'Darling, he has the sea in his blood from both sides of his family. If ever there was a born fisherman, Jeannie, then it's our son.' His glance roamed lovingly over his wife's face as he added softly, 'I'm sorry if it's not what you want for him.'

'Maybe we should have sent him away to boarding school,' Jeannie mused. 'Put some distance between him and the sea. But I just couldna bear to let him go.'

Robert snorted. 'What? And have him turn out like Francis? No fear, Jeannie. Besides, I'm proud of the lad.'

Jeannie glanced up at her husband, a mischievous look on her face. 'Despite my smothering him, so am I. But dinna tell him I said so.'

They laughed together.

Robert put his arm about her and she leant against him. 'Just so long as you know, my darling, that one day he's going to want to go to sea.'

'Aye,' she whispered. 'Aye, I ken.'

Forty-Eight

The moment Jeannie had been dreading came soon after Angus's fourteenth birthday.

'I'm off to sea,' he announced.

'You can go in the school holidays,' she said, valiantly trying to stave off the moment even though she knew it was hopeless. 'I don't mind that. Just for one trip.'

His eyes were twinkling with mischief and he was smiling broadly. 'And then when I leave school, I can go to sea as a real fisherman.'

Now she came to stand before him and place her hands on his shoulders. Already he was almost as tall as she was. As she looked him straight in the face, her heart turned over. He had her red hair but in so many other ways he reminded her of her father. He even smiled in the same way and laughed in that big, head-thrown-back, hearty manner. He was the image of old Angus. And now it seemed, sea water ran in his veins the same as his grandfather had always joked it ran in his.

'Angus, I couldna bear to lose you. I've already lost a father and a husband to the sea.'

'I know, Mother,' the boy said gently. 'But Joe and Sammy are fishermen. And they're all right, aren't they?'

Jeannie nodded, biting on her lower lip. 'Aye, I pray every night to keep them safe . . .' And then she added in a whisper, 'But they're as good as lost to me, for I never see them.'

Now Angus's smile broadened. 'Well, you might soon, Mam, because in the Easter holidays I'm going to sea on the *Arctic Queen II*, the boat Joe skippers.'

Jeannie gasped. 'On Joe's boat? You're going to sea with Joe and Sammy?' It was a Gorton boat, she reminded herself, but even so . . .

At that moment, Robert walked into the room and Jeannie whirled around to face him. 'Did you set all this up?' she demanded.

His glance went from one to another. 'Now what am I supposed to have done?' he asked.

'Did you ask Joe and Sammy to take Angus to sea on their boat?'

But Robert looked genuinely startled and glanced at his son, who spoke up before his father could answer her question.

Angus drew himself up. 'No, Dad knew nothing about it. I asked 'em.'

'You? But – but you dinna ken them.'

'Course I know them.'

'But – how?'

'Every time they dock, I meet the ship. Joe's a great bloke.' He smiled at his mother and added gently, 'I think my half-brother's beginning to like me. And I know Sam does.'

Jeannie opened her mouth to say, of course Joe likes you. But in this family, that was no guarantee. She had not spoken to them since the day she had gone to ask them both to be godfather to Angus. Fourteen long years ago, and since then not a day had gone by that she hadn't thought about them. But until this moment she had had no idea that Angus had even met them, let alone spoken to them. The revelation came as a shock. And yet, rationally, if she thought about it, he had spent such a lot of his young life down at the docks, it would have been odd if he had not run into them. But it sounded now as if he had deliberately sought them out.

'How – how long has this been going on?'

The boy wrinkled his forehead. 'Oh about six months I suppose. I've known for a long time that I wanted to go to sea and I thought the best way would be to go with Joe. And Sammy, too, of course. He's my cousin, isn't he?' He looked towards his father for confirmation. All Robert could do was nod.

They had never tried to keep the fact a secret. Indeed, from an early age, Jeannie and Robert had spoken openly about Joe and Sammy in front of Angus and, when he was old enough, Robert had explained gently all that had happened in their families to cause the rift between them. He had even, Jeannie thought with admiration, told their son of the very first time he had encountered Jeannie, hiding none of his own shame at the memory.

Now Angus took his mother's hands into his own and, looking straight into her eyes, he said quietly, 'I thought I might be able to bring the family together at the same time.'

Tears blurred her eyes and she reached out and touched his cheek with the tips of her fingers but no words would come. He was a deep thinker, this youngest son of hers, with a kind and generous nature. He knew that her dearest wish was to be reunited with Joe and Sammy and, to try to bring it about, he was willing to go to sea with them. All three would be on the same ship at the mercy of the mighty ocean.

No, no, she couldn't let it happen. She must talk to Robert alone. He must stop Angus going.

*

'Now you are being silly, darling,' Robert said. 'This isn't like you at all. Where's my strong Jeannie? The girl who once brandished a gutting knife under my nose? Not that I didn't deserve it,' he added hastily.

'But how do you know they will look after him? How do you know that they're not taking him to sea to – to . . .?'

Even she balked at putting her deepest fears into actual words.

'To tip him over the side in a gale, you mean?' Robert said bluntly, bringing her worst nightmare into the open. 'Oh come now, Jeannie. You're talking about your own son and about my nephew. I know Francis was a bad lot but I don't think even he would stoop to something like that. And as for Joe, well he's your son and Tom's.'

Jeannie faced him. 'Aye, and Tom carried a hatred for you and your family all his life. A resentment that Joe seems to be carrying on. As for Sammy, well, he's his own particular bitterness, hasn't he? I always used to fear for you when you and Tom served on the same minesweeper in the war. More than just the enemy's aircraft and the mines you were clearing.'

Robert stared at her. He opened his mouth to argue but then he remembered. Remembered, suddenly, the times he had felt Tom's antagonism. It had been real, very real. So real that on the odd occasion – strange how he had forgotten it until this moment – the thought had crossed his own mind that he might be in physical danger from the man.

Quietly he said, 'And now you fear for Angus's safety if he should go to sea with Joe and Sammy?'

Wordlessly, because to say it aloud seemed so awful, she nodded.

He was thoughtful for a moment before he said slowly, 'Then I'll go with them. No one would misinterpret that.

He's only fourteen. And after all,' he gave a half-smile, 'I am in the happy position of being able to "pull rank". I own the ship.'

She rushed to him and flung her arms about him. 'Oh Robert, would you? Would you really go?'

He put his arms about her and sighed against her hair. 'You know, Mrs Gorton, that I would do anything in this world for you.'

The day they left, Jeannie refused to come down to the dockside to see them off. Childhood superstition was still strong within her and though her hair now had more strands of white than of the rich, red colour, her fear was still there. 'It might make things awkward if I come with Joe and Sammy there.' She made the excuse that they could not deny, but when she saw Angus's crest-fallen face, she forced a brightness into her voice to promise, 'But I'll come and meet you the day you come back.'

So she did not go down to the dockside, but, unknown to them all, from the window of the Gorton-Hathersage Trawler Company's office, Jeannie watched the *Arctic Queen II* nose its way out of the dock and head for the open sea. Beside her stood her brother-in-law, his arm about her waist.

'Oh Edwin,' she sighed, resting her head against his shoulder for a moment. 'They're all aboard that one boat. The four most important people in my life, and I've let them all go together into the treacherous Icelandic waters.'

'They'll be all right.' Edwin squeezed her waist, still as lithe and trim as a young woman's. 'Joe's a fine skipper. He may be the youngest we've ever had on our boats but he's one of the best. And Sammy too. Not skipper material, maybe, but he's a good seaman. They'll be all right,' he said again, but she had the uncomfortable feeling that he was trying to convince himself as much as comfort her.

Forty-Nine

The 1950s had been a boom time for the Gorton-Hathersage Trawler Company of Havelock. Having weathered the economic problems of the '30s, it had seemed ironic that a world war should smash all that they had built up. At the end of the war, Robert believed he had little to return home to in the way of the business. Caught up in his love for and hopes for the future with Jeannie, he was not too concerned, but after her rejection of him, Robert's only salvation was to plunge himself into work.

Under Edwin's steady hand on the financial side of the business and with Robert's natural flair for dealing fairly with the men in their employ, the company began to flourish. Whilst the brothers themselves might have missed Francis's leadership, amongst the fishermen there was little regret.

By the early 1960s the Gorton-Hathersage Trawler Company of Havelock was reckoned to be the biggest trawler-owning company on the north-east coast of Lincolnshire, and the most modern thinking. And some said they even rivalled the owners in the port of Hull on the opposite bank of the Humber.

'An old man and a boy? Dead weight they'll be. The skipper must be out of his mind teking 'em.'

'He hasn't got a lot of choice, has he? Seeing who it is?'

'Why? Who is it?'

'Don't ya know? Mester Robert Gorton and his young son.'

'Never! I dun't believe you.'

'True.'

'Well, the skipper has lost 'is marbles then.'

The other man laughed. 'Like I said, he ain't much choice seeing as 'ow Mester Robert's the owner of this ship.'

'And I suppose . . .' there was a note of comic horror in the man's tone now, 'you're going to tell me next that I'll get the brat working with me as galley boy?'

The other man laughed. 'No, the young 'un wants to be on deck, so they say. No, old son, you've got the mester as your "galley boy".'

The choice words that followed made even Robert's ears burn. He hadn't meant to listen to the conversation, but had found himself trapped in the tiny cabin stowing his gear when the two men, passing by, had spoken in such loud voices that it was impossible for him not to overhear. He held his breath, hoping they would not step into the cabin and only let it out when the footsteps went on.

The final words Robert heard were, 'Mind you, I dun't reckon the skipper does like it – the old man coming along, I mean. They say he dun't have nowt to do with any of the family even though his mother's married to Mester Robert.'

'What about the lad?' At this point the voices became indistinct and Robert could not hear the reply but he could have told them. Oh yes, he could have told them about the lad.

'The lad' had been in a turmoil of excitement ever since the trip had been finally agreed upon. At first he had argued about his father coming too. 'What'll the crew think? It'll make me look a baby.'

But, credit due to the boy, Robert thought, when he had seen his mother's genuine anxiety, Angus had given her a bear-hug accompanied by his engaging grin of capitulation.

And now he was aboard, his belongings stowed and already he was on deck demanding of Sammy – the third hand – what he could do.

The first two days at sea were awkward. The crew were ill at ease. Conversations stopped abruptly whenever Robert or Angus approached and were virtually non-existent when they all sat together in the messroom. But then, forty-eight hours out to sea, the natural hierarchy aboard ship took over. Though the men all had work to do on the voyage out, there was nevertheless a relaxed atmosphere. When the nets and all their gear had been made ready and the skipper sent down the first tot of rum to 'wet the net', Robert and Angus felt themselves accepted.

'You watch it, Dad, you know what rum does to you,' Angus teased, knocking back his own tot like an old hand.

'And you just wait till I tell your mother about you!'

'Skipper's keeping himself to himself, ain't he?' was the only other remark Robert overheard, though he guessed there were plenty went on out of his hearing.

'Aye, well, awk'ard for him, ain't it?'

'Oh aye. I s'pose it is,' came the reply and Robert, as he carried two mugs of tea and two plates of bread and butter along the rolling deck, felt their glance upon him. But by the third day, they were taking their tea and saying, 'Thanks, mate.'

Ted Gutteridge, the cook, had been blunt. 'Well, Mester Gorton, I can't say I'm pleased to have you aboard, but since you're here and we've got to rub along for the next three weeks, that's the last time I'm going to call you that. From now on, you're Rob and you take your orders from me.'

'Right you are, Mr Gutteridge . . .' Robert had begun, but the man had stuck out his hand, grinned and corrected, 'Ted.'

Robert took his hand. 'Ted, it is.'

Ted had seemed to relax a little. 'It's a dangerous place, the galley. Specially in a force nine gale.' He jerked his thumb upwards. 'Oh I know it's rougher up there, but they don't have a pan of boiling soup slopping over their legs if the ship gives a lurch.'

Robert nodded, respecting the man's trade. 'You just tell me what you want me to do, Ted, and I'll do it.'

Ted slapped his new galley boy on the shoulder. 'Good man.'

Trying not to make it noticeable, Robert still tried to keep a watchful eye on Angus, though it was not easy since he was in the galley most of the time whilst the boy was on deck.

Over the next few days, once the tension had eased, 'Rob' was surprised to find that in a masochistic kind of way he was actually enjoying himself.

He saw little of Joe and nor did Angus, though Robert was thankful to see that Sammy had taken the boy under his wing. In fact, Angus became the third hand's shadow.

'When we get to the grounds,' Ted told Robert, 'he'll have to keep out of his way a bit then. Dangerous job, Sammy's got, y'know. He's the one who releases the knot when the trawl net comes aboard. I've seen a man killed doing that.'

Robert said nothing, but he was wondering if he had been right to go against Jeannie's instincts and allow their son come to sea. Even though he was aboard too, he couldn't watch the boy every minute, nor could he be sure of being able to keep the lad out of potentially dangerous situations.

The moment the ship had nosed its way out of the mouth of the Humber, past the lightship and into the treacherous waters of the North Sea to begin its eight-hundred-mile voyage to the fishing grounds off the north-east coast of Iceland, there was danger.

Suddenly, with a stab of fear, Robert realized, strangely now only for the first time, that the four men who mattered most in the world to Jeannie were all aboard this vessel.

Fifty

With both Robert and Angus away, Jeannie felt lost. Although she saw Edwin every day, either visiting him at the Gorton offices or inviting him to dine with her in the evening, there were still too many hours when she was alone. He took her to the theatre twice in the first week but afterwards Jeannie could not have said what the plays were about; her thoughts were out at sea.

There was one person who would understand how she felt. Thelma. On the first morning of the second week since they had sailed, Jeannie stood outside the terraced house in Wessex Street.

'Hello, Mam. What are you doing here?'

'I hope you don't mind . . .' Jeannie began, stepping into the kitchen but then she stopped as she glanced round in amazement. Every surface gleamed and sparkled. From the scullery came the smell of freshly baking bread and the girl herself was smiling at Jeannie. She had gained a little weight and her face had lost that gaunt, discontented look. Thelma was no longer a girl, Jeannie reminded herself, but a young woman. She must be in her mid-thirties now, Jeannie calculated. As she looked around, everything so tidy and in its place, Jeannie felt a stab of pity. It was too tidy. Immaculate – and childless.

'I'll mek you a cup of tea, Mam, but I'm ever so sorry, I've got to go out at eleven. I've got mesen this little part-time job in Yorks in Main Street.' It was the major department store in the street, the shop where George Lawrence had bought Jeannie the coat all those years ago.

Jeannie nodded. 'That's nice, hen. It's a beautiful shop.'

'It's only part time.' The young woman giggled. 'I wouldn't want owt to interfere with the times Joe's at home, y'know. But it's nice to have summat to do when he's not here. A little bit extra money's handy and it keeps me out of mischief.'

Jeannie made no comment but the two women exchanged a smile.

'Don't let me keep you then.'

'No, no, it's nice to see you. I've half an hour. I'm all ready except for putting me coat on. Sit down, Mam, do. I'll get the kettle on.'

Thelma bustled about, lay a tray with a dainty cloth and reached for delicate china from a cupboard. Jeannie could scarcely believe her eyes. The change in the girl was incredible. She wondered if there was more to it. Surely, oh surely not. Had Thelma got another man whilst Joe was away? Then firmly, she shook herself. I'm getting as bad as Tom in my suspicions, she told herself sharply.

Thelma sat down at the table and poured the tea. 'Do you know, Mam, I'll always be grateful for what you did for me that time. You brought me to me senses. I love Joe and he's a good man. A bit moody at times, maybe, and he gets jealous . . .' She pulled a face. 'Even when there's no need.'

Jeannie knew at once that her fleeting fear had been groundless. She smiled. 'Dinna let's talk about that any more, hen. It's forgotten.'

'Well, I just wanted you to know, that's all. I am grateful, really I am.' Thelma sighed. 'I just wish Joe would see sense and mek friends with you again. He's missing so much, but he's so stubborn. Mind you,' she added, and there was a more hopeful note in her tone. 'I reckon he's coming round to his little brother. And Sammy thinks the world of young Angus, y'know?'

Jeannie's eyes widened and she felt her heart thumping and she could not prevent the tremble in her voice as she said, 'Does he? Does he really?'

Thelma nodded. 'I reckon Joe'll come round, given time. He just doesn't want to admit it, y'know.'

Jeannie smiled, remembering the fights between Joe and Sammy and then the sudden switch to brotherly, or rather cousinly, affection. Maybe Joe was feeling the same towards Angus. He just couldn't decide exactly what he did feel towards his half-brother.

'I just wish I knew what was happening out there,' Jeannie murmured, sipping her tea. 'I just wish I was with them all.'

Thelma laughed. 'Oh, you're best out the way, Mam. The Arctic Circle in a force ten is no place for you an' me.'

Despite the warm cosiness of the room and the hot tea she was drinking, Jeannie shuddered.

As they sailed northwards, Robert pointed out the hazy outline of hills on the port side. 'That, Angus, is Scotland. Somewhere over there is the Fife coast where your mother was born.' He paused and murmured more to himself than to the boy, 'I've been promising to take her back for a visit.'

'We'll take her when we get back,' Angus shouted above the throb of the diesel engines beneath his feet. 'She'd like that.'

The ship passed between the Orkneys and the Shetlands and on past the Faeroes towards Iceland.

As they neared the fishing grounds, Robert went up on

deck. He thought he had never seen such a beautiful sight in the whole of his life. For a moment, he wished Jeannie were standing beside him, seeing what he was seeing.

'It's a rare sight, ain't it?' Sammy said at his elbow. Without taking his gaze away, Robert murmured, 'It certainly is. I wouldn't have missed seeing this for the world.'

They were silent, standing together, watching the small pack ice drift by as the ship nosed her way carefully further and further northwards. The sea was calm, sparkling in the spring sunlight and already sea-birds circled above their heads waiting for easy picking when the fishing began.

'It all looks so – so untouched,' Robert murmured. 'As if no one's ever been here before us. Just look at the blue of the sea and the sky and the whiteness of the ice. It's magnificent. Oh, I'm glad I came – if only for this.'

'It's certainly picture-postcard scenery when it's like this. But get a freezing force ten blow and it's a fearsome place. Mind you,' Sammy nodded towards the bridge, 'I don't know how far north he's planning to go this time. Sometimes he . . .' Sammy stopped suddenly and glanced at Robert in embarrassment.

'It's all right. I'm not on board as The Boss, Sammy,' Robert said quietly. 'Anything you say goes no further.'

'Well, sometimes he goes right to the edge of the ice field, y'know. Fish are often plentiful there.'

More confident now, Sammy grinned impishly, puncturing Robert's romantic image of the magnificent scenery all around him and bringing him back to stark reality.

'You'll be sick of the sight of ice before we've done and so will Angus. He's been down in the ice-room all morning, breaking it up ready for our first trawl. But we've let him up on deck for a bit now, though.' Sammy pointed to where Angus stood on the fo'c'sle, eagerly scanning the horizon. 'He can't wait to get started, can he? But he shouldn't have much longer to wait now.'

'Are we nearly there, then?' Robert asked.

Sammy nodded towards where Joe stood in the wheel-house, a pair of binoculars to his eyes. 'He's got Sparks listening in to the radio to see if he can track the other ships.'

Robert glanced around him, the blue water stretching emptily as far as he could see. 'I don't see any others.'

'You will,' Sammy said, confidently. 'Sparks'll find 'em. Good lad is our Sparks. He listens in to all the radio conversations. He's even picked up a smattering of German and can listen into them, an' all. And he's fath-omed out some of the others' codes. Them that don't change their codes regular like we do. Mind you, Skipper won't join the other ships. He hates bein' in a crowd. But he uses them as a marker, y'know. He's a good skipper, is Joe, and a lucky one. He seems to have an instinct for where the fish are. It's usually us the other ships follow.' Sammy glanced sideways at Robert. 'Course he shares the info with the other Gorton boats . . .' He paused almost waiting to see if Robert would refute his words. Robert managed to keep his face straight, though inwardly he was thinking, pull the other one, Sammy.

The Gorton fleet used a system of codes which their skippers could use to help each other find the good grounds, but Robert knew from overhearing the other skippers as they came ashore that Joe Lawrence was a loner. Rather than fish in a crowded area, he would deliberately steam off and trawl in waters ignored by the other skippers. More often than not it paid off. As Sammy said, Joe was a 'lucky' skipper. But sometimes the gamble failed and Joe had a poor haul.

But now, as they neared the grounds, Sammy was full of confidence. 'If we get a good catch,' he was saying, 'Skipper has everyone on deck. All except the cook. He even has Sparks boiling the livers. So get yer gutting knife ready, he'll mebbe not let you stay warm an' cosy in the galley.'

Robert's expression must have been comical for Sammy laughed and slapped his shoulder just as Angus came running along the deck, sure footed as a goat on a slippery mountain side. 'There's a ship to the north west. Have you seen it?'

Sammy glanced around and squinted in the direction the boy was pointing. 'Where? I can't see. By heck, lad, your eyes must be sharp. Away and tell the skipper. I don't reckon he's spotted it, even with his glasses.'

Robert watched as Angus climbed the ladder to bridge. He saw Joe turn briefly as the boy stepped inside the wheelhouse. Then Angus was pointing and Joe was putting the binoculars to his eyes once more and training them in the direction the boy pointed. The two watching from the deck saw him search the skyline for a few moments and then, dropping the binoculars momentarily, he gave the lad a brief nod and a quick smile and then his attention was once more on the trawler on the horizon.

Angus left the wheelhouse and clambered down the ladder. 'He ses he can see several ships. We're there, Dad, we're there.'

'Right then,' Sammy said. 'There's work to be done. You come with me, Angus. I've a job for you.'

Happily, the boy trotted after his cousin.

Robert watched them go. It was the longest conversation he could remember having with Sammy, he thought, and certainly the friendliest. If only they could carry this camaraderie back to shore, back to Jeannie, how happy she would be.

And work there was in plenty. From the moment they reached the fishing grounds and Joe turned his ship port-side to the wind to shoot the first trawl over the starboard side, Robert lost all account of time and only the cook seemed to keep a tally of whether he should be serving breakfast, dinner, tea or supper.

'You go up on deck whenever you want, Rob,' Ted said. 'I know you want to keep an eye on that lad of yours.'

'You sure, Ted? I'm supposed to be helping you.'

The man grinned, showing a broken front tooth. 'Yer more of a hindrance than a help down here, but I'll give you a shout if I need a hand.'

So Robert was able to watch as they shot the first trawl. When the shout went up, 'Pay away', over the side went the net, bobbins, trawl doors and lastly several hundred feet of three-inch steel cable. As the net sank below the surface to the bottom of the sea, Joe turned the vessel in the direction he had chosen to fish. For the next three hours the ship would trawl at a steady four knots.

Angus was beside him. 'Sammy ses I'm to get summat to eat and some kip, 'cos once the first haul comes up, we're going to be busy.'

Robert smiled at his son. 'Then I'd better go below and see if I can be of any help to Ted if it's "grub up" time.'

'D'you know, Dad,' Angus chattered on as they clambered down the ladder, 'Sammy ses Joe hardly ever lets the mate tek over the ship whilst they're fishing. Once he only had four hours sleep in six days. I can't imagine that, Dad, can you?'

'No,' Robert replied soberly, but in his mind he was thinking, but you may well be about to find out, son.

There was a sense of excitement throughout the ship the first time they hauled in the gear. Everyone was waiting to see if the skipper had got it right. The deckies were all there, some operating the winch whilst others stood by to secure the doors as they came on deck. Up came the metal bobbins and then they heaved on the net itself, leaning down over the side as the ship tilted and rolled and the waves lashed on to the deck. As the cod end floated they could see that the catch was good. Now the cod end was lifted aboard by the derrick. Sammy dodged beneath the water gushing from the mass of fish, jerked the knot undone and, in a second, fish of all shapes and sizes cascaded on to the deck. Robert watched the figure of his son, almost hidden beneath his yellow oilskins, yet he could see the boy's face wreathed in smiles and even above the throb of the engines, he could hear his jubilant shouts.

The boy was a natural, a fisherman born and bred. There was no denying it. Whatever he or Jeannie might do, Robert knew now, they were never going to stop Angus coming to sea.

Despite his size and youth, the boy worked alongside the experienced deckhands. He was quick to learn and, with no serious repairs needed to the net, the trawl was soon back at the bottom of the ocean once more. Then began the hours of work to gut and put away the fish.

Angus, standing close by Sammy now, who was in charge of this operation, watched closely as the man took a cod into his hands, slit open its belly and removed its guts, separating its liver which he dropped into a basket. Then he lobbed the gutted fish into the washer from where it would slide down a chute into the fish-room below. There, the mate, with a deckie to help him, packed the fish in ice and stowed it away.

Robert found he was holding his breath as he watched Angus pick up a sharp knife and take a fish into his left hand. It took the boy a dozen or so fish before he was gutting like an old hand. Robert suspected that this was not the first time young Angus had tried his hand at gutting. Obviously, his hours spent haunting the Havelock fishdocks had not been wasted. Not that he worked with the speed of the other men yet, but that would come. Robert smiled to himself as he remembered, years ago, watching Jeannie at the farlanes. It seemed that young Angus had not only inherited his grandfather's seamanship, but also his mother's dexterity with a gutting knife.

It was a good catch so there was only half-an-hour for deckies to eat and snatch a short rest before the next cod end swung on to the deck and deposited its silver haul.

'Take this to the skipper, Rob, will you,' Ted asked. 'He'll not leave his wheelhouse for the next ten days.'

'You're joking.'

Ted wasn't. 'No, I'm serious. It's his job. He'll stay up there now until the job's done and we make for home.'

'What about sleep?'

The toothy grin was evident again as Ted said, 'Sleep? What's that, mate?'

Six trawls in twenty-four hours with snatched meals and even less sleep had Robert worried for his son. He was only a boy, only fourteen. Surely he couldn't keep up this pace? But Angus was determined and it wasn't until Sammy himself ordered him below for a six-hour period off, that the youngster gave in.

Robert followed him down to help him take off his oilskins, but the boy said, 'Don't, Dad, I can manage.' And Robert was obliged to stand and watch while Angus, reeling with exhaustion, pulled off the stiff, unyielding clothes. Blood and fish guts streaked his pale face. His hands were blue with cold and he winced as he flexed the fingers of his right hand that had held the knife. But the grin on his face was still stretched from ear to ear and even though his eyes were large with tiredness, there was still in them the sparkle of excitement.

'Did you see that huge plaice that came up? "Dustbin-lidders", they call them. Wasn't it huge?'

'It's certainly the biggest I've ever seen.'

'Isn't this great, Dad?'

Robert had to swallow the lump of sheer pride that rose in his throat before he could say, 'Yes, son, it's great. Now, come and eat your supper and away to your bunk.'

It was the first time on board Robert had come face to face with Joe. The skipper, with his own cabin directly behind the bridge, rarely came down to the lower deck and never during the time at the fishing grounds.

'Thanks,' Joe said, taking the meal Robert had carried up to the wheelhouse. As he turned to go, Joe mumbled, his mouth already stuffed, 'He's a good lad, that.'

As Robert turned back to face him, he was amazed to see a grin spread across Joe's face. 'I can tell he's my brother. He looks a bit like me an' all, dun't he?'

Robert smiled, anxious to meet Joe half way, yet at the same time careful not to appear over-eager.

'Your mother always says you both take after your Grandpa Buchanan both in looks and in your love for the sea.'

'Aye well, there's worse to tek after than him.'

Robert wondered if it was a veiled reference to the Hayes-Gorton family, but he said nothing.

Her name was between them now. She was almost a physical presence here in the cramped quarters of the wheelhouse on this heaving ship eight hundred miles from home. And yet she was here with them both. He could see the same hurt mirrored in Joe's eyes that he had seen so often in Jeannie's. He tried to think of something to say, something that could heal the breach yet at the moment he opened his mouth, Joe turned away, his attention once more upon the job in hand. The moment was lost.

But at least, Robert thought, Joe seems to be coming around to Angus.

It was a start.

Fifty-One

'Have you had no word at all from them, Edwin? Don't they keep in touch regularly with their position?'

Edwin smiled at her. 'Not Joe, Jeannie. He's a law unto himself when he's fishing. But,' he shrugged philosophically, 'we've learnt to trust your son. Oh, he'll radio in when he feels like it. And if there's any trouble . . .'

'Trouble?' she said sharply. 'What sort of trouble?'

Edwin swallowed swiftly, realizing his slip. He smiled again. 'That's what I mean, Jeannie. No news is good news, where your Joe's concerned.'

'Oh,' she said, a little mollified, but her shrewd glance at Edwin left him wondering if he had entirely convinced her.

'We'll maybe get a message when they're on their way home,' Edwin said. 'Cheer up. Only one more day and they'll be turning for home. That's if Joe's fish-room is full.' He laughed. 'If it isn't, he'll stay out there as long as he's catching fish and as long as his supplies hold out.'

'But if they've had a good catch, they could be home in four to five days?'

When Edwin nodded, the light came back into Jeannie's eyes.

*

'Last day's fishing today, Dad.' Robert heard the disappointment in the boy's voice.

Sitting beside Angus in the messroom, one of the deckhands shovelled the thick white flakes of fish into his mouth, anxious to snatch a few minutes' sleep before the next haul. It was a shame, Robert thought as he placed bread and butter and a mug of tea in front of the man, that they hadn't time to savour the meals Ted cooked. What that man couldn't do with haddock, wasn't worth knowing. He could teach the chefs in smart hotels a thing or two. That was for sure. Fresh bread buns baked every day. Three main, three-course meals and plenty of snacks in between, to say nothing of gallon after gallon of strong tea. The food was good, Robert was pleased to see, but if only the crew had time to enjoy it.

Picking up on Angus's remark, the deck-hand laughed. 'That's if he can stuff another six hauls into yon fish-room. Have you taken a look down there? We must have got fourteen hundred kits down there.' Grinning at Angus, he added, 'That's almost ninety tons to you, laddie.'

Much too polite to tell the deckie he knew very well the weight of a kit, Angus merely smiled and nodded. 'There doesn't seem much room left.'

The man swallowed his tea and stood up. 'Best trip we've had this year.' He touched the boy's shoulder and winked. 'You must 'ave brought us luck, lad. I have to say it, I thought at first you might be a Jonah, but you're not, you're a good 'un. You can come again.'

The smile on Angus's mouth threatened to split his face in two.

As the final day's fishing began, the weather, which had been kind throughout the whole trip, deteriorated. When the third haul came up over the side, the wind lashed the deck and the ship tossed from side to side in the mountainous waves.

The cod end swung in over the deck and Robert could see at once that it hung limply, devoid of its usually bulging weight of fish.

'What's happened?' he mouthed to Angus. The boy shrugged as together they watched Sammy duck beneath it and release the knot. A pathetically small catch of fish slithered on to the deck. Sammy was issuing orders, pointing and shouting to the men close by and then he was running along the deck towards the bridge.

'He's going up to see Joe.'

Though he passed close by, they did not try to detain him. They'd find out soon enough what had gone wrong.

On his way back, Sammy said briefly, 'We're turning for home. The net's badly torn and it'll take an hour or more to repair. With the weather worsening, it's a sensible decision.' He grinned suddenly, his face drenched beneath his sou'wester. ''Sides, he's got enough fish, if only he'd be satisfied.'

Robert had experienced rough weather during his years at sea aboard the minesweeper, but it was nothing compared with the ferocity of the storm they ran into as they left the Icelandic waters.

The ship was tossed and thrown as the winds, ever changeable, whipped the waves in every direction, so that one moment they were on the crest of a sixty-foot wave, the next being plunged into the trough below.

Grasping Robert's arm, Sammy bellowed into his ear, 'Get the lad below. The mate's going up on to the bridge to help Joe. He's close to exhaustion now. This is all he needs.'

Robert took hold of Angus's arm and was about to pull him towards the ladder when they all felt the ship plummet into a kind of vacuum created by the turbulence of the ocean. Robert and Angus looked up as a huge wave hovered above them and almost in slow motion came down upon them engulfing the ship in a deluge of water.

He put his arms about his son and clasped him to him as they fell together on to the deck. It seemed to last an age that they were tossed and thrown about the deck, bruised and battered. Robert was praying like he'd never prayed in his life before, not even when he had been under enemy fire aboard the war-time trawler. Never, ever had he known such fear. But all the while, he clung on to his son and prayed that they would both live to see Jeannie again.

He was fighting for air and then strong arms were lifting him up and he found that Angus and Sammy were hanging on to him.

'Dad, it's all right,' Angus was panting, gasping through the water and the spray. 'Feel that?'

As he spoke, Robert felt a tremor run through the whole of the ship.

'We're going to be all right, Dad. We're all right.'

Much later, Robert asked Angus what he had meant.

'That shudder, you mean? If you feel that, then the ship's buoyant. I just knew we were going to be all right. That's all.'

Robert stared at his son, marvelling yet again at the boy's instinctive knowledge and understanding. But the dangers were not over yet for the bad weather did not let up. Through the driving rain and sleet, now ice began to collect on every part of the surface of the vessel, but not so much that the crew were called upon to chop it away.

Robert was as busy as when they'd been trawling, carrying tea and food along the heaving deck and up to the wheelhouse.

'This is a bad 'un. I'm sorry you and the lad are having to go through this,' Joe said.

His eyes were dark-ringed with tiredness and the anxiety never left his face. He had the ship and the whole crew, to say nothing of a hold full of fish, for which he was responsible. Grimly, Robert said, 'No apology necessary. I'm glad I came. No, I mean it,' he added firmly as he saw Joe's look of scepticism. 'And you might not believe me, Joe. But it's been an eye-opener for me. I thought I knew about ships and going to sea when I served in the war, but this.' He shook his head. 'My God, this is hell on earth out here. Oh, it's all fine when the weather's good and the fish are there. But face this weather?' He shook his head slowly. 'Joe, I never realized.'

They stared at each other for a moment whilst beneath their feet the ship heaved and rolled.

'So,' Joe said slowly, 'you'll not be letting young Angus come to sea again, then?'

Robert allowed himself a quick, wry smile. 'I shan't be able to stop him. Nor shall I try.'

'You won't?' Joe was obviously surprised.

'No. If he wants to make the sea his life, I shan't try to stop him. Though,' again he smiled, with a tinge of sadness, 'I don't doubt his mother and I will worry every moment he's away. Just,' he added softly, 'as she has always done about you and Sammy.'

The man was silent and he looked away, out of the screen overlooking the deck, unwilling to meet Robert's eyes.

Robert cleared his throat. 'You may not believe me, Joe, but I promise you something. When we get home, I'm going to do everything I can to improve the lot of the fishermen, at least in our fleet. And you know something else too, Joe?' Though he waited a moment, there was no response from Joe, but Robert knew by the rigid set of his shoulders that the skipper was listening to every word. 'Sammy – and you as well – could do so much to help us. If only you would.'

He turned then and left the wheelhouse, clambering down the ladder and along the deck with the waves like walls on either side.

As he was about to go below, he turned and glanced back towards the bridge. Even through the driving rain, he could see that Joe was watching him. Then he glanced sideways to where Angus stood on the deck alongside Sammy. He saw Angus look round and grin at him, but then, as Robert watched, the boy's gaze went beyond him and a look of horror spread across his young features.

As the wave swept on to the boat, lifting Robert high in the air and carrying him over the side, the last thing he remembered was the stricken look on his son's face.

Fifty-Two

'Edwin, you must have heard something? They were due home today. Surely Joe's radioed in by now?'

She could see that Edwin was worried too and she was convinced he was holding something back.

'Even if you've had bad news, I'd sooner know.' All the old fears were crowding in on her. The terrible waiting, the awful not knowing . . . 'Please, Edwin.'

'Dearest Jeannie.' He took her hands in his. 'Try not to worry. Look, let me take you out to lunch and when we come back—'

'No, no, I couldn't eat a thing.' She pulled free of him and began to pace up and down his office coming back each time to stand before the window overlooking the docks. 'You must have heard something.' Jeannie was too knowledgeable to be put off so lightly. 'Are any of the other ships that went out at the same time, back?'

Edwin cleared his throat. 'Er, well, yes.'

'How many?'

He hesitated a moment and she could see the tortured expression in his eyes. Reluctantly, Edwin admitted, 'Most of them.'

Jeannie put her hands to her cheeks and stared at him. She took a deep breath and, her gaze never leaving his face, she asked, 'Edwin, what is it you're no' telling me?'

He sighed and said heavily, 'There was a storm—'

'What! You dinna mean their ship's missing?'

'No – no,' he said swiftly.

'What happened then? Are they all safe?'

But all her brother-in-law would say was, 'Joe's a fine skipper, Jeannie. I promise you. Just put your trust in Joe.'

She turned back to look out of the window once more, across the docks towards the river. Like a figure turned to stone, she stood there the whole day, just watching and waiting . . .

Jeannie refused to leave the office until, at almost midnight, Edwin insisted on driving her home. She lay awake for most of the night, tossing and turning, debating whether she should get in touch with Thelma. At about four o'clock in the morning she fell into an exhausted sleep. Then, as dawn broke over the North Sea, the telephone shrilling in the hall below dragged her back to consciousness.

'Jeannie, that you?' Edwin's voice came down the line.

'Yes. What is it? Tell me quickly.'

'It's all right. Their ship's coming in. She'll be docking on the morning tide in about an hour . . .'

Before he could say any more, Jeannie said, 'I'll be there.' And she dropped the receiver into its cradle and was running back up the stairs before Edwin, at the other end, could draw breath to ask her if she wanted him to come and pick her up.

'Oh well,' he said aloud to his empty office. 'I'll go anyway.'

'Oh Edwin, they're a' right? All of them? You've spoken to them?' She drew him into the kitchen and poured him a cup of coffee.

'This is most welcome, Jeannie. I went back to the office after I dropped you here.'

'You promised me you were going home,' she scolded, but she was laughing, light-headed with relief.

He smiled up at her, but she could see that the anxiety was still not entirely gone from his eyes. 'It was the only way I could get you to come home and try to get a little rest. I knew, if I didn't say that, you'd have stayed up all night at the office too.'

'Aye, I would.'

She watched as he drank his coffee, standing impatiently before him, almost willing him to finish it quickly so that they could leave for the docks.

'What time will she be in?'

'As soon as the dock gates open, I don't doubt. Joe likes to land his fish first to get the best prices.'

'And they are a' right?' she asked again, but Edwin avoided her eyes now. Standing up, he said, 'Come on, time we were going.'

She stood once more at the window of Edwin's office, feeling now as if she had not moved away from it at all in the last twenty-four hours. She squinted towards the place where the dock gates still remained closed, any ships waiting to dock were still drifting on the Humber's tide.

'When will he open the gates?' Jeannie asked for the third time.

'Another five minutes or so, I reckon.'

It was the longest five minutes of Jeannie's life until she saw the gates open and the first ship came nosing her way through.

'Is that the *Arctic Queen II*? I canna see . . .' She almost pressed her nose to the pane in her anxiety.

'Come on,' Edwin said. 'We'll go down. I'll find out where she's berthing.'

Jeannie was waiting on the quayside with Edwin when the first of the deck-hands came down the ladder.

On the bridge she saw Joe and, shading her eyes to look up at him, she knew that he had seen her. He seemed to look down on her for a long moment and then he turned away and disappeared from her view. Several other men came down the ladder and walked away without glancing in their direction. And already the lumpers were gathering near the ship.

Then she saw them. First Sammy came down the ladder followed by Angus. Jeannie sent up a whispered prayer of thankfulness.

Next came Joe. As he stepped ashore, they seemed to hesitate for a moment, standing together, the three of them, as Jeannie's glance went back to the top of the ladder, expecting to see Robert swinging his leg over the side and coming down to join them.

But there was no one else.

They were walking towards her, just the three of them.

Jeannie pulled in a breath and held it. Her hand fluttered nervously to her throat. Oh no, not Robert.

Her glance was darting between them as they came towards her. And then she was aware that Joe's arm was about Angus's shoulders. She looked into their faces, trying to read what she most feared to learn. Her legs felt weak beneath her and, blindly, she stretched out her trembling hands towards them. Towards her three boys.

But Angus was smiling, calling out to her now. 'Mother, Mother, it's all right. Dad's all right. At least . . .' They reached her now and surrounded her, hugging her. All three of them.

'He's safe, Mam,' Sammy said quickly. 'But he's had an accident . . .'

'We had some foul weather, Mother, and a huge wave washed Dad overboard.' Angus was determined to be the one to tell her. His grin widened. 'But, you'd never believe it, the very next wave washed him back on board again.'

'He was badly bruised,' Joe explained, his deep voice calmer than the other two. 'And his leg's broken. He tried to come right home, but we could see he was in a lot of pain. When we got off the coast of Scotland, we radioed ashore to one of the company's agents and he arranged for the local lifeboat to come and take him ashore. He's in hospital in Kirkcaldy.'

Jeannie gasped. 'My home? Near my home?'

'Aye.' Joe grinned and imitated her Scottish tongue. 'You're awae hame, Mam. We're putting you a train . . .' He put his arms about her, holding her close to his chest and resting his cheek against her hair. Huskily, he said, 'You're going home, Mam, just like you always wanted.'

Her eyes brimming with tears, Jeannie looked up into the face of her first-born, unable to speak for the lump in her throat. She wanted to say something, but the words would not come.

'There's just one thing.' He was smiling now, his eyes teasing. 'We're sending my brother, Angus, with you.' There was only the merest emphasis on the word 'brother' but hearing it, the lump in her throat swelled. Again Joe put an arm about the younger boy's shoulders and, as Angus grinned up at him, Jeannie could see the hero worship in his eyes.

'Just to make sure,' Joe was still speaking, his voice sounding a little husky now, 'that you come back to us.'

Now the tears overflowed and ran down her face as she held out her arms, trying to envelop them all.

She'd come back. Oh yes, she'd come back. That was what she wanted to say to Joe, to say to them all. Home was not in Scotland now. Home was here in Havelock. With Robert and her three beloved boys.